An
Orphan of
Hell's Kitchen

Books by Liz Freeland

MURDER IN GREENWICH VILLAGE

MURDER IN MIDTOWN

AN ORPHAN OF HELL'S KITCHEN

Published by Kensington Publishing Corporation

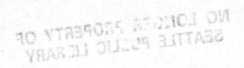

An Orphan of Hell's Kitchen

LIZ FREELAND

KENSINGTON BOOKS
www.kensingtonbooks.com

KENSINGTON BOOKS are published by

Kensington Publishing Corp.
119 West 40th Street
New York, NY 10018

All Kensington titles, imprints, and distributed lines are available at special quantity discounts for bulk purchases for sales promotion, premiums, fund-raising, educational, or institutional use.

Special book excerpts or customized printings can also be created to fit specific needs. For details, write or phone the office of the Kensington Sales Manager: Kensington Publishing Corp., 119 West 40th Street, New York, NY 10018. Attn. Sales Department. Phone: 1-800-221-2647.

Kensington and the K logo Reg. U.S. Pat. & TM Off.

ISBN-13: 978-1-4967-2618-6 (ebook)
ISBN-10: 1-4967-2618-9 (ebook)
Kensington Electronic Edition: March 2020

ISBN-13: 978-1-4967-2617-9
ISBN-10: 1-4967-2617-0
First Kensington Trade Paperback Printing: March 2020

10 9 8 7 6 5 4 3 2

Printed in the United States of America

An
Orphan of
Hell's Kitchen

CHAPTER 1

November 1914

The Thirtieth Street police station was no place to spend Thanksgiving. Across town, my aunt's house would be filled with music, laughter, and the warm companionship of friends and family. Thursday evenings chez Irene Livingston Green were always an event, with guests both invited and uninvited filtering through the house on Fifty-Third Street, but Thanksgiving was the zenith of her social calendar. Here, on the other hand, my company in the chilly basement where I worked consisted of two gum-smacking prostitutes and a woman hauled in on vagrancy and public inebriation charges who was currently on the cot in the second cell, snoring like a bulldog with adenoids. My thankfulness was at its lowest ebb.

The bell above the stairwell door clanged, raising a snort from Sleeping Beauty before she resumed her buzz-saw wheezing. That bell was my summons to go upstairs, most likely to bring down another prisoner for the women's cells. I stood.

"Her master's voice," one prostitute cracked to the other, with an especially loud snap of Beech-Nut gum on molars.

At least going upstairs would get me away from the nerve-jarring basement serenade. I was stiff from cold and sitting too long in the same position. "I'll be right back with a new friend for you."

"Hope she has cigarettes," one of the women said.

"Hope she don't snore," the other wished.

I was definitely going to demand Christmas off. Would I get it? Probably not. I'd been working in this precinct over a year, but I was still the lowest policewoman in the pecking order. Fiona, Evelyn, and Margaret had been with the NYPD since the days when female police officers were called police matrons. Compared to them I was still as fresh as spring's first jonquil, even if at the age of twenty-two I was feeling wind-battered and wilted.

I marched up to the main floor, expecting acerbic Sergeant Donnelly to nod me toward one of the rooms where my new charge would be waiting. Instead, two men standing beside him drew my attention. One, O'Mara, was a constable from our precinct. Burly, freckled, with red hair peeking out from under his hat, he stood beside a reedy old man in a worn overcoat, whose gray pants were frayed at the cuff above unpolished shoes. The older man, slight and runtish, was holding his battered hat, and his unkempt, greasy hair flopped forward. He combed it back nervously with his fingers.

Catching sight of me, Sergeant Donnelly scowled. "You got rocks in your feet, Two?" Long ago I'd made the mistake of bragging about my second-rank finish on the civil service exam, and few around the precinct were inclined to let me forget it in this century. "Grab your hat and coat. You're needed to accompany O'Mara and this man on an errand."

"Yes, sir." That quickly, my spirits lifted. I could have performed a balletic jeté across the precinct hall and danced down the stairs to my basement. Yes, it was a wet, cold November night, but anything that got me out of the station house was a godsend in my book. Though policewomen were no longer called matrons, most of our work still consisted of playing nursemaid to the women in the cells. To be out and about like my male brethren—*like a real officer*, I couldn't help thinking—was a treat.

"Where's our new friend?" the gum-snapper shouted down the hall when she heard me rummaging around the closet where we policewomen stowed our things.

"I have to go out. The sergeant'll send someone else down." Most likely Schultzie, our oldest officer, who at this moment was probably catching a few winks upstairs in the officers' dormitory. Sometimes I wondered if he ever went home, or even had a home to go to.

I shrugged on my coat, popped on my hat, and was winding my muffler around my neck as I took the stairs two at a time. The wool was still damp from my trip uptown to work, hours ago.

Only on the way out the door did Officer O'Mara introduce me to his companion. "Mr. Beggs here's the custodian of an apartment building over on Tenth. Sounds like trouble with one of the tenants."

Beggs, who had anxious, bulging eyes and a breathy voice, nodded at me. "There's a bad smell on the fourth floor, and Ruthie's not answering her door. It's locked."

My footsteps faltered. I understood what was suspected, but I didn't see why I was needed. This sounded like a job for the coroner, and maybe a homicide detective.

Noting my confusion, O'Mara explained, "Woman's got two kids."

"Babies," Beggs said. "Twins." He was practically skipping to keep up with O'Mara. I was having to move fast, too. "Poor little bastards."

"You'll have to take 'em to the foundling hospital," O'Mara told me. He added, "Depending on what we find, of course."

Until I became a policewoman, I'd never realized how often infants came into contact with the police. Most New Yorkers would be shocked at how frequently the most helpless among us were abandoned, and where—in hospitals, in the alley by the precinct, in the grand concourse of Penn Station, or in the ladies' washroom of Macy's department store. Some babies were brought to us when their mothers were arrested, or when a neighbor or landlord reported that a family had cleared out of their flat, leaving the smallest, newest member behind. I was always stunned to be handed one of these tiny discarded beings, whom life had already put at the most grievous disadvantage. For a few hours, I would look after them, and think of another baby—abandoned, too, but now as lucky as a child could be—until we could deliver them to the New York Foundling Hospital on Sixty-Eighth Street.

"It was on account of the babies I couldn't make myself kick Ruthie to the street," Beggs told us between labored breaths. "It's obvious what she is, and having twins didn't help her none. But those poor fatherless babies. I let the unpaid rent pile up, for months. And not like I asked anything in return, like some would've." Frowning, he held his hat against a sharp gust. "These past few weeks, though, I thought Ruthie was doing a little better. Paid her back rent, seemed almost cheerful."

"If she hasn't answered the door, why didn't you just open it with your key?" I asked the man.

He shivered, and I doubted it was just from the cold. "I-I-I must've lost it."

Lost his key or lost his nerve? The latter, I suspected.

O'Mara's long strides brought us quickly to Tenth Avenue, an area of flophouses and illegal barrooms, called blind pigs, selling dregs to winos. I picked my way around the sleeping body of one who'd sampled too much of what was on offer at these dubious taverns. Not too many blocks in any direction, a person could be in the plush velvet-and-gilt interior of a Broadway theater, or dining among millionaires in one of the finest restaurants in America, or stepping onto a luxury liner bound for any of the world's most exotic ports. But in Hell's Kitchen, luxury was ten cents for a night on a mildewed mattress. To afford rent for a flat, by this neighborhood's standards, was to be living high.

Beggs's building had the look of other tenements I'd seen— built on the cheap at the end of the last century before the city had settled on any standards. The edifice was deceptively ornate, fashioned from brick and some kind of light stone that seemed to be as sturdy as chalk. Two cherubs above the arched doorway were chipped, and the whole building had an off-kilter look. The fire escape listed across the front like a zigzagging, rusting scaffold. Inside, the building was airless and dark, the staircase lit only by a weak bare bulb on each landing near a communal washroom. The air reeked of bad plumbing and poverty.

On the fourth floor, a more disturbing smell began to hit us. I took a breath and held my damp muffler over my mouth and nose. Death lay on the other side of the locked door we stopped at, of that I had no doubt. I braced myself. A year and a half ago, I'd seen my roommate's cousin's body after she'd been stabbed to death in our flat. It still gave me nightmares.

"You all right?" O'Mara asked me. He looked a little green himself.

I nodded. There was no sound but the dripping of the faucet at the washroom sink behind me. "I don't hear a baby," I said. Much less two.

The superintendent, who'd stopped at his apartment on the first floor, came up behind us. He handed O'Mara an iron crowbar.

O'Mara made an artless job of cracking the door open. I couldn't blame him. The sooner we got in there, the sooner we could leave. Even the cold, wet air outside was better than this. After a few strong whacks and a swift kick, the door banged open in a spray of splintered wood. A cyclone of putrid air took my breath; my stomach began to heave. Behind my scarf, I tried not to breathe and at the same time swallowed repeatedly against the rising bile in my throat. Beggs fell to his knees. I stepped around him to enter the dark flat.

O'Mara felt along the wall until he found a switch that turned on the bulb hanging from the center of the ceiling. I almost wished he hadn't. At the moment of illumination, my eyes fastened on the large metal tub in the corner, in which a woman slumped forward, her hair covering half her face like a limp, brown curtain. Blood had spilled on the floor, along with filthy water. The woman had drawn a deep bath, a real Saturday nighter. The source of the blood was the woman's thin right arm, which was thrust over the edge of the tub. From wrist to elbow there were multiple slash marks.

Neither O'Mara nor I drew too close to the tub. The woman was obviously gone. Days gone. I sent up brief thanks that this was November. Bad as this was, if it had been July and the body had been sitting in the heat, I would have probably passed out by now.

"Is this her?" O'Mara asked Beggs. The man had pulled himself back to his feet and was leaning against the doorway.

He nodded. "Ruthie."

"Ruthie what?"

"Jones. Anyhow, that's the name she gave me."

I scanned the small room, which was actually the first of two rooms that had been fashioned out of an attic space. Low ceilings slanted down toward the windows, requiring a person of any height to duck a little on that side of the flat. Next to the tub was a stove with a basin leaning against it—probably what had been used to carry water from the washroom tap. Apartments were supposed to have water, but inspectors looked the other way, especially in places like this. Ruthie's wall had several shelves, mostly empty but for a few cans and a tin of crackers, which had been left open. A table and two cane-back chairs were the only furnishings, aside from a traffic-flattened braided rug on the floor. On the table was an unlabeled bottle of liquor, almost empty, and a single glass.

"Where are the babies?" I wondered aloud.

O'Mara and I continued into the even smaller back alcove room, no more than eight-foot square, which two people barely had room to move around in. A cot with a trunk at the foot of it took up one wall, and a dresser with a mirror was wedged in the corner. In one of its opened, disheveled drawers, a baby lay, wan and weak, its tiny limbs barely moving. The stench of soiled diaper added to the already wretched funk. O'Mara lurched to the window and yanked it open.

"Oh, you poor tiny thing." I approached the baby, touching him gently. To my relief, the skin was warm. "He needs food." I turned. "But didn't Mr. Beggs say there were twins?"

Beggs's face, sallow and drawn, peered in from the doorway. "That must be the dummy. Lord only knows what's become of the other."

"He can't speak?" I asked.

"Born that way. They were two boys. Johnny and . . ." His face twisted in thought. "Eddie? Or Teddy. Something like that."

"Who would this one be?"

"How should I know?"

"Eddie," I tried, in a low voice. The baby opened his eyes, which were a startling blue. He sucked in a breath and worked his mouth tentatively, as if testing whether all this were real—whether I was real. Then his face contorted in a silent wail. "You can hear me," I said. "Poor baby."

O'Mara looked puzzled and mournful in equal measure. "I guess he's been alone as long as his ma's been dead. And that seems to be some time."

Alone. Where was his brother? It didn't make sense. I looked again around the room, but there was no place to conceal a baby. I hurried back to the other room, searching all around. But there was nothing to see. Not far from the tub along the wall I spotted a stray brass button that looked as if it belonged to a man's coat, but that wasn't a clue to where the second baby was. God help me, I even opened the oven door. Putting a baby in there would be the work of a madwoman; then again, so would cutting one's wrists. But it was empty, thank heavens. I straightened, put my hands on my hips, and turned in a circle. How could a baby disappear?

"The other one's normal," Beggs said. "Cries louder than a steamship horn. Wakes up the whole blame building sometimes. If he was here, we'd know it."

Could one of the twins have died without anyone knowing? That might account for his mother being distraught enough to kill herself. But in doing so she would have abandoned her other child.

"Maybe the baby was kidnapped," I said, thinking aloud.

O'Mara laughed. "Last thing anyone around here wants or needs is another brat."

"What should we do?" I asked him.

"I'll telephone in." He frowned, itemizing all the things he would have to tell Donnelly. "We'll need the patrol wagon for the baby, and the coroner, and I guess detectives to look at the scene. Though there's not much question what happened."

Suicide. There was even a razor, a barber's straight edge, on the ground with bloody streaks across it. The dull glint of that steel in the bare bulb's glare made my skin twitch.

"I'll run down the street to the call box," O'Mara said. "You see to that baby."

It was hard to know where to begin. Obviously he needed nourishment. But first I had to get him out of his soiled clothes. "I'll need some water." I nodded at the chipped, blue-white basin leaning against the stove. "I suppose it'll be all right if I use that?"

"Don't see what difference it would make." O'Mara reached down and picked it up.

When he handed it to me, my nose wrinkled. "What is that?"

"What?"

"That smell." I sniffed the chipped metal surface.

"Probably perfume. I saw a lot of little bottles on the table in the bedroom."

I nodded. Technically we shouldn't be taking items from the room before the coroner and the detectives got here, but that baby needed tending desperately. First, though, I took a moment to look for milk, on the off-chance that there was any that hadn't gone bad. There was no icebox, but my roommate, Callie, and I kept our milk on the fire escape in winter and Ruthie probably did the same. I poked my head out the front window, sucking in a lungful of air. A milk bottle was on the fire escape, all right, but it was empty. Upright, but empty.

The sound of O'Mara's footsteps receded. Ducking back in, I crossed to the stove, picked up the basin, then checked the shelves to see if Ruthie had left any powdered or canned milk. I tried to avoid looking at the tub, but out of the corner of my eye I noticed something sticking up out of the reddish-brown bath water. It resembled a tiny fist.

I dropped the tin basin, creating a metallic clatter that made both Beggs and me jump. *Dear God, no.* With a shaking hand, I pressed the dead woman's doughy shoulder until she slumped against the back of the tub. My legs turned to jelly and I fell back. It wasn't just the horror of the woman's frozen green stare that transformed me into a quivering mass. It was the infant that bobbed to the surface of the water.

CHAPTER 2

While O'Mara and I waited for the coroner's men and the detectives, I busied myself trying to clean up the surviving baby. I carried cold water in from the hall tap, warmed it on the stove, and poured it into the basin. Meanwhile, the baby took a little water. I bathed him as quickly but thoroughly as I could manage, dried him, and wrapped him in the warmest blankets I could find among Ruthie's things.

Half the building's residents, along with bystanders from the street, lined the hallways and staircases, retreating as we shooed them away and then creeping back out of ghoulish curiosity. One of the crowd turned out to be a godsend, though. A woman approached me, tears in her eyes, and introduced herself as Eileen Daly, from an apartment on the first floor. Her Irish accent made it sound as if she'd stepped off the boat yesterday. "If you'll come with me," she said, "I've got some milk for the bairn in my flat."

O'Mara gave my visual plea the nod, and I followed her.

We edged down past the onlookers. "Poor little mite," was the verdict of most of them. Word of what had happened was now common knowledge, thanks probably to Beggs.

Eileen's flat was bigger than Ruthie's, with a higher ceiling. A plump, older baby lay in a crib on the floor. "My Davy's eight months," Eileen said. While I cradled Ruthie's child, she got a bottle ready, mixing milk, water, cod liver oil, and a bit of sugar in a saucepan. After the bottle was filled and tested on her wrist to her satisfaction, the baby took it eagerly.

"Do you know his name?" I asked, watching his tiny mouth eagerly latch on to the nipple.

"Eddie." She sniffled. "The other one was Johnny."

"Your baby and Ruthie's must be close in age."

"Eddie's a hair under three months." She wiped tears from her eyes. "I don't suppose he'll remember any of this, do you?"

I looked down into his little face, which was crinkled in his concentration of taking the milk. "I don't think so."

"That's a mercy. Though it's a hard thing to hope a babe won't remember his mam. What'll become of him?"

I didn't have the answer to that. "Did you know Ruthie well?"

"Passing well. I'd go up for a cup of tea, that sort of thing."

"Maybe something harder than tea?"

She wrinkled her nose. "Never saw her touch a drop of the stuff. Said she liked to keep her wits about her."

I frowned, remembering the bottle and the glass on her table. That liquor hadn't drunk itself.

"At first my Neal didn't like me visiting with her, on account of what she was," Eileen continued, "but I told him, 'Who else am I supposed to talk to in this godforsaken place?' Neal's a docker."

"A what?"

"He loads ships at the dock. Got arms like granite boulders. Still and all, it was harder for me to be too friendly with Ruthie after the babes came, because of the hours she kept. I didn't want to bother her during the day. I should've popped up more often, though."

"Did she tell you anything about herself? Where she was from, maybe?"

"Somewhere in the midlands, I think."

It took a moment to guess what that meant. "The Midwest?"

Her face brightened. "That's it. She mentioned a state once." Her face tensed again. "Nebraska? That's a state, isn't it?"

I nodded. "I don't suppose she mentioned a city, or town."

Her face pinched in frustration. "If she mentioned a city, it's escaped me. She didn't talk of home much, you know. Just that she'd been unhappy there. I'm thinkin' it couldn't have been much of a place if she preferred this life to the other."

"It must've been hard for her, with the babies."

"Ay. Poor lass was probably at her wit's end." Tears spilled down. "I should've done more to help."

"Don't blame yourself."

"To be honest, I thought maybe she was doin' a little better just lately. Last time I saw her she had a new dress. I told her she looked smart, and asked where did she buy it. She said she'd gone to one of the big stores, and that she was doing all right. She was even thinking of getting out of here." Eileen gasped. "You don't think she was tellin' me she was going to kill herself, do you?"

"Doesn't sound like it."

"And poor Johnny. How could Ruthie have done such a wicked thing? She couldn't have been in her right mind. She was so fond of those bairns, and especially protective of Eddie."

"This baby?"

Head nodding, she said, "I offered once to watch them for her—just in case she needed to go out—but she told me she didn't like to leave Eddie with anyone else, on account of only she understood him." She lifted her apron to her face and sobbed into it.

Why would a woman who wouldn't leave a baby with a neighbor have killed herself and left him behind, alone, forever?

Eileen's account of Ruthie's improved financial circumstances jibed with what Beggs had told me on the walk over—that in past weeks, Ruthie had been doing better. *Paid her rent, seemed almost cheerful.* I could see why financial security could only result in "almost" cheerfulness in this place. The building wasn't just dark, it was dirty and in ill repair. Built before air shafts and other modern improvements had entered the city's building code, the inside felt stuffy and unhealthy. The odor of one-pot dinners, tobacco, and sweat permeated the plaster walls and the cracks of the wood floors. Not a happy place.

My thoughts must have shown in my face as I looked about the room, because Eileen, gathering herself, bristled. "It's not so bad a place if you take care," she said, nodding to the clean, ironed cloth on the table, and her curtains, and the spic-and-span floors. "It's convenient for Neal."

For a longshoreman, that made sense. New York Harbor was the busiest in the world, with goods coming in from all over the United States being loaded on freighters and steamships headed for every port of the globe, and vice versa. Manhattan had just shy of a hundred piers, and across the Hudson, New Jersey had almost as many more. Now, because of the months-old war in Europe, the harbor had never been so crowded. Wilson's so-called neutrality policy banned merchant and military ships docked in United States ports from joining the war effort. Britain had ruled the waves at the time of the announcement of the policy, so German vessels, as well as their crews, were trapped on this side of the Atlantic for the duration. Even the battleship *Frederick the Great* had been towed over to Hoboken. The streets and alleys along the docks swarmed with more than the usual numbers of ship crews, merchant seamen, stevedores, and every other kind of person who fed off the shipping trade. Including prostitutes.

A year in the NYPD had taught me more about prostitution than I'd ever expected to know. Ladies of the evening were practically a policewoman's stock in trade, from the streetwalkers of the docks, alleys, and avenues to the ladies plying their trade in houses with madams providing protection along with a little bit of extortion. Ruthie was obviously the former, which was a tougher life. Yet if she'd managed to pull herself out of debt, she must have attracted a steady clientele, and had managed to find a way to evade the law. She hadn't been arrested during my time in the precinct.

"At heart, she was a good sort, Ruthie," Eileen said. "What would've made her do such a terrible thing?"

It didn't make sense to me, either. If Ruthie loved her sons as Eileen said she did, yet had been unable to take care of them, why hadn't she left them on the doorstep of a hospital before taking her own life? She hadn't written a note and had even locked her door, so she had to have known it could be days before Eddie would be found. She must have been so distraught that she couldn't reason at all anymore. But distraught about what?

"Ruthie didn't mention any specific family members here or back in Nebraska?" I asked.

"No. I got the feeling she was all alone in the world." She sucked in a breath. "She did say once that her father was a strict man. Or stepfather, maybe he was. 'Papa wasn't one for sparing the rod,' she told me. That sounds like he's dead, though, don't it?"

"Maybe when we go through her things, we'll find out." I spoke as if I would be part of this search, but as soon as I took Eddie to the foundling hospital, my involvement in the investigation into Ruthie Jones's death would be finished.

"Why wouldn't she have gone back to her family instead of killing herself?" Eileen wondered aloud. "What would've made her prefer to die?"

Maybe that rod she'd mentioned.

I knew a little about running from home and never returning. I'd left a family I'd lived with since I was a child—uncles, aunts, and young cousins—because they were ashamed of me. Nothing would persuade me to go back, either.

Eileen frowned down at the baby and my inattention to him. "You oughtn'ta feed him too much at once. Here, give him to me." I complied and watched as she laid him at her shoulder and gently patted his back until he burped. "I expect you don't know much about bairns."

My jaw clenched, but I couldn't deny the truth. I'd given birth, but I knew little about babies.

Eileen fussed over Eddie, who seemed more animated since his meal. His limbs kicked, showing a little vigor.

"Did you notice any of Ruthie's visitors?" I asked Eileen.

"Men, you mean?" Her brows drew together, but then she shook her head. "I tried not to pay attention. Poor lamb."

I glanced back at the door to the building's foyer, which stood wide-open. My guess was that it often did. "You never saw anybody, or maybe someone who came back several times?"

She bit her lip. "Well . . ." Her eyes widened, and a shadow fell over me.

When I pivoted to follow Eileen's gaze, a hulking wall of a man stood by the table, frowning at me. Or maybe that scowl was for Eileen. "Engaging in tittle-tattle after the death of that unfortunate woman?" he said.

She nodded at me. "It's a policewoman, Neal."

I stood. "I need to know if your wife remembers any of the men who visited Ruthie Jones."

His face darkened, sending a shiver of fear through me. I realized too late that I had asked the wrong question. *Arms with muscles like granite boulders.* They were, too.

"My wife had nothing to do with that woman beyond the courtesy one neighbor owes another. She certainly didn't pay attention to her customers. Bad enough a decent woman like Eileen had to live in the same building with all that going on."

"I understand. It's just if she remembered anyone, anyone at all—"

"She doesn't."

"Poor Ruthie," Eileen said. "She was never anything but kind to me."

"That doesn't mean you knew her business." The man was adamant about his wife not having seen anything. But presumably he was gone most of the day, so how would he know? He just didn't want me asking questions.

A knock sounded. From outside the door, O'Mara called my name. "Detectives want to see the little one."

I thanked Eileen, nodded at her red-faced husband, picked up the baby, and made my way upstairs past the dwindling number of curious neighbors. Since I'd left, Ruthie's cramped flat had become more crowded. Another policeman had arrived to guard the door, and inside, coroner's men were going through her belongings and sketching the scene. A pale fog of cigarette smoke hung in the room.

The coroner's man was kneeling by the tub, inspecting the pool of blood. "Not as much as you'd expect from gashes like that. But maybe the cold . . ."

His photographer was preparing to take pictures of the victims. At least Johnny had been pulled out of the water and was lying on a blanket someone had pulled from the bed. His diaper was stained red, and I reeled toward the open window, appreciating the cold slap of air. I held Eddie close, making sure the blanket covered his head.

The first detective I saw was one I knew. Lieutenant King was round, with a chubby face now sporting a horseshoe mustache, like a strip of fur forming an exaggerated pout around his lips. King had always struck me as one of the more polite men at the precinct, though I'd had little to do with him up to now.

"Hello, Faulk." The greeting was cheerless, but I appreciated his using my actual surname. "How's our survivor?"

"As well as can be expected, under the circumstances. He took a little milk."

He peered at the baby. "Hm. Guess it's lucky she didn't kill them both."

"Lucky for who?" Another man emerged from the second room. King's partner was a new addition to the detectives' ranks. I'd seen him but hadn't met him yet. He had a medium, athletic build and thick wheat-colored hair with a curl that vats of pomade couldn't quite flatten, giving him the look of an overgrown, mischievous boy. He didn't introduce himself, but approached me and eyed the baby with a curled lip. "O'Mara tells me he's a dummy."

"Are you saying he'd be better off dead?" I asked, incensed.

"He'll be put in an orphanage. What's he got to look forward to?"

"A lifetime," I said.

"Sure, he may learn some kind of trade when he gets older. Like rolling cigars, or sewing, like a woman. He'll never be normal, will he?"

The rules of seniority and precinct politics dictated that I swallow my anger and keep my mouth shut. But I never did like politics. "If a man without a heart can become a detective," I said, "I'm sure a child without a voice will turn out all right."

"That's telling him." King laughed. "Stevens, have you met Officer Louise Faulk?"

Stevens glared at me and tapped his cigarette. Ash drizzled onto the floor. He didn't say it was a pleasure to meet me.

"Poor kid's got a hard road ahead of him though, no doubt about that." King sighed as the coroner's camera flashed. "Not much of a beginning, is it?"

I'd been trying to avoid looking at the tub again, but my gaze was drawn that way. I made myself focus one last time on the scene. Ruthie's torso was not bare, but covered in a thin, armless shift.

"Look at this," the coroner's man said. He reached around the woman's neck and lifted something out of the foul water. It was a little pocket attached to a string. My aunt called those boodle bags—a small bag a person could wear around her neck or waist to carry and conceal money. "It's got dough in it."

The detectives gathered around to count wet bills and a few coins. "Almost forty-six dollars."

For a woman like Ruthie, or anyone in this corner of Hell's Kitchen, that was a fortune.

"Guess she thought she could take it with her," Stevens said.

While the men laughed, I tried to put myself in Ruthie's place. Why hadn't she left the money near Eddie? If I'd been in Ruthie's shoes, even distraught I would have wanted to make sure that forty-six dollars, my only legacy, went toward the care of the child I was leaving behind. I couldn't shake the feeling we were missing something.

Or perhaps it was impossible to second-guess a woman so deranged that she could have done something like this in the first place.

Wrapping the blanket over the baby's head, which still only had wisps of dark hair, I took another turn around the apartment, looking for any other treasure Ruthie might have left behind. There didn't seem to be much. Her clothes filled the pine box at the foot of the bed. Personal items were few. Some combs. Old bottles of perfume and hair lotion, all of which seemed almost used up.

On the top of the dresser stood a picture in a wood frame, half covered by what looked to be a torn envelope, so that all I could see was a woman. I carefully pulled the paper away to reveal a man, too. The middle-aged couple were in their Sunday best, unsmiling. The woman's dark blond or light brown hair was pulled back tight from her face. There was an echo of a onetime beauty in her somber eyes and slightly upturned nose, and she wore a fitted checked dress that emphasized her still-trim figure. The man—her husband, I guessed—was older, and sat next to her in an ornately carved chair that had probably been supplied by the photographer's studio. The man's slate-looking eyes were fixed in a stern, grim expression, and one of his eyes appeared rather cloudy. His caterpillar eyebrows were drawn together in a frown for posterity. He'd donned his most funereal clothes for the portrait: black suit, black vest, black tie, starched white collar. If these were Ruthie's parents, they looked as if they were already in mourning for her.

She'd covered the man's likeness. I wouldn't have wanted to look at him, either, but I assumed Ruthie's reasons were more personal than aesthetic.

"Faulk and I will leave as soon as the wagon arrives," O'Mara informed the detectives.

I hoped it would come soon. There were too many people in too small a space, and I wanted to get Eddie out of there.

"You're not needed here," Stevens said. "For that matter, neither are we. There's no doubt it's suicide."

King's mouth twisted at his partner's pronouncement, but he didn't disagree.

"What about the babies?" I asked.

Both detectives blinked at me.

"Why would Ruthie kill one and not the other?"

King considered my question, then shrugged. "She was suicidal. Not in her right mind."

"But the neighbor said she was very protective of Eddie, the mute baby. Why would she have left *him* behind?"

"Isn't killing one of them bad enough?" Stevens said. "You wish she'd killed them both?"

"No, of course not. But the woman downstairs, who knew Ruthie, said Ruthie was a loving mother. She didn't like leaving Eddie with strangers."

"So she loved him enough to let him live," King explained.

"Yes . . ." I frowned. "But both Beggs and Eileen, the woman downstairs, said they thought Ruthie's financial situation had improved in the past month, and the forty-six dollars bears that out. Who kills herself when her life is actually getting better?"

The younger detective shook his head and gestured around the apartment. "If this was an example of my life improving, I'd down a bottle of whiskey and cut my wrists, too."

"The neighbor also said Ruthie didn't drink."

Stevens laughed. "Sure she didn't. Tell me another one."

"Did the neighbor know anything about next of kin?" King asked me.

"Ruthie told Eileen she was from Nebraska, but she never mentioned any town or person by name."

"Sad," King said. "I'll ask the other tenants if they know any more about her, and maybe get something more out of Beggs."

"There's a picture in the next room. Might be her parents."

Stevens shook his head. "They're not going to pop out of the frame and tell us anything."

Something tugged at my elbow. I turned and O'Mara was frowning down at me. "We'd better go down and wait for the wagon, Two." He escorted me to the hallway and then asked in a fierce whisper, "What do you think you're about, telling detectives their business?"

"I was giving them information I'd learned talking to Eileen. Isn't finding things out what we're supposed to do?"

"It's what *they're* supposed to do."

"They don't seem inclined to," I said.

"And they won't be more inclined to because a young woman decided to boss them around."

Then they were fools. "Ruthie's parents, wherever they are, would be the next of kin of this baby." I nodded at the baby in my arms. He weighed next to nothing. "For all we know, they're all the family he has."

O'Mara's pitying look could have been meant more for either the baby or for me. "He's an orphan. Exactly like thousands of other orphans in this city."

I stared down into Eddie's face. The dazed expression had cleared from his eyes, and now he looked up at me almost as if he trusted me. My throat constricted. I could remember the devastation of losing my parents, who'd died when I was seven. At least I could remember them a little—that was a luxury Eddie would be deprived of. Yet we were both fellow orphans.

"Not exactly like the others," I said, holding him tight. Eddie Jones had at least one person looking out for him. Me.

The patrol wagon took O'Mara back to the precinct before driving Eddie and me to the New York Foundling Hospital. The motorized wagon had mesh windows in the back, but I asked the driver to cover them, both for warmth and so I didn't look like a fallen woman being carted through the streets of Manhattan.

This wasn't my first trip to the foundling hospital. Established by a few Catholic sisters in the last century, the charity had ballooned into an institution responsible for taking in and placing hundreds of orphaned and abandoned children every year. The hospital had an administrative wing, the medical building itself, and a separate wing for the children. New York Foundling also gave care to unwed mothers, and ran a nursery for working mothers. If I had been in New York City two years earlier, I might have ended up there myself. Instead, I had gone to a smaller home in Philadelphia. I tried not to think about those days, but it was difficult when I was holding a helpless infant in my arms as I'd never once held the son I'd given birth to. We hadn't been allowed.

Eddie and I were received by a nun named Sister Eleanor. Though she was dressed in the same long white habit and bonnet as the other sisters I'd encountered on previous visits, her manner was shorter on warmth. She inspected Eddie the way a factory foreman might check out goods: with an eye out for flaws.

"Underweight." She laid him down in the wicker receiving cradle and pulled the blanket off him. The baby kicked unhappily at the cool air or the indignity of her examination, or both. "Needs a good washing." She shook her head. "And mute, did you say?"

"So far as we know. Will he get special care?"

With brisk movements, she folded the blanket back over him. "A doctor will examine him, but there's little enough doctors can do for a child like that."

"I heard him make a noise while we were in the wagon. Maybe he's not really—"

"Was it a throaty sound?"

I nodded eagerly. "More than a gurgle, but not quite a cry."

"That'll be all he's capable of," she said. "You shouldn't let it raise your hopes."

God forbid anyone have hope. "He's very sweet." I put out my finger so he could grip it.

"The slow ones often are. Our Lord's saving grace."

Slow? Not having the gift of speech didn't mean he was slow.

My fears for Eddie's future ramped up a notch. "If it turns out that we are able to find his relatives, would they be able to take him?"

"That would be a desired outcome, if the family members are of good moral character."

Unlike his mother, you could almost hear her say.

"Perhaps someone will claim him."

She looked at me with pity. "You have a good heart, Miss Faulk, but you said that the poor little soul's mother was a fallen woman. Believe me, even if that girl did have family somewhere, they probably wouldn't welcome a dumb, fatherless child any more than they would have welcomed her. That sounds harsh, I know, but it has been my experience."

I wished I was able to contradict her.

She reached out and touched her hand to the coat I wore over my uniform. "Pray for the best, but don't expect happy endings for everyone in this world. You'll go mad."

Behind us, the policeman who'd driven the wagon over cleared his throat. "About time we were getting back, Two."

My heart clenched at the thought of leaving Eddie here. He looked so tiny and helpless. "May I visit him sometimes?" I asked Sister Eleanor.

Her lips pursed. "It would be a kindness, though if he were older I wouldn't recommend becoming attached to a child you're in no position of helping. We don't like to give children false hopes, you know."

Hope obviously wasn't high on Sister Eleanor's list of virtues.

I said goodbye to Eddie and then rode back with the driver in the open front seat of the vehicle, chatting aimlessly with him all the while so I couldn't attend to the trembling sadness in my chest. Facing forward, I let the darkness hide the tears stinging my eyes. Miserable as it was, the steady drizzle that had come down all day added a sheen to the paving stones and sidewalks of the city, especially illuminated by the streetlights and the headlamps of the wagon. Everything glistened. From my perch, it looked as if the entire city had been shellacked. As we turned downtown, the illuminated Diana atop the tower at Madison Square Garden shone like a beacon.

Back inside the station house, I hurried downstairs, shed my wet coat, and ran into the detective on the case, Lieutenant King, who'd returned and was shooting the bull with Schultzie. I was a little surprised. I hadn't been that long at the foundling hospital. King, evidently, hadn't spent much time gathering evidence at Ruthie's.

Schultzie, leaning on a broom, regaled King with his story about arresting the governor's brother-in-law sometime during the last century. I'd already heard it and so probably had King. Yet we both dutifully laughed as Schultzie reached the kicker. " 'Sorry I didn't vote for your sister's husband,' I tells him. 'Don't be,' he says. 'Neither did I.' "

"May I speak to you, Lieutenant?" I asked King after Schultzie was done.

He exhaled a stream of smoke from the cigar he was enjoying. "Sure. Fire away."

Schultzie didn't move, but neither of us expected him to. He knew all the secrets of this station. His droopy eyes watched me as expectantly as King's did.

"I wondered if I could take a closer look at the photograph from Ruthie Jones's flat. The one of the couple."

King shrugged. "Belongs to the landlord now."

"It isn't part of your investigation?"

"Investigation into what?"

"Ruthie's death."

"It was suicide," he said. "The coroner said so at the scene, and the evidence backs him up. We don't investigate suicides, we report them and move on to more important cases. Cases we can do something about."

"There's no room for doubt, then?" I asked.

The impatient look he leveled on me made me question myself. Other detectives were temperamental or dismissive, but King was usually nicer than the rest. "Maybe you don't realize this," he said, "but there's more going on in this city than the death of a prostitute."

"But what about the other clues? The money on her body, the fact that she'd left one of her babies alive, the liquor bottle—"

"What about the fact that the woman was behind a locked door, lying in a bathtub next to the razor she'd used to slash her wrists?"

The retort had come out rat-a-tat, but in the next moment his expression softened. "It was suicide, Louise. Go home and get some sleep."

Schultzie's sagging cheeks puffed up and then he sighed out a long breath, agreeing sympathetically. "Sleep usually makes things clearer."

Arguing with the lead detective would serve no purpose, I knew that. If I'd run into Stevens, I might have tried harder, even though it would have been like hurling words against a brick wall. Perhaps King was even right. He'd seen more suicides and murders than I had.

"It's been a long week," I said. "I'm glad I have tomorrow off."

"That's the idea." King blew a smoke ring. "Wash this place out of your mind for a day. Eat Thanksgiving leftovers."

"If there are any left," Schultzie joked.

King smiled, and the expression in his eyes was achingly kind. "That was a rough thing to see tonight. Sad. Everybody was shaken. You'll feel better tomorrow."

I wasn't sure about that. But at least I'd have a night to consider everything I'd noticed in Ruthie's apartment, and weigh what my next step should be.

CHAPTER 3

When I emerged from my bedroom the next morning, I discovered my roommate, Callie, in the kitchen, humming to herself. Her blond hair was braided and pinned up in an artful pile, with her soft fringe and ringlets framing her eyes. Over an unseasonably thin cotton dress she'd wrapped a wool schoolgirl sweater that hung below her hips. "Who are you today?" I asked.

She beamed at me in greeting, and struck a pose. "Serena in *June Bride*. Do I look dewy and virginal?"

I staggered gratefully toward the percolator. "I'd marry you for your coffee making alone."

She laughed.

This up-with-the-larks version of my roommate took some getting used to. When she was doing stage work, she kept Count Dracula hours, rarely rising before noon. These days, though, she put roosters to shame. Not that there were many roosters in Greenwich Village.

"I was going to wait up for you last night," she told me, "but I conked out over *The Titan* by Theodore Dreiser. Your aunt loaned it to me yesterday. It's better than a bromide. Oh, and she sent you a piece of pumpkin pie."

That was good news. "Better breakfast than Grape-Nuts. Do you want to split it?"

"I already swallowed some burned toast. I need to hurry if I'm going to make it to 175th Street. It's a train, trolley, and long hike to get there."

Callie had already brought in the milk. I poured some into my coffee and then quickly opened the window and put it on the sill. Seeing the milk bottle there reminded me of the one on Ruthie Jones's fire escape, which brought to mind the whole grisly scene at Ruthie's apartment. There went my appetite, even for pie.

I shut the window again as fast as possible. "It's cold out there."

"We're doing a picnic scene today. I'll be shivering in short sleeves."

After her last show closed the past summer, Callie found work in motion pictures to tide her over and had kept on making them. There were film studios all over—in Queens, in the Bronx, New Jersey, on Midtown rooftops, even. While the theater thrived at night, the picture business lived in daytime, and the hours were long. In my opinion it seemed a lot of effort for very little. I'd seen Callie in one of her pictures already, a comedy about a man with a nagging wife. Callie portrayed a shop girl the film's hero flirted with. She'd been the best thing about it.

"You never go on auditions anymore," I said.

"I do so. I went to one just . . ." She thought back. "Three weeks ago."

"You used to get antsy if you'd gone even three days without making the rounds of producers' offices."

"It's almost December, and the Christmas season's a slow time for auditions and casting," she explained. "Besides, I don't have to worry so much now that Alfred Sheldrake at Empire State Pictures is offering me all the work I could want."

"Movies." I shook my head. How gratifying could that be? "You knock yourself out for a few minutes of flickering across a screen in a silly fifteen-minute story."

"I know, you think I should be Ethel Barrymore. But guess what? Even la Barrymore's made a picture. They're the future."

If the future promised nothing but pratfalls and mimed melo-drama, I wasn't sure I was ready for it.

"Last week Alfred paid me ten dollars for a movie idea, too," Callie said.

"That's great, but you should be lighting up Broadway."

"Who are you, my manager? *You* spend a couple of days with your backside polishing benches outside producers' offices and come back and tell me how gratifying the Great White Way is. Anyway, I'll be back in the theater someday. Otto's promised me a part in his new show."

Our friend Otto, a songwriter, and the playwright he was working with had been laboring so long on this show, it was hard to believe it was actually going to come off. Elephants gestated calves more quickly than it took to get a musical comedy on its feet. "Have you spoken to Otto recently?"

"He was at your aunt's yesterday."

Of course. Everyone had been at my aunt's. Except me.

"He says it's a go just as soon as they can line up a producer," she finished.

Which was like someone saying they'll give you a sheet of paper just as soon as they find a seven-hundred-year-old oak tree to pulp. I held my tongue, though.

Callie checked her bracelet watch, drained the last drops of her coffee, and put the cup in the sink. "I've got to go. They promised I'd be finished by three so I can drop off my knitting for the Belgians."

In the first month of the war, the stories coming from Europe had focused on the horrors and depredations committed by the Kaiser's army upon the defiant Belgians as Germans advanced westward. Callie had joined a group of actors who gathered clothes donations and knitted for the Red Cross in the afternoons twice a week. Before the war started, I hadn't known she could tell knitting needles from chopsticks. That fighting had now moved to the disputed territory of Alsace-Lorraine, but the knitters and bundle-gatherers soldiered on.

"I'm getting compliments on the quality of my socks," she said. "Sure you don't want to join us? You're welcome."

"Not this week." I had plans simmering.

Her brow wrinkled as she looked at me. "I don't mean it as an insult to you, you know."

"Why would it be?"

"Well, you know. You're German."

"I'm not a German," I said, my hackles up. "That is, yes, I'm a German-American." Not that I actually thought of myself as what Teddy Roosevelt sneeringly called a 'hyphenated American.' I could speak the language, and many of my ancestors had emigrated from there, but I was two generations removed from the old country. "I'm just as American as people whose ancestors came over on the *Mayflower*."

"I know that."

"Then why, whenever someone mentions that I'm German now, does it always seem as if they're checking to see if I'm hiding a bayonet in my petticoats?"

She touched my shoulder. "Don't get upset. Teddy says the war'll be over in a few months anyway."

Teddy was Callie's boyfriend of over a year now. "Does Teddy have a crystal ball?"

"No, he has Hugh. Hugh's convinced planes will be the key to victory for whichever side wins. Says airplanes will end the war in no time."

Hugh Van Hooten, Teddy's friend, owned an aeronautics business, and Teddy was his most fervent disciple. "So Hugh's not only a fortune-teller, he's a war strategist."

She started putting on her coat, hat, and gloves. "What do you have planned for your day off?"

"I thought I'd go to Aunt Irene's."

"Speaking of fortune-tellers." Callie smiled. "Last night she told me I'm going to meet someone who'll change my life."

My aunt had recently fallen prey to the occult craze. She'd even had her milliner make up a couple of turbans for her to wear when practicing her new art. "Did you tell Teddy about the mysterious stranger in your future?"

"It might not be a love interest," Callie said. "It might be someone in the theater . . . or anybody."

"So in a city of over four million, you might meet someone. Aunt Irene's powers astound me."

"You should get her to tell your fortune. We need a sampling to see how accurate she is."

"I'm just hoping there are leftovers in my future."

"You might get lassoed into housework. You should've seen the herd of people in and out of your aunt's place yesterday. I imagine there's a lot of cleaning up to do."

"I don't mind." It was hard not to contrast the fête my aunt had hosted yesterday with my evening in Hell's Kitchen.

"Is something wrong?" Callie asked.

"Just an unpleasant thing that happened at work last night. A woman committed suicide, and left an orphaned baby."

"How sad."

I didn't mention the other baby. Saddling someone's thoughts with that tragedy this early in the morning didn't seem fair. "The poor woman must have had family somewhere, but no one seems interested in tracking them down."

"A job for you then," Callie said.

"The NYPD doesn't agree. I was basically told to forget all about Ruthie Jones."

"All the more reason it sounds like a job for you. When have you ever done what anyone wanted you to?"

After reading the news from Europe from yesterday's paper over coffee, I bathed, dressed, and then headed uptown to my aunt's. Walter, my aunt's butler, answered the door, feather duster in hand. "Are you here to visit or help?" he asked. "The correct response is help."

"At your service." I held out my hand, and he presented the feather duster to me like a king passing on a scepter.

He ushered me in and led me toward the parlor. The room looked much as it always did to me. The center of my aunt's social universe, the space was dominated by a long sofa near the front bay window, an upright grand piano, and a bar. Glass-paned double doors communicated with a smaller, darker dining room, and beyond that was the kitchen.

"How was Thanksgiving?" I asked.

"One young man got as drunk as a lord and broke a Waterford crystal glass." He frowned and pointed. "Flick that duster over the walnut side table." While I did as ordered, he continued. "Your aunt insisted on the crystal yesterday because it was a special occasion. I warned her that it's special occasions when people act especially foolish."

"I'm sure Aunt Irene will survive being one glass short of a set."

Walter sent me an arch look. "That would be a good description for some of her guests."

I laughed.

My aunt, a writer, had seen her professional fortunes wax and wane over the years, but at the moment she was doing quite well. Recently, she'd moved from writing dewy romances to mysteries. Her latest detective novel, *The Curtain Falls*, was giving Mary Roberts Rinehart a run for her money, and now she was finishing her third. I could hear a typewriter clacking away upstairs. My aunt had returned to doing her own typing again after losing me to the police department and her latest secretary, Miriam, to a job on a newspaper uptown, in Harlem.

The kitchen door swung open and Bernice appeared in the dining room. She positioned a platter of sliced turkey in the middle of the table. Seeing me, she broke into a broad smile. "I told your aunt you'd be here for lunch."

"It's nice someone's glad to see me." Apart from being an extra pair of hands.

"I sure am. Your aunt bet me a dollar that you wouldn't come till dinner."

Walter rang a bell on the hall table and Aunt Irene appeared soon after in a simple—for her—lavender dress trimmed with ivory lace around the neckline and cuffs. Her light brown hair was arranged in an artistic mound held in place by silver combs. Her eyes narrowed in suspicion when she spotted me by the dining table. "Did you tip off Bernice?"

"No, she just knew I wouldn't be able to resist the lure of holiday leftovers."

She swept across the room and kissed my forehead. "I didn't think so, either, but I assumed you'd enjoy a day of rest after your full week at that job."

"It was *that job* that kept me from sleeping in this morning." I waited until Bernice and Walter joined us before giving a brief account of what had happened the night before. Even though I left out the most gruesome details, by the end of my recitation my audience had put down their forks.

"That poor girl." Bernice shook her head at the sad tale.

"She must have felt desperate to have done something so terrible," Walter said.

"Ruthie Jones is beyond our help," my aunt said. "It's that poor little baby my heart goes out to. Losing a mother and a brother like that . . . and now what kind of future will he have?" She lifted her napkin to her eyes.

"Ruthie must have left something behind that would tell who her people are," I said. "Maybe they would take in Eddie. But I'm not sure how to go back to her flat and check without looking as if I were gainsaying my superiors at the precinct. Anyway, the landlord will probably get rid of all her belongings as soon as possible so that he can rent the flat."

Walter cleared his throat. "If that's the case, then a clear way to retrieve the woman's belongings would be to be the ones who clear out the flat for the landlord."

"It's not my place to do that."

"No, it's not," Bernice agreed.

"Would your superiors fire you for looking at the belongings of a murder victim?" Aunt Irene asked.

"I got in trouble last year for following my own initiative. I wouldn't want to be put back on probation again."

"How would anyone find out?" my aunt asked.

I thought of Beggs. "The building manager would know me, and he'd probably mention it the next time he ran across O'Mara, the cop on that beat."

Walter cleared his throat. "The custodian might recognize you, but he wouldn't know Walt the ragman and antiquarian dealer." He smiled at me. "Or my helper, Louie."

* * *

Walter, formerly an actor, had a trunk full of clothes that we dipped into for our disguises as Walt and Louie. Walter wore an old suit, wrinkled and a bit dusty. I got a check-patterned jacket and baggy trousers attached with suspenders. Luckily it was winter, so an old, battered coat covered my chest. He hid my hair beneath a boy's floppy cap and smudged enough dirt on my face to ensure no one would want to approach close enough to get a good look at me.

Bernice, drinking tea in the kitchen, didn't recognize me at first. A good sign. When she realized what I was up to, though, she wasn't impressed. "This looks like the start of something bad."

"We're not going to do anything illegal," I said.

"If you're hiding who you are, you're already in trouble." She frowned. "I know you're thinking about that poor orphaned baby, though, so I'm not going to argue with you. Getting in trouble for a good cause is better than doing nothing at all."

It was as close to a blessing as we were likely to get from Bernice. My aunt, by contrast, had nothing but praise for Walter's handiwork. She even gave us money to buy the belongings I wanted from Ruthie's apartment. A bribe for Beggs.

"I'll pay you back," I promised.

She shook her head. "It's for Eddie Jones. Consider it my first charitable act of the holidays."

I handed over the money to Walter, who pocketed it. We unearthed an old cart in the basement, and though it was laborious as well as tedious, we hauled it across the city. Walter was all for extra work in the name of dramatic believability, and in no time I was feeling authentically grungy, sweaty, and tired. My confidence in our scheme grew during our cross-town trudge, though. As we passed through a poor or commercial pocket of the city, we were ignored. In the wealthier sections, our disguises caused a few women to cross the street to avoid us.

Walter navigated us expertly across Ninth Avenue, dodging cars and wagons as an El train screeched overhead. I rarely saw him out and about like this. It gave me an idea. "You should come over to the flat sometime."

"That's kind of you to suggest," he said, in the stiff, butlery tone he assumed when he wanted to keep someone at a distance. He called it his at-the-door voice.

"I bet you'd enjoy meeting Callie's theater friends," I said. "I don't know why I haven't thought of inviting you before."

"Perhaps because I've been sending telepathic messages to avoid just such a circumstance."

"Why?"

"Because I have an inkling I'd go on my day off and then spend the whole time tidying."

"Callie and I aren't slobs," I said, offended. "At least, not by normal standards."

Walter's look told me that normal standards were merely substandard.

"This is the street, isn't it?" he asked.

Tenth Avenue and Thirty-Third Street looked even worse by day than at night. Old warehouses, tenements, missions, and junk stores weren't visually pleasing, and now I noticed one lot had been turned to rubble, probably after a fire. A man with a pushcart dawdled and clanged in front of us, selling pans and kettles. A beggar approached, only to be repulsed by Walter's stony stare. I was glad to be in disguise, because I recognized a few of the winos and women on the street from the station house. This was their world, and how well Walter and I fit in was a testament to his costuming skills.

I pointed. "It's that building on the corner." It looked as lopsided as ever.

"You take the cart," Walter instructed me. "Keep your head down. I'll do the talking."

I was able to tell him which door belonged to Beggs, and I crossed my fingers that the custodian was in. Luckily, he was, and after a bit of finagling and handing over a couple of bucks, we were allowed into the apartment to take what we wanted, for which we would pay him more when we were done, depending on what we found. It was Beggs's lucky day, and I would have been more resentful if I weren't in such a hurry to see what I could retrieve from the apartment. I feared scavengers had already taken things out. I was especially eager to get my hands on the picture.

My worries were all for nothing. The apartment appeared much the same as it had been the day before. The tub still had quite a bit of blood-stained water in it, although the razor was gone.

Walter paled when we were left alone. "Dear God, this is horrible. That poor woman, and those children. They *lived* here?"

I had seen enough places like it in the past year that I was no longer as shocked at its primitiveness as I'd been before I'd joined the police force. Of course, even the poorest of tenements didn't usually have the stench of death that still clung to Ruthie's rooms. Or was that my imagination?

"I'll open the window." I hurried to let some air in. I also pulled the ratty curtains open, allowing more of the feeble autumn light inside.

It helped. Gulping in a few breaths, Walter recovered his composure. Hands on hips, he inspected the rooms more closely, even running a finger along a shelf where the package of crackers sat. "No dust. Miss Jones was not a lax housekeeper."

"She might have been clean, but she wasn't tidy," I said. "The bed's unmade, nothing in her drawers was folded, and she even left food containers open. And look at the empty milk bottle out on the fire escape."

"So?" he asked. "Everyone puts milk out in winter."

"But the bottle was empty. You noticed she was clean. Why wouldn't she have put it by the door out in the hallway for the milk-man to pick up?" That's what Callie and I did as soon as we finished a bottle. An idea that had been tickling the back of my mind roared forward. "What if someone else caused the mess?"

Walter frowned. "Or maybe this disorder was indicative of a disordered mind."

"Maybe." A voice in my head told me not to get so carried away with my new pet theory that I refused to accept the obvious. Actually, the voice sounded an awful lot like my friend Detective Frank Muldoon. Whenever my imagination ran amok, I could usually count on Muldoon to be my brakeman. If he could see what I was doing now, he'd have a fit. *It's just for the baby,* I told myself. I only needed to find out where in Nebraska Ruthie came from. I wasn't trying to prove her death was a murder.

Next to me, Walter frowned at the floor. "I take back what I said about Ruthie's cleanliness. Look at the mess under the bed. Are those dust moats?"

I followed his gaze. The clumps of fluff seemed too thick for dust. "More like cotton."

Walter knelt and reached under the bed. When his hand appeared again, a piece of mattress stuffing was pincered between his thumb and index finger. "Was this under the bed last night?"

"I think so." When I'd glanced under there last night I'd been more interested in finding a child than in Ruthie's housekeeping skills.

He stood again, and in silent agreement we turned the mattress over. It was cross-hatched with cuts. No wonder the batting was spilling through the slats of the bed frame.

"Someone was looking for something," I said.

"Someone who thought Ruthie kept her money in her mattress, I bet." His eyes widened. "Maybe they killed her for it."

Remembering the boodle bag, I shook my head. "The detectives found forty-six dollars on her, in the tub. Surely Ruthie would have handed over the money before letting someone kill her." And what about her son? "If someone intended to kill her to find the money, they'd probably already killed Johnny as a threat. Surely she would have let the thief have the money before he killed her baby."

I'm not here to solve a murder, I reminded myself. I hurried over to the framed photograph. "I definitely want this. If I can only figure out where the picture was taken . . ."

"It might have a studio stamp on it somewhere."

We'd brought a canvas sack to carry our loot home in, and I put the picture in it. Then I went through every drawer in the flat, hunting for a letter or some clue as to Ruthie's hometown. As minutes ticked by without our finding more, I despaired. A lot was going to depend on that picture.

After a half hour, Walter started to get antsy. "That man Beggs is going to wonder why we've been up here so long."

I relented. "There's nothing more I want here anyway."

"We can't leave empty-handed, though," he said, looking around. "Ragmen aren't picky. Grab some clothes from her trunk."

Thank heavens one of us was thinking straight. I took armloads of Ruthie's clothes and put them in the bags. I could donate them to charity.

"We'll end up spending a lot of your aunt's money for very little," Walter grumbled.

It was true. I took a last turn around the flat, then spotted the button I'd seen earlier. It was shiny brass, with a bird with spread wings, possibly an eagle, in the center. I stuffed it in my pocket. I wasn't sure why. Maybe it was a clue.

Not that I was trying to solve a murder.

CHAPTER 4

The saxophone quintet who lived on the second floor of my building were trying out their version of "It's a Long Way to Tipperary" that evening when I marched up the stairs hauling the bags from Ruthie's. The tenor John McCormack had recently made a recording of the song, and now everyone in New York seemed to be tapping their toes to a tune that, an ocean away, men were singing as they marched off to war.

Though unlocked, the door to our apartment barely budged until I gave it few shoves. "Sorry—the bundles for Belgium are blocking you," Callie called out, rushing to help me.

My friend Otto was right behind her, dressed for evening in a black wool suit with pale gray stripes, tailored to fit his already lean build. His boots were shiny black with gray canvas tops. A purple-and-yellow-check tie gave him a splash of color so that his light-haired, pale face wasn't completely overshadowed by vertical gray-and-black darkness. Since coming to New York, Otto had made the acquaintance of some of the brightest lights of the entertainment world. My friends seemed to be enjoying glamorous lives with entertainment luminaries while I was spending holidays in Hell's Kitchen.

He looked slightly exasperated when I dropped my canvas sacks next to Callie's. "Are you taking part in this madness, too?"

Callie rounded on him. "How is it madness to help people who have been ravaged by the Kaiser's army?"

"Of course I feel bad for the Belgians," he said. "But what's the point of being neutral when we're listening to British marching songs and our newspapers are filled with stories about Germans bayoneting babies?"

These impromptu battles broke out all too frequently these days, and not just in our apartment. Ever since a group of German veterans had staged a march in support of the Kaiser, nearly causing a riot in Manhattan, the mayor had banned parades and the flying of foreign flags. Yet that hadn't stopped lunch counters and even living rooms from turning into war zones from time to time.

"I suppose we should just ignore all the war news, then." Callie's voice dripped sarcasm.

"Of course not." Otto turned to me for backup. "Louise?"

"Helping the victims of war is a good thing," I said, doing my best to bring about a truce. "Even if you don't believe all the stories in the papers, which I don't."

"I only wish I could do more," Callie said.

The Bleecker Blowers repeated their song, this time at a faster tempo. I went down the short hall to the parlor and collapsed onto the sofa. Otto sat next to me, tapping his foot in spite of himself. It *was* catchy.

"Maybe I should pen a counteroffensive," he said. " 'The Neutrality Waltz.' "

I smiled. "The 'Let's Not Tear Each Other to Pieces Rag.' "

"What is this stuff, Louise?" Callie had lagged behind and was rummaging through the bag I'd brought in. She pulled a few garments out and frowned, eyeing them critically.

"Clothes belonging to the woman I told you about this morning."

"The suicide?" A dress slipped from her fingers and back into the sack's gaping maw.

Otto's bulging eyes got bigger. "What suicide?"

I told him Ruthie's story and explained my hope to track down Eddie's family in Nebraska. "There's a picture in those bags somewhere," I said, getting up again. "I need to check it for a photographer's stamp."

"What do you intend to do with these clothes?" Callie asked.

"I don't really need them. Walter and I just took them to fool the landlord. You can send them to Belgium if you think they'll do any good."

"I might . . . but I might take some of them to use as costumes. We lowly film actors have to provide our own. Would that be all right?"

"Be my guest. I just need to get that picture."

I dug through the bags looking for it. The framed photograph lay under a cape that Callie said would be useful. She stood and tried it on while Otto and I huddled on the sofa. After I'd pried the backing off the frame and pulled the picture away from the glass, I felt a surge of hope. As Walter had predicted, the back of the photo bore a stamp in fading inked script *J. Clemsen   Elbart, Nebraska.*

"Glory hallelujah," I said.

"Does Elbart mean anything to you?" Otto asked.

"Never heard of it. But that's good—it can't be a very big place. Which means the photographer might know the people in the picture."

His freckled brow pinched into a frown. "But he's in Nebraska and you're here. And what if those people in the picture aren't even alive anymore?"

I inspected their faces. "They don't look too old."

"You don't know when the picture was taken," he pointed out.

Callie glanced over our shoulders. "That checkered dress with the high neck is identical to one my aunt had. And look at all those pleats. They scream Sears catalog, 1909."

So . . . about five years ago. Assuming Callie was right, and when it came to clothes she usually was. "I'm going to write Mr. Clemsen."

I retrieved a pen and paper and skirted around Callie to get to our compact drop-leaf table. Otto joined me and peered at my paper while I wrote. It reminded me of the days when we'd work on lessons after school together at the library in Altoona. The books were housed in an abandoned Presbyterian church, which always made me feel doubly shamed when Mrs. Dunwoody shushed us. It was like being caught talking in the library *and* church.

"What are you going to write?" he asked in a low voice. Maybe he was remembering Mrs. Dunwoody, too.

"Just the truth."

Dear Mr. Clemsen,
My name is Louise Faulk, and I'm writing to you
for help under sad circumstances. Your business's
stamp was found on the back of a photograph
belonging to a woman who died here in New York
City recently. The woman's name was Ruth Jones,
and she told her neighbor she was from Nebraska. I
am trying to locate any family of Miss Jones.

Otto was reading over my shoulder. "Are you going to tell him she was a suicide?"

"I'm not sure she was. And you know how judgmental people are about that."

It's my hope that you will be able to assist me in
locating the couple who sat for you in the picture
Ruth Jones kept with her, which was obviously a
treasured possession. The picture is of a middle-aged
woman, not unattractive, with light brown or dark
blond hair. In the photograph she is wearing a dress
in a checked pattern. She is with an older man, in his
fifties, I think, clean shaven, with a stern
countenance, salt-and-pepper short hair, and some-
thing wrong with his right eye, which appears cloudy
in the picture. An associate informs me that, judging
from the style of dress the woman is wearing, the
photograph might have been taken approximately
five years ago.

"You're Louise's associate now, Callie," Otto informed her.

She sauntered over to investigate. "Is it a paid position?"

"Paid in cast-off clothing." I looked up at her. She'd tried on a short cape from the bag. "That's nice."

She straightened, twitching her shoulders a little as she frowned at the garment, unsatisfied. "You think so? It drapes oddly."

Otto and I both studied the cape, which was made of dark blue wool with black velvet trim. "Looks fine to me," Otto said.

I turned my attention back to my letter.

Since Elbart is a small town, it's my guess that
you know most of the subjects you photograph. Does
the description of the couple match anyone you
know? The woman looks a little like Ruth Jones, so
I am making the assumption that they are related. I
am sorry to relay news that will surely be a blow to
Ruth's relations, but Ruth's child—a baby, and fa-
therless—is now an orphan and being kept in the
foundling hospital here. The infant had a twin who,
tragically, died with his mother. If there is anyone in
the world who is a relation to the poor little boy,
who might be able to love him as a helpless baby de-
serves to be loved, I think they would want to know.
His name is Edward—shortened to "Eddie" by
Ruth—and he is, after all, a last link to a young
woman who was taken from this world too soon.

I would be so grateful for any assistance you could
lend me in this matter.

Yours sincerely,

Louise Faulk

I closed by writing my address.

"Why don't you tell him you're with the police?" Otto asked. "I bet this Mr. Clemsen would be more likely to take the letter seriously then."

"I'm not sure the NYPD would approve of what I'm up to. Even the nuns at New York Foundling didn't seem to think it was my business to find Eddie's relations. I'd rather keep it a private investigation."

"What the blazes is going on?" Callie said aloud in a fit of frustration, still fussing with the cape. Scowling, she pulled it off and turned it lining-side-out, feeling the hem. "Where's the sewing box?"

"Is the cape ripped?"

"No, but it will be. I'm about to perform surgery on it."

I retrieved the sewing box from my bedroom and watched Callie neatly cut the seam of the lining. She reached in two fingers and brought out a pair of little booklets, which she dropped onto the little table by the sofa.

"What are they?" I picked one up and unfolded it.

"Passports?" Otto was looking at the other. "This one's an Englishman's."

"Mine's in . . ." I wasn't sure at first, but then I saw the word *Stockholm.* "Swedish."

"There's another one, I think." Face tensed, Callie worked the lining until another document was in a position to be pulled out. When it was free, she opened it. "Dutch?" She pulled a torn sheet of paper out of the folds of the document. "*The Silver Swan,*" she read, showing it to me. The words were written in a careful, looping script. Ruthie's writing? I suspected so, but I couldn't be sure.

"I wonder where the Silver Swan is," I said.

"Not *where,*" Otto said. "*What.* 'The Silver Swan' is a new song by Scott Joplin." He looked around as if a piano would materialize in our apartment. We didn't have one. "He released it as a piano roll but didn't publish the music." He hummed a few bars. "Catchy tune."

"How likely would it be that Ruthie Jones heard it?" I asked.

"Or liked it so much she decided to write down the title and tuck it into a passport." Callie shook her head. "Bet it's something else. A tavern, maybe."

"I can check the business directory at work." Meanwhile, I was faced with a bigger puzzle.

I spread all three passports before me, picking out what information I could of the three passport holders. All three had men's names. The Swedish one was a challenge to decipher, but it also contained the most entry stamps from ports all over the world. The British passport belonged to a man named Gerald Hughes, who according to what was written was thirty-eight, with brown eyes and hair. From what I could pick out in the foreign languages, the youngest was the Dutchman, who was twenty-three.

"Why would Ruthie have passports?" I wondered.

"She probably took them off her"—Otto's face reddened— "customers."

"Why?" Callie asked. "They're not worth anything. And she sewed them into a cape. Why go to such lengths to hide them?"

"Because she was a thief," Otto said. "Of course she wanted to hide them. She probably took their money, too."

I wasn't so sure about that. Prostitutes were different than pickpockets, shoplifters, and badger-game girls. A prostitute, especially one with a fixed address and no protector, didn't steal from her customers if she hoped to ply her trade—or live—for long. Even in seedy areas like Hell's Kitchen, word of mouth about various girls got around.

Then again, Ruthie *hadn't* lived long.

"What are you going to do with the passports?" Callie asked.

"She's going to turn them in," Otto said. "That's what a person's supposed to do, right?"

Callie shot him an incredulous look. "A person, sure. But Louise is cop who just snuck into a crime scene in disguise and swiped all this stuff."

I was in a pickle, all right. "Bernice warned me this would be trouble."

"Of course she did," Callie said. "She's always the voice of doom."

"Or reason." Otto straightened. "I can take them to a police station—or do they need to go somewhere else? Is there a sailor's aid society in town? I bet they were all sailors."

My eyes narrowed. "I'm not going to get anyone else involved in this."

Although that wasn't exactly true. There was one person I needed to get involved, simply because I didn't know who else to turn to.

After work the following evening I made my way via the subway to Brooklyn, to an address on Henry Street I'd discovered by slightly devious means. The building was a brick row house that many years ago had been ill-advisedly painted yellow. The yellow was now flaking off the brick, although the black trim paint on the windows and front door was still adhering. A smile tugged at my lips as I stood on the stoop and knocked. I never imagined Detective Frank Muldoon's home would resemble a giant bumblebee.

From inside, footsteps clattered down stairs. When the door swung open, a short young woman with round, dark eyes and cinnamon hair blinked up at me.

"Is Detective Muldoon at home?" I asked.

She looked me up and down as she wiped her hands on her

pinafore apron. I'd stopped at home and changed into a fresh white shirtwaist and camel-color skirt, which were barely visible beneath my long coat. "Not yet. I'm expecting him any minute. Although 'any minute' for a detective isn't something you can set a clock by, if you get my meaning."

I did. Detectives worked on a rotating shift schedule like all policemen, but for them the hours in a workday expanded if a case required more attention.

"I'm sorry I missed him. Would you tell him Louise Faulk stopped by?"

"Louise Faulk?" She repeated my name the way Callie might have said "Maude Adams" if I'd told her that her stage idol had knocked at our door. The next thing I knew, she had grabbed my arm. "Don't go. Frank'll be back soon, and I'm sure he'll want to see you. Won't you come in?"

I peered behind her, weighing the wisdom of taking her up on her offer. I wasn't sure Muldoon would appreciate me entering his house in his absence. Quite the contrary. I'd known him a year and a half and he'd never invited me here. But the way the woman's hand was clamped on my arm, I felt like a fish on a hook.

"Are you Anna?" I asked. Muldoon had mentioned his sister a few times.

Her head bobbed. "Please come in. I've got dinner warming."

"I shouldn't intrude."

"Nonsense." She practically yanked me over the threshold, shut the door and turned the key lock. "Louise Faulk. Frank's told me about you. Let me take your things."

I unbuttoned the coat and she tugged it off from behind with a deft hand. She offered to take my satchel, but I looped it over my shoulder. I'd need it if Muldoon ever arrived. The passports were in there.

"You're practically the only woman Frank's ever mentioned," Anna said. "A policewoman! And he brought me a few of your aunt's books, autographed. I love them all. Especially *Shy Fern*. You can guess why."

I didn't have a clue. "Why?"

"Because I'm shy myself." She piloted me toward the cozy front sitting room of the house, where a small blaze burned in the fireplace. The walls were papered in a dark green trellis pattern, and a few Muldoon family portraits hung next to landscapes and a decent copy of Gainsborough's *Blue Boy*. Antimacassars graced every chair and sofa, and lace doilies covered two side tables.

Anna gestured to the sofa. "Please sit down. Do you want tea?"

"No, thank you." I sat, and though there were three other chairs free, Anna took a seat inches next to me. "Louise Faulk." She studied me so intently, I squirmed. "Frank's never brought a girl home before."

"He didn't bring me home, either," I reminded her.

"Oh, but he'll be delighted." Her words made me wonder if she was some imposter posing as Frank Muldoon's sister. I'd never known a man who liked surprises less. "Usually it's just the two of us now. I've done my best since our mama died, but it's a lot of work, taking care of a house and a hardworking brother. Lonely sometimes, too. But think how it is for Frank! I'm sure no man dreams of coming home every night to his drudge of a sister."

No woman seemed less of a drudge than Anna Muldoon. She was pert, talkative, and certainly attractive. Her light blue wool dress fit her petite figure like a glove.

"You wouldn't believe how worried Frank was about you after the two of you fell into the river last year chasing that murderer," she said. "I was the one who suggested he send the fruit basket. He never sent any other girl fruit, and believe you me, there's more than one girl in this parish who'd be over the moon if Frank Muldoon brought her so much as a single grape. But does he care a snap for any of them? Not at all. And even though I had to give him the nudge about the fruit basket, it was him who brought it to you, wasn't it? That has to mean something."

"It meant he wanted to encourage me to get well. That water was freezing."

A laugh trilled out of her. "You're birds of a feather, you two are. He would have put it the same way."

"Well . . . it's the truth."

She nodded and laughed. "The pair of you—it's like one of your aunt's old books. The reluctant lovers."

Those last words gave me a jolt. "No, it's not."

As if I'd said nothing at all, she inhaled a deep, happy breath.

"A few more visits and you'll be wanting to move in and take over the household, and I'll just have to step aside."

"Anna, I came here to talk about a case."

"Mm-hm, I know." She winked.

"You should put whatever you're thinking out of your mind. Completely."

She patted my knee. "One thing I *don't* want you to worry about is me. Frank's never wanted me to work, but maybe I'll take a job in a shop in Manhattan. I could save and go traveling. Now wouldn't that be something?"

Had the IRT dropped me down a rabbit hole? It was all madness here. My gaze sought the door, and I wondered if I could make an escape. The only time Muldoon had spoken of his little sister at any length, it was to tell me what a good head she had on her shoulders. Little did he know it was a head crowded with fantasies. Not much of a detective in his own home, evidently.

"I should go now." I half stood, but Anna tugged me back down.

"There's stew for dinner. A whole pot of it. If Frank's not here in five minutes, we'll start without him." She patted my hand. "It would serve him right for taking you for granted."

"He doesn't know I'm here."

Did she hear me? I couldn't tell. She'd already flitted to another topic. "You probably live in Manhattan. So sophisticated!"

"Greenwich Village. Not exactly Millionaires' Mile."

"To me it would be. I've only been to Manhattan a handful of times. Frank thinks people there are all frivolous and loose. Of course *he's* there almost every day. He can't imagine why I'd find it exciting." A dreamy smile touched her lips. "I'd love to go to interesting places, wouldn't you? I was just reading a book set in Ceylon. It sounds intriguing—so *torrid*." She sighed.

I bolted up before she could stop me. "I really should go." Just as I turned toward the door, the sound of a key turning in the front door reached us. Anna also hopped up in anticipation. When Muldoon appeared, divested of hat and coat, we were both planted in front of the sofa, an awkward two-person welcoming committee.

Seeing me, Muldoon did everything but take a step back. His frame filled the entrance to the parlor. For a flicker of a second, a smile lit his face, but when his dark-eyed gaze traveled between me and Anna, he assumed a more guarded look.

"Louise." His voice didn't exactly fizz with enthusiasm. "What are you doing here?"

Before I could answer, Anna scolded him. "Right now she's here to eat dinner. I'm hungry, and I'm sure you both are too. Come into the dining room."

The four-person table was set for two, which Anna quickly remedied. The consternation on Muldoon's face as she did so didn't ease the situation.

"Anna insisted I stay," I explained in a low voice when the swinging door to the kitchen had shut behind her.

"Why did you come out all this way? You could have found me at the precinct."

"A delicate situation came up. I need to talk to you in private."

Anna swung back through with a serving bowl and spoon. "Sit down, you two, and I'll serve you."

We did as instructed. Anna ladled stew into our bowls and then brought out a loaf of bread. She handed her brother the bread knife, and he did the honors with the slicing and divvying.

Over the past year, my first year in the police force, Frank Muldoon had become a mentor to me. Of course my fellow policewomen had been essential to me in settling into my work, but I'd known Muldoon six months before I'd joined the police. He'd been my introduction to the NYPD, and despite the fact that he didn't particularly like the idea of policewomen, he'd written a letter in favor of my application when I applied for the job. He'd also helped me catch two murderers—although he'd say it was the other way around. Sometimes he visited my aunt, who adored him. There had been occasions when a feeling of intimacy had sprung between us, but those moments were rare. And thank heavens for that. A staid traditionalist like Muldoon didn't want a fellow police officer as a girlfriend, and for many reasons I didn't want a romance in my life.

In short, Muldoon was more than a friend, but far less than what Anna was hinting at.

Just the thought made my face redden, which unfortunately occurred as my eyes met his over the hunk of bread he was offering me.

"Thank you." Taking it, I vowed to make it through the meal without more awkward eye contact. I even considered not looking at him at all, but that proved impossible. I was too curious not to observe him now. This was his habitat. I felt as if I'd stumbled into one of the dioramas in the Museum of Natural History. *A Muldoon feeding in his natural surroundings*, the informative marker would read. *Note how intently he chews and avoids the gaze of the female intruder.*

"You're smiling, Louise," Anna said. "Penny for your thoughts."

Not for a million dollars would I speak those thoughts aloud. "I was challenging myself to find something to talk about that doesn't involve war." Out of thin air, I pulled the first thing that came to mind. "I heard the stock exchange is opening again, finally."

Muldoon lifted his napkin to his mouth. "They wouldn't have closed it except for the war in Europe, so that still qualifies as war talk."

Foiled. "What about the arts? That must be safe. Did you know Ethel Barrymore is making films now?"

During the meal, I talked too much. Every time I tried to make myself stop, though, a gaping void opened up. Muldoon still seemed too taken aback at finding me at his dinner table to speak easily. And Anna, who was especially interested in what I could tell her about Callie and her film career, egged me on. Though bright-eyed and attentive, she added little more than the occasional question, agreement, or interjection, or to ask if I wanted the salt. Quite a contrast with the chatterbox she'd been before her brother came home.

As the meal drew to a close, my nerves began to frazzle. Muldoon wasn't going to be pleased when I explained exactly why I was there. His common sense was what I was seeking, but now his dark countenance reminded me that his common sense often came in the form of a stern lecture. Desiring to put that off, I asked Anna to let me help with the dishes.

She drew back as if I'd scalded her pride. "You're a guest."

"An uninvited one," I reminded her.

"I won't hear of it," she insisted. "Besides, you and Frank probably have to talk, otherwise you wouldn't be here."

Muldoon and I returned to the parlor.

"How did you find me?" He lit a pipe, something I'd never seen him do.

A Muldoon at leisure in his den.

"I'm a good investigator."

"You don't have to tell me." He eyed me steadily. "This delicate matter you mentioned. Is it something about Cain?"

Leonard Cain was a nightclub-owning crime lord who had his hand in all the vice this city could offer. I'd helped put him away in Sing Sing last year, and once he'd gotten wind of that he'd vowed to make me pay. The only way he could have heard of my involvement in his downfall would have been if someone in the department had told him. I'd been unable to completely trust my colleagues at the precinct ever since.

Cain's promised vengeance hadn't come, though, even though nearly a year had passed since he'd been sentenced last December twentieth.

"Why I'm here has to do with a suicide case. A prostitute." I told Muldoon about the grisly scene on Tenth Avenue, the dismissive way the detectives had seemed to handle Ruthie's and her baby's deaths, and my desire to find Eddie Jones's remaining kin. So far so good. Then I explained about Walter and I taking the things from Ruthie's apartment, and Callie finding the passports. By the time I produced them from my satchel, Muldoon's face had become the stern mask of doom I was familiar with from previous instances when he'd thought I'd acted unwisely, or rashly, or both. Usually both.

"You should have let your precinct captain or at least Sergeant Donnelly know what you were up to."

"But Detective King dismissed the idea of looking further into Ruthie's death."

"You didn't need to tell them that you were suspicious about the death. Just that you were going to look for items that might help you trace the child's kin."

"And Sergeant Donnelly would have told me that I needed to leave that work to the foundling hospital."

"He would have been right. The sisters at New York Foundling are good at finding homes for children. Some of the children even end up out West."

For decades, New York City had been dealing with its over-population of orphans by sending them by the trainload to other parts of America. Some childless couples adopted the children to fill a void in their lives, but many people who took the orphans were people on farms for whom another pair of hands was sorely needed.

"You can't tell me that all of those families want a child and not free labor."

"Maybe some do, but would the children be better off here, in the streets?"

"They'd be better off in loving homes. Which is why it's prefer-able to find Ruthie's family. Eddie's not going to be like other chil-dren, the ones who get sent to farm families. A regular boy in that situation can at least stand up for himself. Eddie's not going to have a voice."

Muldoon looked thoughtful, but when he spoke again, it was to return to my dilemma, not Eddie's. "All right. With the best of in-tentions, you went back to the apartment, and now you have these passports. Turn them in."

"What if one of the passport men was Ruthie's murderer? Someone went through the apartment looking for something—why not passports? Her drawers were gone through and her mattress was slashed. There was all sorts of evidence that someone had been in that flat, but the detectives on the case didn't even care. The sec-ond they saw signs of a prostitute who'd committed suicide, they were ready to pack up and go home."

Muldoon shook his head. "If you took the subway all the way to Brooklyn to convince me to try to investigate Ruthie Jones's death, you've wasted a nickel. I can't second-guess another detective's work."

"Why not?"

"It's not my precinct."

"So?"

"Louise, you know that's not how we work."

"And you know someone at my precinct is corrupt. Maybe sev-eral someones. Can I trust them to treat the passports as evi-dence?"

"Those passports might only be evidence of Ruthie Jones being a thief. Maybe she stole money along with them, then didn't know what to do with the documents."

"Burning them or tossing them in the trash would have been much easier than sewing them into her clothes," I said. "Anyway, I don't think she was a thief. Prostitutes can't steal from customers and expect to stay alive for long."

"And Ruthie didn't." The moment the words came out of his mouth, he frowned at the trap he'd just talked himself into.

I folded my arms. "You see? The passports *could* be evidence that Ruthie's death wasn't a suicide."

He leaned back in his chair. "I knew my life had seemed too calm lately."

"I just want your advice."

"Then you should heed it. Hand in the passports and tell your sergeant as close to a version of the truth as you can manage. At least give the detectives a chance to link them to the investigation—or not. You might get a reprimand for going back to a crime scene to look for information to help track down the baby's family. The brass won't be happy to have this question mark added to a case they considered open-and-shut, but no one will fire you for being overzealous for helping out the sisters at the foundling hospital."

As frustrating as it was for me to admit, he was right. At least as far as precinct politics went. "I should have figured that out on my own."

"You would have."

"But you saw it in minutes."

He gave me one of his rare smiles. "Because I've been there before. Do you think you're the only police officer who's ever been in a bind?"

A rustle sounded in the doorway. Anna was eyeing us with satisfaction. "This is cozy, isn't it?" She crossed to a phonograph cabinet in the corner. "I hope you two aren't going to talk about work all night. Would you like to hear a record, Louise? Frank bought the phonograph for me last year, to entertain me. Wasn't that generous?"

Muldoon shifted in his seat. "It wasn't entirely unselfish. I like music, too."

"I got a new record last Saturday." Anna pulled a record out of the cabinet shelf and put it on the felt turntable. The opening strains of "You Made Me Love You" by Al Jolson began.

Of course it would be Al Jolson. Not only were his records selling like hotcakes, Muldoon had seen Jolson hamming it up at one of my aunt's parties last year. No doubt Muldoon had told Anna all about it. And now I remembered that day, and how kind he had been to me. I'd felt a real closeness with him then.

"Wouldn't you two like to dance?" Anna asked.

"No," we said in unison.

Our eyes met in mutual surprise and dismay at the other's vehemence.

We sat in silence as Jolson tortured every drop of emotion out of the remainder of the song. The minutes crawled. As soon as the record was over, I hopped to my feet.

Muldoon rose, too. "I'll walk you to the subway station?"

"That's not necessary."

"Nonsense." Anna sent me a significant look. "Frank would be delighted to do it. Right, Frank?"

"Of course."

On Henry Street, I turned to him. "I'm sorry if my coming out here causes trouble for you."

"What kind of trouble?"

"Your sister is very . . . fanciful."

"Anna?" His brows drew together. "I don't know about that. She reads a lot of books. She sneaks out to the pictures, too."

"Why should she sneak? Surely you don't care?"

"Of course not. I want her to enjoy herself, although I don't see much joy in sitting in the dark watching a screen." His expression was serious, and a little worried. "Anna's had a hard time of it, living alone with just me since our mother died. For a while it seemed she was getting involved in helping at the church, but I think she perhaps got *over* involved. Some of the ladies who'd been there longer didn't seem to appreciate her help. She stopped going."

I had a few guesses why that would be. "She seems to like to take charge. Once I arrived at your door, she wouldn't hear of my leaving."

"Maybe she doesn't get enough company. She's been dedicated to her housekeeping."

Not so dedicated that she wouldn't run off to torrid Ceylon with the first man who asked her. It wasn't my place to get into an argument with Muldoon about his domestic arrangements, however.

We reached the entrance to the subway station. "Thank you for your help," I said.

"Just remember that you don't have to take everything on your shoulders. Let the detectives do their work."

"Wise advice," I said, waving goodbye to him. And it was advice I had every intention of following. To a degree.

CHAPTER 5

Sergeant Donnelly wasn't at his desk the next morning when I arrived at the station. In his place stood his second-in-command, Officer Jenks. His long face cracked into an unconvincing smile as he saw me approach.

"I need to speak to Donnelly," I said.

"He's not here."

"Is Lieutenant King on duty now? I've come across something relating to the Ruthie Jones case."

The officer tilted his head, his brow a complicated map of lines. "What case? She committed suicide."

"Is King here?"

He leaned forward. "What did you find?"

I hesitated, but finally told him about the three passports, giving my rehearsed explanation of coming across them in a blanket I'd taken from the apartment for Eddie the night we'd found Ruthie. Naturally I left out all mention of disguises and my suspicions.

"Nothing better to do with your time, eh? You should get yourself a steady fellow." He held out his hand. "I'll pass 'em along to the detectives for you."

"I want to make sure they go to the right people."

His expression darkened to a glower. "I told you I'll pass them along. But if you don't trust me to do that, I'll tell Donnelly that he'll need to talk to you. And that maybe he ought to question you a little more on that story of yours. A little bird told me a ragman and his son carted away a lot of stuff from there yesterday. Know anything about that?"

"Of course not." But he knew I was lying. Reluctantly, I handed over the passports.

Jenks opened a desk drawer to his right, dropped them in, and slammed it shut. "There. Safe and sound."

"Thanks." I imbued my voice with as little gratefulness as I could get away with.

Downstairs, I made a quick roll call of all the lady prisoners in my cells. There were quite a few, and they had the usual complaints, requests, and insults for me. After a year, the taunts were water off a duck's back. Besides, I was preoccupied. I found the city directory and thumbed through it, looking for a business called the Silver Swan. I found nothing.

Maybe Ruthie really had just written down a song title she'd liked. Or maybe the owner of the Dutch passport had. I still didn't know if that was Ruthie's handwriting on the scrap of paper. I needed to concentrate my efforts on what I did know.

I sat down on my bench and removed a paper from my jacket pocket. The night before, I'd copied down all the information from the three passports. I studied the names and the vital statistics of the three men and decided to focus on the hardest first: the Swede. Lars Holmgren, his name was. His passport was the one that had been stamped most recently, and the most often.

Muldoon had counseled me to let the detectives do their jobs, and I agreed with that advice. In theory. But if the detectives weren't inclined to do their jobs, and Jenks's dismissive behavior seemed more confirmation that they weren't, I was going to do a little detecting myself.

Locating a single Swede in a city of four and a half million was not quite the equivalent of finding a needle in a haystack. For one thing, needles didn't have consulates, and the Swedes did.

It was on Sixth Avenue near Fourteenth Street, a quick hop down the El. My lunch break gave me just enough time to go there. The building was a simple brick edifice, narrow and modest, with just the blue-and-yellow flag giving away its tenants. It certainly wasn't the busiest place in the city. As soon as I walked in, I was directed to speak to Mr. Berglund, who sat studying the contents of a folder with the intensity of an employee who was trying to look busy. He was slight-framed and older, with wire spectacles perched on his long nose.

He half stood as I approached him, and directed me to take the chair opposite him. "How may I be of help to you?" he asked in precise, accented English.

"I'm looking for a countryman of yours who lost his passport." Before I'd even finished spinning a brief yarn of finding Lars Holmgren's passport on a park bench, Berglund was extracting a cloth-bound book from a file drawer to his left.

"Where is the document?" he asked.

"I gave it to the police. Or, rather, they took it from me when I showed it to them."

His eyes narrowed. "Then, Miss—"

"Frobisher," I lied. "Idelle Frobisher."

The real Idelle Frobisher, a tightly corseted dragon with a fondness for rapping small knuckles with rulers, had been my least favorite teacher in elementary school. I'd decided to use an alias just to be safe. If Ruthie's death was in any way being covered up at my precinct, for whatever reason, I didn't want my snooping about those passports to be traced back to me. Also, as Muldoon warned, it wasn't politic to be seen second-guessing the work of my detective superiors. Though I was wearing my uniform, my long coat disguised all but the bottom of my blue skirt, which wasn't giving much away.

Mr. Berglund, who until this point had been poised to take down all the information I could give him, put down his pen. "Miss Frobisher, it would seem to me that you've already done your duty by Mr. Holmgren."

"If you trust the police, you must be the only one in this city who does." I gripped my satchel, sending up an apology to the patron saint of the NYPD. "No, I'd feel better if I could contact Mr. Holmgren myself and tell him who has his passport."

"I wish you luck, but in this I cannot help you. Mr. Holmgren has not been to this office."

"You think Mr. Holmgren would know to come here, then? I didn't think to until after I went to the police."

He considered this. "You said the passport had many stamps?"

I nodded. "Two from entering New York, and several more from the East—Hong Kong, Tokyo . . . lots of places."

"He certainly sounds worldly enough to know to come to the consulate, but we would have a record if a man had come here to report a lost passport. We would have taken steps to get him a new travel document."

"And how long would that take?"

He shrugged. "A matter of a week or so to give him a temporary traveling document."

I believed him when he said he knew Holmgren hadn't been here. All the action in the consulate seemed to take place at this desk, and he looked as if he hadn't left his post for a few decades. It was possible he could help me in another way, however. I rummaged in my satchel for the notes I'd taken the night before. "Could you translate this word for me?" I pointed to some words I'd copied from the passport. "I think that means 'eyes: blue.'"

"That is correct, yes."

I moved my finger down a line. "And this word?"

He frowned. "Blond."

"And these would be height measurements?"

"Mr. Holmgren is five feet ten inches and weighs one hundred and sixty pounds."

"And he's twenty-six years old."

"Yes."

Catching on to my intentions, Mr. Berglund bleated out a laugh. "You intend to go looking for this man on your own?"

I nodded.

"Please, Miss Frobisher, I am touched at your concern for my countryman, but you will waste your time. New York is a large city."

"It is, but visitors to New York generally congregate in certain parts." I knew the Swede had spent a little time in Hell's Kitchen, but I couldn't say that, or how I knew. "I'm fairly certain Mr. Holmgren is a sailor. The stamps on his passport were all ports of call where a sailor on a merchant ship might stop."

"Or an adventurous traveler." That bespectacled gaze homed in on me. "Are you sure you don't know Mr. Holmgren?" Clearly, he was beginning to suspect I was some kind of lunatic. An obsessive Swede fancier.

"I told you, I'm just concerned about him. Is there anywhere people of your country would tend to go?"

"There are thousands of Swedish people in New York City, Miss Frobisher. Many own restaurants, bakeries, bars. We are like people of any country. Even in foreign lands, especially in foreign lands, we seek out what is familiar and reminds us of home."

Bakeries, bars, and restaurants. "Have you ever heard of an establishment called the Silver Swan?"

He shook his head. "I do not recognize the name."

When I finally stood, he looked relieved. He rose and bowed slightly. "Goodbye, Miss Frobisher. *Lycka till.* That means 'Good luck.' "

"Thank you."

"*Jag tror att du behöver det.*"

I smiled. "And what does that mean?"

" 'I think you will need it.' "

Back at the station, as the afternoon wore on, I sifted through my options. Maybe Berglund was right and I had set myself an impossible task. Should I start combing the waterfront, hunting for Swedes? Make the rounds of all the Swedish bakeries and restaurants? How much lutefisk was I willing to consume in this quest?

Midafternoon, a new female offender was brought in, someone I already knew well. Light-fingered Lettie had been collared for stealing a bracelet from Gimbels, the second time she'd been caught thieving in that particular establishment.

"Why would you go there again?" I asked her as I ushered her into a cell. "Surely you knew the store detective would spot you."

"I'd never been there as a redhead, though, had I?"

The last time she'd been in my care, she'd been a dishwater blonde. Now her tresses were an eye-popping, brassy red. "I thought the point of a disguise was to *not* attract attention."

"Faulk's right, dearie," one of her cellmates chimed. "That hair's as good as a lighted billboard."

"That was the idea," Lettie muttered. "Stupid dick was supposed to look at my hair, not my fingers."

The woman who'd spoken before suggested helpfully, "Maybe you oughta change up your routine, Lettie. Or try a new city."

Lettie glowered at her. "This is my city and I don't need to be told my own business. You think I don't change up my routine? Sure I do. But sometimes you have to aim for the easy pickings or you just end up getting discouraged. That store used to supply me with a reliable income, till they started bringing in all these damned detectives."

"Very selfish of them," I said, earning some appreciative laughs.

Lettie's words made sense when I applied them to my own situation, though. There was something to be said for aiming for easy pickings. I could wear myself out looking for the Swede just as I was beginning my quest to find the passport owners. Maybe I should try for the easy pickings. After all, the Englishman, Gerald Hughes, would probably be the easiest for me to track down.

As soon as I was done for the day, I hurried across town to the British consulate, which was located in a spacious new building on the East Side. There were more people milling around there than at the Swedish consulate, and initially I worried they would never get to me. But within a half hour, again in my guise as a distraught Miss Frobisher, I was presenting myself to an official. This time I was checking on the whereabouts of my long-lost cousin Gerald, who'd left his passport at my home in Camden.

The clerk I spoke to, a middle-aged English gentleman who looked as if he were composed of equal parts clotted cream and arrogance, heaved a sigh. "And where is he now?"

"That's just it—I don't know."

"You've lost touch?"

"We're only distant cousins, so it was a surprise to see him when he showed up. Said he was just passing through Camden. He only was at the house a few hours, and that was weeks ago. It wasn't until last night that I found the passport."

"Let me see the document. Perhaps I can help."

Though he pronounced that "perhaps" in the most doubtful tone, I opened my satchel and rifled through it. My bag really was a wonderful accessory for traveling about town. At that moment, it contained a folded newspaper, the latest Booth Tarkington, an apple, three pencils, a pad of paper, powder, extra handkerchiefs, and a baby's rattle I'd picked up at a five-and-dime for Eddie. But of course no passport. After I'd upended the contents on the man's desk, I let out a distressed gasp. "Golly, I must've left it back in Camden."

Dark brows drew into a V as the clerk examined the pile on his desk. "Is there anything left in Camden *but* the passport? You seem to have brought everything else."

I clucked at my fictitious forgetfulness. "I'm such a scatter-brain."

The man heaved himself out of his chair and went to investigate the contents of a cabinet a few steps away. After extracting a folder, he waddled back. "As it happens, Miss Frobisher, you needn't worry at all. Mr. Hughes was issued a new passport just two weeks ago."

His words sent an electric current through me. Two weeks! Ruthie must have lifted his passport a few weeks before that. Maybe in October? And now Gerald Hughes had had two weeks to leave New York.

Catching the clerk staring at me, I smiled in feigned relief. "Well, that *is* a comfort—dear Gerald has his passport. I worried he was trapped."

The man's head tilted. "I'm surprised he didn't contact you before coming here."

"Oh, he was only at my house for a short time. Probably didn't realize it was missing till later." I cleared my throat. "Did Gerald leave the address of where he was staying? I thought I heard him mention a place called the Silver Swan, but I haven't been able to find it."

"We're not a directory, miss."

"Of course not. I only thought, since the war . . . Well, you understand how worried I am for him. I might never see him again." I lifted a handkerchief to my eyes.

Whether the man's face showed pity or impatience to be rid of me I wasn't quite sure. "Your cousin's last address was the Hotel McAlpin," he said.

The McAlpin? That was just a few blocks from the Thirtieth Street station house. Right under my nose.

"That's where we sent notice that his new travel documents were ready," the man continued. "He came by for it here."

It was all I could do not to sprint to the McAlpin hotel. What were the chances Hughes would still be there? Not good, I was afraid. But I wasn't going to waste a second.

I wasn't familiar with many hotels in New York City, but the brand-spanking-new McAlpin, the biggest hotel in the world, was hard to miss. At twenty-five stories, with distinctive white brick-and stone top floors, it dwarfed every other building around it.

The interior was like something out of a palace in Italy—or what I imagined such a palace would be. Entering through the southeast entrance door on Broadway, I found myself in a long hall with a vaulted stone ceiling from which three massive chandeliers hung. Marble pillars held up balconies on each side of the room, and below these, in the manner of a loggia designed for business purposes, the male clerks stood at desks, helping guests. I made my way past islands of velvet-cushioned benches positioned around stone urns to ask one of them about Gerald Hughes.

Unfortunately, the clerk told me Hughes had checked out not long after receiving his passport and hadn't provided a forwarding address. My lament about his being in England might be true. With a passport, Mr. Hughes was as free as a bird. He could be anywhere by now.

Feeling defeated, I made my way out of the hotel.

"Officer Faulk!"

A girl was standing by a door marked Hotel Staff Entrance. I knew her at once, though I'd almost walked right past her. "Hello, Lena." The last time I'd seen her, she hadn't been wearing a black uniform with a starched white pinafore and maid's cap. "I didn't know you worked here. What happened to the job at the market?"

Several months ago, Lena had landed in one of my cells, brought in on a solicitation charge. It was her first offense, and the story she gave was a familiar one: a father who'd abandoned the family, younger siblings, a sick mother, an impatient landlady. I'd heard it before, and seen first offenders sink into pitiable lives.

Lena was young and bright, and thinking that she still might have a chance, I did the thing I'd been warned by my colleagues never to do. I got personally involved. Just to the tune of a few dollars—well, ten—and a little pressure on a grocer not far from my apartment. I'd once helped him discover the source of the thieving problem at his store, so he agreed to give Lena a job at the register.

"Mr. Otway was all right," she explained. "But this job pays better, and I can work evenings and take care of Mama during the day. Harry watches her at night."

Harry was her little brother. "She's no better?"

"But no worse, thank the Lord." She frowned at me. "What are you doing here?"

"Looking for a guest at the hotel, named Gerald Hughes. He checked out, according to the clerk I spoke with."

Her face brightened. "Mr. Hughes? With the limp?"

I had no idea. "He's British."

"Sure, that's him. He's gone, but I bet he'll be back. He's a salesman—at least that's what I guess he is, from all the cases in his room."

My mood ramped up from gloomy defeatism to full-steam hope. "You remember this man?"

"Of course. A real gentleman. Gave me a fifty-cent tip once for bringing him a tea when he was feeling poorly. I don't care if he has got a wooden leg. Fifty cents on a cup of tea that costs fifteen? If that's not handsome, I don't know what is."

"A wooden leg?"

She nodded. "Doreen, another girl who works here, said she walked into his room and saw it propped up against the chair—a leg and a foot with the shoe on it, just leaning there. 'Bout scared her to death."

You'd think Eileen, Ruthie's neighbor, would've noticed a one-legged man with a limp if he'd visited repeatedly, but she hadn't mentioned him. Yet I knew Gerald Hughes had visited Ruthie at least once, because she'd stolen his passport. Unless she'd stolen it from him somewhere besides her flat. A distinct possibility.

"You think Mr. Hughes will be back?" I asked. "The clerk didn't think so."

Lena's lips twisted in a dismissive sneer. "Them clerks don't know half so much, for all their airs. Mr. Hughes'll be back, wait and see."

I didn't have the leisure to wait and see forever. "Any idea when?"

"I saw something about the Great Lakes on his chair one day. Bet he's up there for a spell. Michigan, maybe? Or Chicago. He won't want to stay *there* in the winter."

Probably not, but New York City in December wasn't exactly the Riviera, either. "Let me know if you see him again, won't you?"

"I hope he's not in any trouble."

"No . . ." I didn't want to scare Lena away from helping me. "Just need to talk to him."

She nodded. "I'll send word if I ever see him around here."

I thanked her. At least I had some eyes working for me. But the man might have relocated to Chicago permanently, or he might be on his way even farther west.

Though it was full dark now and my feet were starting to ache from crisscrossing the city, I couldn't forget Eddie. Maybe it was silly to worry about a baby who certainly didn't know me from any of the nuns around him. His needs were being seen to. Yet my heart twisted at the idea of letting the day go by without checking up on him. He was all alone in the world now, with no prospects, not even a person to lend him a little special attention. Except me. The rattle in my satchel hurried my steps toward the foundling hospital.

A sister named Mary Grace greeted me with a bemused smile when she heard whom I was there to visit. "The most popular baby in the ward. He's asleep now, though, worn out after his busy day. He had the doctors in to see him."

"What did they say?"

"That he's fit as a flea." Her lips tightened. "Except for being mute, poor thing."

I tried to hide the stab of disappointment. Against Sister Eleanor's warning, I had begun to hope that the doctors would discover his muteness was all a mistake. "Is he too tired out for me to see him?"

She considered. "Well, there's no harm in a peek, I suppose. You being his rescuer and all."

"I didn't do anything special."

She walked ahead of me at a rapid gait. "False modesty is as bad as a boast. From what I've heard, you plucked the babe from the jaws of hell."

"Hell's Kitchen. Any police officer would've done the same." Still, her description of my supposed heroics made me walk taller in my boots.

After entering a long room set up with a fleet of cribs spaced at regular intervals down both sides, the sister tiptoed me over to one in the middle. I was used to thinking that babies all looked alike, but Eddie had made an impression on me. I let out a sigh upon seeing him there, his eyes gently closed, his small chest moving almost imperceptibly in sleep. I stared at him for a long minute, taking in the yellow footed sleeper he wore. I didn't recognize it from the things I'd grabbed out of Ruthie's chest of drawers the night we found him.

I wrote away for news of your family, Eddie.

Would the photographer send a response? I could only wait, and hope.

I unbuckled the clasp on my satchel and pulled out the bright red rattle. "I hope it's all right to give him this?"

The nun inspected it with only a trace of a smile. "Oh yes. Except we don't want to wake him now, do we? Him, or any of the others. I'll just put it with his other treasures."

Treasures? That's not how I would have described the bare necessities I'd salvaged from Ruthie's. I followed Sister Mary Grace to the chest of drawers against the wall. When she opened the one that had Eddie's name on it, I gaped. Inside were several adorable little suits either in fine linen or soft knit wool, complete with matching bonnets and booties. For the first time, I also noticed the teddy bear on top of the dresser, which was the only large toy of any kind displayed in the room. Next to the bear was another rattle, larger than mine and elaborately carved and painted with a smiling sun at one end and a man on the moon at the other.

"Where did all this come from?" The items certainly weren't the kind the orphan asylum issued its tiny inmates.

Two cribs away, a baby fussed.

Sister Mary Grace put her finger to her lips, then gestured toward the hallway. I gave Eddie a last look as she tucked my rattle in the drawer and closed it.

Once we were out of the nursery, she explained, "Some Good Samaritans came by today."

"Who?"

"They wish to remain anonymous."

My mind sifted through all of the possibilities. Fellow officers sometimes took up collections for particularly unfortunate widows or orphans. But as far as I knew, no one had passed a hat around the station recently. Anyway, I couldn't imagine the men of my precinct buying the beautiful baby items I'd seen in Eddie's drawer.

"Were they policemen?" I asked.

"You understand what anonymous means, I trust," Mary Grace said. "Their anonymity makes the gift all the sweeter, don't you think?"

It certainly made the puzzle more frustrating. "Was one a woman?" I couldn't imagine a man picking out those clothes.

For a moment she weighed how much to tell me. She relented only enough to confess, "It was a man and a woman who came—and that's all I'll say to you about it."

A couple? Now I really was intrigued. I'd told no couple about the baby . . . had I? There was Ruthie's downstairs neighbor . . . but she and her husband didn't have money to throw at extravagant clothes for someone else's child.

I left the asylum with my curiosity unquenched, and with a new mystery: Who besides me was looking after Eddie?

CHAPTER 6

The streetcar home traveled down a glistening Fifth Avenue. The first Christmas displays of the season were drawing crowds in front of store windows. At Lord & Taylor, a lighted Christmas carousel had people spilling into the street to watch the reindeer pulling Santa's sleigh. Those children who couldn't muscle their way to the glass to gawp at the moving tableau sat on their fathers' shoulders for a better look.

On my streetcar, so many people lurched to the side with the best view that it felt for a moment as if the vehicle might topple over. Having maneuvered to secure a seat, I remained where I was, deflated over how little I'd accomplished that day. I was not much closer to finding any of the three men than I'd been when I'd opened my eyes this morning. *Early days*, I told myself, trying to buck up.

I stepped off the streetcar and trudged my way across Greenwich Village toward 391 Bleecker Street. More than anything, I longed first for a soak in the tub, where I could think over what I'd learned since Ruthie's death and ponder what to do next. After my soak I pictured falling into bed for a long sleep. Bliss.

My landlady's son, an unappealing troll of a young man named

Wally Grimes, met me as soon as I walked through the front door. "You gals ain't renting out a room, are you?"

"What room?" Callie and I only had two bedrooms, and there were two of us. "We don't have a spare."

His head tilted in suspicion. "You two could double up and rent out one of the bedrooms. Ma says two unmarried girls in an apartment is enough. She doesn't want the place to become a hen house. Too many in one apartment . . . you know."

Was it worth pointing out that just below Callie and me lived a rotating group of *five* male musicians? "By the Beautiful Sea," being rehearsed at that moment, was an audible reminder of their presence in the house. None of them were married, either, though of course that was different. They were men. Mrs. Grimes had never complained about the Bleecker Blowers, to my knowledge.

"She doesn't want this place to get a reputation," Wally said.

"What do you mean?"

Those lips twisted. "You know."

"I'm a police officer and my roommate is an actress, so perhaps you mean you don't want to rent to hardworking women. Or is it the police connection in particular that bothers you? Because I could have a few officers come talk to you about that. And while they're here, maybe I could point out the stoop of the building and the loose masonry regulations you're flaunting."

Wally backed off. "Did I ever say I had anything against the police?"

"Did I ever say I had any intention of subletting a room?" I turned to go up the stairs.

"No, but when some little doll comes in and asks which apartment's yours and how much rent do you pay, that makes me wonder."

Some little doll? Now I really was confused, though I wasn't about to let on to him that I didn't know what he was talking about. "You can stop wondering. We're not looking for a roommate."

"Nice girl, though," he called after me, picking his front tooth with his pinky nail. "Cute."

Who was this girl, this doll? I heard laughter upstairs, and as I climbed the two flights to our apartment, it grew louder. My footsteps slowed when I reached our door. It sounded like a party. So much for my tub-and-bed plan. When I opened the door and looked in, Otto stood in the middle of the rug at the center of our cramped parlor, gesticulating broadly. Teddy and Callie were watching from the threadbare velvet sofa. To my shock, on our equally battered chair perched Anna Muldoon, hair tied back neatly in a bun with ringlets for bangs.

What was she doing here?

The four of them, smiling, stopped whatever it was that they'd been doing to stare at me.

"Am I interrupting a performance?" I asked Otto.

Callie stood. "We're acting charades. Come join us. You can play with Otto and me."

"Not fair," Teddy protested. "Louise should play on our team."

His team obviously meant him and Anna.

"How do you figure that?" Callie asked.

"We're ahead." He grinned at her. "First dibs."

Anna stood. The crown of her head barely reached Callie's chin. "Please, Louise can take my place. I'm just a guest."

"Don't be silly," I said. "I'm going to make tea. You all keep playing."

Before they could protest my not joining in their fun, I crossed to the kitchen. As I put the kettle on the stove, Callie called out, "Box! No? Trunk? Oh dear. It's *something* square. Portmanteau!"

"It's a sound-alike word," Otto reminded her in exasperation. "How is anything supposed to rhyme with *portmanteau*?"

"I can only guess from what you're acting out. Believe me, you're no John Drew."

"You could at least *try*," he shot back.

"No discussion among teammates," Teddy objected. "It's supposed to be a pantomime, remember?"

Callie muttered in frustration. "Go ahead, Otto."

I peeked out and looked at Anna perched in our chair, grinning happily. Did Muldoon know his sister had come to town and was spending the evening in our apartment? Or had he sent her here?

Sister Mary Grace had said a couple had visited the orphanage and given all those things to Ruthie's boy. Could the couple have been Muldoon and Anna?

But why, in that case, would Anna be here on her own?

Why should she be here at all?

"Carton!" Callie called out as I reentered the parlor area.

Otto looked as if he might expire with relief. "Finally—a correct guess!"

"No talking," Anna and Teddy called out in unison.

"Oh! I've got it!" Callie smiled. "Sydney Carton. *A Tale of Two Cities.*"

"It's a book title, not a character," Otto said. "And it's just the first syllable."

"Carton is two syllables," Callie objected.

"All right, two syllables. And it's a sound-alike, don't forget."

Callie put her hands on her hips. "What rhymes with Carton?"

Teddy laughed. "That's what you're supposed to be guessing, nitwit."

She glared at him.

Teddy and Callie at odds... Callie and Otto bickering... Anna sitting there delighted... Everything about this situation alarmed me.

"Martin Chuzzlewit," I blurted out.

Everyone turned toward me. "That's it!" Otto shouted with glee. "We got it!"

"Louise isn't on your team," Teddy protested.

"She just guessed the answer, so she was de facto declaring herself on our team," Callie said. "Isn't that right, Louise?"

I nodded. "Who wants tea?"

"I wouldn't say no," Teddy said. "To tea, or something stronger."

"Or do you need to leave?" I asked Anna.

My question might have been pointed, but her hide was thick. "Oh no," she said. "I can stay."

That declaration made me wary. Wally had intimated that "the doll" was moving in. I didn't spy any baggage, but she appeared to be making herself at home.

"Your brother knows you're here?" I asked when Callie and then Anna followed me into the kitchen.

She shook her head. "If I'm not there when Frank gets home, he'll just think I've snuck out to the pictures."

Callie put her hands on her hips. "Imagine a grown woman having to sneak anywhere, especially to a picture show. It's medieval."

I recalled Muldoon's saying Anna could do as she pleased. Had he been lying for my benefit, or was Anna vying for sympathy?

"Tell your brother the days of women being under men's thumbs are over," Callie said.

Anna's eyes brightened with a worshipful glint. "Louise says you're in pictures. I love the movies. I go see them all." She moved over a little as Otto sidled into the kitchen to hear what we were talking about. "Do you know Charlie Chaplin?"

"No," Callie said.

Anna tried again. "Lillian Gish?"

"Only to nod hello to."

Anna sighed. "That must be marvelous. I'd love to see how pictures are made."

"Of course, Callie really belongs on the stage," Otto put in. "Once Jimmy and I finish *Double Daisy*, Broadway won't be able to get enough of her."

Double Daisy was the show Otto had been working on for the past ten months, laboring over songs, and then laboring over the book with a writer friend. Now their efforts were focused on rewrites and trying to find a backer for the show.

"Once you boys finish *Double Daisy*," Callie admonished, "I'll be ready for granny roles."

Otto was stung. "Art takes time, as opposed to children's pantomimes captured on celluloid."

"Pantomimes!" Her hands fisted on her hips. "Another crack like that and I'll be calling you a song scribbler."

"Stop bickering," I said. "We have company."

"Don't mind me," Anna said, wide-eyed with interest.

"I thought we were having tea," Otto said.

Callie's brows arched. "Like great art, tea takes time."

Otto retreated.

Callie turned her attention back to Anna. "If you're so crazy about pictures, you should come with me someday and see how they're made. I'm working on one now with Maurice Costello."

It looked as if Anna's soul might leave her body and float straight up to the heavens. "Me, visit a movie set? I wouldn't be in the way?"

"Of course not. It's not like a theater rehearsal. These movie studios are like Grand Central Station. Everyone's in the way. But it's fun. You'll get a kick out of it."

"I'll have to keep pinching myself to assure myself I'm not dreaming."

"That sensation won't last thirty minutes, believe me. The first time you see us all with chalk all over our faces, you'll see it for the ridiculous business that it is."

"Chalk?"

"We use it for a makeup base sometimes, especially if the light's bad. Chalk makes facial features stand out more on film."

"When can I go?" Anna asked.

"Whenever you have time. Just let me know."

"How about tomorrow?"

Pouring water from the kettle to the teapot, Callie laughed. "No one could accuse you of not being eager."

"Is tomorrow too soon?" Anna's expression changed to worry. "Of course it is. And maybe you were just being polite, inviting me."

"No, I wasn't," Callie assured her. "Tomorrow will be perfect."

I couldn't help asking, "Did Lieutenant Muldoon bring you into the city today?"

"I came on my own," Anna said.

She and Muldoon couldn't have been the couple at the foundling home, then. It was foolish to entertain the notion they could have been. A man who has to be nudged into buying a fruit basket wasn't going to go shopping for teddy bears and baby rattles for orphans.

"I'll tell my brother all about it, of course." Anna winked at Callie. "When my day at the motion picture set is over."

"Now you've got the idea." The two shared a conspiratorial nod, and then Callie glanced at me and laughed. "Louise, you look like the dance chaperone who's just seen a couple canoodling behind the punch table."

"Small wonder she and my brother are drawn together," Anna said.

I couldn't let that stand. "I hardly ever see him."

"That's exactly what he says about you. 'I just bump into her sometimes,' he'll say."

"Detective Muldoon talks about Louise?" Callie's voice was full of curiosity.

"Of course, whenever her name comes up he'll usually roll his eyes, or mutter something unflattering."

Oh he did, did he?

"Just to throw me off the scent," Anna added quickly.

Both Teddy and Otto appeared in the doorway. "Is there really going to be tea, or are you going to sit gossiping forever?" Teddy asked.

"I was just telling them about my brother's well-hidden fondness for Louise."

"Ah—the detective." Now Teddy was all ears. Never let it be said that women were the only sex who enjoyed gossip.

"It's so well hidden that half the time he seems to positively dislike me," I pointed out.

Anna rocked on her heels, smiling. "Time will tell."

"Speaking of time..." Otto took out his pocket watch and scowled at it. "Tea or no tea, I need to go. I still have a long night of songwriting ahead."

Anna sighed. "And I still have a long trip home."

"I'll walk you to the subway," Otto offered.

"How kind," Anna said.

Callie cleared her throat in a way that caught Teddy's attention. After a brief exchange of glances, he piped up, "Never mind the subway. I can take you in my car."

Anna gasped, thrilled. Otto's offer was forgotten. "But I live in Brooklyn."

Teddy laughed. "There's a bridge, you know—my buzz wagon will have you home in two shakes."

"But it's so much trouble," she protested.

"Certainly not," Teddy said with enthusiasm, really seeming to enjoy being the gallant knight, once Callie had nudged him into donning his armor.

"And I'll come back tomorrow and go to work with you?" Anna asked Callie.

They arranged a time to meet.

After the others left, Callie and I finally had tea.

"What was Anna doing here?" I asked.

Callie gave me a strange look. "You invited her."

"I did?"

"She said you did. According to her, you insisted she come visit you."

I didn't remember that. Or at least, I didn't remember insisting.

"She's a cute kid," Callie said. "It'll be a lark taking her around the studio." After a moment of thought over a sip of tea, she added, "I guess Brooklyn, even if it is just across the river, can't be all that much different than Little Yawns."

I sputtered. "Anna's not getting up at the crack of dawn to milk cows," I pointed out, reminding her of just how life in her upstate village, Little Falls, had been.

"Okay, but you weren't here to see her eyes light up when she described coming out of the subway and being in Greenwich Village. It reminded me how I felt a few years ago."

"She's a bundle of enthusiasm," I said, without enthusiasm.

Callie put her saucer down with a clatter. "What's bit you this evening? You came home late, then acted as if Anna was a trespasser."

"I just wonder why she was here."

"She was bored, poor kid."

That's what Muldoon had said—that Anna didn't get to see people as much as he thought she should. At least not since the church ladies kicked her to the curb.

How pushy did a person have to be to be ostracized by the church altar guild?

"Wally thought she was moving in," I said. "She asked him how much we pay in rent."

"Probably just curious about how much it would cost to be out on her own." She sighed and stretched. "I feel good about this. That poor girl's been stuck in Brooklyn under her brother's thumb, but now I'm emancipating Anna." She laughed. "Makes me feel like a suffragette."

Or an altar guild lady, I thought, unable to share her zeal for her Anna project.

CHAPTER 7

"That kid got me thinking," Otto said.

We met for our standing date at our favorite haunt, Ziggy's, a German sausage pushcart operation. Ziggy got our business rain or shine, and judging from the lineup along the sidewalk in front of Pennsylvania Station, he got the business of half of Midtown, as well.

The spot was not too far from my precinct house, convenient for a quick lunch, and Otto was always nostalgic for the German fare of our youth. A brat on a bun was the next best thing to a trip home for him. For me, there were no trips home, but I was still fond of the food.

I had a special favor to ask Otto today, but he was distracted right out of the gate. This was the second time he'd brought up Anna Muldoon.

"Kid?" I shifted from foot to foot, both from irritation and trying to warm myself. It was forty degrees out—balmy compared to last week's temperatures, but still chilly for al fresco dining. "She's older than us, I think."

"Really? She's got this innocence about her."

Even after a year in the city, Otto was still green himself, so his calling someone else innocent made me smile. "You mean she's short. She looks like a kid because she's short."

I swear his eyes misted over. "Right—a half-pint bundle of enthusiasm for life. It got me thinking . . . what if we had a kid sister?"

I blew on the fingers of my wool gloves. This was a bad idea, like drinking sea water in a lifeboat. The moisture just made the gloves all the colder when the breath froze, creating a frost coating on my fingers. But for those few seconds of warmth . . . "My mother died, so you'll have to take up the matter of siblings with yours."

"I'm talking about the show. Jimmy and I could write in a little sister for Daisy—give her a real fun novelty number or dance."

"You said the show needed a better second act," I said. "A little sister would just be more business, wouldn't she?"

"But she'd add pep."

"The main character has pep—both of her."

Double Daisy was a story about identical twins, separated at birth yet both improbably sharing the same first name, who meet up on the Riviera. One is a jewel thief, the other is a socialite. They trade places and end up switching beaux, too. Mostly it was a framework for musical numbers and a chance for the leading lady—Callie—to show off her comedic talents.

The idea that the show needed *another* ingénue riled me on Callie's behalf. "You've got a showstopper already."

"Yeah, but—"

"You really think it would be a good idea to take attention away from the leading lady?"

He shrugged. "Audiences like girls."

"Let 'em go to a burlesque, then."

He frowned at me. "What's eating you?"

"You just met Anna once and she's making you rethink something you've been working on for months."

He tilted his head. "She's your friend."

"I barely know her."

"According to her, the two of you got on like a house afire."

"As far as I can tell, Anna gets along with everybody, until she doesn't."

"What's that mean?"

Before I could respond, Ziggy interrupted us. I hadn't even noticed that we'd made it to the front of the line.

"*Wie üblich?*" he asked. *The usual?*

Otto and I both answered with enthusiastic *ja*s. Though we'd both grown up speaking English, our immigrant elders had used their mother tongue to make us casually conversant. I'd also taken German in high school and could read and write the language passably well.

It surprised me, then, when Ziggy handed over my lunch wrapped in a newspaper that shouted a headline in German, in letters as tall as mason jars: ENGLISH LIES POISON AMERICAN-GERMAN RELATIONS.

I crooked my head, trying to read through the grease. "What paper is this?"

"*Das Auge*," Ziggy said.

In English that translated to *The Eye*. Presumably the name was supposed to conjure up the image of intrepid reporters keeping a watch over Manhattan, although it struck me as sinister.

"You can't trust the American papers," Ziggy said in a low voice. "They lie about us."

"Us?" I asked. When he nodded, I said, "I'm an American."

Otto tugged my elbow. "C'mon, Louise. Let's eat in the station today."

I allowed myself to be yanked away, but I couldn't quite let the subject go. "How do you like that! Bombarded with propaganda in the lunch line."

"It's counter-propaganda," Otto said. "You can't blame Germans for wanting to remind people that they're not bayoneting babies."

"But the paper's in German. That's not correcting the record—it's just stirring up the Germans who live here."

"It's got you stirred up, all right."

I tried to shrug it off, but as I sat on one of the long benches in Penn Station's main waiting room, in the light of its massive semicircular windows, I couldn't savor my lunch as I usually did. The idea of another continent's troubles spilling over onto mine made me uncomfortable. We had problems of our own. Which reminded me . . .

"I need your help, Otto."

He'd been chewing happily, but now his gaze grew wary and his Adam's apple bobbed when he swallowed. "This is the kind of help that brings trouble, isn't it?"

"Not at all." I hoped. "I just need someone to accompany me to a few waterfront saloons to look for that Swede whose passport Ruthie swiped. Tomorrow, if possible. I have the day off before my shift changes again. I'd go myself, but a woman alone in a bar isn't going to get much more than come-ons, and a policewoman is likely to get the cold shoulder. Anyway, I don't want anyone to know I'm with the police. What I'm doing can't get back to the station."

He chewed, thinking it over.

"It's for a good cause," I told him. "A woman and her baby might have been killed, remember? This Swede, Lars Holmgren, could be the key to finding a murderer."

"Or he might *be* a murderer."

I wiped my greasy hands with my handkerchief. "I doubt it. If so, why wouldn't he have made Ruthie give him back his passport?"

"Maybe he tried, and when she wouldn't, he killed her."

That didn't seem likely. "From what I've heard of Ruthie, she loved those babies more than she would have cared about a pilfered passport. If someone had threatened her sons, she would have handed over the passports in a second. But there has to be some reason she sewed them into that cape."

"Maybe she was crazy. The police said she committed suicide," Otto reminded me, "not to mention infanticide."

Infanticide was what really bothered me. Accusing someone of suicide was one thing, but saying Ruthie killed her baby boy if she was in fact innocent felt like calumny. "They're wrong. I feel it in my bones."

His worried, doubtful gaze studied my face. "Nice opinion you have of your colleagues."

"Not all of them. But no one is taking Ruthie and Johnny's deaths seriously, just because she was a prostitute. As if their lives didn't matter."

"Okay—step down off the soapbox. I'll go with you."

"Thanks, Otto."

"You knew I would."

He had been involved with me on other cases. He'd been accused of murder himself, had been tossed out of a nightclub with me, and had spent late nights trying to piece together clues with me.

"I knew you would," I agreed, "but I was hoping it wouldn't take the entire lunch to convince you."

With a deft hand, Walter worked his magic on Otto, transforming him from a sport about town to the kind of down-on-his-heels youth who might escort his young lady to a waterfront tavern. Gone was Otto's tailored gray broadcloth suit, traded for striped pants and a brown wool jacket that had seen better days. His carefully center-parted, pomaded hair was mussed to a less fussy coiffure and topped with a workingman's cap.

I looked in the mirror, wondering how I could complement Otto. "I should be a shopgirl. What can I do to transform myself?"

Walter peered critically at my blue crepe de chine blouse, which I wore over a newish wool skirt in navy, with a tunic overskirt in a navy and gray vertical stripe. I worried I looked too chic.

"You're fine," he said.

I drew back. "This skirt cost me $10.95."

"There's a saying about fools and their money that I won't mention," he said. "Just frowzle your fringe a bit. You'll be perfect."

I grumbled but did as told. Minutes later, Otto and I hit the streets.

As we approached the first watering hole, which didn't even have a name—just the word TAVERN painted on cloudy plate glass—Otto had second thoughts. He turned an anxious face to me. "What precisely are we going to say?"

"Just follow my lead." I added quickly, "But act as if you're the one who thought of it."

"Thought of what?"

"Of whatever I come up with."

I pushed through the heavy door. The patrons inside, all men, swiveled toward us as one, and their gazes locked on me. Conversation ceased momentarily, and an awkward frisson disturbed the smoky air. The barkeep, a heavy man with an elaborate mustache whose twisted ends curled up like a smile, narrowed his eyes at me. When Otto took my arm and steered me toward a barstool, the barman leaned toward us. "What'll it be?"

This was unfamiliar ground. "Beer?" I said.

Otto elbowed past me, more authoritative than I was prepared for. "Sarsaparilla for the lady, a horse's neck for me."

I frowned at him. "Wait just a moment—"

"We can't have you drinking this afternoon," Otto said, cutting me off. Rather cleverly, I realized. The bartender, who hadn't seemed comfortable with a woman coming into this masculine redoubt, seemed more contented now that the woman had been put in her place.

He served us, and I nudged Otto. "Aren't you going to ask him?" I nodded to the barkeep.

Otto gaped at me, eyes both clueless and frantic.

"About Cousin Lars," I prompted.

"Oh!" He cleared his throat and turned to the man. "You wouldn't happen to know of a Swede named Lars Holmgren, would you?"

The bartender didn't respond. Neither did any of the other men not-so-subtly eavesdropping on us.

"He's my cousin," I explained. "We haven't heard from him in over a month."

"Why do you think he'd be here?" the barkeep asked.

"He mentioned this place," Otto said.

"Or an establishment much like it," I said. "He's a young fellow, about twenty-three. Might've been dressed like a seaman. Blond hair, blue eyes. His name's Lars Holmgren."

"This ain't the Waldorf, lady. I don't make the customers sign in." Chuckles from his listeners encouraged the barman. "And there's lots of Swedes, sailors, and what have you comin' in and out all the time. Maybe he was here, maybe he wasn't."

I hadn't really expected success on the first try. I swallowed a sip of my drink, and so did Otto. He choked, coughed, and turned to me in shock. "This has whiskey in it!"

I tried not to laugh. "What did you expect?"

"Ginger ale and lemon juice. That's how they always made them at Arnie's Tavern back in Altoona."

"That's how they made them for *you*."

We moved on to try our luck at another tavern. Unfortunately, we didn't have any more success on our second try, or our third, or our sixth. By that time, I felt nauseous from so many sips of sarsaparilla, the quality of which seemed to deteriorate the farther south on the waterfront we went. Otto, who stuck with horse's necks, grew glassy-eyed, even a little loud. "I told you nobody'd have seen him," he said to me when we struck out yet again. He downed his drink and pushed the empty tumbler away on the waxy bar. "Lars is probably halfway to China by now. And good riddance."

The proprietor of the latest establishment, listening in on us as he wiped a glass with his filthy apron, frowned. "If it's a Swede you're looking for, you oughta try the Swedish Lutheran Immigrant Home."

I froze in astonishment. "There's a Swedish Immigrant Home?" This was the first I'd heard of such a place. The man at the consulate hadn't mentioned it. Naturally. That would have been helpful.

"Over on Water Street, I think. Somewheres near there, leastwise. Run by Lutherans."

I stood and tugged Otto's coat sleeve. He slid bonelessly off his stool. "Thanks," I told the man. "That's the first helpful tip I've had all day."

He shrugged. "Still a long shot you'll find your cousin there. Chances are your friend's right. The guy's probably at sea by now. But the home might could tell you if he came through there."

We hotfooted it to Water Street. Thankfully our afternoon of wandering downtown had landed us not too far from the Battery, and a few inquiries led us right to the Swedish Lutheran Immigrant Home, which looked nothing like a home on the exterior. The charity was housed in a faded white-stone five-story office building on a corner. It appeared about as homey as a savings and loan.

Somewhere in the building, though, a hot meal was being served. The smell of salt cod and cabbage almost knocked me off my pins when I stepped inside.

A dour-looking woman took one look at us and stopped us at the entrance. We couldn't pass ourselves off as either Swedes or immigrants, so I trotted out the distant cousin story, which now fell so easily off my tongue I half believed it myself. The woman frowned sympathetically at my tale of familial estrangement, but she didn't seem inclined to give me hope, or give me access to look around the building. "We serve immigrants here," she said, with a slight accent. "Most of whom lack family."

The reception room was filled with furniture—wooden chairs for people waiting, desks, file cabinets, bookshelves, and everywhere papers stacked high. On the walls were a few brightly painted pieces, a calendar, and the ubiquitous portrait of long-faced President Wilson. In one corner a man with white-blond hair sat on one of the uncomfortable chairs reading a Swedish newspaper. Maybe he'd decided to skip dinner. From the stench of that cabbage, I couldn't blame him.

"Lars is only a distant cousin," I explained. "He dropped round our flat to say hello, but we haven't seen him since. I don't know where else he could have gone."

The woman shook her head as she perused what looked like an overlarge ledger. "I don't believe your cousin came here. If he's a sailor, perhaps he found a ship."

"He lost his passport," I said. "I have it, but there's no way to let him know that."

"He could have gone to the consulate and applied for another."

"I've been there. They hadn't seen him."

She lifted her shoulders. "I'm afraid I can't help you. He might have been taken on as a ship's hand without papers—some captains will look the other way, although with the war the documentation requirement is getting more stringent."

"She can't help us, Louise." Otto pawed at my sleeve. "Let's go."

I realized belatedly that he smelled of whiskey and looked unsteady. Perhaps this was the reason the woman wouldn't let us in any farther. I needed to get him home, but frustration built up inside me, especially when I peered through plate glass into an adjoining room and saw people eating. Blond heads. So many Swedes in one place. There was a chance someone in there had come across Lars Holmgren, and this might be my only opportunity to talk to them.

"If I could just speak to some of the people here," I said.

"These are immigrants," the woman replied. "Many don't speak English, and if I'm not mistaken, you don't speak Swedish."

"I don't," I confessed, "but I'm sure I could get my questions across somehow. Especially if someone would help me..." I sent her a pleading look.

For all her determination not to let me pester people in her care with questions, the woman didn't strike me as unkind. "Give me your name and how I can reach you. If I hear of your cousin, I will try to get word to you."

It seemed the best I could hope for at the moment. I jotted down my name and address, and silently cursed my landlady, Mrs. Grimes, for not putting in telephone service yet.

I handed the scrap of paper to the woman and thanked her. "Come on, Otto." I steered him toward the door.

One good thing about leaving the Swedish Immigrant Home was that we could go back out into the air that smelled of smoke, burned chestnuts, and refuse—the pungent winter air of Manhattan—and away from fish and cooked cabbage. I sucked in a few gulps of damp air and tried to decide where to go next. I needed to get Otto back to his place, which was an apartment just off Union Square. Perhaps we should take a cab.

As I contemplated which direction to turn, someone tugged on my sleeve. A face I recognized—ruddy complexion, white-blond hair—looked up at me. The man who'd been reading the newspaper in the lobby of the immigrant home.

"Pardon me, miss," he said, in a rasping shallow voice that sounded like consumption. "I couldn't help overhearing your conversation."

My heartbeat sped. Yes, the man appeared a little disreputable, but I wouldn't hold that against him if he could help me.

"I think this man—this Lars Holmgren—might not be your cousin, no?" His lips curled up in a toothless smile.

That wasn't what I'd expected him to say. "What's it to you if he is or isn't?"

He lifted his shoulders in exaggerated innocence. "Nothing, nothing. The question should be, what is it worth to you to find him?" When I didn't answer right away, he tilted his head. "Or perhaps you don't want to find him. Maybe you just want to make sure he's gone."

Otto stepped forward. "What's your game, mister?"

I put my hand on Otto's arm. "It's all right." I turned back to the man. "I *do* want to locate him."

"Ah. Well..." He shrugged again. "Then that's a shame. Mr. Holmgren might be worth more to you if you didn't find him."

"I don't understand."

"You say you have the Swede's passport," the man pointed out. "In certain quarters, that's as good as cash."

I frowned at him. "You mean I could sell it? To whom?"

"To me." He smiled. "If I could just see it?"

"I'm not carrying it with me," I said.

"Perhaps I could get your address from the woman at the immigrants' home, then."

Lord, I hoped not. I didn't mind her contacting me, but I certainly didn't want every Tom, Dick, and Sven to know where I lived.

Otto stepped forward again, striking an uncharacteristically pugnacious stance. "Don't think you're going to follow Louise to her house and try to steal the passport," he warned.

I tugged at his coat. "It's all right, Otto."

"No, it's not—this man's got a dirty venture going, or knows someone who does." He planted his hands on his hips and sneered at the man. "You've made a big mistake, buddy. You think you're talking to some lady you can just bully or steal from?"

"Otto, never mind, I—"

"It just so happens you're speaking to a cop!"

The man's eyes bulged as he gazed up at me. "A lady cop?"

"Wait—"

But it was already too late. The moment it dawned on him that I really could be a policewoman, and that he'd just implicated his participation in an illegal scheme, the man backed away, turned, and then legged it as fast as he could.

"Stop!" I sprinted after him up Water Street before the man dissolved into a crowd at Hanover Square. A gust of frustration huffed out of me just as Otto trotted up behind me, out of breath.

"What did you think you were doing, chasing that man?" he asked. "He's obviously some kind of criminal!"

I rounded on him. "That was the idea—to find out what kind of activity he was involved in."

Otto began to speak, then understanding dawned in his eyes. He sagged slightly. "Oh."

"What did *you* think you were doing, telling the man I am a policewoman when the whole point of this outing was to try to find out Holmgren's whereabouts without letting on that this has anything to do with a woman's murder."

"*Possible* murder. It's only you who thinks so."

I scowled into the distance where my passport swindler had disappeared. "I'm more convinced now than I was before." Illegal activity . . . a woman with no reason to kill herself, much less her baby. Murder seemed more likely than suicide.

Otto sighed. "I'm sorry, Louise. I saw him menacing you and just blurted out that you were a cop. I wasn't thinking." His eyes focused for a moment. "Do you know, I suspect I drank one too many horse's necks."

I bit back a sarcastic retort. Whose fault was it that he was in this condition? I should have been paying closer attention to him.

He took out his watch and stared at it, disbelieving. "Is it really after five o'clock? I'm supposed to meet Jimmy at seven to work on *Double Daisy*."

"You'll make it. We should get you home and back into your regular clothes, though. I'll take those back to Walter the next time I visit Aunt Irene."

At Otto's flat, I brewed strong coffee while he changed clothes. He was still living in rather primitive rooms, although he had snapped them up with a fresh coat of creamy white paint, blue curtains, and several good pieces of furniture he'd bought new to replace the items he'd found on the street when he'd first rented the flat. The grand piano that had been the previous tenant's still dominated the main room, which was only fitting. Otto spent most of his days hovered over those ivories.

I set a cup of coffee in front of him as he shaved before the washstand and mirror he'd set up in the short hall leading to his Pullman car–sized bedroom. There was a shared bathroom for tenants down the corridor, but Otto liked the convenience of having his washstand. He claimed to do a lot of thinking while he shaved. That might explain the carved-up look his chin had sometimes.

He stopped now to take a sip of the coffee, pooching out his lips like a fish to avoid getting shaving lather on the mug. He already looked much better. "Sorry about today, Louise. I hope I didn't ruin your investigation."

I leaned back against the wall. "You didn't. I learned some useful information today—more than I expected, to be honest."

"Like what?"

The first thing I'd learned was that it was sometimes better to be on my own, although I couldn't tell Otto that. He'd spent a day tagging along with me, when I'm sure he'd rather have been working on his music. And I would've had to deal with a lot more harassment if he hadn't been with me.

"The most important thing I learned is that there's a market for counterfeit passports in this town."

Otto's mouth turned down in a frown as he moved the razor carefully over his right cheek. "You think Ruthie Jones was part of that?"

"It's the best explanation for why she'd steal passports from her customers. It also might show how she'd been able to save up money. She'd discovered a lucrative side business."

He rinsed his razor in the shaving bowl, dried it carefully, and then wiped the towel over his face, getting rid of the last of the shaving soap. He dabbed aftershave on his palms and began to slap it on his face.

"But why did she *hide* the passports?" I wondered, stepping away from the pungent odor. "Sewing them into a cape . . . that's not something you'd do if you were about to hand them off for money, is it?"

"Depends on how much money was at stake, and who she was dealing with."

I narrowed my eyes on my friend. His insights often surprised me, but they shouldn't have. Songwriting required a knack for getting to the heart of a matter.

"The question isn't why Ruthie hid the passports, is it?" he elaborated. "It isn't even simply their dollars-and-cents value. It's whether or not someone was willing to kill her for them."

Yes. That was just it. Why did those three hidden passports

prove deadly? Unless it wasn't just three. Maybe there were more that hadn't been found, or that had been taken by Ruthie's killer. Although . . .

I drew in a breath. Could it be I was underestimating the extent of Ruthie's involvement in this passport scheme?

"What?" Otto asked.

"Maybe Ruthie Jones wasn't just a cog in whatever this passport scheme was. Maybe she was the mastermind."

CHAPTER 8

During my break the next day, I went upstairs to search as incon-
spicuously as I could for Lieutenant King. There were questions I
needed to ask him about Ruthie Jones's apartment, and I wanted as
few of my colleagues as possible to witness my nosiness. No one I
asked had seen King today, however, or knew where he was.

My manner must not have been as surreptitious as I'd hoped.
When I was making my way downstairs again, a detective caught
up with me in the stairwell. Not Lieutenant King, unfortunately.
His partner, Stevens, caught my arm. "I want a word with you."

My instinct was to slap his hand away. I shrugged it off instead.
"I can hear you just fine. No need to maul me."

Some women might have found Detective Stevens attractive.
His individual features were appealing, but there was something
taunting in his expression and tone, no matter the subject under
discussion.

It was there in his voice when he asked, "You were asking after
my partner?"

He stood on the stair above me, which gave him a height advantage. Even at the risk of being closer to him, I stepped up to his
level.

"Yes, I was. Is Lieutenant King in today?"

"What'd you want to see him for?"

"I have a question to ask him."

His lips tightened in impatience. "What you want to know?"

"Do you speak for him now?"

He studied me, then took a step back. "I see." He gave his head a knowing shake.

"What?"

"A girl like you could do better than a fat, middle-aged fellow like King." He shrugged. "But widowers are like catnip to some of you ladies, aren't they?"

I crossed my arms. "Dry up, Detective. I only wanted to ask him about the Jones case."

"The who case?"

Was he really that forgetful, or was he playing obtuse to get my goat? "Ruthie Jones—the woman who died in her flat a few days ago?"

"Oh, the crazy whore who killed her kid and herself. What burning questions concerning that mess made you chase after King?"

Oh, for Pete's sake. "I wasn't chasing him. I have no designs on your partner, aside from wanting to ask him about what was found in Ruthie Jones's apartment."

"I could have told you that. Why not ask me?"

Because I want to talk to a person who's capable of acting like a human being.

Then again . . . why not talk to Stevens? I was already in an unpleasant conversation with him, so I might as well get something out of it. "I wondered if any kind of special materials were found in Ruthie's flat."

"Such as?"

"Well, parchment or other types of paper, or stamps, or ink . . . that sort of thing."

I was ready for more argument, or more sneering, but his brows drew together in thought. "Not that I recall. The flat was just full of what you'd expect. Clothes, cookware, crockery, little gewgaws a cheap woman like her would collect. Perfume bottles, paste jewelry."

"And it didn't appear as if anything had been taken?"

He chuckled. "You think burglars kill whores over ink wells? That's a new one."

My jaw clenched tight enough to crack a molar, but I managed a nod. "Guess you're right."

I hadn't seen anything that looked specific to the forgery game when I'd searched the apartment, either, but I thought there might be a chance that the detectives had removed items during their search. I should have known better. The investigation had been perfunctory.

"That answer your question?" Stevens asked.

"It does." I forced a smile. "Thank you."

He grinned. "That's more like it. You're not half bad to look at when you smile, you know. What's the expression? 'You can catch more flies with sugar.'"

Instinctively, I leaned away from him, even though there was nothing but a wall at my back. If only I could have vanished through it. "I generally try to avoid flies."

"You must like some fun, Two. You have to admit, I'm better looking than my partner."

"Are you?" I asked earnestly. "I hadn't noticed. But why would I? Whenever we meet, we're at work. I try to keep my mind on the job."

He seemed miffed that I didn't melt at his having noticed me, though he covered it with a smirk. "Work isn't everything."

"That's why I'm lucky to have so many good friends. Unfortunately, there's rarely a moment to catch my breath. Like now—I really must get back to the cells. Thank you so much, Detective."

"Maybe some other time," he said.

I descended the stairs briskly, eager suddenly to be back at my usual post. The women's cells might be in the dank, airless basement, but at least every step toward there took me farther from the loathsome Stevens. I turned the corner at the bottom of the stairs, where a short hallway led to the cells. A tall figure in front of me stopped me short. We only avoided a collision by inches.

"Officer Jenks." Here was a frying-pan-into-the-fire situation. Sergeant Donnelly's right hand always had an eye out for infractions large and small. "I thought Schultzie was filling in for me during lunch."

He shook his head. From the look in his eye, I could tell he'd been eavesdropping on my conversation with Stevens. Damn. The way the grapevine worked among policemen, my name would probably be linked with Stevens's within hours. I braced myself for teasing.

"Why all the questions about Ruthie's place?" he asked.

"Just curious."

His head tilted. "You asked Stevens about her flat. What was that about?"

"If you were listening—and obviously you were—you heard him tell me that there wasn't a burglary."

"Uh-huh. And you were asking specifically about paper and ink. That's what you were really curious about, wasn't it?"

He hadn't just been casually eavesdropping, then. He'd picked up on details. I reached quickly for any plausible explanation for my curiosity. "Well, no suicide note ever turned up, did it?"

"No."

"Isn't that odd? After all, there was the baby."

"The one she didn't murder, you mean."

Hearing of her spoken of so off-handedly as a killer made me bristle, but I tried not to show it. "Exactly. She spared him, so you'd think she'd want to leave a note for someone to take care of him."

"Ruthie was insane—she must've been to have killed that baby. And then after, I imagine she was insane with guilt and grief."

Yes, she would have been. If that's how it had happened.

"Anyhow," Jenks said, "not all suicides leave notes. You probably haven't seen that many, but I have. Besides, a lot of people can't even write. Did you see any books in Ruthie's place?"

I frowned, trying to remember. "Not books, no." Nor magazines. "There was a short stack of old newspapers in the front room."

He sniffed. "Newspapers. What're they good for but taking out the trash?"

He had a point. There were so many newspapers in New York, the whole city could have been carpeted anew with them every day. Wrapping for garbage was just one of their ancillary uses. Having a stack of them wasn't proof she could read.

"She couldn't have written a note if she was . . . whatever-you-call-it," Jenks said.

"Illiterate." If she couldn't write, it couldn't have been she who wrote the name Silver Swan on that scrap of paper we'd found in the passports, either.

And she couldn't have been the ringleader of a passport forgery operation. She would have been incidental to any scheme involving those passports. A cog. And yet, something about her involvement may have cost her her life.

"You've given me a lot to think about," I said.

"Leave thinking to the detectives. I only mean this as friendly advice, you know. I've been waiting a long time for a promotion, and do you know why?"

I had a few guesses, but none that he'd want to hear. "Why?"

"Because sometimes I seem a little ambitious. The brass don't always like that."

"Sergeant Donnelly seems to trust you."

He raised his hands. "There again—maybe I come across like I'm in Donnelly's pocket. So Donnelly doesn't want to show favorites by putting me forward for anything. See what I mean?"

"It's very considerate of you to warn me of possible missteps."

His long face broke out in a grin. "You're a nice girl. No reason we shouldn't be pals."

"Uh-huh."

"Just think about it," he advised. "Go easy on these questions about Ruthie. Last thing men around here want is pushy policewomen telling 'em how to do their jobs."

He patted my arm, nearly earning a reflexive swat. But I nodded instead, and we parted amicably. Had he really been imparting collegial advice, or was that his awkward method of flirtation? Or maybe there was something else entirely going on. His eavesdropping couldn't be denied. My suspicion that Leonard Cain had a spy in the precinct rose another notch.

That evening I stopped by my aunt's. Discovering she was out, I headed to the kitchen to see if I could beg something for dinner from Bernice. "I want to make something for Callie," I explained. "She's been working so hard."

Bernice leveled a dry look on me. "You mean you want *me* to make something, and you to take all the credit."

"No one appreciates your culinary genius more than we do, Bernice."

She wasn't impressed by flattery. "You're turning into an old scarecrow under those uniform rags of yours. Can't you even bother to learn how to make yourself supper?"

"Who has the time?"

"If you haven't got the time to learn how to feed yourself, you've got no business breathing air. You don't have to slave over a stove. Get yourself a ham. Cut it up and cook yourself some vegetables. Any fool can do that."

"Ham," I repeated.

"Smoked ham. It's the meat that keeps."

I laughed. "You should go into magazine advertisements."

She wasn't amused. "Might as well. I'm wasting my breath with you."

"Do I hear Louise?" my aunt called from inside the house.

In the next moment, she swept into her gleaming white kitchen, providing an eye-popping contrast in a blue silk crepe poplin dress with orange velvet insets at the neck and waist. Lace adorned her cuffs and fluttered when she raised her arms to embrace me. She'd obviously just come from the hairdresser; her curls looked almost as if they'd been shellacked in place. Circling the narrow hobble skirt of her dress were her two toy spaniels, just in from their walk. Walter had taken them out, Bernice had informed me when she and not he had met me at the door a few minutes earlier.

"Did you *see* what was delivered?" Aunt Irene asked, a light in her eyes.

"I haven't been here long. I brought back the clothes Otto borrowed from Walter." I didn't mention my ulterior motive of cadging food.

My aunt bobbed with excitement. "You must come to the parlor."

I let her lead me away, albeit not without casting a longing glance back at the pie Bernice had made, which she'd informed me was pear-apple. She'd just been preparing to slice off a healthy wedge for me.

"I'll wrap some up," she promised.

The assurance helped me focus on whatever it was that had

Aunt Irene so excited. Her hands, still cold from being outside, held mine in a firm grip as she tugged me toward the parlor. When we arrived, she stopped before a beautifully carved rocking horse, two feet high, gleaming white with a red saddle and black bridle with gold-painted trim.

"Isn't it wonderful?" Before I could answer, she followed up with the question, "Do you think he'll like it?"

"Who?" I had two boy cousins back in Altoona, but they were in their teens now, far too old for a toy like this, exquisite as it was.

She blinked at me. "Who else? Eddie."

I glanced back at the rocking horse, biting the inside of my cheek. "It's . . . a little large for him, isn't it? I mean, he's just a baby."

"Oh, but he'll grow into it." She gave the horse a tap on its flank that sent it rocking. "In the meantime, we can hold him while he sits on it."

We?

Pleased, she folded her arms as she watched over the horse's slowing movement. "It was the nicest one at FAO Schwarz's toy bazaar. Walter and I were there for over an hour."

My aunt and Walter at the children's toy store was an image it would take a while to wrap my mind around.

I remembered something that had puzzled me a few days earlier. "Was it you who visited Eddie in the orphan's hospital and took him such nice toys?"

Her eyes twinkled. "Did you see them?"

"Sister Mary Grace showed me." I didn't mention that her rattle had put mine in the shade. "That was very generous of you."

She crossed to her sofa. Dickens and Trollope hopped up after her. "After you told me what had happened to that unfortunate woman, my heart when out to the poor little soul."

"The sister told me that it was a couple who'd brought Eddie the toys."

"Walter was with me. He was concerned for Eddie's welfare, too. And Walter lives here, so he'll feel the changes that come about almost as much as I will."

I frowned. "Changes?"

"Concerning little Eddie."

"How..." Understanding dawned. "Are you thinking of taking him in?"

"Wouldn't it be wonderful?"

"Yes, but..." My mind reeled. Was this desire to help an orphaned baby sincere, or a mania like her interest in fortune-telling? Either way, I worried my aunt was getting her hopes up and not considering all the obstacles before her. "From what I've heard, the foundling hospital is particular about adoptions."

My aunt's face fell. "Do you think I would be a deficient candidate for adopting a baby? Am I too old? Am I not loving enough?"

"Not at all." I rushed to her side, displacing a dog. My aunt had a heart as big as a mountain. But I knew something of adoptions, even if I couldn't tell her how much, and I doubted her path to becoming Eddie's guardian would be smooth sailing. "Any child would be lucky to have you looking after him or her. But these hospitals... don't they try to find married couples to adopt babies?"

She bridled at that. "Marriage—what does that mean? It means a man provides for his wife and children, but isn't it always the woman who does the actual work of raising a child? Well, I am a woman, and I have a regular income of my own. I could be father and mother. And I have a nice home to offer him, and a brilliant future."

I worried the hospital wouldn't see it that way. Then again, if anyone could convince them, I was pretty sure Irene Livingston Green was that person.

"Besides," she added, "Eddie's not just any baby. How many couples are going to want a mute child? But I can provide him with a good life. What's more, I *want* to."

Where had this maternal instinct come from? "I never knew you wanted children."

"I never did, either. But then you told me about Eddie, and I couldn't stop thinking about him. I guess I hadn't realized how alone I felt, especially since poor Ogden... went away." Her friend, Ogden McChesney, was in jail. "Here I am, a successful woman, and yet I've lost my dearest friend, and though he was an old fool, I've found nothing to fill that void. Not really. Even a full house on Thursday evenings just makes the place seem emptier the rest of the week."

"I had no idea you were feeling this way."

"No reason you should. I'm no mope. I have a good life. But when I heard about Eddie I thought, there's that boy alone in the city, an orphan, and here I am, a spinster writer with room to spare in my house and my heart. Ever since Walter and I went to see him, I haven't been able to concentrate on anything else." She gazed at me. "You're young, and your ambitions are young, too. Perhaps you don't understand what I'm feeling for that little boy."

I understood more than she could ever know. An empty ache took up residence in my chest in moments of idleness, in the small hours of the morning when I couldn't sleep, and on days that seemed like unavoidable traps now set throughout the calendar year—the anniversary of my leaving Altoona, or arriving in New York, or a child's birthday I couldn't acknowledge, much less celebrate. I understood, and I sympathized. And if my aunt's dreams of adopting baby Eddie were realized, I would be happy for her.

But what about that letter I'd sent to Nebraska? "I have to tell you something."

"You look as if someone's died. What is it?"

"You know Walter and I went back to Ruthie Jones's apartment, looking for evidence that she'd been murdered . . ."

"Yes."

I cleared my throat. "Well, while I was there I found a picture of a couple on her bureau. It had a photographer's stamp on the back. I wrote to the photographer to ask if he remembered who the couple was, and if they were any relation to Ruthie Jones."

Her rouged lips pursed. "I see."

"It will probably come to nothing. For all I know, the photographer has gone out of business, or died, or has no recollection of the couple at all."

Aunt Irene looked thoughtful. "Of course, you did what you had to. Due diligence, isn't that what they call it in legal circles?"

"Everyone I've told so far seems to think it was a hopeless effort."

"Yes. I suspect it was, too. But quite proper."

"If I had known your feelings . . ."

She let out a mirthless laugh. "What? You *wouldn't* have tried to locate the baby's true family? That wouldn't have been right."

"But . . ." I lifted my shoulders. "Well, what will you do?"

She petted Dickens absently, thinking. Then she shook her head, as if sloughing off negativity. "I'll do what I intended all along. I'll see about giving the child a home for as long as I'm able. At the very least, he won't spend his first Christmas in a cold orphanage."

"That's generous of you."

"Nonsense—it's selfish. You wouldn't believe how much pleasure it's given me to do even as little as I have so far."

"Eddie's lucky to have run into such a wonderful benefactress."

"It was through you, don't forget."

And what if it's also through me that he loses his benefactress? I tried to push the vision of the dour-looking couple in the photograph out of my mind. A few days ago I'd thought any family would be better than no family at all. But that's when I'd thought he'd had little hope of finding a good home. I'd had Detective Stevens's words echoing in my brain.

"Have you come any closer to understanding what really happened to Eddie's poor mother?" she asked.

"Not really." I explained all I'd learned so far, including information about the passports. It seemed woefully little. "And my feeling that her death wasn't a suicide at all is still just a hunch."

"Your hunches are usually reliable."

"Muldoon always tells me that gut feelings are weak notions to base an investigation on."

My aunt sniffed. "Detective Muldoon can say what he likes. Who is the better crime solver, you or he?"

I laughed. "Don't let him overhear you ask that question."

"Well, perhaps I'm a tad biased. And yet I do remember being present when you solved cases that had stumped the good detective."

I stood. "I should go."

"You aren't staying for supper?"

"I can't. In fact, I was hoping to get home before Callie and prepare a supper for her. She's been working so hard, what with movies and knitting bundles for Belgium."

Aunt Irene hopped up from the couch so quickly, Trollope woke up and let out a yip. Both dogs followed her across the room, where she rang a bell. In a few moments, Walter was at the door, eyeing the dogs sternly.

"Again? They just went out."

"The boys are fine. I just remembered that I had a bag of old clothes to send Callie. Do you remember where I put it?"

"Oh yes. I'll bring it right away."

I went back to the kitchen, where Bernice had prepared a box for me. "You're a soft touch," I said. "What would I do without you?"

"Ham," she said sternly.

By the time I circled back around to the foyer, Walter was standing next to a large carry sack. That wasn't going to be easy to lug home, especially with my bounty from Bernice's kitchen. Still, I was doing little enough for the Belgians. The memory of that German newspaper made the idea of hauling a bag on a streetcar downtown more palatable.

"Callie will be ecstatic," I said, hefting the bag.

"It's just a few cast-off items."

It felt like an entire wardrobe.

Forty-five minutes later, after taking the slowest streetcar in Christendom, I slogged home over wet sidewalks to our apartment. I was relieved to be home . . . right up to the moment I climbed the last stair of the two flights leading to our apartment's floor. I was practically wheezing with the effort, although the wheezing turned to an appreciative sniff as a heavenly, savory scent hit my nostrils. It couldn't be coming from our apartment. Callie never attempted anything more challenging than boiled eggs.

As I stopped and struggled to shift the bag, the box, and my satchel to reach for the doorknob, the door flew open. Instead of my roommate, Anna Muldoon greeted me at the door.

CHAPTER 9

"Oh my goodness—let me help you!" Anna lunged forward to take the box containing the bounty from Bernice's kitchen. Then she twisted back toward the apartment's interior. "Callie, look who's here—it's Louise!"

Who did she expect to come home to my apartment?

Callie darted out of the kitchen holding up a wooden spoon, with one hand cupped beneath it to catch possible drips. Seeing me, she stopped short. "Oh!" she said, as if surprised, too. "You're home."

Before I could answer, Anna peeked into the bag she'd taken from me. "And look—she's brought more food with her."

"*More* food?" I said, dropping the sack of clothes at my feet.

"Anna's making me—us—Irish stew."

That accounted for the heavenly smell. The dish seemed to be her specialty.

"Or as my people call it," Anna said, "stew." She laughed a little too boisterously at her own joke. She was wearing a long flour-sack tea towel pinned over a confection of a dress that looked suspiciously like one of Callie's. I glanced down. Sure enough, the hem was being kept off the floor by scores of pins.

Callie swept forward. "I invited Anna to stay the night, so she offered to cook for us. Isn't that nice?"

"Wonderful." I tried to muster up enthusiasm for the altered evening ahead, but my attention was focused on the large evergreen tree now taking up a corner of our parlor. Callie followed my gaze.

"Anna and I saw it this evening and couldn't resist—the first Christmas tree of the season. Remember?"

Last year, not long after I'd survived an attack on my life, Callie and I had dragged home a tree from the first vendor we saw on Sheridan Square. The labor to get that tree up to the third floor had caused much blue language and fits of hysteria. It had been our first Christmas together in our own apartment, and life had seemed golden.

"We'll have to find some decorations," Anna said. "Or better yet, make some."

I fixed a smile on my face, trying to tamp down a foolish spike of jealousy. It was just a tree. Callie and I would have wanted one anyway. Their going out to get one had saved me trouble.

I tried not to think of Wally's warnings that Anna was going to be moving in.

"The dress looks nice on you," I said to Anna.

"*I've* been telling her so this past hour, but she wouldn't take my word for it." Callie surveyed her handiwork-in-progress with a critical eye. She was a deft hand at quick alterations, or the fortunate placement of a sash or other ornament to hide a flaw. "Anna needed something smarter to wear around the movie set."

"Something less dowdy, she means," Anna said, fluttering at the attention.

"Alfred thinks Anna's my assistant." The two of them exchanged a look and then broke up laughing. "I've been getting the royal treatment for the past two days," Callie said. "It's amazing how much better people treat you when you have an entourage."

"Even if it's just an entourage of one," Anna said.

"You were at the studio today, too?" I knew she'd been there the day before.

"I've been enjoying myself so much! I wish I really could be Callie's assistant, but even so, it's fun just to watch."

We slowly made our way into the flat's main room. Callie took the sack from Anna and peered inside. "Is this from Bernice?"

"Soup and a wedge of pie." I'd intended it to be our dinner.

"The pie will be good," Callie said, "and the soup will keep on the fire escape."

"What kind of pie?" Anna asked.

"Pear-apple."

"Oh, I can make a terrific pear-apple pie." She practically clapped her hands as an idea occurred to her. "I could make one and we could do a side-by-side comparison."

Callie laughed. "Let's not get too ambitious."

"Right," I said, "this isn't the state fair."

I'd intended the comment as a light jest, but the two of them turned to me as if I'd thrown a bucket of water at them.

"It was just a thought." Anna took the foodstuffs off to the kitchen. "Anyway, you two relax. I'll have supper ready in two shakes."

After she disappeared, Callie threw me a questioning glance.

"I was just joking," I said.

A constrained atmosphere pervaded the apartment. Callie and I made a desultory stab at chatting, but it felt rude to exclude Anna, who was slaving in our small kitchen ten feet away. Yet including her when there was a wall between us was also a problem. I went to see if I could help, but Anna shooed me away. Expelled from my own kitchen.

Perhaps I was the only one who felt the awkwardness—Callie seemed perfectly serene. She'd put on her favorite kimono wrap and treated herself to a cigarette. We both ended up staring at the Christmas tree, and I felt that odd tingling of jealousy again.

I got up to freshen up for dinner. When I came back out of my room ten minutes later, Callie had shifted to the drop-leaf table, and Anna was bringing out the last bowl of stew. When we were all seated and Callie lifted her spoon to her mouth, she was in raptures. "This is splendid! What on earth did you do? It's so good."

"Secret ingredient." Anna winked at me. "Paprika."

"Not secret anymore," I said.

Callie swung a curious gaze at me. "Are you feeling all right? You seem grouchy."

What was the matter with me? Why did it matter that Anna stopped here for an evening? She'd even made us dinner, for heaven's sake. Callie and I had been living together for two years. It wasn't as if we'd never had an unexpected visitor.

"I've been so absorbed in what's going on with this case I'm working on, I'm forgetting my manners." I smiled at Anna. "Excuse me. This really is delicious."

"Gracious—no need to apologize to *me*," she said. "Besides, now I feel right at home. You're just like Frank—he's always in a mood when he's on a tough case. He gets all silent and grumbles that he doesn't want to talk about it, until I finally *force* him to tell me what the case is about. And half the time I'll listen and tell him something he's never thought of before! I bet I've solved a case or two for the NYPD just by listening and blurting out some idea that occurs off the top of my head. So feel free to tell me what's bothering you—I just might help."

I nearly grumbled that I didn't want to talk about it. Why should I seek the opinion of a woman who seemed to misjudge just about everything?

Callie prompted me, "Is it still the orphan case?"

I nodded, and then, for Anna's sake, I roughed out the facts of what had happened—Ruthie's death, the drowned child, the surviving one, my suspicions, my lack of any proof to support my suspicions so far.

Anna frowned. "It's the passports that make the thing funny, isn't it? If it weren't for them, you'd probably be looking at different people entirely."

"Or not at all," Callie said.

"Exactly." Anna gestured at me with her soup spoon. "You might believe it was a suicide. But even if she did kill herself, I'd bet my last nickel that a man was behind it all. A very bad man. Why do women commit suicide in books? Men! I've read a dozen books where some poor heroine throws herself in front of a train or walks into a raging river."

"That's fiction," I said.

Anna dimpled and turned to Callie. "See? She *does* sound like my brother. Frank is always telling me fiction isn't reality. As if I didn't know that!"

Her mention of fiction sent my mind down the path Jenks had

opened up this afternoon. If Ruthie couldn't read, the chances that she was at the heart of some passport-forging scheme were very small. Perhaps her death was less complicated than I'd been thinking. *A very bad man.* Ruthie had encountered her share of those, certainly. Hell's Kitchen was crawling with toughs, thieves, desperate men, and louses. Enough to keep the precinct cells at capacity most nights. In which case, finding the specific one who'd killed Ruthie would be like looking for a needle in a haystack. Unless he was a regular . . .

"You said that the woman who lived downstairs from poor Ruthie Jones had a husband," Anna said. "Maybe he would have more idea than his wife about the men who Ruthie knew."

"Why?" I asked.

"Because he might have known men who went to see her—or even told them about her."

Or he might have been one of Ruthie's clients himself. I remembered the way he'd cut Eileen off when she'd been talking to me. I hadn't thought that much of it at the time. A lot of people don't want to talk to the police—especially men who might have been in trouble with the law once or twice themselves. Could there have been something more sinister in his impulse to keep his wife from talking to me?

"You've put Louise into a blue funk," Callie said.

Anna laughed. "That's a policeman's cogitating look. Frank gets it all the time. That's why he and Louise would be so perfect together."

Not this again.

"Leave Muldoon out of this," I said. "He doesn't approve of me or what I'm doing."

"Oh, he never approves of anything at first," Anna said breezily. "Takes him forever to get used to new things. You wouldn't believe how long it took him to start using a safety razor! For years he held on to this cutthroat-looking razor our father gave him. Surprising he didn't end up with lockjaw, or whatever it is people get from rusty metal."

"You see?" Callie's eyes were bright as she looked at me across the table. "You'll wear him down, just like Mr. Gillette did."

"Hopefully sooner," Anna said.

"I'm not trying to wear anyone down," I insisted. "I just want to catch a killer."

"Then you should follow Anna's advice and look at the men around Ruthie." Callie glanced around at our empty plates. "Is it time for pie?"

"I'll get it!" Anna said.

Callie and I overruled her this time. We weren't going to let our guest do *all* the work. Any more than I was going to let Anna dictate my investigation. Except she had given me a good idea.

"Where is Anna going to sleep?" I asked Callie when I could snatch a private moment with her as we made tea in the kitchen.

"On the sofa, I guess."

Anna poked her head into the kitchen. "If that's all right with you, of course."

Well, I'd thought it was a private moment.

"Of course it's all right," my roommate assured her. "We're old hands at having three people living in this flat, aren't we, Louise?"

"Mm."

"Oh! Did you have another roommate?" Anna asked.

"A houseguest," I corrected. "Callie's cousin. She was murdered."

The moment the words were out of my mouth, I could have kicked myself. I couldn't seem to say anything right tonight. Callie's face paled at the memory of what had happened a year and a half ago to Ethel, her cousin. Anna was staring at me as if I were a ghoul to have blurted it out so matter-of-factly. The truth was, I was becoming inured to the city's horrors. Which wasn't to say certain things—like Ruthie's death—still didn't shock me. The grisliness of that curdled my blood. But I was used to processing the awful scenes and moving on to the next problem.

Maybe I *was* becoming ghoulish. Belatedly I added, "It was terrible."

"Well, *I* have no intention of being murdered," Anna declared. "Besides, who'd want to kill me?"

How long do you intend to stay? lollopped on the tip of my tongue, but by the grace of God I managed to keep it there.

"Does Detective Muldoon know where you are?" I asked.

"Detective Muldoon?" Anna flicked a smile at Callie. "Doesn't she ever call him Frank?"

"Never," Callie said.

Anna sighed. "Don't worry, I left word that I'd be staying the night here."

"You left a note at his precinct?" I asked.

"At home. He'll see it when he gets in tonight."

There was something odd about that, but Callie was sending me the evil eye, so I let the subject drop. And to make up for any lack of hospitality I might have been guilty of showing, I washed the dessert dishes while the two of them made up the sofa for Anna. Callie called a good night to me, and I heard the door to her room close.

"Good night, Louise," Anna said a few minutes later as I went to my own room to turn in. She was sitting up on the sofa, knees tucked up to her chin under her sheet and blanket. Only one small table lamp next to her illuminated the parlor. "Sweet dreams."

"You too," I said.

"We'll be quiet as mice in the morning so as not to disturb you."

"Don't worry about that. I sleep like a log."

She turned off the light, and I proceeded to walk right into the Christmas tree. I stubbed my toe and let out a yelp.

The light flicked back on and Callie emerged from her room. "What happened?"

"Just a collision with an evergreen," I said, wincing.

"Oh!" Anna looked stricken. "Did I turn out the light too soon?"

"Of course not." Callie put her hands on her hips. "Honestly, Louise, you ought to be able to walk across a room without hitting a tree."

Anna and Callie looked at each other and smiled, as if this incident confirmed something they'd talked about together. Some private joke. *Louise is so clumsy . . .*

I shook my head. I was being paranoid because I was embarrassed. Also, my toe was throbbing but I didn't want to whine about something so trivial.

"Do you think you can make it the rest of the way," Callie asked me, "or should I escort you?"

"I'll make it by myself," I said with a rueful smile. "I'll take it slowly."

"All right, Granny," Callie said.

Anna laughed, and so did I. One of those laughs wasn't as genuine as the other.

CHAPTER 10

Eileen didn't look glad to see me standing in her doorway, but that might have had something to do with the wailing baby in her arms and the washtub of laundry I spied in her kitchen. The flat was steaming, close, and almost dizzying with the smells of lye and bleach. I was interrupting what was obviously a busy morning, and I don't think she recognized me at first.

"Officer Faulk of the NYPD," I said, raising my voice to be heard above the baby's cries. "I was here the night your neighbor Ruthie Jones was found."

Recognition dawned, along with unhappiness at the memory of that event. "Poor Ruthie. You know how the wee bairn's getting on?"

"Eddie? He's at the foundling hospital, doing very well. He might even be adopted."

"That's a mercy." Her eyes narrowed. "What're you here for, then?"

"May I come in?" I asked.

She hesitated, less the helpful neighbor now that there was no crisis afoot. "I'm very busy."

"I won't be long," I said. "Here—let me take the baby."

The offer was a gamble. I'd had more than one baby go from

placid to arch-backed, red-faced hysteria the moment I touched them. Fortunately, little Davy had the opposite reaction. Being in unfamiliar arms shocked him into silence. Quickly I reached into my satchel for the nearest thing to a toy and came up with my key chain. His fat fingers latched on to it with a clawlike grip.

"You've got a way, haven't you?" Eileen said, hands on hips. "First peace I've had all morning."

Dumb luck, but I'd take it. "May I sit down?" I was already edging my way into the flat's interior.

Resigned to my intrusion, Eileen said, "I'll put the kettle on. It can't get any worse in here, can it?"

I wasn't so sure. Hard to describe how a flat could feel both steamy and dank, but this one managed it. The hot-and-cold moisture made me feel as droopy as the long johns, linens, and shirts hanging across the clothesline that bisected the kitchen. Now that I got a better look at her, Eileen also seemed to sag in her clothes. Some hair had come unpinned and hung in lifeless hanks. Her hands were red from scrubbing clothes in lye, and more troubling yet, there was a purplish bruise on one cheek.

"You've been doing a lot of work," I said, sinking into a chair at the small table. There were only two, so I doubted Eileen and Neil did much entertaining. All at once I absorbed what her life must be—caring for the baby, keeping the flat habitable, getting food on the table. Dinner, washing up, and then falling into bed with little hope that tomorrow would be any different.

"Ay, every week seems like there's more chores than there was before," she lamented. "How's that happen, I wonder?"

"You're lucky you've got your husband to help you."

The mention of Neil was like poking her with a stick. "Don't make me laugh. Him's gone at the docks from sunup to sundown, and the evenings it's the pub, or taverns, whatever they're called. Days I wish the whole city would slide into the harbor out where that statue is." She laughed bitterly. "Liberty, a woman? Not a married woman."

I couldn't keep my gaze away from that bruise. "Is he violent?"

"Show me a man who hasn't got a temper," she said, defensive.

"He's as loving as you please most of the time. We're expecting our second."

"Congratulations." Under the circumstances, the words came out flat, but I didn't know what else to say.

She slapped a pitcher on the table. "There's no sugar for tea, but I've got a bit of milk."

"Lovely, thank you."

"Dribble some on his highness there, so's we might have a little more peace."

I dipped a cloth in the milk and Davy sucked on it happily.

Eileen placed a cup and saucer in front of me—dainty china in a blue pattern. When I complimented it, her shoulders straightened. "A wedding present from me mam. I brought it across the ocean in a crate. One of the cups shattered when I unpacked it. I cried like Davy here an entire day." She sighed. "What did I ever think I'd do with six?"

I nodded and drank the tea. It was dark and bracing, even after a splash of milk had diluted it.

Eileen regarded me across her cup, which she held with two hands as if there was no delicate handle at all. Her pointy elbows were propped on the table.

"It's very good," I said.

"The police send officers around just to drink tea, do they? What is it you're after?"

I set my cup carefully back down in its saucer. "I wanted to know if you could tell me any more about Ruthie."

"What for? She's gone." Her expression turned grim. "She gave up."

"That's not entirely certain."

Something lit in her eyes for the first time since I'd entered the flat. "What, do the police think somebody done for her?"

"Not just as yet . . ." I was wobbling on a tightrope, presenting myself as a police officer on an official investigation, when it was only official in my own head. If my snooping got back to the precinct, there would be no end of trouble. Or, rather, there might very well be an end—the end of my career in the NYPD.

Eileen thumped the table with her bony hand. "I knew it wasn't suicide. That first night I told Neil she wouldn't have done for herself that way. Not Ruthie."

I wish she'd told me. "What did Neil say?"

"What do you think? He said I was only wishing, on account of Ruthie and me were friendly."

I looked toward the door, which was left open as it had been on the night Ruthie's body had been discovered. Sitting where I was, I had a fairly good view of the apartment's foyer, between the entrance door and the staircase. I imagined Eileen spent a fair amount of time sitting here, as well.

"Did you ever see any of the men who visited Ruthie?" I asked, repeating the question she hadn't answered that night.

Her gaze darted toward the floor. "I might've."

"Did you recognize any of them?"

She looked at me again, her brow pinched. "Were any of them famous, do you mean? You think the mayor or someone like that was coming to this place?"

"I mean did any of the men come here more than once, or frequently?"

"They might've done."

Her manner had changed, as it had the other night before Neil interrupted us. That sullen expression told me she knew something, though. I was going to have to pry it out of her.

"Was there a man who had any special characteristic you noticed, like a scar . . . or a limp?"

Her gaze sharpened. "You think one of them men killed Ruthie and her baby?" she asked. "He would have had to drown Johnny and then made Ruthie look like a suicide."

"It's possible." Whoever it was would have had to slash her wrists while there was still a sign of life flowing through her. There was blood, but not as much as the coroner's man on the scene said he would have expected.

She took a swig of tea, then set the cup down again with a clatter. "No. There would have been an unholy row if someone had hurt one of Ruthie's boys in front of her. You think she would have stood for that without screaming the house down?"

The question startled me. In all my thinking over Ruthie's death, that angle hadn't occurred to me. Of course she wouldn't have stood for any man laying a hand on her baby, much less drowning the poor thing.

"It couldn't have happened *that* way," Eileen continued, and I knew then she'd been thinking this over as much as I had. Of course she had. Who but Ruthie had come down to sit at this table with her and drunk tea from these precious blue china cups? Who else had sympathized with her over the trouble with the babies— there was always troubles with babies. Crying. Colic. Rashes. Two young mothers. That was a bond that not even the stigma of Ruthie's profession would break. "Whoever it was, he would've had to kill her first." Her face was hard, angry. "The demon."

"I want to find him."

Her eyes told me she wanted me to succeed, but something held her back. Neil, I assumed. He'd told her to stay out of it, to stop thinking about Ruthie, even. Ruthie's death had been on her mind and she probably hadn't been able to stop talking about it. Had that been the origin of Eileen's bruise? First he'd told her to shut up, then he'd hit her.

What if Neil himself had been Ruthie's client? What if *he'd* killed her?

"One of my colleagues"—yes, that was stretching the truth— "wondered if your husband might've told someone about Ruthie. Recommended her, I mean. One of the men he drinks with, for instance."

Eileen's demeanor stiffened. "You think my Neil would do that?"

"Would he?"

"He's no angel, but he had no time for Ruthie. He didn't even like a woman like her living in the same building as me. He certainly wouldn't have been drumming up trade for her."

"I had to ask. Any connection at all would help us."

Her eyes narrowed. "Next you'll be wanting to know if Neil himself visited Ruthie, and I'll tell you straightaway that the answer to that would be no. He would never—"

"I didn't ask—"

"You think I'm so daft I wouldn't know what my own husband was doing right under my nose?"

"He seemed very intent on your not talking to me the other night."

"Sure he was. And you know why?" She didn't give me time to answer. "Because you're with the peelers."

"The what?"

"The police," she translated. "What good's talking to you when you're just looking to pin the blame on someone?"

"I want to catch a killer. Ruthie's killer, her son's killer. They were your neighbors. She was your friend."

"Catch a killer? Measure my Neil for prison stripes, you mean." Her long, strong arms reached across the table and plucked the baby out of my arms. A chubby foot nearly knocked over a second teacup but I lunged for it in time. Eileen dislodged the keys from Davy's little hands and tossed them at me. My sympathy with her plight might have won me this conversation, but now the finger was too close to pointing at her husband, and threatening her home. Unhelpful and violent Neil might be, but without him Eileen would be alone in a strange country with one babe in arms and another on the way.

"I'll give you a hint," she said, eyeing me resentfully. "Look closer to your own home."

Her words brought me up short. "What?"

"You heard me. Sure, Neil didn't want me telling about the man I remembered seeing Ruthie with most. It never does any good pointing the finger at police. You all cover for each other."

"I never would," I said.

"Certain of that, are you?"

"You're saying someone from our precinct was one of Ruthie's regulars?"

"I don't know one precinct from the next, and I don't know how regular he was. All's I know is I saw an officer going up to the third floor once, and after he'd left I rushed up to see Ruthie. I worried she was in some kind of trouble. But she just met me at the door—a little the worse for wear, if you follow me—and assured me everything was fine."

"Did you ever see the officer again?"
"Didn't I! Several times."
"A uniformed officer?"
"Sure."
"He wasn't the policeman I was with the other night, was he?"
"Nah, he was a tall, skinny one. Bristly brown hair. Long face."
Recognition flushed through me in a wave of disgust that began in my heels and rippled up to my hairline.

My reaction brought a scornful curl to Eileen's lips. "Know him, do you?"

I knew him, all right. What I didn't know was what I was going to do about it.

Indignation blew me all the way back to the Thirtieth Street station. *Jenks.* Of course. Why hadn't I seen it? Why else would he have been eavesdropping on me and Stevens that day? Why else would he have seemed so invested in my believing that Ruthie's death was a suicide?

I'd foolishly assumed he was just being a busybody because that's what he always was—a noscy parker ready to run to Sergeant Donnelly to report any infraction. He'd been borderline hostile toward me from my first day at the precinct. I should have noticed that while everyone else referred to Ruthie as "that whore" or something equally dismissive, to Jenks she was always Ruthie. Just Ruthie.

I marched east on Thirtieth, one hand on my satchel, the other balled in a fist at my side, preparing for a confrontation. Or should I talk to one of the detectives first? Or even the precinct captain, Captain McMartin. What exactly would I say?

"I have evidence that Officer Jenks was a frequent client of the prostitute Ruthie Jones."

And what would they say? *"You mean that whore who killed her baby and then herself?"*

"I believe it was a murder, not a suicide."

"And what is your evidence, Two?"

"A hunch . . . and the neighbor's hunch."

Half a block from the station, my outrage had been doused by reality. Feeble hunches wouldn't carry water, not if I was going to be pointing the finger at one of our own. Especially when that man was Sergeant Donnelly's own creature.

My footsteps slowed. I wasn't an innocent. A majority of the men in the precinct had probably visited a prostitute at some time in their lives. No doubt most saw nothing wrong with it. Periodically scandals broke concerning policemen who looked the other way at brothels operating in their precincts in exchange for money or sexual favors, or both. For all I knew, Jenks had some arrangement like that with Ruthie. Perhaps many of my colleagues did. The Tenderloin district had been swept clean before, but the broom that kept dirt from collecting again had yet to be invented.

The sergeant and the captain could be part of that corruption. I didn't want to think so, but how could I be sure? After a year as a policewoman, nothing about men surprised me.

I looked across the street to the station house. It was an impressive edifice. Ten years old, half of gray stone more befitting a medieval castle than a modern police station, with turrets built into the design. The upper floors, though clad in a more pedestrian red brick, were topped by a crenellated roof. Only the green globe lights at the doors clearly marked it as a police station.

Near those lights, about five feet in front of the steps, Jenks stood talking to a man wearing a black coat and a hat pulled low over his brows. Both the stranger's hands were buried in his coat pockets. The only part of his face I could really see was his jaw jutting out of a fat neck, and a nose that looked as if it had been flattened by a few encounters with someone's fist. I'd seen his like before. I'd even met some thugs like him, back when I had come up against Leonard Cain. Cain was in jail now—thanks, in part, to me—but he still had associates and former henchmen looking after his business interests for him. And perhaps looking to take his revenge against me.

I hung back in a doorway, observing them. There was no way this was a chance encounter. The beefy man in black wasn't simply asking directions. He and Jenks were discussing something intently.

Heretofore, I'd viewed Jenks as a nuisance, not something evil. Was he capable of murdering a woman and her child, and staging it to look as if she'd killed her own baby and herself? That required malevolence beyond what I'd given him credit for. Yet if he was associating with Cain's men . . . *They* were capable of anything. They might have even done the deed for him, if they owed him.

But why would Cain's people owe anything to Jenks? That question worried me more than any other.

Not that I had proof positive that this was one of Cain's men.

I was glad now that I hadn't charged into the station hurling accusations like an ancient god tossing thunderbolts. Six months before I might have. Even six minutes ago. Now I sensed that my next step was going to require more calculation and finesse.

I was getting ready to cross the street and go around to the station's back entrance when I saw a young woman exit the police station. Male instinct made the gazes of Jenks and the man in black swing toward her, too. Neither man appeared to comment on her, but they tracked her young, shapely figure, taking in the flash of delicate ankle that peeked between her skirt and the black pumps on her feet.

Lena. She'd come to find me, I was sure. Nothing else would have possessed her to set foot inside a police station. I hurried to the corner, hoping Jenks wouldn't notice me crossing the street to try to catch up with her. I splashed across a puddle and practically had to sprint several yards so that I didn't lose her. I didn't dare call her name until we were both safely around the other side of the building and out of Jenks's line of vision.

"Lena!"

She stopped and turned. "There you are—they said you wasn't here."

"I just got back. What were you doing there?"

"I come to tell you about that gent you asked me to look out for."

My pulse leapt. "Gerald Hughes?"

"That's him—the gimp. He checked in to the hotel this morning."

Finally, I'd be able to talk to one of the elusive passport men. Someone with a real connection to what had been going on with Ruthie before her death. "Lena—that's wonderful. Thank you."

"The way your face lit up, anyone would think you were sweet on him."

"I've never even seen him before. I do want to talk to him, though."

"He's in room 815."

I filed the information away, then frowned as new difficulties reared in my mind. It wasn't as if I could barge up to a man's hotel room door and start interrogating him. No—I would need a little more finesse for this, too. And possibly an alias.

"If you see me in the hotel in the next few days, Lena, you must pretend you don't know me."

"I get it. You going to be a detective?"

"That's it. What does Mr. Hughes look like?"

She bit her lip. "I don't know if I could say much about him. There's the limp, of course. And he wears nice suits—tweedy looking things. Browns and grays. He's some sort of salesman, I guess, because he usually carries a case with him, like a drummer. And he's not bad looking, even if he is a cripple. Brown hair, clean shaven, thick brows over the darkest brown eyes you ever saw. Like coffee beans. He's tall but a little on the thin side, and might be self-conscious about it. He stoops a bit."

I laughed. "You should be the detective."

"Will that do?"

"It will definitely do."

"Got to hurry back to work before my lunch break's over," she said. "I don't want to lose my job."

"Thank you."

She smiled, turned, and disappeared into the crowd flowing uptown, a river of people being swept toward a world of big billboards and lighted marquees.

Gerald Hughes. Though just this morning I'd admitted the chance that the passport men were unconnected to Ruthie's death, I was happy to return to the possibility that they were. It was much more comforting than the troubling prospect of trying to prove the guilt of one of my colleagues.

"*You all cover for each other,*" Eileen had said.

And I'd denied it. But I couldn't deny now that the prospect of pinning blame on my own colleagues made my stomach clench in dread. It was a relief to turn my attention to investigating Mr. Hughes.

CHAPTER 11

Lucky thing the Hotel McAlpin was so impressive to look at, because I began to fear I'd be there long enough to inspect every square inch of it. I wandered from one seating area to another in the three-story-high marble and stone thoroughfare of its lobby, armchair to bench to velvet-upholstered circular banquette, trying to find the best vantage point to scope out the passing parade without drawing attention to myself. I drank in the splendor of the arched columns decorated with painted murals of women representing the colors of jewels, all the while keeping one eye on the building's entrance and elevators. For a break, I strolled to the candy store and purchased a copy of *The Smart Set*, hoping to blend in with the fashionable crowd coming and going. I chose another bench beside a potted palm from which to observe the lobby over the top of my magazine.

I worried my chances of spotting Gerald Hughes this way were slim. The hotel was so massive and self-sufficient, someone could spend a week there without feeling the need to see the city outside. Why should they? In addition to the newsstand and candy store, it contained a grill, a Chinese tearoom, a spa, barbershop, a miniature hospital on the twenty-third floor, a Turkish bath, a pool, and a club on a floor set aside specifically for male visitors. And to show that they were a progressive-thinking hotel, one floor was reserved exclusively for women, with its own registration desk so that women traveling alone could register without feeling awkward. The building was a city unto itself.

After two hours of watchful loitering I was definitely discouraged. And that was before my luck took a turn for the worse.

A finger poked me on the shoulder. "Time to move along, sister," a gruff voice said.

I looked up into the face of a middle-aged man with hard blue eyes. His brusque voice mimicked the way cops often spoke, but this character wore a baggy brown suit gone shiny in the pants, which even our plainclothesmen would shun. His look was topped by an old fedora tipped low on his forehead. His shoes weren't even properly polished.

"Who are you?" I asked.

"House detective."

That explained it. House detectives were often former, and sometimes disgraced, policemen.

"Am I doing something wrong?"

"Not so far, lady. That's why the management would prefer it if you pushed off."

"I have a right to sit here, don't I?"

"Depends. Are you a guest at this hotel?"

"I'm waiting on someone who is." Technically, this was true. That Gerald Hughes didn't know me was another matter entirely.

"You mind giving me his name?"

By this time, I was livid. "I certainly do mind. Why I'm here, or whom I'm meeting, is none of your business."

"Wrong. It's my business to keep respectable guests from becoming marks of females like you."

I rose to my feet. *Females like me?* I had half a mind to show him my badge . . . except the station was just six blocks away. If the detective happened to mention this incident to one of the neighborhood's beat cops, I'd be in for it.

Better, I decided, to act a part. I straightened my shoulders and raised my chin. "The management of this hotel will hear about this."

"Sure," the odious man said. "I'll tell 'em about it myself."

Were men ejected from hotel lobbies this way? I felt frustrated.

Thwarted. How was I supposed to get any investigating done at all if people wouldn't leave me in peace?

I couldn't afford to cause a scene—and I doubted my plight would have mattered to a management invested in keeping women of ill repute away from their guests—so I was out on my ear. Outside, I stood a few yards from the lobby doors, squinting at the winter sun in a clear sky that had just begun to beam directly down on the concrete city. Adjusting my hat to shade my eyes, I was wondering where to go next when a man emerged from the hotel. At a glance, he fit Lena's description of Gerald Hughes—tall, slightly stooped, dark eyes, carrying a large case.

"Do you need a cab, sir?" the uniformed doorman asked.

"No, thank you. It's a fine day," he answered with a pronounced English accent. "I'll walk."

A few paces assured me I'd found my man. He moved with a distinctly uneven gait.

Hughes only walked as far as the Sixth Avenue El that came within a stone's throw of the hotel on the corner where Sixth and Broadway intersected. A newsboy thrust a paper toward him, and the gentleman shook his head. He then went up the stairs to catch the train. I followed, my heart beating a little faster. I'd been pushed in front of an elevated train once, so I hung back a little from the tracks until I could feel and hear the downtown train rumbling toward the stop. Plenty of people got on and off, but I managed to step into the same car as Hughes.

Now that I was finally seeing him in the flesh, Gerald Hughes intrigued me. I could tell why he'd stood out to Lena. Even if I hadn't seen his passport or heard him speak, I might have guessed he was a foreigner. His clothes seemed cut slightly differently from American men's suits. The collar wasn't so high that it looked as though it might strangle him, and his jacket was fitted a little more neatly than the loose tailoring Americans favored now.

I settled into my seat, pretending interest in my magazine, expecting Hughes to be heading to the financial district. Instead, he got off after only two stops. Luckily he wasn't quick or I might have lost him then and there. I darted off the train at the last minute, then remained a safe distance behind as he carefully descended the staircase.

Hughes headed to Sixth Avenue, walked north a block, and then entered a brick building with *Koster Brothers* stenciled in block letters above the door. Staying well back, I surveyed the block. Callie would have known it. This area was her old stomping ground from her days as a mannequin. The garment industry in New York was booming and spreading north. Koster Brothers, from the age of the paint on that peeling sign, had been here a while.

Hughes remained inside for a half hour. When he came out, case in hand, he walked north two blocks and went inside another garment manufacturer called Smithe Designs. Another half hour. He visited two more businesses before stopping for lunch.

The restaurant was one I hadn't noticed before, even though we were nearing the bounds of my precinct. I'd never walked a beat policewomen didn't do that job—but over the course of a year I'd visited what I'd considered most corners of the area on various errands. The White Rose had never drawn my attention. After I waited five minutes and followed Hughes inside, I understood why. It was a place Callie would have called pokey—white tablecloths over too-small tables; ivory wallpaper in a cabbage-rose pattern; narrow, high-backed chairs from back when women wore such constricting clothing that it didn't matter if furniture was comfortable or not.

The clientele veered toward the female and aged. Hughes had been shown to a table in the back, while I seated myself at the front counter on a metal stool facing a display of cakes, tarts, and fussy cookies. The menu the frilly-aproned waitress handed me offered a variety of sandwiches, soups, and a few specialties like steak-and-kidney pie.

"See anything you like, dearie?" the woman asked in a strong English accent.

That was probably the reason Hughes had stopped here. Like Otto and I going to Ziggy's. Nothing scratches that itch for one's home like the sounds and tastes you've grown up with.

From the fuss the waitress made over him, I assumed he'd been here before. She paid him more attention than any other customer, and practically drowned him in tea. As soon as he'd taken a few sips, she was back at his table to pour out more from the pot she'd left at his table. She delivered his food—the steak-and-kidney pie—with a flourish completely lacking when my roast beef sandwich was unceremoniously pushed across the counter to me. Hughes accepted all the attention with cordiality and even humor—something he said to the waitress made her toss back her head and laugh. Then she suggested he choose a dessert and nodded in the direction of the dessert tray.

Quickly, I buried my head in *The Smart Set* until the woman had come and extracted a tart—lemon, not a bad choice—from the case. I ate the rest of my sandwich quickly and paid before Hughes could finish so I would have time to position myself across the street and see where he headed next.

The remainder of the afternoon was more of the same: garment houses and a few smallish sewing factories farther west, toward the river.

Maybe it was here that he'd encountered Ruthie, I thought as I stood waiting for him to emerge from one of the factories. It wasn't too far from her flat. Or maybe he might have heard of her from another customer, a recommendation from one out-of-towner to another.

I was working the night shift at the precinct, so I followed Hughes all the way back to the McAlpin and then went straight to work. My legs were killing me. I'd been on my feet most of the day, and what had I discovered? That Hughes was a salesman. Lena had already told me that. Not much return for a day's surveillance. A day when I should have been resting. It was going to be a long night.

"Evening, Louise. You on graveyard again already?"

I smiled at Schultzie. "I told Evelyn I'd take her shift this week. Her father's on a night shift and she didn't want to leave her kid sisters alone all night."

"Best time of day to leave 'em alone," he insisted. "At night, all they do is sleep. Of course, kids are coddled now."

It was a familiar refrain. According to Schultzie, all the kids in his neighborhood growing up were put to work by the age of six and were thoroughly jaded and battle-scarred by the time they'd reached ten. If his stories were even fractionally accurate, I wasn't sorry to be living in modern times.

While he expounded more on the spoiled youth of today, I found myself staring at his coat. Even he finally noticed.

"What's the matter?" he asked, looking down. "I spill something on myself again?"

"You're missing a button." The observation set off a queasiness in my stomach. The buttons on his uniform jacket were the same size as the one I had at home—the button I'd found at Ruthie's.

"Darn things are always coming off," he said with a cluck of disgust. "Hope I can find it at home."

I hoped so, too. I leaned in closer to inspect the buttons that remained. They were brass with a design in the center. Some kind of whorl. Not a bird.

I released a sigh. "I thought I had one at home that matched it, but yours is different."

I wobbled downstairs and relieved Fiona. "I don't want to jinx you," she said, "but it's been quiet so far."

It was quiet for the rest of the night, too, except for the thoughts storming through my mind. What was wrong with me that, even for an instant, I'd suspected Schultzie—old, sweet, talkative Schultzie—of being mixed up in Ruthie's murder? The man was seventy if he was a day. Of course, seventy-year-old men were still men.

But was it Jenks whom Eileen had described, not Schultzie? I still hadn't decided what to do about Jenks, or given more thought to what his conversation with the man in black the day before portended.

I'd been up too long. During the night I had to transport a woman prisoner to Bellevue. It would have been the perfect time for an escape; if she'd chosen to make a dash for freedom I would've been too exhausted to put up much of a chase. At the end of my shift, I dragged myself home, envisioning my head sinking into my feather pillow with each step. It was a wonder that I didn't fall asleep standing up at a corner, waiting for a produce wagon coming from the Gansevoort Market to pass.

When I let myself in, the curtains were pulled and it was still dark inside the apartment. Shrugging off my coat and hat and hanging them on the tippy coatrack, I noticed a strip of light beneath the bathroom door. Callie was up. There was no hurrying her out of there when she was readying herself for a day of filming, so I went straight to my room, prepared to hurl myself onto the bed just as I was, boots and all. What I wasn't prepared for was finding a half-dressed woman in my bedroom. I yelped, leapt back, and slammed the door shut.

Disoriented, I stared at the closed door. There *had* been a woman in there, hadn't there? Or was I so tired that I was having weird waking dreams?

The door opened again and the dream emerged, all apologies. Anna—of course it was Anna—had pulled another of Callie's dresses over her head and was buttoning up as fast as she could. "I'm so sorry, Louise. You see, you weren't here, and Callie swore you wouldn't mind. Anyway, it's almost like we're family now, isn't it?"

What? Was that some reference to an imagined relationship between her brother and me? "I don't—"

Callie crashed out of the bathroom—it always sounded like people were crashing out, because the door had begun to warp, requiring several mighty yanks to unstick. "What's all the ruckus?"

"Anna took me by surprise," I said.

"I'm so sorry," Anna piped up, to both of us this time.

"It's okay," Callie assured her. "Louise is always out of sorts after working nights."

I was?

"The bathroom's free if you want it," she continued, addressing Anna.

"Thank you." Anna scuttled into the bathroom.

"Honestly," Callie muttered after Anna managed to shut the door on her third attempt. "This flat." She turned on her slippered heels and headed for the kitchen, passing the tree, which still stood undecorated on its crossed-slat stand. It smelled good, at least.

I trailed after her, giving up on the idea of sleep for the moment. "What's the matter with our place?"

She laughed incredulously as she poured herself a coffee from the pot sitting on our little range. "What isn't? It's inadequate in every way."

"You loved it here when we moved in."

"We were both broke when we moved in. It was the best we could do."

"Two bedrooms and no going down the hall for the bathroom," I reminded her.

"What seemed luxurious then seems shabby now. Surely we can do better."

A feeling of panic filled me. Not that I was overly attached to our flat—certainly not to the constant intrusion of saxophone music at all hours, and our grumpy landlady and her nosy son. Mostly I worried this change of attitude wasn't entirely about the apartment. "Did Anna say something about it?"

Her long-lashed eyes blinked at me over her coffee cup. "What's Anna got to do with anything?"

I hesitated, then plowed forward. "She seems to be staying here quite a bit."

"Alfred's taken a shine to her and decided to give her a little part as my kid sister. Staying with me saves her time getting uptown—and it wasn't as if you needed your bed last night."

"I might've liked some warning that my room would be occupied when I got home."

"So I should've made a special trip to the station house on Thirtieth Street to ask your permission for someone to stay in a room you weren't even using?"

Of course not. I felt silly for saying anything now. "I was just wondering if Anna's being here has made you suddenly feel as if you don't like the apartment."

"Well, you have to admit that there's not much room for company."

We'd found that out when her cousin Ethel had stayed. And stayed.

"I didn't even know Anna could act," I said, despairing at the idea of Anna as a perpetual guest.

"I can't."

Her bright voice at my back startled me. How had she gotten out of that bathroom without my hearing her? She must have tried extra hard to pry it open without making a sound.

"I expect I'll be booted back to Brooklyn after I try to do my little scene," she continued, bobbing on the balls of her feet, "and that will be the end of Anna Muldoon's career in moving pictures."

"You'll be terrific," Callie assured her. "She's playing the part of the kid sister who interrupts my beau and me when we're canoodling on a settee. It's a funny little bit."

"We *hope* it's funny," Anna said.

My guess was that she was a little older than Callie, but her short stature and round-cheeked face did give her a youthful, innocent appearance.

"I'm just so grateful everyone's taken me under their wing like they have," she said. "It's like a little family, isn't it?"

Again with the family. "What is?"

"Show business."

Callie snorted into her coffee cup, then glanced at the locket watch around her neck. "We'd better scoot, little sis." She gave Anna a nudge.

"Oh! Already?" For the first time, Anna looked flustered. Her anxious gaze met mine. "Wish me luck."

"Good luck," I said.

Callie herded her protégée out the door. Someday we were going to finish the conversation we'd started about the inadequacy of this apartment. But the moment I heard the flat's door click closed, exhaustion overtook me again, and I went back to my room again and collapsed on the bed. As I drifted off, a scent of jasmine reached me.

It was Anna's, I realized. A sweet smell. Too sweet.

A few scant hours of sleep later, I was up, dressed, and, following a hunch, standing across the street from the White Rose. I got there at an hour I hoped was early for lunch and stayed outside, scanning the street. Sure enough, Gerald Hughes came ambling up Sixth Avenue, case in one hand and using an umbrella as a cane with the other. Nearing the corner, steps away from the restaurant, he stopped to watch an elderly woman across the intersection fumbling with her handbag. His eyes narrowed beneath the brim of his homburg. He seemed to be calculating something.

Was that look menacing?

I also studied the old lady, who was standing about ten yards to my right. If there were any purse snatchers in the area, she would provide the perfect mark. She dug through the open bag, and dropped a handkerchief that blew onto the avenue without her seeming to notice. In the next moment, still searching for something, she stepped into the street.

Hughes leapt to action. I wanted to shout a warning to the woman, but I was too slow—slower even than the man with only one real leg, who raced across the street in a flash. I don't know what I expected—did I really think he was going to snatch her bag?—but instead he nearly threw himself in front of an oncoming delivery truck making a sharp left turn. My heart leapt to my throat. Hughes clearly intended to shield the elderly woman, but had the truck's brakes been a fraction less strong, they both would have been run over.

At the sound of squealing tires, the woman dropped her bag. Hughes scooped it up for her while the truck honked at them. Taking his time—maybe to spite the driver, who was now blocking traffic and being honked at himself—he returned it to the old woman and escorted her across the street. They exchanged a few words, he tipped his hat, and the woman continued on her way. He watched her for a moment, then turned and walked into the White Rose for his lunch. His limp seemed more pronounced now than before.

My pulse rate had jumped, almost as if *I* had nearly been run down. Hughes had risked his life to help that woman. Another man might have yelled out a warning, or simply watched in shock, but the Galahad spirit was alive and well in him. Did that preclude his also being a killer? I doubted following the man on his rounds to more clothing makers would answer that question.

Not wanting to run the risk of him seeing me and possibly remembering me from yesterday, I didn't follow him inside the tearoom. A plan was forming in my head, but I needed someone to help me execute it.

To that end, I spent the rest of the afternoon at Otto's, playing cards, convincing him to again be my partner in crime—or crime fighting—coming up with a routine, and then catnapping in his chair while he played me selections from *Double Daisy*. I worked the night shift again, and once more found that Anna had stayed over in my room when I returned home. I tried not to let it bother me.

It bothered me.

The following day, Otto and I met at one o'clock at the White

Rose. I managed to finagle a table near the back, where I hoped Gerald Hughes would be sitting. That he wasn't there yet made me nervous, and preoccupied me while Otto told me all about *Double Daisy*'s latest woes.

"We've found a money man, but he thinks we ought to have a star."

I peeled my gaze away from the view of the street and took a sip of tea. "That would be good, wouldn't it? Who could you get?"

"I mean, he thinks we should get a star to play Daisy."

Alarmed, I crashed my teacup into its saucer. "That's Callie's part."

"I know." He drooped miserably. "What am I going to do?"

"Didn't you tell him that you have your Daisy already? You wrote that part for Callie."

"I can't just put the kibosh on the whole musical because they won't give my girl the part. She's not even my girl. *That* at least they'd understand. They might not cast her, but they'd understand my wanting to."

Biased as I was, I could still see his conundrum. There were more people than Otto invested in the show, and Callie's only experience on Broadway so far had been limited to one bit part and a show that had closed in its first week. Not exactly a track record that would lead investors to gamble thousands on.

"Callie will be heartbroken," I said, and then wished I could unsay it. Otto looked more depressed than ever.

Having been Otto's friend for ten years, and watched him struggle to try to transform himself from butcher's assistant to Broadway wunderkind, I understood what was at stake for him. Songwriters needed hits. Shows were vehicles for creating song sensations. He had poured six months of his life into this show, while Callie had been making movies and pursuing other projects.

"What am I going to do?" he moaned.

"You have to think of your own career," I said, unable to believe how quickly I was turning from my roommate's advocate to his. They were both my friends, though. "Callie can audition for every show in this city, but this *is* your show. You can't give up on it now because she might be disappointed. You have to live."

"Yes, but I also have to live with myself," he said. "I promised her."

"Callie's not a fool. She's been in the business longer than you have. She'll understand how these things work."

I hoped.

My mind was so full of anguish for Callie—for both of them—that it was a few moments before I glanced to my right and saw Gerald Hughes being seated a table away, by the window. *Take your mind off the task at hand for one minute . . .*

I straightened and said in a louder voice, "I don't know why you care so much about what happens to that woman."

Otto's face twisted in confusion. "Huh?"

Under the table, I gave his shin a sharp tap with the toe of my shoe.

It took him a moment to catch on. He pulled his shoulders back, shifting gears. "What are you complaining about?" he growled. "We're not married."

I made my voice as quavery and woebegone as I could manage. "But we're engaged, Otto. If you love this other girl—"

"Did I say I loved her? Can't a man talk without some woman putting words in his mouth?"

"I'm not just some woman. I'm your fiancée. It's been three years. The family keeps asking questions . . ."

His sneer almost frightened me, it was so realistic. "Your family never seems to question how I'm supposed to support you once I do take you off their hands."

"I told you I'd keep my job."

"And we're supposed to live on sixteen dollars a week? Can't you find something better?"

"Doing what?"

"I dunno—you're the one who's supposed to have the imagination. You're not bad to look at. If you'd try a little harder, maybe someone in that building would take notice of you."

"Oh, Otto. It almost sounds as if you want me to seduce these men just to get ahead."

He snorted. "Well, isn't that how most women operate?"

We had the ears of most of the restaurant now. I lowered my

voice out of self-consciousness. Gerald Hughes would still be within earshot.

"If that's what you think of me, then I'm not sure I'd want to wait another three years."

He threw his head back. "And if you're going to be so clingy and stupid, I'm not sure I'd want to stick it for another three hours."

I gulped.

"Oh, don't start blubbering now."

I yanked the ring I'd borrowed from Callie's jewelry box off my finger and tossed it on the table.

Laughing, he swiped it up and put it in his pocket. "You'll be calling me tomorrow begging for it back."

"Just go."

He pushed back from the table, his chair legs screeching against the floorboards. "Good riddance. At least I'll never choke down any more of your aunt's goulash."

It was a detail too far—Otto's aunt Bertha was the one who made the awful goulash. I had to lift a napkin to my face to hide my struggle to keep from laughing. But out of the corner of my eye, I saw Gerald Hughes's pitying gaze pinned on me.

Otto turned and stomped out, even slamming the door upon his exit. For him, this show of callousness was especially impressive. It proved what a little exposure to theater people could do.

Now I was on my own. The waitress, the same one from two days ago, realized at once what that meant. She was at my table before the door had closed behind Otto. "See here, we don't like arguing in my establishment. This isn't the Automat."

I dabbed my eyes with the napkin. "I'm sorry," I said feebly.

Her gaze took in the full table in front of me. "And who's going to pay for all this food now? I hope you have money."

"I . . ." I looked down at my purse. "Oh . . ."

The waitress crossed her arms. "This isn't a charity."

"I left my house with just enough for the streetcar," I said.

"You ought to have thought of that before you sent him on his way then."

A strained silence stretched, with all the patrons of the little restaurant staring openly at the showdown between the waitress and me. In fact, they seemed more curious about this than they had about my argument with Otto.

"I'll cover the young lady's lunch," Hughes said at last.

My Galahad. I'd begun to worry I'd misjudged him.

"Thank you," I said, "but I couldn't possibly accept your generosity. You don't even know me. If this lady could just wait until tomorrow . . ."

The waitress scoffed. "And what's to keep you from scarpering out of here and never showing your face again?"

"Nonsense," he said, although I couldn't tell who the comment was directed to. "Of course I'll pay. It's the smallest thing." He smiled at me, and there was nothing at all wolfish in his eyes. Part of me wanted to clear him as a suspect right then. Just reach into my purse, pull out a dollar, and end the whole farce. But Ruthie had taken his passport, and he might be the only one of the passport men I'd ever get a chance to speak to.

"Bring her plate to my table, Cora," he said. "She'll be my guest."

"And the young man's meal?" the distrustful Cora asked.

"I'll pay for that too." He looked at her and laughed. "Unless you don't think I'm good for it."

Cora jabbed her thumb at me. "The trouble is this one. I'm not sure what *she's* good for."

Before she could talk Hughes out of his charitable impulse, I grabbed my plate and moved to his table by the window. "Thank you very much, sir."

Hughes was a little late to pull my chair out for me, so he brought my teacup over. "The pleasure is all mine. My name is Gerald Hughes, by the way."

I smiled. "I'm Louise F—" Too late, I remembered I was supposed to be someone else. Blurting out one's name is so instinctive. I was just able to salvage something of my disguise at the last minute. "Frobisher."

"And what is it you do, Miss Frobisher, besides breaking hearts in tearooms?"

"I work as a secretary at a publisher's." This was almost true—I'd worked at a publisher after first coming to New York. Better, I decided, to keep my fake persona's life story somewhat close to my own.

"Fascinating work, I imagine."

"If you consider typing and making coffee fascinating." I smiled. "Oh, and answering the telephone. Enthralling!"

"I'm sure you do it very well."

If I had really needed bucking up, Gerald Hughes would have been a good man for the job. His voice was deep and had a pleasant burr to it. His manner came across as kind and conscientious without being fussy. He wanted to put me at ease, but I sensed his interest in what I had to say was genuine. It was something about the eyes. They were, as Lena had said, deep, dark brown. Kind eyes. *Not the eyes of a murderer* was my first thought. But first impressions like that were unreliable. Probably some of the biggest villains of history had kind manners and faces women deemed trustworthy. Bait for easy prey.

I was glad for the chance to observe him up close. Hughes looked every one of his thirty-eight years. The corners of those brown eyes had deep lines, as if he'd spent a decade or two of his life in the sun. Not what I would expect from a salesman from England.

"I'm sorry you had to have your lunch interrupted by that scene Otto made," I said, sensing he was waiting for me to speak on that subject. I tried to think what a long-suffering secretary would say about a ne'er-do-well beau. "He's not usually like that."

"Don't make excuses for him. I saw what kind of man he is."

"He's had . . . disappointments."

Gerald wasn't moved. "Nothing excuses acting boorish in public, especially towards a lady."

"You're from England, aren't you?" I asked.

He nodded. "I grew up around Manchester."

"That's in the North."

He smiled. "Right in one."

"Everything I know about England I learned from novels. Mrs. Gaskell."

"*North and South*. A good book. Haven't run across many here who've read it."

"Oh, you should meet my aunt. She loves the Victorians. She named her dogs Dickens and Trollope."

"Sounds to me as if quite a bit of your whole life revolves around books," he observed.

"Too much, sometimes. I often find myself wanting to live life instead of just reading about it. I bet you've seen things, traveling as you have."

The grooves that lined his forehead grew deeper. "Yes, I've traveled."

"Where?" I leaned forward eagerly. "I'd love to hear about some of your adventures. I don't even know what you do for a living, do I?"

"Right now I'm a representative for a business in Manchester. A mill, as a matter of fact." He smiled again, acknowledging the *North and South* parallel.

"Like Mr. Thornton?"

"I'm not a mill owner, just a salesman." He added quickly, "But I started adulthood as a soldier."

"In India?" I asked. "That's where the British sent most of their soldiers, isn't it? Before the war, I mean."

He shook his head. "In my day it was a different war. Africa. I joined up during the second fight against the Boers." His mouth tightened. "I was wounded."

No elaboration on how badly he was wounded. "I'm sorry."

"I was luckier than some. That's what war shows you—as long as you're breathing, you're luckier than the lads who never saw home again. Who never got a chance at life, really. There will be even more of them this time around."

More casualties than the Boer War, which dragged on for years? I doubted that. "This war can't last, can it? Everyone says it will be over quickly."

"When has 'everyone' ever been right?" he asked.

"But conflicts can't go on and on nowadays, with the whole world reporting every movement. Everything is blasted across the world instantly via telegraph, and with pictures. Film, even. Men can't wage war for long with the whole world watching."

A bitter laugh escaped him. "There have been witnesses to wars who've written down their impressions going all the way back to the Greeks."

"Yes, but this is the modern age. We're not barbarians."

"And we've found more modern ways to do battle." He shook his head. "No, Miss Frobisher, I fear this will be a long, costly conflict. My only regret is they won't let me in it."

Was he mad? A long and deadly conflict, and he wanted to be in the thick of it. "Surely you've seen enough fighting in your lifetime."

"Who better to continue than the men who've fought before? But of course, it's hopeless."

He looked truly unhappy about his ineligibility for service. Did that show an honorable if overactive sense of duty, or a lust for violence? My mind whirred. A frustrated soldier. He felt left behind, far away from home when the war broke out in August. Had he taken his disappointment out on Ruthie?

Hughes smiled. "Not doing a very good job cheering you up, am I?"

For a moment I almost forgot what he was talking about. "You've helped me immensely. I never thought it was your job to cheer me up."

"But *I* did, and still do. I hope you'll allow me to see you again. This evening, perhaps?"

"Oh, I don't know . . ." I grasped the first excuse that popped into my head. "I've taken such a long lunch, I'll have to stay late at work. And I promised to visit with my aunt this evening."

"I see. Tomorrow evening, then?"

The timing might be a little difficult to work out, but how could I pass up this opportunity?

"All right," I said.

"Wonderful. Where shall I pick you up?"

It never occurred to me that my plan would meet with so much success so quickly. My mind reached for a fast dodge.

"That's very kind of you, but my flat's so far from Midtown—

the back of beyond in Brooklyn. It would be easier for me to meet you after work. Say, at your hotel?"

"How did you know I was staying at a hotel?"

"Oh . . ." I swallowed, kicking myself. "Aren't you? You said you were a salesman, so . . ."

"I'm at the Hotel McAlpin," he said.

As we arranged to meet in the lobby the next evening, I couldn't believe my good fortune. No girl had ever been happier to have procured a date with a man she suspected might be a murderer.

CHAPTER 12

When I met Gerald the following evening, he presented me with a corsage of flowers—an arrangement of hothouse rosebuds that must have cost him a pretty penny. He'd made reservations at the McAlpin's grill, which would be quick, he said. As the white-coated waiter was pouring our wine, Gerald revealed why time was of the essence. He'd managed to procure a pair of opening-week tickets to *Watch Your Step*, the new Irving Berlin musical starring the ballroom dancers Vernon and Irene Castle.

I gasped. "How on earth did you manage it?" Callie would melt with envy.

He shrugged modestly, in a way that told me that it hadn't been as easy as he wanted to let on.

In spite of myself, I began to look forward to the fun of the evening he'd planned. I hadn't expected to like the man I was investigating. As we talked over dinner, I kept having to remind myself of Ruthie. The gentleman in front of me had known Ruthie Jones—possibly in the Biblical sense—and might even have been responsible for her death. That horrible scene from Hell's Kitchen was hard to keep in mind, though, when the wine flowed so freely in such sumptuous surroundings. The grill was all dark paneling and walnut furniture, with attentive waiters ready to hop at the least sign of diner distress. Yet we were a mere ten minutes' walk away from the flat where Ruthie had died.

I was here to find out things, not for pleasure. I asked Gerald about himself as often and discreetly as I could. He was the second of three sons of a physician, though neither of his parents were still living. He'd gone to good schools—sent away to boarding schools, of course—where he'd caused the usual amount of trouble. Then he joined the army. He didn't want to talk about that, or the years directly after he returned home with the injury that had ended his military career. He loved books, some opera, and popular music, but he said he was starting to feel too last-century for modern times.

"That can't be true," I protested. I knew his age from the passport but feigned ignorance. "You can't be much over thirty."

"Bless you for that, dear girl, but I'm thirty-eight." He winced. "Now you'll think I'm entirely too long in the tooth to be seen out with."

I lowered my voice sympathetically. "I could ask the waiter to bring you some soft foods and a push chair."

We laughed and talked through the rest of dinner, and then laughed even more during *Watch Your Step*, which was such a wondrous confection I never wanted it to end. The Castles danced so energetically yet gracefully, they didn't seem quite human. The story was the usual comedy fluff, but there were wonderful bits throughout, like Verdi protesting *Rigoletto* being done in ragtime. Throughout, I tried to remember songs for Otto, and bits of dialogue for Callie. When the show was over, I wanted nothing more than for it to begin again. I floated out of the theater humming, "Play a Simple Melody."

"Did you like that song?" Gerald asked as we joined the hordes of just-released theater patrons hoping for taxicabs.

"I loved it," I said. "I can't wait to tell—" I didn't say the name, but Gerald heard enough to know. I reddened at my mistake.

His face fell. "But surely . . . That's over, isn't it?"

Recovering from my blunder required Broadway-worthy theatrics. I wilted back a step, my hands fluttering toward my face. "I don't know why I said that, or even thought it."

He laid his hand on the shoulder of my coat, nodding in understanding, though it was obvious that my words had wounded him. "After three years, you can't expect to forget someone in a single day." His lips turned down. "I know that better than anyone."

That last statement made me bird-dog alert. "Have you had a . . . disappointment?"

He shook his head. "Never mind. I need to get you home."

This was the awkward bit I'd been dreading. "Please don't feel you have to bother. I just need to take the subway."

"At this hour? Nonsense. We'll hire a taxi."

Even if I had been an honest-to-goodness resident of far-flung Brooklyn, I wouldn't have let him escort me all the way there in a cab. Going there and back again would have taken him an hour. Convincing him of the folly of this—and the waste of time—took precious minutes of arguing on the emptying sidewalk in the cold. I was already later for work than I'd ever been.

Relenting at last, Gerald waved down a cab, handed me in, and paid the driver handsomely in advance to take me where I needed to go in Brooklyn. With a gentle squeeze of my hand, he bade me good night.

The cab driver was bemused but very happy when he discovered he only had to drive me fifteen blocks, not to Canarsie. I was probably his most profitable fare of the week.

"Just drop me near the police station," I said when we were approaching Thirtieth Street, then added quickly, "but not too close."

"You in some kind of trouble?" he asked.

"It's where I work. I'm a policewoman."

He twisted to gape at me, and for a moment I worried he might wreck the car. "Honest?"

I dug in my purse, leaned forward, and showed him my badge.

"I've never seen a police lady dolled up before." His brow furrowed as he pulled to the curb. "You want I should split the difference with you for the cab fare? I don't want you to think I was trying to chisel your boyfriend."

"What I most want is for you to forget you dropped me here should you ever see that man again. Understand?"

He nodded and winked as if we were in cahoots, which I supposed we were.

I scooted into the station, self-conscious in my finery. Luckily, the place was having a moment of quiet for that time of night. Someone on one of the long wooden waiting benches whistled, though, which caught the attention of Jenks, who—just my luck—was at the desk. "Your highness!" he said. "You deigned to join us this evening."

"I'm sorry," I said. "I'm late."

"Don't apologize to me. Save it for Schultzie, who's downstairs watching over your loyal subjects."

So Fiona, who'd had the shift before mine, had left. That was good. Schultzie was probably napping on a bench.

"Being late's no joke, Two."

"I know. I'm sorry."

"Do you want to be a police officer or a debutante?"

I didn't dignify that question with a response.

"I'll have to tell Captain McMartin about this." His gaze raked up and down my body. "Unless you want to give me a little incentive not to."

The blood flowed into my cheeks, but I didn't care. I kept a hard, even stare on him.

He lowered his voice. "I know corners of this station nobody else ever goes to."

I couldn't hide my disgust. "Tell Captain McMartin I'm very sorry and that it won't happen again."

His lips turned down. "I might do that, unless you change your mind."

"I won't, so you can write up the memo now."

As I stomped down the stairs, he called after me, "It was just a joke, Two. Don't you have a sense of humor?"

I yanked off my coat, and checking that Schultzie really was napping on a bench—he was—I placed it and my nice skirt into the upright locker where we policewomen stowed our things. I put on my blue wool uniform jacket and skirt. I didn't have a spare pair of shoes or boots, so my nice slip-on heels would have to remain on my feet. Once I roused Schultzie, thanking him profusely for covering for me, I was able to sit down myself and calm my buzzing nerves. A fine world when policemen were more predatory and insulting than the man I was investigating as a possible murderer. The evening's music and laughter went mute then, and I tried to concentrate on the female prisoners and their needs, and the chores I was expected to do every night shift. Half of my job was being a custodian, which was tedious but at least it helped the hours pass.

As the night dragged on, remembered snippets of *Watch Your Step* would pop into my head, bringing a smile that would buoy me. When my shift was over, I opened my locker again and the fragrance of rose wafted toward me. I hadn't received a corsage since my high school graduation, and that one had come from Uncle Luddie, so it really hadn't counted.

This one didn't count either, I reminded myself.

My aunt needed to know that Gerald Hughes might call her house looking for me.

I hadn't wanted to give my address to Gerald, of course, but it was necessary to provide someplace where he could reach me. Obviously the police station wouldn't do. I wove an elaborate fiction of an inconvenient boarding house that was both time-consuming to reach by car and without a telephone. When I saw that he was about to ask how to telephone me at work, I waylaid the question by giving him Aunt Irene's phone number instead.

I arrived at East Fifty-Third Street around noon. Right away, I sensed something was afoot. Walter opened the door wearing a full pinafore apron over his immaculately pressed suit. In his right hand he held a baby bottle.

"Don't just stand there gaping," he said. "You're letting the cold in."

As soon as I was whisked inside, he shut the door. The place could have used some cold air, in my opinion. *National Geographic* magazine had once featured a story on Indian sweat lodges. I no longer needed the descriptive powers of journalism to imagine how it felt inside one. Just the effort of taking off my coat, hat, and gloves made me break out in a sweat. If only I could have shed my wool dress, as well.

Hammering came from upstairs.

"What's happening?" I asked.

"Little visitor, big changes," Walter said.

The parlor had been transformed since my last visit. The rocking horse was still near the now-roaring fire in the hearth, where Trollope and Dickens were lying side by side like two baking bricks. A crib stood in the center of the room. Inside it Eddie lay on his tummy, his head up and alert. My aunt stood over him, her green silk crepe de chine dress covered by a pinafore like Walter's, only with more ruffles. Her fretful expression changed to relief when she saw Walter.

"Oh good—the bottle." As an afterthought, she greeted me, "Hello, Louise." Taking the bottle from Walter, she dashed a little on her wrist. "Is that too hot?"

She passed the bottle back and Walter repeated the experiment on his own skin. "It seems just right to me."

"The book says milk shouldn't be too hot. Or too cold. It's supposed to be just the temperature it would be if it came from"—she lowered her voice—"the bosom."

Walter and I exchanged a perplexed look.

"Body temperature," my aunt explained. "Or the same temperature cow's milk would be fresh from a cow's udder."

"I know nothing of cows," he said. "My father was a blacksmith."

Hearing my aunt and Walter discuss bosoms and udders was a diverting novelty, but I sensed they could dither over milk temperature all day. Meanwhile, the temperature in that room was causing me to feel like a damp rag. "Speaking of blacksmiths, if I were metal, I'd be ready for smelting."

"Eddie needs warmth," my aunt explained.

"He's a baby, not an egg. He's already been incubated."

My aunt ignored the comment. Evidently it was my turn for the bottle. "Try this, Louise. Does it seem right?"

"*She* doesn't know," Walter said in disgust. "The longer we stand around debating, the colder it will become."

"I wouldn't bet on that." I plucked a copy of *The New York Times* off a side table and fanned myself.

"We don't want Eddie to get indigestion," my aunt said.

All this while, Eddie was tracking the bottle intently. My aunt finally picked him up, and after much fussing with various blankets, towels, and bibs, the baby was finally allowed to take some nourishment. If the temperature was off by a few degrees, he didn't seem to mind.

"Isn't he enchanting?" Aunt Irene said, staring down at him.

"How did you manage to wrest him from the nuns?" I envisioned Aunt Irene snatching the baby from his crib and making a run for it.

"Didn't you hear?" My aunt's eyes widened. "There's flu at the foundling hospital. Several children were hospitalized, so I asked if I could bring Eddie home with me—through the holiday season, at least. And they agreed."

"Just like that?" I asked.

And Irene shifted. "Well, a substantial financial contribution smoothed the way. But they needed the money, and poor Eddie needed out of there. It was the perfect solution for everyone."

The sound of hammering upstairs crescendoed until it was so loud that the pendant fixture hanging from a medallion in the center of the ceiling started to sway.

"What's going on up there?" I asked.

"I hired some men to build shelves for the nursery."

"Nursery?"

"Well, it's the guest room, and Eddie's a guest, isn't he? I couldn't have him sleeping in the big bed that you usually sleep in."

Bernice came in, wiping her brow with a handkerchief. "You're going to need to keep giving that poor child bottles all day long, he'll be sweating so much."

I could have used a bottle myself. A bottle of ice.

"Nonsense. He's done, and now he'll be fine for two hours and forty minutes." She looked at me. "That's how long Mrs. Toomey says they should go between feedings."

Whoever Mrs. Toomey was, Bernice didn't look impressed. "He's not going to be fine if you just sit there dandling him after all that milk and don't burp him."

She extracted the baby from my aunt's lap, cradled him against her shoulder without the benefit of even one towel, and patted his back until he emitted a loud belch.

"Good heavens!" Aunt Irene said.

Bernice laughed. "That's nothing. I had a baby brother who could almost make the earth shake."

It was gratifying to know that there was at least one person in this house who knew something about taking care of an infant. "Don't you think it would be a good idea to open a window?"

Aunt Irene and Walter gasped. "And let in a draft?" he asked.

"If the draft saves him from suffocating . . ."

Bernice nodded. "That's what I've been saying."

"How many books have you read on the subject of babies, Louise?" my aunt asked.

"None," I confessed.

"Well, there you are." My aunt pointed to a fat volume on the bar nearby. "*Mrs. Toomey's Guide for Modern Mothers* tells me everything I could possibly need to know."

I doubted even Mrs. Toomey advocated saunas for three-month-olds. But, since my aunt was clearly a true believer in Mrs. Toomey's modern methods, I decided to withdraw from the argument and leave the battle to Bernice.

"I actually came to ask a favor." I told them about following Gerald Hughes, our "accidental" meeting at the tearoom, and our date last night. Walter and my aunt were riveted. Bernice, predictably, was less so.

"You mean you didn't want to let a murderer know your address," the latter said, "so you gave him this one."

"I doubt very much he's a murderer, and I only gave him the phone exchange and number," I said. "If someone calls to leave a message for Miss Frobisher, that's him."

Aunt Irene threaded her fingers together. "And how should we relay messages to you?"

"I'll telephone every day to check."

"How many times do you intend to meet with this killer?" Bernice asked.

"I'm not sure. The more time I spend with him, the less I suspect him."

Bernice handed the baby back to my aunt. "But you don't know."

"He certainly doesn't *sound* like a murderer," my aunt said. She wrote murder mysteries—often rather similar to real-life cases I'd been involved in—so she considered herself an authority on homicide. "In fact, he seems quite civilized. A gallant war hero, wishing he could join up again. And giving that corsage to Louise was a sweet gesture."

"I just need to talk to Gerald Hughes a few more times. He's already started to trust me and tell me things."

Walter frowned. "He's not likely to confess that he murdered a woman, especially not to someone he's sweet on."

Before I could respond, the phone rang in the front hallway, and Walter hurried to answer it. A few moments later he was back. "Call for Miss Frobisher."

I stilled. "He knows I'm here?"

"Did you expect Walter to lie, too?" Bernice asked.

Frowning, I hurried out, trying to come up with some excuse for not being at work in the middle of the day. I decided to use my aunt. "Aunt Irene has a child who's . . . getting over influenza," I explained after we'd exchanged greetings. "I wanted to check on him."

Gerald sounded genuinely concerned. "I hope the poor thing's better."

"Much better, thank you."

"Well, since you've slipped your traces for the time being, perhaps I can persuade you to go out and enjoy a sunny day. We could take a carriage drive in the park."

"No," I said. Too quickly. "I mean, that wouldn't be a good idea today. My aunt's house is at sixes and sevens, and I do have to return to work."

We decided, though, that we would meet again at his hotel that evening. Remembering my encounter with Jenks last night, I told him, "I can't make it a very late night tonight. I was so tired today I nearly fell asleep at my typewriter."

"I'll try to send you home in time for you to get some beauty sleep." A light laugh came down the line. "I could use some of that myself."

I hung up feeling strangely uplifted. I immediately started wondering what activity he would have planned for us, and what I should wear. If I could just catch Callie at home this evening, perhaps I could borrow something of hers.

"Well?" my aunt asked when I returned to the parlor.

I said, in as even a voice as I could manage, "I'm meeting him again tonight."

"Wonderful!" Aunt Irene said.

Bernice shook her head. "What's wonderful about this girl eating dinner with a killer two nights in a row?"

"Because *this girl* just might find out who killed Eddie's mother." Aunt Irene looked at me, and then winked. "And if he isn't a killer, he sounds rather fascinating. Maybe we could have him to one of my Thursday nights."

"A murderer would probably fit right in with all the other characters," Walter lamented.

CHAPTER 13

"When You Wore a Tulip and I Wore a Big Red Rose," courtesy of the Bleecker Blowers, shook the floorboards beneath my feet as I climbed the stairs to our flat. Once I'd been entirely ignorant of saxophones. Now I could discern the different pitches of instruments from the soprano down to the bass. I could also tell when Charlie was playing alto as opposed to Mick, who was always a little sharp. Occasionally my downstairs neighbors played something so melodic and lovely it would bring tears to my eyes. Most days I wished Adolphe Sax had never been born.

Today was one of those days. After forty-eight hours of night work and day sleuthing, I craved sleep like an underfed dog craves food. The next nap or longer doze was never far from my calculations. This afternoon I'd come home from my aunt's hoping I'd find the apartment empty and quiet so I could catch a few winks before dashing off to meet Gerald. I was wondering how effective plugging my ears would be against the boom of the bass saxophone when I mounted the second flight and found Teddy's friend Hugh Van Hooten, of all people, seated on the top step. His knees poked up before him, making him look like a crouching insect. His overcoat was unbuttoned, so I wasn't sure if he was coming or going. His face was drawn into a frown.

"Does that racket go on every day?"

Though our paths hadn't crossed in nearly a year, I wasn't at all surprised by the lack of greeting. Our interactions had always been on the contentious side. He personified the worst of all worlds—a patrician who took for granted all the benefits of wealth but practiced none of the niceties of polite society. Why was he camped in my hallway?

In answer to my unspoken question, something thumped against my apartment door from the inside, and shouting came from within: Callie's voice—loud—calling someone a fool. And then Teddy's voice, a little softer, responding in a pleading tone.

"I wouldn't go in there if I were you," Hugh warned. "Lovers' tiff."

"It sounds like more than a tiff," I said. "More like a knock-down, drag-out."

"Exactly. I got out of there as soon as I could, but we came in Teddy's car. I'm not keen on finding my own way back to the airfield."

Hugh's aviation business was in New Jersey.

I glanced anxiously at the door. "No one's getting hurt, I hope."

"Callie's winging objects around, but Teddy's a fast ducker." He scooted closer to the wall and crossed his spidery legs. "You might as well sit down. They're a while from the reconciliation stage, I imagine."

Exhausted, I sat down next to him.

From inside, Callie shouted, "England!"

"What happened?" I asked.

"Ah." Hugh had taken off his gloves, and now slapped one against the other. "You may be surprised to find out that it's actually my fault."

It didn't surprise me a bit. "What did you do?"

"Nothing but what I've been trying to do for years and have finally, through ingenuity, intelligence, and hard work succeeded at—perfecting my Van Hooten aerial photographic brace."

In the year I'd known Hugh and Teddy, their joint obsession had been a device that allowed airplane pilots to mount photographic equipment on their machines. The idea struck me as impractical, but Hugh swore the device would be indispensable to people such as cartographers.

"You know that I've spoken with the US Army, thinking perhaps they would like to invest in my device for their little fleet of planes?"

I hadn't heard this. "What did they say?"

"No soap." He shook his head. "Very short-sighted and ignorant of them. But through the to-ing and fro-ing of letters, I happened to catch the name of this chap in England who said he thought the idea would be very useful. I wrote to him months ago, and he finally responded to ask if I would object to Britain's using the photographic mount on the planes they're using in the war."

"What for?"

Hugh gave me one of his long, exasperated stares. "For surveillance, jinglebrain. Surveillance and charting the lines of the armies, as well as regular mapmaking. It'll be invaluable."

"And you don't mind?"

"Why should I?"

"It would be used in a war, by a foreign country."

"Oh, that's right. Teddy said you were pro-German."

"I'm no such thing. I'm American, and we're not fighting a war."

"We will be, sooner or later."

"Very much later, I hope."

"So does Callie, and there's where the argument came in. Because Teddy and I are going over not only to demonstrate my device, but also in the hopes of getting involved."

I blinked. "Involved in what?"

"Flying. For the British. Or the French—whoever will have us."

He said it so nonchalantly, as if it were nothing to think of joining up with a foreign army and putting himself—and his friend—in harm's way.

"Have you lost your mind?" I couldn't believe it. "You could get killed!"

He chuckled. "Well, yes, I suppose so. It is a war."

His flippancy infuriated me. "It's their war, not yours."

"All of Europe is involved, and someday the United States will be, too. And Teddy and I will have experience by then learning how airplanes can help the efforts of our allies."

Now I understood why Callie was so angry. Frankly I was surprised that she wasn't out in the hallway shouting at Hugh. His zeal for his photographic mount had rubbed off on Teddy, and now he'd probably infected him with the desire to join some slapdash air outfit for whatever country would take them.

"It wasn't too long ago that they first flew over the English Channel," I pointed out. "Now every plane from England going to the Continent will have to perform that feat just for starters, won't they?"

He flapped a glove dismissively. "Flying the Channel's old hat now. In aviation terms, Blériot's feat of crossing the Channel might as well have happened in the Bronze Age. Fifteen years ago, no one had flown at all except in hot air balloons."

"Actually, wouldn't balloons be safer, in terms of maps and things?" I asked.

"Safer until someone figures out a way to shoot them out of the sky. That won't take long. Mount a gun on a plane and a hot air balloon won't stand a chance."

Guns on planes? I frowned. "Neither will other planes."

"Nonsense. Planes are fast. They can dive, and roll. Pilots will be the safest people in the war."

Safe? I'd flown in one of his contraptions. It had been the most terrifying hour of my life.

The apartment door opened and a very ruffled Teddy emerged, carrying his hat and coat.

"We'd better go," he said in a harried voice.

Hugh unfolded himself and stood, plopping his own hat on his head. I got up, too.

"Oh, hello, Louise," Teddy said. "I suppose Hoots told you all about our plans."

I nodded.

He put a hand on my arm. "Try to explain it to Callie, won't you?"

"I'm not sure—"

But Callie's voice interrupted me. "Yes, Louise, come explain to me why a young man should chuck away his entire future to fly around battlefields for a country that isn't even his own."

"Well, he survived *this* battlefield," Hugh said. "We really should be going, Teddy."

"Goodbye, Louise." Teddy looked back at the apartment door. "Goodbye, Callie." His face reddened. "Darling."

She turned on her heel and went inside the apartment again, slamming the door behind her.

Once the hall door had stopped echoing from that slam, I assured Teddy, "She's just upset."

He rubbed his jaw. "You're telling me."

"We really should be going," Hugh said. "I was still hoping to stop by Mother's." The Van Hooten mansion was located just off the Millionaires' Mile section of Fifth Avenue.

I bid both of them goodbye. "Write and tell us how you get on," I said. "And whatever happens, good luck."

Impulsively, Teddy leaned forward and kissed me on the cheek. "You're a good egg, Louise."

Hugh stuck out his hand and wrapped it around my gloved one. "We'll be safe as houses," he assured me. "You'll see."

I watched them descend the staircase, and then even leaned over the railing to see them all the way down to the foyer. Teddy looked up through the railings and waved goodbye again. I waved back, feeling rather strange. The Bleecker Blowers had launched into "It's a Long Way to Tipperary" for the hundredth time that month. For once it seemed achingly apropos. I couldn't help thinking of Gerald Hughes, and his limp. And how much he would have given to be in Hugh and Teddy's shoes right now—going back to England to take part in the war.

Swallowing past an unexpected lump in my throat, I turned and went inside the apartment. I expected to find Callie still raving mad, but instead she was sweeping up. An ashtray had been one of the victims of the fracas.

"Can you believe those idiots?" she said. "They're mad, both of them. Mad fools. I can almost understand Hugh. It's his invention, so naturally he wants to see it finally put to use. But Teddy! What excuse does he have?"

"It's an adventure."

"Exactly—they're like two Boy Scouts setting off on a hike. And Hugh is the arrogant leader Teddy will follow right into the grizzly bear's den."

"England might not even want them," I said, flopping down on the sofa.

"It doesn't matter. Teddy said if England didn't take them, they'd go to France and who knows where else."

Given how avid a supporter of the Belgian cause Callie had been, I was a little surprised by her attitude now. "I thought you supported the war against Germany."

"*Support*, yes. Knitting and gathering clothes—of course. I didn't expect Teddy would try to volunteer. Besides, Hugh would probably fly for the Kaiser If Germany offered him money for that stupid little invention of his."

"Hugh said—"

Callie cut me off. "I've heard all both of them had to say, and now I don't want to hear another word about airplanes, Europe, wars, Hugh, or Teddy." She slid the ashtray remnants into our kitchen dust bin, hung the copper dustpan on its peg, then came and sank onto the other end of the sofa.

I tried to think of something to say that had nothing to do with the war or Teddy. I gazed around the apartment, appreciative of the privacy we suddenly had. It wasn't just that Hugh and Teddy had gone. It was also the first time Callie and I had been alone in the apartment together for several days. "Anna finally went home?"

Callie sighed. "I left her at the studio. Alfred figured out another little scene for her to do. I wasn't involved in it, so I left."

"He must think she has something."

"She's got a little natural talent, actually. It's gratifying. I feel like Svengali." She frowned. "Is that the right guy?"

"I think so."

"Teddy would know. He knows all kinds of things from those highfalutin schools he went to." She bit her lip. "Did he say anything to you before he left?"

"He said I was a good egg."

She rolled her eyes. "He would say something stupid like that."

"I thought it was sweet."

She crossed her arms. "I'm done talking about him. Done even thinking about him." She frowned at her shoes, evidently cudgeling her brains for something else to talk about. "To be honest, I think Alfred has a little crush on Anna."

"Really?"

"She can be a little charmer, especially when I put some snappy clothes on her. I have a hunch Alfred wants to make a whole lot more movies about the little sister now."

Anna was either a very good actress or a very fast worker. Maybe both.

"Alfred Sheldrake's married, isn't he?" I asked.

"With three children. He's the kind who has trouble remembering his domestic life, though. I warned Anna."

"Was she listening?"

Callie shrugged and sighed. "It's probably a good thing I still have Broadway prospects, because I'm not sure how many more of these movies I can stomach anyway."

At the words *Broadway prospects*, my insides quaked. I remembered Otto telling me about his prospective producer wanting someone famous for *Double Daisy*. "I thought you like making movies."

"I did too. But just look—Anna can walk off the street and be a movie actress. You were right, Louise. It's not real acting." Her brows beetled. "Or maybe Teddy said that."

"Sounds more like Hugh."

She crossed her legs, sighing again. "I can't wait till *Double Daisy* gets up on its legs. I wonder when rehearsals'll start."

Obviously Otto had not spoken to Callie since our conversation at the White Rose. Coward that I was, I didn't want to be the one to break bad news to her. Especially today.

"Would you mind if I borrowed a dress tonight?" I asked her.

She leveled a curious stare on me. "Are you still stepping out with that murderer?"

"Before you turn up your nose, you should know that last night my suspected murderer took me to *Watch Your Step*."

I'd never seen a lightning bolt hit anyone, but I imagined the result would look something like what happened to Callie in that moment. She straightened, eyes saucer-wide, face slack. "Those tickets are like hen's teeth!"

I couldn't help preening a little. "Fourth-row seats."

"What did Irene Castle wear? Her costumes are supposed to be divine."

"They were"—my limited couture knowledge had me fumbling for words—"fancy. Lots of silk."

Lines furrowed her brow. "And?"

"Well, there was one with sort of flowery appliqués on it. It was green."

She sank back. "You're hopeless. I bet your murderer could describe the dresses better."

"He's not a murderer."

"What is he like?"

I gave a detailed description—I was better with people than clothes—but of course Callie's attention homed in on one detail. "He lost a leg? How?"

"The Boer War. He was in the British Army." I explained all I knew about him, which admittedly wasn't much. "He was telling me about the battles, and about his friends who didn't come back. He was saying that in spite of his injury—he lost a leg, but he won't tell me too many specifics about *that*—he feels lucky. That's why I want to see him again. I think he's really starting to open up a little to me. And I've let my wardrobe suffer this year, since I spend so much time in uniform . . ."

It wasn't clear exactly when during my speech Callie stopped paying attention, but she was miles away now.

"Callie?"

"Just take whatever you want out of my closet," she said.

Something was very wrong. Callie wasn't stingy, but she tended to be very particular about which clothes I could borrow and which were off limits. I was harder on clothes than she was and tended to have small accidents with ink pens and mud puddles. Now she was giving me carte blanche to take what I wanted.

"Are you feeling all right?" I asked.

She leapt to her feet, her face almost as green as Irene Castle's dress had been. "What if it's too late?"

"Too late for what?"

"To find Teddy!" She made a dash for the coatrack. "It'll take me forever to get to—" She yanked hats off the rack, nearly tipping it over to find one she liked. "Where would they have gone? Are they catching a boat tonight?"

I thought back. "They mentioned the airfield."

A distressed keen came out of her. "How will I get out there with no car?"

I snapped my fingers. "No—Hugh said he wanted to go see his mother."

Callie brightened. "Oh thank God! If I can just find a taxi . . ." She shrugged on her coat, and then ran to retrieve her little bag from the table. "You understand, don't you?" she said. "I have to say goodbye to him, even if he is an idiot. What if I never see him again?"

"You will."

"If I hurry, maybe." She ran out the door, then popped her head back in and smiled. "You are a good egg, Louise."

During the next few days, my life underwent a strange transformation. Evenings, I was like a young woman with a steady beau. Before, I'd occasionally stepped out with some young man or another, usually in the company of Callie and her many friends. But the kind of young men who'd escorted me places in the past were nowhere as courtly as Gerald Hughes. Gerald was a gentleman.

Often I enjoyed myself too much to remember my primary purpose. I had to remind myself that he was a gentleman mixed up in what was possibly a murder. That maybe he was a gentleman-murderer.

Both as an escort and as a subject of investigation, however, he wasn't a perfect specimen. He talked, but tended to be short on information about himself and long-winded when it came to the subject of textiles and the effect the war would have on manufacturing.

"The reason I was sent here is to find buyers for our cloth. The government, of course, wants to buy up wool fabric for uniforms, but our best quality products could suffer as a result, and that worries investors. So here I am, trying to secure buyers for the luxury-grade wools, but the war has businessmen on this side of the Atlantic afraid that there will be disruptions in production because of the war. And if the war drags on, as I fear it will, they'll be right."

We were taking a walk, and I was nodding off on my feet—it wasn't the first time I'd heard about this textile conundrum.

No matter how closely I watched Gerald for clues to a mercurial temper—for some possibility that he might have killed Ruthie after discovering she'd stolen from him, for example—he remained doggedly phlegmatic and basically decent. I still couldn't understand how he'd ever met Ruthie. Perhaps even the most straitlaced of men sought out ladies of the evening, but I could hardly insert the subject into casual conversation. *"By the bye, have you ever visited a prostitute?"* Coming from me, demure Louise Frobisher, that probably would have shocked him back across the Atlantic, and I wasn't about to let him go just yet. He was still my only connection to any of the men whose passports Ruthie had stolen.

Instead, during our walk, I tried to bring the conversation around to passports. "I've thought about seeing London and Paris and all those places. I don't even have a passport, though. Is it a lengthy process?"

He frowned. "Is what?"

"Getting a passport."

"Certainly not. At least, not for an Englishman. I don't know about Americans. As a matter of fact, I lost mine not long ago and had it replaced as fast as you please."

There it was at last. A nibble. "Lost it? How?"

His blank expression gave nothing away. "I don't remember, honestly. I just reached for it one morning and it wasn't there."

"Was it stolen?"

His eyes narrowed. He looked wary. "Why would anyone do such a thing?"

"Pickpockets aren't always accurate in what they steal, you know. You'd be surprised."

He laughed. "I'm surprised *you* would know anything about it."

He leaned closer and asked confidentially, "Have you been considering a second profession?"

I blushed, more in anger at drawing him away from the circumstances surrounding his stolen passport than from my own near-blunder. "They report things in the newspapers."

"Girls shouldn't read newspapers so much," he said. "Too much ugliness in them."

"I don't think women should be sheltered from the world."

"Not sheltered, exactly. But so many of life's burdens fall on the fairer sex, it seems to me. Why go out of your way to read about troubles?"

I revised my opinion of him from old-worldly to antediluvian. "To be informed."

He smiled. "You must think me very old and stuffy."

"You talk as if you could be my grandfather. There's barely ten years difference between us."

"Sixteen," he said. "And I feel every one of them."

"I don't."

Occasionally that was even true. The man, who had one leg fewer than I did, could walk from one end of Manhattan to the other on a chilly day, at a pace that sometimes had me trotting to keep up. He had an indefatigable curiosity to see things. We spent an entire afternoon in the Metropolitan Museum of Art looking at paintings, Greek statuary, and ancient pottery. He also loved New York itself, and was fascinated by the vertical direction it seemed to be taking. That's why we'd made a special trip downtown to look at the half-constructed Equitable Building on lower Broadway, which was already casting a considerable shadow over the Singer Building and everything else within a seven-acre path. It was planned to be forty stories high, with the largest area for office space in the world.

"Aren't there skyscrapers in England?" I asked as we stared up at what was, to my mind, just another behemoth being added to Manhattan's skyline.

"About twenty years ago someone constructed a fourteen-story building of luxury flats that blocked Queen Victoria's view of the parliament buildings. After that, a law was passed restricting building heights to eighty feet."

I'd almost forgotten what it was like to live in a world that wasn't slowly laddering its way up to the heavens in brick, steel, and stone. "I'm sure it's beautiful, though. I'd love to see it."

He looked down at me. "Do you mean that?"

I rubbed my hands together, too distracted by the cold to realize his expression had changed. "Of course. There's so much history there, and"—my teeth were chattering—"and literary landmarks, and so on . . ."

"It's not the first time you've brought up the subject of England, and your interest in it."

"Well, you're English."

"You also ask me a lot of questions about myself. Are you this inquisitive with everyone, Louise?"

Did he suspect what I was up to? I faltered a bit before coming up with an answer. "I suppose I am curious, but you've been so kind, and so generous with your time."

"And you have no idea why?"

Boredom, I'd assumed. He was a salesman in a foreign city, with holidays approaching. Companionship in those circumstances was probably hard to come by. Which might explain why he'd found Ruthie.

"Louise?" he prompted.

"Well, you're far from home, and I came along. Someone to spend a little time and share a few laughs with until you leave on your next trip."

"Share a few laughs," he repeated.

"Any port in a storm, and all that."

He buried his gloved hands in the pockets of his coat. "I see."

"Did I say something wrong?"

"Just a bit of a blow to my pride, that's all."

I saw at once what he meant. He had thought that he and I were building up to something.

I looked down at the sidewalk, my deceit filling me with shame. That was the problem with living a double life—the duplicity of it. I hadn't thought Gerald would become attached to me. Or, rather, I figured I would simply see him a few times, and get an idea whether he had anything to do with Ruthie's death. I had failed to do that, but succeeded in leading him down a garden path.

"I'm sorry," I said.

His struggle with wounded pride showed in his expression. How much more wounded would he feel to know that I suspected he'd killed someone? "Don't be sorry. I've enjoyed our time together."

"I've only known you a short time, Gerald."

"Of course! And you've made it clear how you feel." His voice strained to remain calm, but the resentment in it burned through the chilly air. "Museums, shows, walks . . . a few laughs. Nothing more."

This was the flash of temper I'd been waiting for.

"You've kept me at a distance from the beginning," he continued testily. "I suppose I should have taken my cue from that. I've never seen your flat, or your office. You've spoken often of your aunt, but you've never suggested taking me to meet her. It's very awkward telephoning her house for you, and yet not being able to present myself at her door."

This revelation of his feelings panicked me, especially if he were about to cut me out of his life for fear of breaking his heart. If he pushed me away now, how would I ever find out what I needed to know?

I grabbed hold of the first lifeline that came to me. "I never thought you would want to bother with my family."

A sad smile turned up his lips. "Haven't you noticed, Louise? I'm rather old-fashioned."

"A last-century man." I smiled back, a rash plan taking shape in my mind. Doing what I was thinking would be a mad roll of the dice—reckless, and possibly even dangerous. I would be involving others in my subterfuge, which was always a risk. And there was Eddie to consider.

But wasn't it for Eddie that I was doing all of this?

"It just so happens that my aunt usually has a get-together at her house most Thursday nights," I said. "I was going to ask you if you'd like to go with me tomorrow night."

Heaven help me, the question immediately lifted the man's spirits. You'd think I'd just agreed to marry him and sail back to England.

"Are you sure, Louise?"

I put my arm through his, feeling grubby yet strangely excited. This had to be what the women I saw in the cells at the jail felt like as they led their marks into dingy hotel rooms for their badger schemes. Poor Gerald thought he was going to be a gentleman caller meeting my family. Instead, he'd be stepping right into a trap.

CHAPTER 14

In the week since I'd last dropped by Aunt Irene's house, the halls had been thoroughly decked for Christmas. A fat wreath hung on the front door and the foyer's chandelier was festooned with mistletoe and ribbons. Tinsel and more ribbon wound around the banister, and greenery brightened every surface, from arrangements on tabletops to the Christmas tree next to the sofa in the corner of the salon. Half the electric lights were left off, replaced by candelabras and hurricane lamps surrounded by fragrant pine. Everywhere flickering candlelight made the familiar rooms glow. My aunt and Walter had done a beautiful job, and from the aromas of cinnamon, nutmeg, and ginger coming from the kitchen, Bernice had been spinning some culinary holiday magic as well.

It wouldn't have surprised me a bit if Aunt Irene had put her foot down and refused to let me bring Gerald Hughes to her Thursday night. As much as I liked to assure everyone that he probably wasn't a murderer, there was no escaping the slight chance that he actually was. Aunt Irene had not only her guests to consider, but the people who worked for her, and now Eddie. Flu or no flu, the foundling hospital didn't hand over babies to people who played hostess to criminals.

But when I telephoned my aunt to discuss the matter, she greeted the idea with as much enthusiasm as if I'd suggested bringing royalty. "Your slightly dangerous English gentleman sounds fascinating."

"He's only possibly dangerous. The most certain danger is that he'll talk your ear off about looms."

"It's all research to me, sugar plum."

My aunt was never one to let experiences go to waste when she could find a way to shoehorn them into her latest book. No doubt there would be a mystery about a textile salesman in her future. *Woven in Death*, or something similar.

"You realize I'll have to pose as Louise Frobisher."

"That's no problem. Everyone just calls you Louise here."

"And you don't mind my using Eddie?"

Tinny silence stretched on the line before she answered. "It's our duty, isn't it, to find out what happened to poor Ruthie Jones and her baby? This is all for Eddie, and for the sake of his mother and the twin brother he'll never know."

When Gerald and I arrived, the parlor was already full of revelers, most of whom seemed already full of spirits both of the emotional and liquid variety. I took Gerald's hand and threaded my way across the room to my aunt, who couldn't have been more enthusiastic in her greeting. "Mr. Hughes, my niece has told me so much about you." The dogs, both with plaid bows around their necks, panted up at the stranger. One let out a yip. My aunt's voice rose on a peel of laughter. "Dickens is glad to meet you, too."

Gerald would have been more gratified by the welcome if he, like most of the other guests who hadn't been warned, wasn't already tugging at his collar against the heat.

"It's for the little one," my aunt said in a confidential voice, watching him mop his forehead with a handkerchief. "A little mite visiting for Christmas."

"Not your child?" he asked, confused.

"For now I'm calling him my ward. That's more accurate. Have you met him?"

"Not yet," Gerald said.

"Louise needs to take you upstairs to the nursery, then. I've just done it up. Eddie just adores it!"

"We just arrived," I told her.

"Of course—show your beau off to some of the other guests

first," Aunt Irene said. "But don't wait too long. I don't want Eddie to be pestered too far past his bedtime."

"Eddie is the child I told you about," I said as we moved along. "An orphan."

"How sad," he said. "Yet how lucky that he's fallen into your aunt's orbit. She's a charming woman."

I snagged a glass of champagne off Walter's tray. Gaping too intently at Gerald, he asked, "Would you rather have a hot drink, Louise?"

Was he crazy?

"I've made it special this week," he continued in a meaningful tone. "I call it the Hell's Kitchen Hot Chocolate."

Very subtle. "What's in it?"

"Hot chocolate with a deadly kick of brandy. Perhaps your friend would be interested."

We both glanced at Gerald to gauge his reaction, but his gaze was entirely focused on someone on the other side of the room. And that someone was staring very intently back at him. Muldoon. I barely suppressed a groan. What was he doing here?

Gerald leaned closer to me. "That man keeps looking this way. Do you know him?"

I gulped down half a glass of champagne. The last thing I needed right now was for Muldoon to muddle up my plan. Before the detective could take a step toward us, I held fast to Gerald's arm and steered him in the other direction. Unfortunately, that's when I noticed Otto sitting down at the piano.

I'd been so concerned with Walter and the other regulars that I'd forgotten that Otto—not an unfamiliar face at Aunt Irene's Thursday Nights—might be here.

In a nod to the season, Otto launched into a peppy rendition of "The Boar's Head Carol." Gerald might have been charmed under other circumstances—Otto played very well, and a small coterie around him were singing along—but the reappearance of Miss Frobisher's former fiancé had thrown him off balance. For a moment he looked almost apoplectic.

"What is *he* doing here?" Gerald asked.

"I suppose my aunt forgot to disinvite him. We were engaged three years, you know."

"So? He has a nerve to show his face after how he treated you."

"I didn't expect him to." I drained the rest of my glass.

"Of course you didn't. I'm surprised by your aunt, though. Surely she knows he's a blackguard?"

I nearly coughed up my champagne. I would have to remember to tell Otto that he'd been called a blackguard—when I next spoke to him, which I hoped would not be at this party. I scanned the room for some way to escape. It was becoming more and more difficult to avoid bumping into someone I didn't want to speak to. I felt like a rabbit in a forest full of snares.

"Why don't I take you up to Eddie?" I suggested. "It's quiet up there. This crowd—"

"And this heat," Gerald agreed. "And to think that butler chap wanted to give us a hot drink."

"Walter's always dreaming up new things," I said as I led us through the dining room. From there we got back out to the hall and doubled back to the stairs. In that way I was able to avoid Muldoon. "He wandered through Hell's Kitchen a few weeks ago. It gave him ideas."

Gerald grunted as we mounted the narrow staircase. I forgot about his leg for a moment and ended up three steps ahead of him before slowing down. The champagne had made me feel odd, lightheaded. For some reason, I was aware of the rustling of my rough silk dress, and of Gerald behind me.

"You did say you liked children, didn't you?" I asked as I reached the landing ahead of him.

"Louise, wait."

I stopped. At first I didn't know what was wrong and backtracked to the stairs. "Is something wrong?"

He climbed the last stair and walked a few steps beyond, stopping where someone had dangled a sprig of mistletoe from the light fixture finial on the landing. "As you said, Louise, I'm just happy to have a moment of privacy with you, away from that crowd."

He took hold of me then, clamping a hand around the upper sleeve of my dress and drawing me to him. "You look so lovely tonight," he whispered.

"I—"

His lips pressed against mine before I could even think to duck away. Having acted like a perfect gentleman all during our rambles across the city, he caught me off guard now, and I put a hand against his waistcoat. It was just for balance as I leaned away from him, but he interpreted the touch as encouragement, and suddenly his arms were around me, squeezing me. Memories of another man catching me off guard welled up and I pushed him away with a surprised protest.

"Stop."

My shove knocked him back a step on his bad leg, and he grabbed the banister for balance. He looked stricken. "I'm sorry. I thought—"

"This is my aunt's house." Part of me wanted to flee back down the stairs, yet another wanted to laugh at the prudish outrage in my voice. "I hope you didn't think I suggested coming up here for *that*."

"No, of course . . ." I'd never seen him so flustered. "Excuse me, Louise, I—" At that moment, he glanced down to the bottom of the staircase. And there stood Muldoon. Looking more thunderous than ever. Thunderous and astonished.

My heart dropped to my heels. Was he spying on me now?

"Come on." I tugged Gerald toward Eddie's room, hoping he wouldn't interpret this as further encouragement—and that Muldoon wouldn't follow.

"Does that man have some claim on you?" Gerald asked in a low voice.

Oh, for heaven's sake. "No man has a claim on me. Detective Muldoon always looks like that."

"Detective?"

Did I hear a note of fear in his tone? Good.

I hadn't seen the guest room since its transformation into a nursery. The room still smelled of fresh paste from the paper, which was decorated with little animal drawings in blue and yellow and red. Eddie's crib was in the center of the room. I'd seen it before, of course, but a yellow painted dresser was new. His rocking horse was opposite the crib, and a mountain of toys was piled on a chair that had been reupholstered in a fabric embroidered with fairy-tale scenes.

Eddie was sitting up as I approached the crib, which seemed

quite an accomplishment for under four months. Slow, Sister Eleanor had predicted. Just showed what she knew. "Look at you!" I greeted him. "Do you like your new room, Eddie?"

His gummy smile grew bigger, and I picked up his teddy bear and held it in front of him, moving its arm like a puppet that wanted to shake hands. Eddie reached out and grabbed the bear's furry claw.

"Quiet little chap," Gerald said slowly.

"He's mute," I said. "He doesn't really make many sounds—just gurgles and incidental noises like that."

I continued to focus on Eddie for a few moments until I noticed that someone else in the room had gone mute: Gerald. His face was as pale as plaster, and his hands trembled slightly.

So it was true. Ruthie hadn't just lifted his passport off him on the street. He knew Eddie—he'd been in that shabby flat. He'd been with Ruthie. His mild-mannered salesman demeanor, his vulnerability as a wounded soldier . . . had that all been an act to cover up a darker self? All this time, I'd known there was a possibility that Gerald was tied up in Ruthie's death, possibly even responsible for it, yet part of me hadn't wanted to believe it.

"Is something wrong?" I asked. My pulse was racing. It took effort to stay calm and feign ignorance.

He backed up a step, and then had to catch himself on the dresser. "It's . . . the heat. I'm sorry, but I find that I'm feeling unwell. Perhaps that's why . . . that incident earlier . . . I hope you'll forgive that mistake . . ." He took another step toward the door. "You'll have to excuse me. Please make my apologies to your aunt."

He fled the room.

I'd envisioned Gerald's guilty conscience leading him to a confession—as in one of my aunt's books, where the murderer always blurted out his guilt to the detective at the end. A foolish expectation. Yet Gerald had reacted so violently to seeing Eddie that I knew now that I hadn't been wrong about his involvement.

I hurried toward the door to follow him when Muldoon's figure appeared, blocking me. "Rather old for you, isn't he?"

"It's not what you think." The trouble was, when he found out who Gerald really was, he would think it was worse. "Would you mind stepping out of the way? He's a suspect and I need to catch up to him."

"You kiss suspects?"

"*I* didn't kiss *him*. That was Gerald Hughes, and he wasn't kissing me, he was kissing Louise Frobisher."

"What—" Muldoon's voice cut off, and his face registered the effort of putting all the pieces together. "I've heard the name Gerald Hughes before, haven't I? Please tell me I'm wrong."

"He was one of the men who had his passport stolen by Ruthie."

"And you have been following him around under a false name in the hopes of getting him to confess to Ruthie's murder?"

"He was the only passport man I could track down. I wanted to see what I could find out about Ruthie from him."

"What did you find out?"

"That he knew Ruthie."

The moment I said it, I felt ridiculous. Of course he'd known her. I expected Muldoon to point this out, but he'd become distracted by Eddie in his crib. The baby was watching us.

"What's this?" he asked.

"It's Eddie."

Frowning, he moved toward the baby, who opened his mouth in welcome to the newcomer. He really was cute.

"Where did he come from?"

"Hell's Kitchen, by way of New York Foundling. He's Ruthie's surviving child." I told him about the flu, and my aunt's bringing him home for the holidays.

Just as I had done minutes before, Muldoon gazed around the room in amazement. "Your aunt doesn't do anything by halves, does she?"

"No."

"And so you brought Gerald Hughes here to meet Ruthie's child."

I nodded, again feeling the excitement I had when I saw Gerald reacting to Eddie. "You've never seen a man so spooked."

"Yes, I have. I saw Hughes himself fleeing out this door not five minutes ago."

"And why would he do that?" I asked. "There was guilt in his eyes. He looked frightened—I'm sure of it."

Muldoon buried his hands in his pockets. "He doesn't know you're a policewoman?"

"No."

"And so a woman he's been seeing happens to drag him to her aunt's house and show him the baby of a dead prostitute of his acquaintance. If you were in his shoes, what would you think?"

"You don't understand. He looked like a trapped animal."

"Because that's what you did—you trapped him, and I don't like to think about by what means you managed it."

He was acting as if I were some tawdry, treacherous female who'd tricked a good man through seduction. Salome of Greenwich Village. "It's not what you're thinking. It was all very innocent—a night at the theater, a few walks around town, meals . . ."

His eyes widened. "Sounds like quite a campaign. How long did this go on?"

"Not even two weeks."

"How far did you intend to lead him on?"

"Is it my fault that Gerald Hughes is a lonely soul, susceptible to kindness from any woman?"

"Why didn't you simply ask him about Ruthie?"

"What if *he* killed her? Do you think it would have been smart to ask him that straightaway? He would have lied, or maybe decided to do away with me, as well."

"If he's guilty, he still might try to do away with you," he pointed out.

I froze. I'd known all along that Gerald *might* be dangerous, but I'd been downplaying the possibility for so long I'd begun to believe my own reassurances to others.

"But the chances are he simply had his passport stolen by a prostitute," Muldoon said.

"I wish I could find something that would actually tie him to Ruthie's apartment. If only I could have gotten into his hotel room to search his things . . ."

Muldoon raked a hand through his coal-dark hair. "I'm very glad you didn't."

"But don't you see? I've come this far—and now I lack a way to *really* frighten the truth out of him. It's frustrating."

"I can't believe you've been gadding about town with a strange man in order to pursue some half-cocked investigation. It doesn't show the best judgment, Louise."

"The NYPD not pursuing its own investigation of Ruthie's death doesn't show very good judgment to me."

"I understand you feel that Ruthie's death hasn't received the attention it deserved, but detectives have to work with the evidence we're given. Part of surviving in the police is accepting that justice isn't always meted out evenly, and occasionally it isn't served at all."

I couldn't accept that. I couldn't believe he could, either.

A short silence marked the impasse we'd reached.

"Is there a reason you came here tonight?" I asked. "It couldn't have been simply to watch me getting mauled in hallways, or to sweat."

"Why *is* it so hot?"

"My aunt has a theory that babies need warmth. She read a book about it."

"Someone needs to chuck that book out. Surely with your talent for subterfuge you could manage that?"

Very funny. "You still haven't told me why you came tonight. Not that my aunt won't be delighted to see you."

"I thought perhaps you and Callie might have brought Anna here. My sister's a stranger these days. She occasionally leaves me notes telling me she's staying with you, but when I went to look for her there this evening in the hopes of escorting her home, no one answered my knock. I remembered it was Thursday night, so I came here."

"I haven't seen her, but my irregular schedule makes it hard to keep up with people. Callie says everyone at the studio loves Anna, though. They're building up her part."

The lines around his mouth deepened. "She'll never get over being in a movie. It's really turned her head."

"It's good for her, surely." Muldoon brought out the devil's advocate in me. "She's got so much energy and drive—even the church ladies thought she was too much for them. Now she's found a productive outlet for all her energy."

He mopped a handkerchief across the back of his neck. "Well, maybe she'll get bored with it after a little while."

When we went back downstairs, I dreaded Muldoon's talking to my aunt, who naturally would want to know what had happened with Gerald Hughes. The less said about that at the moment the better.

But when we came down, a woman I didn't recognize had sat down at the piano and started to play with such effortless brilliance, Gerald Hughes was now the farthest thing from my aunt's or anyone else's mind. Guests circled the old Chickering, which produced the most beautiful sounds in its half-century of life. The woman at the instrument played a long piece based on Balkan tunes, rousing and sad by turns.

"Who is it?" I whispered to Otto, who was rapt.

"Amy Beach," he whispered.

I'd heard of her, but couldn't imagine how she'd managed to find her way to my aunt's house. Mrs. Beach had written the first ever symphony by an American woman, and had traveled around Europe, only coming back at the start of the war. I remembered hearing about her because she'd said she was pro-German, but only pro *artistic* Germany, not militaristic Germany.

When the piece finished, I turned to see Muldoon's reaction, but there was an empty space next to me, and no sign of him anywhere in the room.

CHAPTER 15

The next morning I was supposed to begin with the dog's watch, so I set my alarm early. My sleep patterns were so confused now, I lay awake half the night and spent my first full day shift feeling like a sleepwalker.

My aunt's party had marked an end to my half-baked investigation, I knew. I had proven nothing. Perhaps, as Muldoon had said, I had to accept that justice couldn't always be served. But why was it always the Ruthies of the world that justice bypassed?

Justice or no justice, at the end of my shift I was happy to shrug on my coat and go home. For the first time in a long time, I was determined to relax over a leisurely supper, read a little, go to bed at a decent hour, and return to work the next day refreshed. A little peaceful domesticity—that was what I needed. For the first night since Thanksgiving, I was not going to think about Ruthie Jones.

On my way home, I passed a butcher who advertised smoked hams in the window. It was as if Bernice were calling out to me. All I had to do was slice it up and boil some kind of vegetable to go with it. It was time to focus on living my life, not obsessing over murders.

I ducked into the butcher shop and bought an ambitiously large ham, which the man behind the counter wrapped up for me. I put it in the string shopping bag I carried in my satchel. After a block,

I realized I might have gone overboard and bought too much; my arm started to get tired carrying the thing. When I couldn't get a seat on the streetcar downtown, I ended up balancing it on my hip as if it were an infant. In the close confines, the ham seemed to smell even stronger. Everyone in the car was probably salivating by the time I got off at Eighth Street.

I made my way home, crossing Sixth Avenue and then turning down my street, which was practically deserted. And dark. The days were now so short, it was fully dark by six. The puddles of light let out by the streetlamps were inadequate.

A block from my building, on a quiet residential street, I heard footsteps behind me, almost as if someone was following me. *You're just imagining things.* When I sped up, however, so did the footsteps. I strained to hear better, placing my feet on the sidewalk as quietly as possible.

A horrible thought entered my mind. What had Muldoon said last night? *"He might still try to do away with you."* And to be done away with so ignominiously—me on the way home with my ham, bludgeoned to death in the street by a one-legged textile salesman.

Then an even more chilling thought occurred to me. What if this wasn't actually Gerald, but one of Leonard Cain's goons coming to exact Cain's final revenge? December twentieth, the anniversary of his sentencing, wasn't far away.

Taking a deep breath, I forced myself to slow down. As the steps grew louder and more rapid behind me, my grip around the string bag tensed. Much like Bernice, my Aunt Sonja, who'd raised me, had always despaired of my ever learning to be of any use in the kitchen, but I had absorbed one bit of cooking wisdom that she'd imparted: sometimes it was best to use what you had on hand.

I waited until I'd passed out of a puddle of light from the streetlamp. I wanted the advantage of being able to see my foe better than he could see me. I slowed almost to a standstill until the quickening steps were almost even with me. Then I grabbed the string bag with both hands and whirled like an athlete executing the hammer throw. I angled my string bag so that the heavy weight moved in an arc and clipped the man on the jaw with a satisfying smack.

Gerald Hughes cried out and stumbled to the ground. Not

about to relinquish my advantage, I scurried over and towered above him while he tried to push himself up from one knee. If he made another move toward me, I was ready to slug him again with the ham.

He groaned.

"Why are you following me in the dark?" I asked. "You could have called my name."

He cupped his jaw, wincing as he looked up at me. "What did you hit me with?"

"A smoked ham. How did you find me?"

He worked his jaw, testing it. "How do you think? I followed you last night."

Last night? And I hadn't noticed him. Worse, I hadn't even considered the possibility that he might do such a thing. I just assumed he'd fled out of guilt and wouldn't want to be seen by me again.

"I watched you go into a house," he continued, "but when I asked a man coming out of that same building today to tell me which apartment was Miss Frobisher's, he said there was no Miss Frobisher living there. Only a Miss Gale and a Miss Faulk."

Thanks, Wally.

"Miss Faulk, I presume?"

It was pointless to try to deny it. He knew my name, my address, everything.

Although . . . not quite everything.

"Imagine what a fool I felt—after I'd practically poured my heart out to you. I don't know what kind of scheme you and that aunt of yours are operating. Is she really your aunt?"

"She is." I was glad, in that moment, that there was something about me that was true.

"You must think I'm an idiot. I *am* an idiot. I knew women in this city lured men into traps, but you were very good. You seemed so genuine, and kind. It was the baby that gave me a jolt—I'd met his mother. I'm sure it was the same baby. What were you trying to get out of me? Money?"

"No."

"So you say, but it's always about money, isn't it? Although if it was blackmail you intended, you took your time about it." He was in a self-righteous swivet. "I should have reported you to the police. Or that detective you pointed out last night—maybe someone else hired him to follow you."

"I *am* the police."

He gaped at me. "You're . . ."

"Officer Louise Faulk of the New York City police." I purposely left out my precinct information and kept my badge in my satchel. I wasn't through deceiving Gerald Hughes quite yet.

Hughes faltered back a step, and his face collapsed into the expression of a man who had just had shackles placed around his wrists. "Why would the police be watching *me?*"

He seemed genuinely puzzled. Lots of criminals were excellent actors, though. "I was looking into your connection to a woman named Ruthie Jones."

"The mother of that mute baby. I knew it had to be the same one! That's why I was so confused."

"Ruthie, as you well know, was also a prostitute who lived on Tenth Avenue in Hell's Kitchen."

He nodded, but in the next moment, his nod became a shake. "*Was?* I don't understand."

"I told you Eddie was an orphan. Ruthie died several days before Thanksgiving, when her body was finally discovered in her apartment. It was a grisly scene."

"Are you saying she was murdered?" Even in the dark, I noted Gerald's face went two shades paler. "I had nothing to do with that. I swear it."

"But you did know Ruthie. She stole your passport."

He blinked. "Yes. Or, rather, I'm fairly certain she did. When I confronted her, she denied it."

"And that made you angry."

"Of course—but not enough to kill a woman. Can you really think so little of my character?"

"Anything can happen in the heat of an argument, even over the most trivial matters."

"But there wasn't an argument," he said. "When I discovered my passport missing, I went back to her apartment and asked her if she'd found it. I was sure she'd taken it and my money."

"And?"

He lifted his arms. "She denied it, and I left and never saw her again. What else could I do? I got another passport through the British consulate here."

"That's how I found you."

He shook his head sadly. "After what happened with Ruthie, I should have known better than to trust a woman in this town."

"How did you meet Ruthie?" I asked. "The usual way?"

He blinked. "Louise, please."

"Officer Faulk."

"I don't care who or what you are. There was nothing sordid about my evening with Ruthie, at least not in the way you mean. I bumped into her at a picture show."

I'm sure my brows arched at that. "Really."

"Yes. There was a Charlie Chaplin and Mabel Normand picture on the bill."

"There usually is." Those two seemed to make half of the pictures shown. "Go on."

"I must be the easiest mark in the world," he lamented. "I first noticed her behind me in line. I'd just finished buying my ticket, but she was a few pennies short, so I offered to pay for her. Afterwards, when I was leaving, she caught up with me to thank me. She seemed like a very pleasant young woman. I offered to treat her to a light supper, and we had some wine. I walked her home—a very shabby neighborhood—and she asked me to come up. I . . . I feel foolish saying this, but I felt I should accompany her. The building was so . . ."

I nodded. "I've been in it."

"Yes, of course. Well, I went up, and she offered me another drink. I took it more out of politeness than anything else. I saw her children. There were two of them, and she'd just left them there—she said she didn't trust anyone else to take care of them. One was normal, but the other, I remembered, couldn't make a sound. She called him Eddie. Well, children or no children, I began to understand what she was. I was shocked, to be honest. I was going to give her money, not for services but out of kindness. But the next thing I knew I was barely able to keep my eyes open. It was worse than when you hit me with that ham."

"You think she slipped something into your drink?"

"I'm sure of it now."

I remembered something. "Do you recall a sweet smell from when you were at Ruthie's?"

He frowned in thought, then shook his head. "No. I think it was something in my drink. Later, she either pushed me out of the flat, or I escaped on my own. I was awakened later on a park bench by one of your police brethren poking me with a stick. It was only when I was trying to catch a taxi back to my hotel that I realized that my money and my passport were gone."

"You carried it with you?"

"I thought it was safer that way. Before I came to America, someone warned me of hotel maids stealing."

I'd have to make sure Lena never heard that.

"I was so groggy," he continued. "I walked to the hotel, rested, and looked for the passport. It took me a little time to piece what had happened all together, but when I went to confront the woman—Ruthie—of course she denied it."

"And you were too embarrassed to tell the police."

"Oh no. I went to them straightaway."

His answer set me back on my heels.

"It *was* embarrassing," he explained, "but I thought it my duty to try to keep others from becoming victims. Evidently I needn't have bothered. They said I had no evidence of anything."

"Where did you make this report?"

"At a station the desk clerk at the hotel directed me to. It wasn't far. On Thirtieth Street, I believe?"

My heart felt heavy in my chest. "Do you remember which officer you spoke to?"

"I don't think so. He didn't give me much hope of retrieving the money."

"Can you remember what he looked like?"

"He had a sort of long face. Perfectly friendly, if a little supercilious. He had an odd name." His face tensed in concentration as he tried to remember it.

"Jenks."

"That's it."

I felt like the biggest fool in the world. Jenks had been right in front of me all along, as big as a Times Square billboard. I should have been investigating him, not Gerald.

"Doesn't my going to the police show I didn't harm that woman?" Gerald asked. "I was trying to help her and I was taken advantage of. Is being robbed a crime?"

"No," I said.

"Maybe the police should find out what they already know before persecuting innocent people."

"You're right about that."

It was entirely possible, of course, that Jenks had told King and Stevens about the incident of Ruthie stealing Gerald Hughes's passport. Maybe the stolen passport incident was the reason Ruthie's neighbor saw Jenks going to Ruthie's apartment.

Except she said she saw him on more than one occasion.

A more sinister scenario was forming in my mind: Jenks and Ruthie working in tandem, with Jenks at the nearby police precinct to absorb any complaints about her and make them disappear. He could also steer other officers' investigations away. Even when it came to Ruthie's murder.

Terrible thoughts entered my mind. A policeman would have known how to kill someone to make it look like a suicide. But why would Jenks have killed Ruthie? A mundane lover's tiff? A business disagreement? Had she threatened to expose him to the brass?

The possibility that I'd stumbled on a case of police corruption made me feel ill. I already believed one of my colleagues was in league with Cain, even if I didn't know his identity. And now I suspected Jenks of the vilest murder I'd been a witness to, and I didn't know how many others were complicit in his crime. Whom could I go to with this information about Jenks? Was anyone at the Thirtieth Street station trustworthy?

"Well?" My silence had made Gerald anxious. "Are you going to arrest me?"

Luckily for me, he seemed to have forgotten who assaulted whom this evening. "No."

"I'm sorry about that woman. She drugged and robbed me, but she was someone's daughter."

"Someone's," I echoed. "I wasn't able to track down her family."

He thought about this, but finally shrugged. It wasn't his problem. "Then am I free to go?"

"Of course." I couldn't blame him for wanting to get away from me as soon as possible. There was no covering the awkwardness of the parting. "Good-bye, Mr. Hughes. Good luck."

As he hobbled away, it felt as if something had cracked inside me. A piece of me was broken, too. I wouldn't have a limp. No one but myself would know that I'd become so comfortable with trickery and lies that I'd driven a man to follow me down dark streets, hurling accusations of blackmail at me. He hadn't deserved deceit, and my double dealings with him seemed even worse in retrospect, now that I knew he'd done nothing.

On the other hand, I had gleaned information. I was closer to knowing the truth. My clumsy investigation hadn't produced the result I'd expected, but facts weren't always convenient. Now I worried I would have to create another antagonist in my own precinct. How was I going to handle that?

"I just need to screw up my courage."

No one had ever looked less like a man summoning courage. Otto resembled a cornered rabbit so much, he was almost twitching.

"Be honest with her." I hunched deeper in my coat. Light flurries floated through the air and were beginning to dust the sidewalk around Pennsylvania Station. I peered ahead to see if Ziggy's line was moving and noticed the men in front of us. One of them was a man with startlingly clear blue eyes. He and his companion were speaking in what sounded like German, from the few snatches I caught.

"That's what you said last time we talked," Otto said. "You must think I'm an awful coward."

"I think you don't want to disappoint her because you're still infatuated."

His mouth dropped open, but no denial came forth. "What difference does it make? She's in love with Teddy."

"Teddy's off to England."

"That's even worse. Teddy, here, she might have gotten tired of eventually. Now he can be her romantic ideal—the one who dashed off on an adventure."

Maybe Callie *was* going to romanticize Teddy now. "She was cooped up in her room last night, knitting."

"Probably socks for Teddy." He looked even more discouraged. "He's her new Belgium."

I laughed but then became distracted by the two in front of us. They were an odd pair. The blue-eyed man was tall, with a strong, clean-cut jaw. Blond hair peeked out from under his homburg, and he wore a mink-brown cashmere coat. His companion was stouter, and sloppier looking, with a belly that pushed against his overcoat. The two were speaking German at a clip difficult for me to keep up with. One phrase caught my ear, though. *Die Reisepasses.*

Passports.

Were my ears playing tricks on me?

"Jimmy was pointing out that there was a lulu of a part that Callie would knock 'em cold in," Otto said.

My attention ricocheted back to my friend. "What part?"

"Agnes, the chambermaid. She has a fun novelty song in the second act. 'Dust Away Your Troubles.' "

I rubbed my gloved hands together for warmth. "Give me warning before you tell Callie she's being demoted from the title role to Agnes the chambermaid. I want to remove any breakable valuables from the apartment."

"You don't think she'll go for it?"

Ahead of me, I heard the words *mehr beschaffen.*

Procure more . . . what? It was all I could do to keep my body from tilting forward to eavesdrop.

"*I can't do everything myself,*" the plump one said. "*I need help.*"

"Louise?" Otto prompted.

I tried to focus on his problem. "I don't want to speak for anyone when a job's in the offing, but I doubt she's going to be tickled pink."

"Oh." He drooped.

"A person expecting champagne doesn't jump for joy over a bottle of beer."

"You're right." He sighed. "I just wish you weren't."

"Then again, she might think beer is better than nothing."

When we got to the front of the line and placed our orders, I questioned Ziggy while he loaded our brats. "That man who was just here . . . the one with the blue eyes . . . is he a regular customer of yours?"

"More faithful than you two," Ziggy said.

"I like that. Otto and I are here every week—even in the snow."

"That is nothing. Herr Neumann comes *twice* a week." He winked at me. "A handsome man, *ja*?"

I made a show of fluttering and hoped Otto wasn't staring at me as if I'd lost my mind. "Is he? I didn't notice."

"Sure, you notice nothing—only his blue eyes." Ziggy laughed and tilted his head toward Otto. "Your taste in men is improving, fräulein."

I smiled as Otto and I each handed over our fifteen cents in exchange for our food. It had taken me years to get Otto used to going dutch. Ziggy didn't approve.

"What was that all about?" Otto said, bristling a little as we walked toward Pennsylvania Station to get out of the snow.

"Ziggy was just needling you."

"I *know* that. But why were you simpering over some fellow in the bratwurst line?"

"Didn't you hear the two men in front of us?" I asked.

"No, and I'm surprised you did, either. I thought *we* were having a conversation."

"I can't help it if my ears pick up snatches of what other people are saying. You can hardly blame me. They were talking about passports."

"So?"

"They were keeping their voices very low, like they didn't want anyone else to hear. Even so, I caught the phrase *procure more*."

"That could mean anything."

"Procure more passports? Who does that?"

"Government officials?" Otto guessed. "Consulate workers?"

"Passport thieves?" I added.

Otto chewed, shaking his head.

"Those two looked shady," I said.

"Up until yesterday, you thought Gerald Hughes was shady," he reminded me. I'd given him the whole story about Gerald. "Turned out he was just a luckless salesman who'd been fleeced."

True. "I'm glad he wasn't a murderer."

"Ziggy's blue-eyed customer probably isn't a murderer, either."

I forced myself to take a little of my own medicine and really listened to what Otto was saying. He was right, of course. There were almost five million people in New York City. What were the chances that I would bump into another man who'd known Ruthie Jones? From snatches of probably innocent conversation, I was imagining conspiracies.

But what else could the men have been talking about? *Passports . . . procure more . . .*

Resignation settled into Otto's gaze. "You're not going to let it go, are you?"

"I'll have to file it away for a later date," I said. "I have other matters to contend with this afternoon."

Namely, Jenks. I wasn't fool enough to think I could handle him on my own, though.

CHAPTER 16

When I pushed through the doors of the station house, Muldoon was there, having his ear talked off by Schultzie. He caught my gaze and raised a hand in a way that let me know he'd been watching the door for me. I hurried over.

Looking from Muldoon's face to mine, Schultzie smiled. "The lieutenant here was asking about you in a way that would've made me jealous if I didn't already know that you are dedicated to our humble precinct." He poked me in the side. "Don't let these downtown dandies steal you away from us."

The idea of anyone calling Muldoon a dandy made me smile. "No need to worry about that."

Muldoon steered me downstairs. Curious at the lack of anyone else down there, I peeked around to the cells. There was just Sleeping Myrtle conked out in the back of one. A slow day, which is how Myrtle liked it. When her rooming house got too rough, or she just didn't have any money, she'd arrange to get picked up and stay for a day.

A slow day was fortunate for me, too.

"You got my note?" I asked Muldoon.

He nodded. "I was on my way here anyway. I could've sworn you said you were going to hand over those passports to the detectives on the Ruthie Jones case."

"I did."

"King told me he didn't know the first thing about them. Never saw them."

"Why were you asking him about the passports?"

"A man was found stabbed in the Bowery. His description matched one of the men I remembered from the passports you brought to my house."

It felt as if someone had plugged me into a socket. "Lars Holmgren, the Swede?"

"Might be. The victim had krona in his pockets, and a piece of paper with Swedish writing. But nothing else very helpful in identifying him. That passport was a long shot, but I thought I'd check."

Could it really be him? I'd just been assuming he'd caught a ship and was half a world away by now.

"I gave the passports to Jenks, who said he'd pass them along to King and Stevens."

"Must've slipped his mind."

"Accidentally on purpose." I related the confrontation I'd had with Gerald Hughes the night before. "Jenks has been obstructing us from the very beginning. He knew Ruthie. Eileen, the neighbor on the first floor, said she saw a cop who matches his description visiting Ruthie. I'll bet he knew about the scam Ruthie was running. He might even have put her up to it."

"What scam?"

"A man outside the Swedish Immigrant Home told me there's a black market for passports. He offered to buy one from me. That could explain how Ruthie accumulated so much cash before she died. Well, for a woman living in a dump like that building she and her kids were in. And then, when she was killed—"

"Found dead," Muldoon corrected.

He could think that if he wanted to. "Maybe Ruthie and Jenks were in on a passport-stealing-and-selling scheme together, but she started to hold out on him. Could've been why he killed her."

"We don't know she was killed."

"A cop would've known how to make her death look like a suicide. Even the coroner said she hadn't bled much. He was trying to float all kinds of reasons like the cold, but isn't the more obvious answer that she was already dead?"

"Your mind certainly wanders down some gruesome trails." He sighed. "I need to have a word with Jenks. Could be we're jumping the gun. I don't want to accuse the man of covering up something if it was just a thoughtless oversight."

"That's what he'll probably tell you." Prudence might be Muldoon's watchword, but my inclination was to scare the daylights out of Jenks and make him confess. "We'll both talk to him. Otherwise he'll just hand you a load of malarkey. Besides, I know how to get him down here so we can ask him a few questions in private, with the benefit of surprise."

It didn't take much. Upstairs, I spotted Jenks and waited until he was heading down a corridor to a room where old files were kept. It was secluded enough that no one could hear me call out, "Hello, Melvin."

He turned, surprised, and then a little suspicious.

"You don't mind my calling you by your Christian name in private, do you?" I asked, sidling closer.

One of his eyebrows shot up. "Why would you?"

"It's only fair. You call me Two."

"Sure . . . but everybody does." He eyed me warily. "What do you want?"

I put my hand on his forearm sleeve. "I thought this was what *you* wanted."

He looked into my eyes a moment, then glanced around the hallway to see if anyone else was around. A sheen of sweat broke out on his forehead, which didn't make my siren-of-the-precinct act any easier.

"You were pretty high-hat about my offer that time," he recalled.

I cast my eyes to the floor. "I didn't expect a man like you to give up so easily."

I was afraid to look up—afraid I'd see that he was seeing right through me. But keeping an eye on him probably would've been wise, because the next thing I knew he'd pounced and I was shoved up against the wall by my forearms. At first gasp I thought this must be anger, but no, this was apparently Jenks's way of expressing passion. His groin ground into me and his mouth, which seemed to be buried in my hair, blew hot breath against my scalp.

His action summoned an unwanted memory, one I'd tried to bury. Every muscle in my body exploded with unexpected energy. I pushed him away, harder than I intended, and smoothed my hair, which felt as if a spaniel had licked it. What was the matter with men? "Not *here*, for Pete's sake."

He was breathing hard. "Where?"

I kept my voice low, confidential. "The women's cells are practically empty today." Feathering my fingers across his palm, I added, "Just give me a little head start."

For a moment, I worried he'd attack me again. I broke away and hurried downstairs, biting my lip. Callie might be the actress, but it was shocking how easily lying was starting to come to me.

"Well?" Muldoon asked when I came downstairs.

"Better tuck yourself away."

Muldoon stepped into the small closet where the locked cabinets for our things were. I stood waiting, but not for long. Jenks wasn't far behind me, and within seconds he was snuffling into my hair again. I'd need to wash it tonight.

"Call me Mel," he panted into my scalp. "Only my mother calls me Melvin."

"That's enough, Melvin." Muldoon stepped out of the closet, looking like doom.

Jenks, turning, flung me aside. He shrank away from Muldoon, then looked from him to me. "You bitch."

Muldoon's hand shot out, quick as an adder, slapping him with a sharp crack that made me jump. "Watch yourself, Jenks. I asked her to bring you here so I could talk to you away from the brass. To save you embarrassment, if possible."

"*Save* me from embarrassment?" he repeated, touching his cheek and eyeing me resentfully. "That's not how it seems."

"We know about you and Ruthie," I said.

His eyes widened. "Know what?"

"That you visited her. Often. You were seen going up to her flat on multiple occasions."

"So?"

"Prostitution is against the law, Officer," Muldoon reminded him.

Jenks laughed. "So's baseball on Sundays. Show me the man who's never gone to a park and played a game."

At the flip answer, Muldoon's scowl deepened. "Officer Faulk gave you the passports found at Ruthie Jones's flat to hand over to Stevens or King. You didn't."

"I forgot." His eyes were beginning to register worry. "Anyone could forget a thing like that. What difference did it make anyways?"

"We think Ruthie stole those passports. She might even have been killed for them."

"Ruthie committed suicide," Jenks said.

"And now one of her passport theft victims appears to have turned up dead in the Bowery. That makes two suspicious deaths surrounding those passports," Muldoon said. "I can bring you downtown for questioning in this matter, or you can clear it up right here and now."

I held my breath. Muldoon was tossing the dice. Jenks could refuse to talk and then go running to Sergeant Donnelly. The link between the passports and the dead man downtown was tenuous, but if my tactics and Muldoon's high-handedness were aired, it could cause more of a stink than my shaky position in the NYPD could weather. Men were already leery of policewomen; having one around who'd tried to snitch on a fellow officer wouldn't go over well.

Like a balloon deflating, Jenks sank onto the cot. "I knew her," he confessed. "She . . . well, I won't say I *loved* her, but we were close. She was a fun girl."

"When did you last see her?" I asked.

"Nearly a week before Thanksgiving." His face paled. "I couldn't believe it when I heard what happened to her. And when they told me about the baby . . ."

"Were the twins yours?" I asked.

"No." Alarm squeezed his voice a pitch higher. "At least, she never said. Who knows whose they were? Ruthie didn't seem to care. As far as she was concerned, they were all hers. She was blooming."

"She loved them that much, then," I said.

"Yeah, she did," Jenks said. "You can say what you want about Ruthie. She was no saint, but she was a pretty good mother to those boys."

"Do you think Ruthie would have killed her baby?"

He shuddered. "I couldn't believe it. But . . . well, people do all sorts of things you don't expect, don't they?"

"Did she ever mention another man who might've had a grudge against her? A client? A relative?"

"She didn't have any relations here. Those were all back west. Ruthie said her sister wrote to her, but she didn't think they'd want her back. Especially not after the babies came. She burned the letter. Burned her bridges. She never wrote back, as far as I know."

"So Ruthie *could* write," I said.

He sent me a contemptuous look. "Sure. I just told you she couldn't to throw you off the scent."

For some reason, this made me even angrier on Ruthie's behalf than on my own.

"Why did Ruthie steal passports?" Muldoon asked.

"I don't know anything about that," Jenks said. "Weeks ago, a man came here and said she'd stolen his passport and money. I assumed she'd just been stealing the money, and the passport was just by the bye."

"You never asked her?"

"I asked her about the money, of course. I told her she needed to cut that out. She swore she hadn't stolen money, and maybe she didn't. The man said he'd spent a night on a park bench. Anybody could've taken his money."

"You didn't ever talk to any of her other clients?"

"It wasn't my business. I wasn't going to marry her or anything, so it wasn't like I could ask her to give up her living."

Muldoon sighed. "So you don't know anyone who would've wanted to kill her. And you don't know why she would've had three stolen passports sewn into a cape?"

Jenks rubbed his jaw. "No idea."

I squinted at him. He really did seem not to know what she'd been up to. "You don't know how she'd saved forty-six dollars?"

He frowned. "A while back, she told me she was onto easy money. I thought maybe she'd found a good regular customer— and like I said, I wasn't jealous. I was happy for her. She'd been destitute there for a while, waiting for the babies. I'd had to spot her some money myself, and paid for a nurse to go see her once or twice."

Muldoon shook his head. "If you didn't know anything about the passports, why bother hiding them when Officer Faulk brought them to you?"

"I didn't want the detectives poking into Ruthie's life and finding out I'd been going to see her, especially if she'd been up to something. I tried not to leave anything there, but I couldn't be sure. If they went over the place with a fine-tooth comb, some little something tied to me might turn up. I didn't want the brass to wonder if I was involved in some whore's death. I've been waiting two years to get a promotion." Looking at Muldoon, he sighed. "I guess I'll never get it now."

"You might," Muldoon said, "if you'll swear this is all you know about those passports and the death of Ruthie Jones."

What? I gaped at him. We couldn't just cover this up now, could we? We needed to drag Jenks up to King and Stevens and let *them* decide whether or not he should be turned over to Captain McMartin.

Jenks nodded violently. "I swear it on my mother's life. I don't know anything more about Ruthie's death than either of you do."

"Then you can forget you've spoken to us," Muldoon said. "But I'd like to have those passports."

Bullets moved slower than Jenks shooting out of that basement.

I rounded on Muldoon, unable to hide my incredulity. "You're just going to take his word for it?"

"Didn't you believe him?"

"It's *you* I don't believe. You're the one always telling me to let detectives handle matters."

"I am a detective."

"Not on the Ruthie Jones case."

"There is no Ruthie Jones case," he replied. "Not according to King and Stevens. She committed suicide. Having Jenks confess to having known her isn't going to change their minds about anything."

"But he was lying and covering things up."

"To protect his career. Any cop would understand that."

"Any guilty person would, too." I crossed my arms.

"Antagonizing Jenks further isn't going to help you, Louise. You're not a detective. If you stick your neck out about Ruthie

Jones on flimsy evidence, and try and fail to bring down a fellow officer, your career will be dead in the water."

I lifted my arm, pointing down the hallway that led to the women's cells. "I've been cooped up here for a year now. I'm dead already."

"You knew what the job was."

I'd known, somewhat. And yet I'd had hopes that I could do more. Now I looked at my fellow policewomen and it felt as if we were being wasted. There was work we could be doing besides babysitting female prisoners. We could be out policing communities in ways that men couldn't. The brass thought brawn was all that mattered in police work. They were wrong.

"You have to deal with reality," Muldoon said, making me wonder if he could read my mind. "Not how you want the police department to be."

He was right, of course. My male colleagues would take a dim view of my insinuating that Jenks had been involved in Ruthie's death. A ragged, resentful sigh tore out of me. "All right. I see your point."

"I'll go upstairs and have a word with Jenks," Muldoon said, "and see if I can smooth over his ruffled feathers."

The idea that he was concerned with *Jenks's* ruffled feathers aggravated my sense of injustice. "What about the passports? You'll tell me if the Bowery victim was Holmgren, won't you?"

"If we can make an identification from the information in the document," he agreed. "It might not be possible."

He was getting what he came for while I'd hit a brick wall, but I couldn't dwell on that or I'd end up mired in resentment. "I'm grateful for your help," I forced myself to say. "I might not always show it, but I am."

"It's the least I can do, given that you've been putting up with my sister for so long."

"How is Anna?"

Muldoon, who'd already been turning to go upstairs, pivoted back. "You tell me. She's staying with you."

"Not for the past two nights," I said.

Muldoon stood frozen. "She hasn't been at your apartment? You haven't seen her?"

Uh-oh. I'd stepped into something. "Perhaps we just missed each other."

Muldoon wasn't convinced. "Damnation, Louise. I thought she'd be safe with you."

"Who said she isn't safe?"

"From what you're saying, my little sister could be anywhere in the city." He slapped his hat against his thigh. "I should've known better than to entrust her to you and that flighty roommate of yours."

It felt as if he'd slapped me. "Flighty?"

"What would you call it? Running around with men all the time, working with stage people. Everyone knows what actors are."

"I only know the actresses and actors I've met. They're not flighty." *Unlike that sister of yours*, I barely kept myself from adding.

His lips tightened. "Of course. You're such a grand judge of character."

His words stunned me so, I could barely choke out a sentence. "Why would you say that?"

"For one thing, this refusal of yours to believe a degraded woman like Ruthie Jones would kill herself."

My mouth dropped open. I'd thought we were on the same page about Ruthie, but now he was dismissing her . . . and dismissing my concern. I was so mad I was starting to see spots. "You think I'm deluded?"

"I think you've spent so much of the last two years stewing in the worst elements of society that you've lost perspective."

I tossed my head back. "You also spend your life 'stewing' in bad society—how is it Anna is only in danger of being polluted when she stays with Callie and me?"

"I didn't mean it like that," he said.

"That's how it sounded. My ears aren't faulty, although you seem to think my judgment is."

"No one's judgment is always right all the time. But you're so prickly about criticism."

"Only when I'm criticized for doing my job."

"Your job." He shook his head in frustration. "Why does it matter to you so much? Why can't you be like normal women?"

My first instinct was to strangle him, my second was to laugh. I opted for the second, which made him flinch. "Because there is no such thing. I don't mean to frighten you, Lieutenant, but there are millions upon millions of women, and we're all different, with different dreams and ambitions—some modest, some outrageous. You might have an imagined ideal of a normal woman in your head, but believe me, that's the only place she lives."

He was scowling. "I can't figure you out. You're so single-minded, sometimes it seems as if you're on a quest to right a wrong. Has your life been so bad?"

I wavered. I could confide everything about my past to him, relive the horrible moment of being attacked and then the months of feeling shunned by my own family, culminating in the shock of giving away my own flesh. Maybe Muldoon would understand and offer some comfort. But there was also the chance, especially given the things he'd just said to me, that he wouldn't sympathize; the chill of his distancing himself from me and my past and the emotional tangle it had left me in was a possibility I wasn't ready to face here and now. I'd rather him think me irrational than recoil from me.

"This isn't about me," I said. "This began with your sister. She latched herself on to Callie, and Callie's done a lot for her. If you object to Anna's choices, you should speak to her. Better yet, find yourself a time machine like H. G. Wells wrote of and travel back to three weeks ago, before she caught the mania for acting. I don't think there's any stopping her now."

"Right now all I care about is finding her." He put his hat back on this head and turned to go. "I'll worry about the rest later."

After he'd left, I stood unmoving until his footsteps were no longer discernible from the rest of the foot traffic above. What the hell had happened? One minute we were on the same side, and the next minute it had all blown up. I grabbed a broom and marched over to the cells. Myrtle was just waking up and pulled a package of cigarettes out of her blouse. "Noisy in here today," she complained, yawning. She offered me a cigarette. "Smoke, Officer?"

We weren't supposed to, but I snatched the proffered cigarette. "Thanks." I leaned in and she lit it through the bars. Matches were considered contraband, but I let that pass, too. I sighed and exhaled a cloud of noxious smoke as I picked up the broom again. Tobacco never did much for me, but I felt better exhaling smoke—less like a lowly police drudge, more like a dragon.

And evidently nothing like a normal woman.

Stewing in the worst elements of society. What a thing to say. I thought Muldoon and I were friends. More than friends—colleagues, and . . . well, I didn't like to acknowledge it, but there had been times when I thought I detected something more. Like the jealousy in his eyes when he'd seen Gerald Hughes and me at the top of the stairs. Apparently he'd just been marveling at me—a sponge of immorality and licentiousness.

"You're sweeping that dust around the floor like my ma used to before she'd give me a blistering," Myrtle croaked. "What's got you bothered?"

"Men," I said.

"Say no more, sister." With a wave of her hand, she shuffled back to a bench seat in the back of the cell. "I always say, don't waste your thoughts on men. They usually show you how shady they are right off the bat. But fool women have been taught to doubt ourselves and give *them* the benefit of a doubt. Quite a racket the males of the species have going, if you ask me."

Another thing women were taught was to shun women like Myrtle. Yet during my year on this job, I'd heard more hard-won, useful wisdom coming out of the mouths of "degraded" women than I had from my Aunt Sonja in Altoona in twenty years. Maybe that was stewing in the worst elements, but so be it. If the world truly wanted to arm young girls with knowledge about what to watch out for, they should sit them down for an hour with the Myrtles of the world.

At the flat that evening, I found Callie in her homeliest robe and slippers, cupping a piping hot mug of tea in her hands like an invalid. She was ensconced on the sofa, next to the still-undecorated tree. Hard to tell which looked droopiest—her or that sad, neglected evergreen weeping needles onto our floor.

I seated myself in a chair near her. "Are you sick?" I asked, alarmed.

"Not physically."

So what was the problem? I took a shot in the dark. "I don't suppose you've heard from Teddy?"

Her body sank further into the sofa. "No, he's probably still bobbing somewhere over the ocean, or across the English Channel. Who knows."

I wondered if that was what was bothering her. Thanks to the Kaiser's submarines, ocean travel was less safe now than it used to be. Another reason to hate the war. Not only did transatlantic passengers have to worry about hitting icebergs, warring countries were now threatening to launch torpedoes at ocean liners as well as warships.

"I'm thinking of becoming a Red Cross nurse," Callie said, tapping a cigarette out of a packet and lighting it. "Or maybe I should just go to California. That's what Mary Pickford did—and now look at her. She's a bigger star even than when she was the Biograph Girl. She's got her name up in lights on theater marquees."

"Movie theaters," I said dismissively.

"Someday there won't be a difference."

I doubted that. At any rate, someday wasn't now. "I don't think you should go to California, and I certainly don't see you as a nurse."

"Why not? I'd like to do something useful for a change. Something where my fate didn't rest in the hands of men. Fickle men."

Now I understood. "You've spoken to Otto."

"You *knew*?"

Heat filled my face. "He mentioned something about a producer wanting a star . . ."

"Agnes the chambermaid!" She blew out a long stream of smoke. "I can just see it now. Me knocking the audience cockeyed in my maid uniform and feather duster. If I do great, I'll get a line of praise in a paper or two like I did in my last Broadway show. Then, when the show closes, I'll be just as unemployed as I was before. Nothing's adding up."

It was no use my counseling patience and perseverance. I'd left publishing because so much of the work seemed thankless. And that had been a steady job—at least until the publishing house burned down. But an actress's life could be unstable as well as unrewarding.

Thinking of actresses reminded me of someone else. "Have you seen Anna lately? I told Muldoon she hasn't been here for the past two days and he blew his stack. I think he believes she's been kidnapped. Has she been by today?"

Callie's eyes flashed. "Of course not. Even she wouldn't have the gall to show her face here now."

I shook my head in confusion. "What's happened?"

Callie frowned at how uninformed I was. "She stole my movie. They decided to turn the scenario into a vehicle for Anna—*my* scenario. Alfred told me I wasn't needed for the rest of the week. That's five dollars a day I'm not getting, thanks to your houseguest."

"*My* houseguest?" I repeated.

"You invited her here."

"You were the one who took her under your wing," I pointed out.

"I thought she was your friend. Some friend!" She shook her head. "I really regret the day you brought her into our lives."

First I'd had to deal with Muldoon's blaming me for Anna's disappearance, and now I was getting blamed for Anna's ever being here at all. I felt like a whale being harpooned on both sides. "I didn't tell you to make her your protégée."

"Go ahead," Callie said. "Blame me for my own misfortune." A tear streaked down her face.

"I'm not blaming you, but you certainly can't point the finger at me when you're the one who promoted her on the set."

Callie lifted a handkerchief to her eyes. "Honestly, Louise, if *you're* going to turn on me like this, I might as well become a nurse."

"You go woozy at the sight of blood," I reminded her. "How would you hold up on a battlefield?"

"See?" She shot to her feet. "What kind of friend are you? You don't even support me in my decisions."

She ran to her room and shut her door firmly. I collapsed back in my chair. Below, a single saxophone was moaning out a new song in their repertoire called "Saint Louis Blues." I was coming down with a case of the blues myself. First Muldoon attacked Callie and I stood up for her. Now Callie blamed me for the Muldoons. The feeling that the world had gone topsy-turvy settled over me.

Thank heavens tomorrow was my day off in the rotation. I needed to rest and clear my head.

My brain wasn't ready to relax, though. I thought about what Myrtle had said about women mistrusting themselves. I'd had my suspicions about Anna, and look how that had turned out. I should have trusted in myself more.

Was I right about Jenks, too?

Or what about that blue-eyed man in Ziggy's line? He seemed worth another look, if I could find him. Luckily, Ziggy had handed me a big fat hint about where I could bump into him again.

That quickly, my day off got kicked to the curb. The world might be spinning out of control, but I at least had one thing I knew I could do, even if I had to pursue it on my own: find out what really happened to Ruthie Jones.

CHAPTER 17

I tried not to feel self-conscious as I stood in the back of Ziggy's line, hoping Blue Eyes would return. Maybe it was a long shot, but Ziggy had said the man was a regular. Pretending to wait for someone, I let a steady stream of people cut ahead of me. When I turned to extend the same offer to another newcomer, it turned out to be Blue Eyes himself, absorbed in a copy of the German paper Ziggy had shown me a few weeks ago. TRAVESTIE IN ARGENTINIEN! blazed across the top of the page. The article detailed the rout the Germans had received in the Falkland Islands at the hands of the British Navy. Bold print highlighted the disaster for the Germans:1800 casualties, and only one ship had escaped unscathed.

"*Schrecklich*," I said. *Terrible.*

Annoyed, the man looked up, then did a double take when he realized I'd just spoken in his native tongue. "*Deutsche?*"

The thrill an angler must experience at that first tug on the line zipped through me. "*Nicht ganz.*" *Not quite.* "I was born in Pennsylvania, but my father was from Bavaria."

"He taught you well, that is obvious."

"I'm not fluent. My parents were, but they're both dead now."

The hard planes of his face softened a fraction. "I'm sorry. That is unfortunate for you."

"I never considered myself unfortunate—at least not till I came here." I shrugged. "I'll just have to make my own way." Remembering the man's companion complaining of having to do everything himself, I looked down at the newspaper he held and asked, "Are there any employment ads in there, by any chance?"

"It is a paper of ideas." His brow furrowed, then he offered the paper to me. "You should take it to practice your German."

"Thanks—*danke*, I mean." I accepted the propaganda rag from him. "You've given me an idea. Maybe I could find someone who could use a not-quite-fluent-in-German secretary."

"You are a secretary?"

"I graduated third in my class at secretarial college."

He seemed sincerely interested. *Maybe he's like Gerald*, I warned myself. A lonely foreigner in New York City. This man didn't *seem* lonely, though. He exuded a vitality and focus that made me suspect he didn't spend much time hankering after things he couldn't get. Especially women. But one thing I'd learned about men: Their vanity was almost as strong a force as the libido. I kept an admiring, grateful gaze on him.

When we reached the front of the line, Ziggy took in the German and me arriving together. I held my breath, hoping he wouldn't reveal that I'd been asking about this man on my previous visit.

"This is good," Ziggy said. "My two favorite customers. *Es war Schicksal.*"

At this mention of fate, the German did not look amused. "The young lady was reading my newspaper."

"She is full of curiosity." Ziggy winked at me. He didn't even ask what we wanted, but went about putting our lunches together.

"I hoped I might find a job," I said. "Any ideas would be welcome."

Ziggy regarded me with compassion. "I did not know. If only I could help, but I regret I have only one sausage wagon, and one worker—me!" He roared at his own little—very little—joke.

I expected the German to hurry away from me as soon as our food was handed over to us. Instead, he stuck with me and even paid for my lunch despite my protests. "Don't speak of it," he said when I thanked him profusely. "It is the least I can do for a *nicht ganz* German. My name is Holger Neumann. I am a businessman."

He led me toward an unoccupied bench near the post office. I would have rather gone into the relatively warm train station, but maybe it would be easier to talk here. We sat on the cold seat within view of Ziggy's cart. He nodded toward it. "That man is too familiar," he said.

"Ziggy? He's harmless."

"I do not like to see a countryman act like a buffoon. Especially not in these times."

Here we go. The war. I took a breath. "Much as it pains me to contradict the gentleman who bought my lunch, I must. When the papers are full of such terrible things about our people, don't you think it's important for Germans now to put forward a friendly demeanor? Otherwise, it would be easy for everyone to assume we're all bloodthirsty, bayonet-wielding monsters."

His eyes narrowed on me. "That is a point I had not considered. Very shrewd. You are right. Ziggy is a clown, but in circuses clowns serve a useful function, to entertain and distract."

I sputtered out a laugh. "Distract? I don't see why Germans would need a distraction here. It's not as if they're doing much in New York. Just watching our ships going to rust in port."

My use of "our ships" wasn't lost on Neumann. Chewing, he contemplated my face so long I worried I'd blush. I tried to concentrate on my food, bolting down my sandwich as if I hadn't eaten in a while.

"Why did you come to New York, fräulein?"

"Same as most people—for work. I have a friend who's had some luck here, and she invited me to stay with her. But she's an actress and I . . ." I wrinkled my nose. "That sort of thing doesn't interest me."

"Very sensible."

"Hard to take make-believe seriously when the world's gone mad. I wish there was something I could do to be useful." I remembered Callie's lament last night. "If only I'd trained as a nurse, not as a secretary. Maybe I could go to Europe and help."

"Help the war effort, for the Germans?"

I glanced around. The only person nearby was a man leaning against a light pole, eating his lunch as we were. He was one of the men I'd let move ahead of me in line. "I wouldn't talk about my preferences too loudly around here, Herr Neumann. I haven't been in New York City for long, but already people have accused me of being pro-German."

His face tensed in indignation. "As if that is a bad thing."

"*I* don't think it's bad. But you know public opinion. It's the papers. They just take the one side."

His jaw tightened. "Yes, the British cut Germany's transatlantic cable. Now the news that reaches this country first is all from the English."

"It doesn't seem fair," I said.

"You are a good girl, Fräulein . . ."

"Frobisher," I blurted out. "Leisl Frobisher. I've been thinking of changing it to Lisa, though. Just while I'm searching for a job, you understand."

His face creased in disgust. "I understand too well."

"A lot of people here change their names to sound more American."

"More English, you mean." He sighed. "I don't blame you for being a realist. But Leisl is a beautiful name. You should keep it."

I smiled at him. "You don't know how it's helped my morale to talk to someone like you. It's given me a little hope that there's good in this city."

"It is you who has given me hope," he said. "I would like to help you more."

I leaned toward him eagerly. "You mean with a job? Do you know of a position?"

"I might."

"That's wonderful! I'd be so grateful for anything."

He recoiled instinctively from my enthusiasm, but I don't think he was entirely displeased. "Where may I reach you?" he asked.

The phone was always the sticking point. "The building where I'm staying doesn't have a telephone," I said, biting my lip. "But if you could tell me where to go—"

"Never mind." He muttered something to himself in German. "*Nutze den Tag.*"

"Carpe diem?" I translated uncertainly.

He nodded, stood, and took my hand so I would follow suit. "I will seize this day to do a good deed for—what is the expression?—

a damsel in distress. And for myself, as well. I do have a job that needs doing, Fräulein Frobisher, and you are just the person to help."

He led me to a side street, where a car and a hulking driver in a black suit and cap awaited him. Ziggy's attracted everyone, rich and poor, but I was surprised by this man's having wealth enough for a car and chauffeur. When the driver opened the back door, all sorts of grisly ideas caromed through my mind. Where was I being taken? One thing about working for the police, it filled the imagination with all sorts of unsavory scenarios. All I had to do was think of poor Ruthie.

But even as these worries cropped up, so did a little excitement. I didn't have a very clear idea of my objective in accepting his offer, but it was a chance I couldn't let pass. I had to seize the day, as well. In terms of working covertly, it was almost a Cinderella moment, and Holger Neumann's Dodge touring car was the gilded coach taking me to meet my destiny.

I was so pleased with myself, in fact, that I was oblivious to being watched. I was a slow learner.

"*Das Auge,*" Holger told his driver.

The car lurched into traffic, cutting off a bread wagon.

"Where are we going?" I asked.

"To 335 East Eighty-Sixth Street."

Eighty-Sixth Street? That was farther than I'd expected. Despite my jangling nerves, I made myself smile. "We're very much alike, aren't we? Willing to travel across town from where we live for Ziggy's."

"Where I am taking you is not where I live," he said. "I am not that kind of man."

"Oh, I never thought—"

"We are going to the offices of the paper I showed you. *Das Auge* is a financial investment of mine."

"You mean I get to work on a real newspaper? Just like Nellie Bly."

"You will work for a man called Johann. But you will really work for me. *Verstehst du?*"

Did I understand? It took me a moment to catch on. "You want me to spy for you?"

"I want you to keep your eyes open, Fräulein Frobisher."

In other words, I would be spying for the man I was spying on. "If we're going to be confederates, you should call me Leisl."

The corners of his lips tucked down. "The man you will be working under, Johann Schmidt, is a very sloppy man. I want to ensure he is sloppy, but honest. You will keep a log of everyone who goes in and out of the office, and what passes between them. The paper is a very expensive concern, and has grown more expensive of late. Do you see?"

"Yes, sir."

"You have no problem with this . . . how would you say it?"

I said it in the language he understood best. "*Duplizität.*" Duplicity. If only he knew how little trouble I was going to have with it. "I don't mind, as long as it's for a worthy cause."

"We both want the best. To oppose the lies being spread in English newspapers so that the world will be peaceful again."

"Don't worry," I promised. "I'll tell you everything I see and hear."

He gave my thigh a quick, pleased pat with his gloved hand—from anyone else it might have seemed fresh, but from him it bore all the intimacy of a man giving praise to his spaniel. "Good girl," he said. "You will meet me the morning after tomorrow. Eight thirty, where Ziggy's cart is."

"Ziggy's not there at eight thirty, is he?"

"No. It is not a social engagement. You will simply tell me what you have observed."

The car turned sharply and then stopped in front of a hydrant on Eighty-Sixth between First and Second Avenues. We were in Yorkville, one of the most heavily German areas in Manhattan now, after the German population, the most prosperous of immigrants, started abandoning Kleindeutschland on the poorer Lower East Side. The many four- and five-story buildings along the busy street were well kept, the sidewalks clean. There was an air of middle-class prosperity, with a very distinct German flair. Nearby businesses bore names like Muller's Shoes, Schneider's Bakery, and Lange's Hofbräuhaus. Number 335 was one of the brownstones that must have been the bread and butter of New York City architects. I looked up at five stories of the plain-fronted edifice. "Here?"

Neumann took my arm. There was little about the building to draw attention, besides a simple black-and-white stenciling of *Das Auge* on the plate glass of the door. Inside, we walked down a narrow hallway to another door. Neumann held it open for me.

A man I assumed was Johann—he was the only person there—hopped up from a squeaky chair and hurried forward, glancing at me repeatedly as he greeted Neumann. I recognized him right away as the stout man Neumann had been speaking to at Ziggy's when I was there with Otto. My nerves spiked. If I had seen him, he might have seen me.

"Allow me to introduce Leisl Frobisher," Holger said. "Just like you, she is an American but also German by blood and eager to help." He turned to me, and that smile of his made me realize I preferred his usual dour expression. There was something unnatural about that flash of white teeth across his face. Like seeing a lizard break into a grin.

Johann, on the other hand, smiled and laughed as easily as he breathed. Glue a white beard on him and put him in a red velvet hat and suit and he could have stood in as a store-window Santa Claus. His big paws clapped over the hand I held out to him. "A friend of Holger's is a friend of mine."

"But not *too* good a friend, Johann," Neumann warned. "She is here to work, not for romance."

"Ha! Never fear. I've never been lucky with the ladies, except of course the ones who own bakeries." He rubbed his protruding belly, which itself was covered by a wrinkled shirt with what appeared to be mustard stains, and laughed.

Neumann was impatient with his nonsense. "Perhaps you should show Fräulein Frobisher where she will do her work."

"Of course, Herr Neumann, of course."

Johann led me to a small desk piled high with papers—whole newspapers, clippings, stacks of receipts, carbons, open correspondence that had all been tossed into unruly mounds on the desk, even onto the old chair whose dried leather upholstery was crazed with cracks. The platen of a tall old fossil of a German typewriter poked above the mess. As far as I could tell, Johann and I were the only ones working here, but there were two other desks in similar states of disorder. If this had been my first day of a real job, I would have been tempted to turn tail and run.

Only one corner of the long room remained uncluttered and that was the far back wall where a contraption that looked a little like a steam roller that had been torn apart and ineptly put back together stood. This, I gathered, was a press. And a table next to it was lined with narrow drawers. It, too, was conspicuously neat.

The walls of the long, low-ceilinged room were covered with various prints of German scenes, two framed copies of *Das Auge*, one announcing the declaration of war, the other—I assumed the first issue—proclaiming itself to be *Truthful news for Germans in our city*. A tear-off calendar with a woman in braids holding a stein of Geyer's beer hung not far from a portrait of Kaiser Wilhelm and his odd Viking-boat mustache. A mismatch of wood and metal file cabinets lined one wall.

It's only for an afternoon. Two days at most. If I felt it was worth coming back tomorrow, I could send word to the station house that I was ill. Was it madness to risk getting caught malingering and losing my job—which, whatever its faults, I had taken pains to secure—in order to spy on the producers of a foreign language newspaper that reached a few hundred gullible readers? Perhaps the death of Ruthie Jones had sent my judgment off the rails.

"I will leave you to work," Neumann said. "I have other business."

The moment he was gone, the tension I'd noticed in Johann relaxed. He sighed and sank into his squeaky chair. "That cold fish lowers the temperature of a room, doesn't he?"

"Herr Neumann? He seems a little distant, but kind."

Johann laughed bitterly. "You mean he's tall and handsome."

"No, I mean he gave me a job. And I'm grateful."

"Oh yes. I'm grateful, too," Johann said. "And I'm certainly grateful he hired *you*."

For the next hours, I was the traveler who'd washed up on Johann's deserted island. Anyone would think he'd spent decades alone in this cavernous pile of paper debris. He told me all about his family. He was from Pittsburgh. We shared a few laughs at the expense of our Pennsylvania hometowns, and then he went on to regale me with his spotty academic history, culminating with his leaving college early—"No one there appreciated originality"— from which I extrapolated that he'd flunked out. He produced a tin of cookies from his desk and talked about the great novel he'd begun to write but abandoned. Then he demonstrated a new dance called the bunny hug and showed me three card tricks.

No wonder Holger wanted to keep an eye on him. I barely managed to do any work, and Johann did even less. He viewed the role of editor mainly as a sort of impresario. Throughout the afternoon, several men stopped by, usually just to hand him sheets of paper and then shuffle out again, sometimes with as little as a few dollars in their pockets for their trouble. He would glance over the work and drop the handwritten pages into my basket to be typed.

Of these visitors, one man stood out. He was older, grizzled in appearance, and wore a boat captain's cap and black pea coat. Johann called him Skipper, but he said it almost laughingly. The man stayed just long enough for Johann to open one of the drawers of his desk with a key and hand over an envelope he had stored there. The Skipper took the envelope and left with very few words.

"Does that man have a boat?" I asked, pecking at the unfamiliar keys of the German typewriter.

"He lives on one. A houseboat, he calls it."

"Did he bring you pages for me to type?"

Johann's lips turned down. "Not today. He just wanted paying off."

That explained why the envelope had been in a locked drawer. But the envelope had appeared thick—how much money could Johann have owed him? Was this what Holger had wanted me to look out for? I tried to concentrate on my typing so I wouldn't appear too nosy.

The articles all seemed like boilerplate pro-German interpretations of war news, just as I'd seen in the paper the two times I'd had the misfortune to read a copy.

"On Friday our typesetter will arrive," Johann said after I handed him a typed page. "We can only afford to pay him for two days a week." He frowned at me. "Can *you* set type, by any chance?"

"No."

He shrugged fatalistically. "No—that would be too lucky. I do a little when I can, but when is there ever time?"

"I could learn. Is there a book about typesetting?" Perhaps I could acquire a skill while I was here. Something to fall back on when the NYPD found out what I was up to and fired me.

"No need to go berserk on your first day," he said.

Nevertheless, I went to investigate the shelves for information on typesetting, using my search as a pretext for more snooping. When I looked back a few moments later, Johann's head was on his desk blotter and he was snoring lightly. I glanced through all the cabinets, too, which were crammed with old newspapers, correspondence, and, in the case of one file drawer, food wrappers. I detected nothing suspicious.

Like Jack edging around the sleeping giant, I maneuvered around Johann's slumped-over body and pulled the handle of his desk's file drawer, the one he'd unlocked when Skipper came around. Before I knew what was happening, a hand darted out and clamped around my wrist.

"What are you doing?" The tone of his voice was sharper than it had been.

"I was hungry," I blurted out. "I was going to sneak another cookie."

His grip relaxed and he let go of my arm. "No need to sneak. And they're not in that drawer anyway." He smiled at me. "You're not very observant, are you?"

"I'm afraid not. I'm sorry, I should have asked, but I didn't want to disturb your nap."

"I wasn't napping," he said defensively. "I was thinking. Creative people have to think."

I'd never heard a man snore while awake, no matter how creative he was being, but I let that pass. He produced the cookie tin again and I took one. He grabbed two. "They're not bad once you get used to them, are they?"

They weren't Bernice's, but I ate mine gratefully as I leaned my hip on his desk. He looked me up and down. "How did you meet Holger?"

"In the line of a bratwurst cart by Pennsylvania Station. When he discovered I had no job, he insisted on buying my lunch."

He snapped his fingers. "Ziggy's! I *knew* I'd seen you somewhere."

"You've been there?" I asked, dreading what might come next.

"I was there just the other day." His eyes narrowed. "Were you alone?"

I made a show of thinking it over. "I might have been there with my cousin, Otto . . . but I don't remember seeing you. As you said, I'm not very observant."

"I was there with Holger. He must have gone back." He shook his head. "He's a fast worker."

"I'm surprised Holger's not in the war," I said, wanting to change the subject.

"He says he's doing something just as important here."

Something just as important. It made it seem as though Holger expected the fighting in Europe to be won by tactics carried out here in America. Could the opinion of *Das Auge* readers really be so vital?

By the time Johann informed me it was time to go home, I was unsure whether I would return the next day. As curious as the goings-on at *Das Auge* were, I'd seen nothing at all to connect either of these two to Ruthie's death. The workings of a propaganda paper weren't worth jeopardizing my future in the NYPD over.

"Good night," I told Johann.

"Night, Leisl." He winked at me as he locked the door. "It sure has been nice having someone else around."

"Thanks. Do you live nearby?" I asked.

He shook his head. "Downtown. You?"

"The same."

"Then we can go down together."

I didn't want Johann to know where I lived. "That would be nice, but I've got a little shopping to do close by."

He looked disappointed. "Of course. Good night."

I watched him walk toward the corner to catch the Second Avenue El before I turned in the opposite direction. I was far from home, though not so far from my aunt's. A long, brisk stroll would do me good, I decided, so I went to First Avenue to avoid walking in the shadow of the elevated train tracks. I liked the neighborhood with all its German shops, which reminded me of parts of Altoona. I'd have to bring Otto here.

Except that I couldn't do that now, without risking Johann or Holger seeing me. The drawback of living a double life.

At Eightieth, I leaned against a building on the side street to retie the lace on my boot and looked furtively around me for signs of Holger. Given his suspicious nature, I wouldn't have put it past him to have *me* watched. Convinced all was clear, I straightened again and continued on.

Within moments, a hand clamped down on my shoulder. "Stop right there."

My fight instinct kicked in. I pivoted back, ready to swing my pocketbook at the man if he didn't let go of me. He wore a dark blue double-breasted wool coat and a black hat, and had just a bit of red hair showing at his nape and on the sides. My heart thumped. Was this one of Cain's men? He had a square jaw and an unsmiling countenance, but something about his freckled face didn't fit my idea of a hoodlum. "What is this?" I asked.

"This is you coming with us, miss."

I drew back, shrugging my shoulder out from under that hand. "Why should I? You're not the police."

"No, we're not." A long black car pulled up to the curb and another man with a steely, determined expression got out and opened the back door. I recognized the man I'd let pass me in Ziggy's line, who'd been leaning against the lamppost while I talked to Neumann.

The red-haired man nodded at the car. "You'd better come along."

I dug my heels into the pavement. "I'm a policewoman. Officer Louise Faulk, NYPD."

"Got a badge?" he asked.

I didn't, as luck would have it. I'd been told always to carry it, but I'd gotten out of the habit when I was going around with Gerald. I hadn't wanted to risk his getting a glimpse of it and realizing I wasn't who I said I was. "Not on me. But if you'll just take me to my flat—"

He nudged me toward the car. "Right now we need to ask you a few questions."

"If I'm being arrested, I want to see *your* badge." I twisted away from him. "If you have one."

With the straightest of faces, he pulled out a silver badge in the shape of a star. The blue inlaid lettering read United States Secret Service. My insides twisted into a knot. What had I gotten myself into?

CHAPTER 18

"You have no right to kidnap me," I said.

The red-haired man sitting next to me smiled and looked at the driver. "Ever heard of a right to kidnap, Fred?"

"Nope. Kidnapping's a crime, last I heard."

They shared a laugh.

Wiseacres. "Now I know why Gallagher and Shean busted up," I said. "They must've heard you two comedy geniuses were on the horizon."

The red-headed one got a chuckle out of that. "Halloran and Luft—the great comic double act."

"Oh, you have names?" I asked.

My neighbor in the backseat nodded. "I'm Operative Halloran, and my partner is Operative Luft."

The driver looked back at me and smiled. As if we were all going on a picnic.

"Operatives?" I asked. "Don't you have ranks in the Secret Service?"

"Only higher up."

"Then how can I tell who's the senior officer in charge?"

"I am," they said in unison.

The car passed within a stone's throw of the NYPD's Centre Street Headquarters. "You can drop me off right there," I said, nodding toward the building with its great domed clock tower. "Captain Percival Smith works there—he interviewed me for my position last year."

"Captain Percival Smith," Halloran repeated, though the car didn't stop. Or even slow down. "Wonder what he'll make of all this."

I wondered too, and shuddered at the memory of the beak-nosed, irascible Captain Smith. Before getting the brass involved, it might be wise to ferret out how much trouble I was in. The car drove a dozen more blocks, to an office building on Chambers Street, not far from City Hall.

There, I was escorted to a room with shades drawn and left sitting on my own for an hour. I knew this tactic: letting the suspect stew alone in worry until they were ready to blurt out anything to regain their freedom. Though I understood what the Secret Service men were up to, the strategy was still effective. There was nothing in the room to focus on—just a picture of Woodrow Wilson hanging in the middle of an otherwise bare wall. I looked at the long, solemn face of the man who was pledging to keep us out of war. Nice thought, yet I had the unsettling feeling I was now under attack from my own country.

When next I saw Operative Halloran, I didn't even wait till he was seated before asking, "Why would the Secret Service be interested in me? Isn't your job to look into counterfeiters?"

"Usually," he said.

"And to guard the president." A terrible thought occurred to me. "Is someone at *Das Auge* planning to assassinate President Wilson?"

His eyes widened in alarm. "Are they?"

"I'm a police officer, not an expert on threats to the president. And the NYPD doesn't look lightly on their officers being abducted off the streets."

Halloran sat. Luft, joining us, remained silent and stayed on his feet, pacing from one side of the room to the other. I understood this, too, as an attempt to keep me off balance.

"The government of the United States of America doesn't look lightly on its citizens colluding with foreigners we suspect of conspiring against our nation," Halloran said.

My blood went cold. What he was describing sounded like treason. They executed traitors. "Y-you must be joking. I've done nothing except work for a day—not even an entire day—at a newspaper."

A reddish-brown eyebrow jutted upward. "You said you were a police officer."

I swallowed. "It's a little hard to explain . . ."

Nevertheless, I tried to make the situation as clear as I could, starting back with the discovery of Ruthie's body in the bathtub.

When I finished, the two men looked incredulous. "You took it upon yourself to investigate a man you believe—for reasons no one else credits—was responsible for the murder of a prostitute who actually committed suicide?" Luft asked.

"*Allegedly* committed suicide," I corrected.

"So none of your colleagues knew what you intended to do today?"

"No, because I wasn't sure it would amount to anything. I didn't expect the man in the bratwurst line would take me into his confidence, much less give me a job. Would you?"

"No," Halloran said, "but I don't have your figure."

Oh brother. "I didn't even tell my roommate where I was going today," I said, "and she's my best friend."

"Look here, Miss Faulk—"

"Officer Faulk," I corrected, still holding out hope that a police officer stood a better chance of surviving whatever was happening to me than a mere civilian would.

"All right, Officer Faulk. We want to believe you're not involved in any illegal activity. But you need to tell us what you know about the offices of *Das Auge*."

"Is Johann Schmidt plotting against our government?" I asked, unable to swallow back my curiosity. "What made you watch him? He must have been acting suspiciously."

"It's actually the newspaper itself we're curious about. We found a scrap of paper and the address of *Das Auge* on the person of a German sailor who was picked up with a forged document. We've been following Holger Neumann, the owner, until today, when we saw the two of you seemed to be meeting clandestinely."

"*I* met him clandestinely, because of my suspicions about the matter I just told you about," I said. "He knew nothing about me.

He bought me lunch and offered me a job—he wanted me to keep an eye on Johann Schmidt, who works at *Das Auge*."

I told them about the office, the locked drawer, and the furtive handovers of envelopes. "It might be Schmidt you should be watching. Even Neumann wants to keep an eye on him. For that matter, if you were curious, why didn't *you* send someone undercover?"

A cloud traveled across Halloran's expression. "We don't have the personnel right now to cover every report of suspicious activity. Anyway, we had no way of knowing the newspaper was looking for help."

"We'd only recently received information about Neumann," Luft added.

"If you don't have the men," I asked, "who's giving you information?"

"Up till now, our country hasn't had much use for international espionage," Halloran said. "The British, for instance, have more people in New York looking into suspicious activity among foreigners than we do."

I was not only surprised by the information, but astonished that he was sharing it with me. Was that a strategy, too?

How could I be sure they were telling me the truth about anything?

He saw my skepticism. "The Europeans are accustomed to spying on each other. We Americans have some catching up to do."

"What can you tell us about Schmidt?" Luft asked.

I relayed to him every detail I could remember from that day, right down to the bunny hug and the strange way Johann had reacted when I'd tried the wrong drawer to find the cookie tin. I again mentioned the envelope that had come from that door—the one he'd handed to the Skipper as "payment."

Halloran's eyes narrowed. "And that was the only drawer you came across that was locked?"

I nodded. "He could have anything in there. Dodgy financial records, or evidence of something else incriminating . . . or it might just be naughty pictures."

"Might be." Halloran stroked his chin.

His obvious suspicions stoked my own. Despite how nervous I

was, it was almost a joy to finally come across someone who was taking this situation as seriously as I did, albeit for different reasons. They were looking into document forgery, but I was trying to find a connection between passports and a suspicious death. "You need to be careful," I said, considering another angle. "Neumann wasn't too specific about what his suspicions of Johann were. He might even think Johann's working for you."

Halloran looked doubtful. "Nothing we've done so far should have drawn anyone's attention."

"Then it would be unwise to take any action that would put them even more on guard." At his questioning look, I elaborated. "For instance, if a woman who worked at the offices of *Das Auge* for a day were to suddenly disappear, wouldn't that raise suspicions?"

By the time help arrived, I was fairly certain I'd won over Halloran. I at least felt the firing squad, electric chair, or hangman's noose might be avoided. On the other hand, I had time to float plenty of doubts about my future in the NYPD. My outlook became even gloomier when the door opened and Captain Percival Smith appeared, looking more imperious and irritable than ever. I hadn't seen him since my initial interview after passing the police exam. I shot to my feet.

Percival Smith was the tallest man in the room, slender and straight with an aristocratic way of carrying himself. His iron-gray hair was still thick, and he sported a full mustache under his beaky nose. Stopping just inside the door, he squinted at me for a moment.

"I remember you." He pushed his spectacles up to the bridge of his nose. "You're the one who got into that mess at the Woolworth Building last year."

"Yes, sir," I said, standing rigidly at attention. "Officer Louise Faulk."

"I had my doubts about you—obviously I was right. Good policewomen don't end up being hauled in by the Secret Service," the captain said in clipped tones. "We've never even had a police*man* brought here." He narrowed his eyes on me. "You'd better have a good excuse for this."

Halloran came forward. "Officer Faulk explained the circumstances to me, Captain, and if her story is all true, we think there is a way we could use her."

My knees practically went noodly with relief, until Smith voiced his reply.

"That's fortunate. Officer Faulk might soon be at liberty to work for you on a permanent basis."

I winced . . . although the word *might* did allow for some hope. I started to speak, but Smith raised his hand, palm out, to stop me, like a traffic cop. "When I want to hear from you, Faulk, I'll ask you a direct question."

He then demanded Halloran go over the afternoon's events—starting with the account of my day, my observations, right through to the moment they picked me up. I could have told him what he wanted to know much more succinctly, but Captain Smith was old-fashioned, and would always listen to a higher rank before a lower one, and to a man before a woman. And of course Operatives Halloran and Luft were no longer the flippant jokesters they'd been with me. I bit my tongue, seethed, and worried.

On one hand, things didn't look good for me. But I felt energized by the fact that Halloran had said he could use me. How?

When Halloran was done, Smith finally turned back to me.

"So, Officer Faulk, you undertook this little investigation on your own, without telling any of your colleagues at your precinct."

"Yes, sir."

"I don't like independence in an officer."

"It's fortunate for us that she found trouble," Halloran interrupted. "As long as she's at *Das Auge*, what she discovers there might be of use to us. We would like someone to trace the people who come and go there, and see if there is a subversive group congregating at those offices, or if any codes are being worked into the paper. If we can keep her there with the NYPD's blessing, so much the better."

"How long would this operation last?" Captain Smith asked.

"With her watching from inside the newspaper, a week or less should be sufficient to let us know if there's anything we should be concerned with."

Smith frowned over steepled fingertips. "We'll have to think of an excuse for taking her out of Thirtieth Street."

I couldn't hold my tongue any longer. "I could be escorting a female prisoner to Albion Prison." The fictional trip upstate would explain a few days' absence.

Percival Smith's bushy iron-gray brows climbed into his forehead, as if a chair had turned sentient and piped up with a suggestion. I worried I was about to be verbally slapped down, but he said, "Well, as long as you're offering ideas out of turn, at least they're sensible ones."

The comment was as close to a compliment from him as I would likely ever receive.

The men conferred on strategy. If I hadn't been so elated at the prospect of an interesting assignment before me, it would've been more irksome to hear myself talked about as if I were a piece on a chessboard. But I was too focused on the job ahead to get angry. In fact, it was hard not to fall to my knees in relief. Not only had I escaped a charge of treason, I was going to be placed into an official secret assignment. With the NYPD's blessing.

CHAPTER 19

The next morning, a remade Johann greeted me with kuchen he'd bought at the bakery down the street. "To celebrate your second day."

The stark difference between Johann today and the Johann of yesterday? Grooming. His shirt and collar were white, relatively unstained, and stiff with starch, and his coat and pants appeared to have been pressed. A trip to the barber had also occurred since I'd seen him last. Gone was the whiskery shadow on his jaw and cheeks, and his hair was trimmed and slicked back. The pungent odor of witch hazel with an undercurrent of pine—that fresh-from-the-barber-chair olfactory hallmark—wafted my way when he moved closer.

"You smell nice," I said.

He stuffed an oversized piece of kuchen into his mouth to cover his self-consciousness. His full cheeks made him look like a well-fed squirrel. "Passed by a barber's this morning," he said through his mouthful.

Passed by a barber, passed by a bakery. This couldn't be all a co-incidence.

I bit into a piece of the cake. Crumbly, buttery, and drizzled with sugar over the top. Not my usual breakfast, but who was complaining? "Delicious. Thank you."

Another difference was that Johann wasn't quite as gregarious as he'd been the day before. I wondered if he'd simply run out of things to talk about and show me. I did my best to accomplish the tasks at hand. I typed, cleaned, rearranged piles of papers. Again, various people appeared, dropped off stories, and left, and I discreetly logged names, times, and descriptions. I kept my eyes open for anything shady going on, for money changing hands, and most of all, for the Skipper to come back. This evening I would copy my list of observations for Operative Halloran, whom I would meet the evenings following my every-other-morning tête-à-têtes with Holger Neumann.

I paid close attention to the articles I was given to type. The intention of *Das Auge* was to digest the news, especially the European war news, down to nuggets of indignation and spit it out in headlines for their readership. Interspersed with OUTRAGES! happening on the European front and to German ships at sea were the INJUSTICES! taking place right here in New York. I skimmed recent issues to see if there was any mention of a German sailor held for forged documents. There wasn't, but there was plenty of anger directed at the supposedly neutral Wilson, who evidently was hatching plans to funnel backdoor aid to the allies.

Nowhere could I detect a coded message. But how would I? I had no background in that type of investigation. In this, I was out of my depth.

The few times I found myself alone in the office; those moments when Johann left for any reason, I hurried to the locked drawer. It remained locked, always. I searched everywhere for a key, but Johann must have kept it on his person. Why hadn't I paid more attention when the pickpockets and lock pickers in my jail talked about their trade? Without those skills, the best I could hope for would be to pry the drawer open.

Once, while rifling through the top drawer of Johann's desk, I ran across a hefty brass letter opener that would work very well as a lever. I needed to find a stretch of time when I could be certain of having the office to myself. A busted lock would be hard to disguise, but if I found vital evidence in the drawer, at that point I could walk out of *Das Auge* and never return.

On the other hand, if I *didn't* find evidence, that would put me in a tricky spot. I doubted my Secret Service overseers would want me to abandon my post with nothing to show for myself, especially if I was going to leave anything suspicious in my wake, like a drawer that had been pried open. Times like these, I wished for a partner in spying, or even someone to confide in, as I used to confide in Muldoon . . . before he'd insulted me and Callie. The memory of that encounter still stung. I felt very much on my own.

Holger didn't come by the *Das Auge* offices. His absence fueled my suspicion that Johann was actually at the bottom of whatever subversive activity the Secret Service suspected was taking place at the newspaper.

I lured Johann out to lunch at the local German eatery, a low-ceilinged room with timbered rafters, heavily textured plaster walls, and amber lighting to finish off the Olde World effect. The menu was suitably heavy on spaetzle, schnitzel, and cabbage. "This reminds me of my Aunt Sonja's," I said, taking a deep breath. "It's almost enough to make me homesick."

"I'm never homesick." He spoke so adamantly that it made me doubt him. "I have a good life here."

"You must have fallen into happy circumstances. Do you have a girlfriend?"

He blinked. "No. I thought you knew that."

"I just assume every man in this city is living the life of Don Juan. I read so many stories in the papers."

"And you believe them?" He laughed. "You've seen now who writes for the papers."

"Such interesting characters."

He took a drink of beer. "Not particularly. Just people who understand how to write what we'll print."

"What about the Skipper?" I asked.

"He's the least interesting of all."

He looked more interested in the bread and butter than talking about *Das Auge*'s contributors, so I asked, "What do you do in your free time?"

He considered the question longer than necessary, as if weighing how truthfully to answer. "I draw."

I hadn't expected this. "You're an artist?"

"Not a serious one."

"Do you do portraits?" I asked.

"Sometimes."

"Could you draw one of me?" I asked. "I'd love to have a picture to send to my cousins. Maybe I could visit your rooms sometime."

Interest and anxiety filled his eyes. "Truly?"

"Of course."

By the time we'd devoured the food on our plates, I'd made a date to meet him at his flat the following evening. I had to invent an excuse why I couldn't simply accompany him home directly from work, since I was supposed to meet with Operative Halloran at that time. Johann seemed pleased, and made so bold as to take my arm as we hurried back to the office. A peek into Johann's home life would be invaluable. A man could hide a great deal at the office, but at home a person tended to relax his guard.

The next morning I left home early and was outside Pennsylvania Station a good ten minutes before Holger's car drew up to the curb. He beckoned me inside. "I will drive you uptown. That way we can talk."

I stepped into the car and settled on the velvet upholstery. "I'm afraid I don't have anything much to report." His initial frown of displeasure disappeared as I gave him my list of people who had been to the office, how long they had stayed, and what had passed between them and Johann. My list might have lacked anything noteworthy, but it was exhaustive.

"The only suspicious thing I've seen is whatever passed between Johann and the man called the Skipper," I said.

Holger sniffed as if a bad odor had wafted in. "I wouldn't worry too much about him."

"Don't you want to know what was in the envelope?"

"I have a strong guess," he said.

"Money?" I asked.

He smiled patiently at me. "Just keep watching, fräulein. You are doing very well."

"Johann seems nice. I don't want to get him in trouble, but why not just fire him if you suspect him of something underhanded? There are lots of young men in this city who could do his job, aren't there?"

"Johann cares about our cause."

Did he? I hadn't seen much evidence of that.

Holger continued, "He also knows . . . a great deal."

"About the office, you mean?"

"Yes. Exactly. But I have put much faith in one man at *Das Auge*. I want to make certain that faith is not being exploited." We pulled up to the curb a block from the offices. "I will let you out here."

I understood his intention in letting me off out of sight of the *Das Auge* offices. He didn't want Johann to see him dropping me off at the office, early in the morning.

The moment I walked into the offices, it was clear the atmosphere had shifted. I shook some flurries off my hat and coat and hung them up, then looked over at Johann, who was immersed in that morning's copy of *The Sun*.

"Anything happening?" I asked.

"The Russians are retreating toward Moscow."

It took me a moment too long to remember how Leisl Frobisher would react. "More good news. Will you write that story?"

He ate a chunk of kuchen. He had two pieces, but this morning he wasn't sharing. "Probably," he said in a clipped, resentful voice. "I do work very hard here, you know."

"Of course." I sat down at my desk and began typing an article. "German Navy Victorious in North Atlantic!" My stomach felt queasy as I pecked out the feverish excitement over one hundred and thirty-seven Allied sailors meeting their deaths in the frigid waters. Of course, the Germans would suffer the same fate if they lost these battles, but . . .

Maybe Holger and Johann were wrong about *Das Auge*. The more exposure I had to their propaganda, the more I sympathized with the other side.

The morning dragged. Tension radiated from Johann's desk, and I couldn't account for it.

At eleven o'clock I looked up as Johann put on his coat and then twined a long scarf around his neck. Flurries floated through the air outside our window. "I think I'll go to the Hofbräuhaus. I have a few friends who often meet me there."

No invitation was extended to me.

He donned his hat and was out the door. As soon as he disappeared from sight, I hopped out of my chair and hurried over to his desk. The top drawer, at least, was still unlocked. I seized the letter opener and began to work on the locked drawer on the right. There was barely enough room for me to wedge the tip of the letter opener between the sliver of space where the top of the drawer met the desktop. I needed to work the brass shiv in farther to give myself more leverage. I pushed, moving the letter opener back and forth, hoping to force it in so I could pry the lock open.

My progress was slow. I didn't want to damage the wood so obviously that Johann would guess what I'd been up to. Finally, I was able to work the letter opener in about half its length. Now all I had to do was keep tugging on the opener's handle and hope the movement forced the locking mechanism to give. I sent up a prayer that I'd find something in that drawer. Because the more I worked the letter opener back and forth, the more obvious it became that someone had been tampering with the wood above the lock, which was indented and chipped.

Though the office was kept chilly, I was sweating from both effort and nerves. Pushing gently wasn't getting me very far. I decided to really throw some force behind it and pushed hard. Finally, something happened: The letter opener bent from the fulcrum into a perfect V. A victory of oak over brass.

"Damn," I muttered.

And that was before I heard the building's front door open and close.

My heart pounded so hard it almost made me feel as if I were vibrating. Footsteps came down the hall toward our door as I yanked frantically to free the letter opener from its trapped position. Johann whistled tunelessly out in the hallway as I gave a last mighty tug. When the letter opener popped free, I was launched onto my backside, on the floor.

The door opened.

I thrust the opener into the nearest wastebasket. It hadn't been emptied recently, so I was relieved the brass sank into the mound of wadded paper. I'd have to retrieve it later. For now, my problem was explaining why I was on the floor to Johann, who crossed the threshold and gaped at me sprawled there.

"What happened to you?" he asked.

"I . . . slipped."

He surveyed my surroundings for any object I might have fallen over. "Did you trip over your own feet?"

"Are you going to make me go through the humiliation of explaining?" I asked as I accepted his offer of a hand up. "I was practicing the steps of that silly dance you taught me."

"You mean you were bunny hugging in here all on your ownsome?" To my relief, he laughed.

" 'He jests at scars that never felt a wound.' My shoes are almost new, and the soles are still slick."

I hoped he wouldn't check on that last detail too closely, and heavens be praised, he didn't. He was all concern. "You didn't hurt yourself, did you?" he asked, still holding on to my hand.

"Just my pride," I said, smiling at him.

For a second, he smiled back, but then he dropped my hand and backed up a step. "I'm apt to trip over my own feet, too. Nothing to be embarrassed about—at least not with me."

"Didn't you find any of your friends?" I asked, tugging my hand away from his.

"No, I just got a sausage on a roll and came back." He took off his coat and tossed it on his chair. Then he hiked his hip onto his desktop—just above the place where the letter opener had damaged the desk drawer, I was happy to see. Unwrapping his lunch, he said, "You don't expect *Holger* to bunny hug with you, do you?"

It was a startling question, especially when I tried to envision the high-collared, unsmiling German giving in to the latest dance craze. "No. Why would I?"

"You don't have to lie to me, Leisl. I saw you with him."

"With Holger? When?"

"This morning. Early. Getting out of his car." He put heavy, equal emphasis on each bit of evidence, and I could tell at once the sordid impression he'd received. So that accounted for his strange behavior this morning.

"He saw me walking and offered me a ride," I explained.

"And let you out a block from work?" He shook his head in disbelief. "I know it's not my business, Leisl, but you can't say that you really care for him."

"You've got it all wrong," I insisted. "But why couldn't a

woman care for him? He's been generous with me. Not to mention, he's handsome."

The response caused him to put his wax-paper wrapped food aside. "Handsome, with a rancid heart."

His bitter words took me aback. But emotion was a good thing if it made him reveal a little of his feelings about what went on here.

"I haven't seen anything rancid about him."

"He's . . ." He looked at me directly. "He's not kind, Leisl."

"He plucked me off the street and gave me this job."

"Sure, but if you don't do what he wants—"

His words broke off, and a tense silence rent the air.

"If I don't do what he wants . . . ?"

He picked up his sandwich again. "Just watch yourself. He's not—"

The door opened, and the Skipper walked in. Frustration filled me. Johann had been on the verge of divulging something interesting. Now his attention pivoted to the old man in the cap.

"Nothing today," Johann told him.

"Ah, a wasted trip, then." He caught my eye and removed his cap. His scalp was mostly bald with a dusting of gray bristles. Did I detect suspicion in his gaze? "As I walked in, you were having a conversation. Very intimate, I would have guessed."

Johann looked alarmed. "You're all wet. I was just having lunch, is all." His denial didn't cover the splotches of red that appeared in his cheeks, though, and he lowered his gaze. To my dismay, he was looking at the indentations the letter opener had made against the wood of the drawer. He ran his finger along it.

I jumped out of my chair. "Would you like something hot to drink?" I asked the Skipper. "It's so chilly out, and snowing."

The man scoffed. "This? This is nothing." His lightly accented voice reminded me of relatives back home. "You young people are spoiled. I moved here in the winter of eighty-eight."

Johann, who'd taken up his food again, chewed through a half laugh and winked at me. "Here comes the blizzard story."

The Skipper scowled at him. "You laugh? Fifty inches of snow, delivered in a wind like a hurricane. Snow drifts reached the second stories of buildings and people trapped on elevated trains had to be rescued with ladders. Overhead wires snapped and fell, making it treacherous to clear snow. Scores of people froze to death. Sure, laugh at the hardships of the past—and then howl in outrage when bad things happen in your lifetime." His sneer took in both of us. "Do you expect always to be comfortable, that tragedy will not touch you? I envy your ignorance. And I pity you for what you'll learn before too long."

I wouldn't have been surprised if he'd spat on us in disgust. At least the Skipper's diatribe had turned my coworker's attention away from the drawer, though.

"Who said anything about being comfortable?" Johann's voice arced up defensively. "I do nothing but look over articles about war, for Pete's sake."

"That's right. You sit on your fat duff *reading* about war. No one's going to pin a medal on you for that."

Johann's face went red. "My country's not at war."

For a moment I thought the old man might spontaneously combust. "Isn't it? Wilson's got Germany's ships in America's harbors, German sailors marooned in her ports. And are they blockading the British? Of course not. How is choosing sides like that not considered being at war?"

"That's what *Das Auge's* telling the people," Johann said. "The work I'm doing here is just as important as a soldier's."

"Exactly," I piped up loyally. "The pen is mightier than the sword."

The man's mouth turned down in a sour frown. "Not when the bullets start flying."

After the old man stumped out, Johann sagged in his chair in relief. "What's eating him?"

I went back to my typewriter. "I guess anyone who looks at the situation as closely as you and he do every day must feel frustrated about the war."

"Sure, but why take it out on me? I don't understand these people sometimes."

These people. Was Johann experiencing friction with Holger and his associates?

I pecked at a few keys—wishing I hadn't forgotten my German

spelling from school. I was prone to leaving out umlauts, or worse, putting them in where they weren't needed, like two eyeballs staring pointlessly back at me.

"What does the Skipper do, exactly?" I asked.

Johann stared through me as if he weren't actually seeing me. A few seconds ticked by before he roused himself to answer. "He just . . . runs errands." He shrugged. "You could ask Holger about him, but I doubt you'd get a straight answer."

"So many mysteries," I said.

Johann, evidently still smarting over his interchange with the Skipper, let out a huff. "Imagine that old man telling me I wasn't doing anything. He's got a crust."

"Well, so might you if you'd lived through the Blizzard of Eighty-Eight." I tried to imitate the old man's accented, dramatically quavering voice when he'd talked about the blizzard.

Johann laughed, and for a moment our camaraderie fell back in place. In the next instant, though, any trace of a smile disappeared and he resumed our prior discussion. "You don't have to step out with Holger just because you're grateful to him, Leisl."

What was it about my relationship to Holger that bothered him? "Anyone would think the two of you weren't friends."

"Friends!" He snorted. "I should say not. This is his newspaper, that's all. As for the rest . . ."

I wasn't about to let him leave that thought dangling. "The rest of what?"

"Nothing," he answered quickly. "Only I don't like the way he deals with people."

"Why?"

He opened his mouth to speak, then shook his head.

I don't like the way he deals with people. What did that mean? Did he realize Holger was the type who hired people to spy on his employees, or was something worse going on?

I blinked in my best approximation of dewy-eyed confusion. "Now *you're* being very mysterious."

"You have to be, around here." His lips quirked self-deprecatingly. "He gave me my job, too. Do you think positions like this are easy to come by?"

"I know they're not," I said. "I've had a hard enough time finding anything."

"Then stop asking questions."

I smiled, trying to lighten the mood. "Maybe you'll tell me tonight, when you're sketching me."

He wadded up his waxed-paper wrapper. Without meeting my eye, he said, "I forgot. Something came up. Maybe we can meet some other time."

"Of course," I said, but I could tell that "some other time" meant never.

He was convinced I was Holger's girl, so he was going to steer clear of any intimate situation between us. There seemed to be a paranoia about this beyond simply not wanting to offend his employer.

My objective for the next day, I decided, was to worm my way back into his good graces. Whatever he knew about Holger, I needed to wheedle it out of him by any means necessary.

CHAPTER 20

It was only a week before Christmas, but no one would have guessed by looking at our apartment. It seemed strange, especially in light of last Christmas, when we'd taken such joy in our little tree and tucking our wrapped gifts beneath it. The tree had reminded us of the best moments of our childhoods, which Callie and I both wanted to remember as a little happier than they actually were. I missed the camaraderie of those days last December, that feeling of having survived a turbulent year. We'd felt invincible, indivisible.

Now . . . I didn't know. The dry, undecorated tree sagged in its corner. Callie and I hadn't had a good chin-wag after our argument about Anna Muldoon, and neither of us had mentioned plans for celebrating Christmas. The only packages in evidence were bundles for Belgium—and even Callie's enthusiasm for that worthy cause seemed to have waned a little since Teddy left.

When I emerged from my room the next morning, Callie was at the table, dressed smartly in a fitted, dark blue rough silk dress. A mug of coffee sat before her.

"Oh good," she said, not looking up from the latest issue of *Motion Picture News*. "I was hoping to get a chance to talk to you." Her voice sounded tense.

"What about?" Still barely awake, I wasn't ready for another argument.

"I have an audition this morning."

I let out a breath. Her tone had led me to expect something terrible. "Didn't you say Christmas is a slow time for theatrical casting?"

"A road tour needs a replacement," she explained. "The second lead in a comedy bit had her appendix go out on her in Omaha. If I'm lucky, I'll catch up to them in St. Louis."

Missouri? *A bit?* "Vaudeville?"

The surprise in my voice registered in her ear as disdain, if her stiff-backed reaction was any indication. "Listen to you, Miss Hoity-Toity, the theater snob."

"I thought you didn't want to do vaudeville."

"Maybe I did say something like that a year or so ago, but that was when my career felt like it was taking off like a shooting star. I forgot that shooting stars are in the process of flaming out."

"You're not flaming out," I protested. "Is this because Alfred Sheldrake took a shine to Anna? There must be other directors who'd jump at the chance to have you work for them. It's not as if you're desperate."

"Tell that to the Calumet Savings Bank." She nodded toward the kitchen. We kept our housekeeping money in an old Calumet baking powder tin. Until recently, the balance in the tin had been getting healthier, but I hadn't checked it lately.

"If you need money..." Goodness knows she'd floated me often enough.

"I'm not going to take your cash when I've got a perfectly good way to make some on my own. There's nothing wrong with vaudeville. Ethel Barrymore's toured the circuit."

The exceptional Miss Barrymore. She did pictures... toured in vaudeville... what next? A trapeze act for the Ringling Brothers?

"You'll be gone for months," I said, sinking into a chair.

She set her magazine aside. "I'll send postcards."

The look in her eyes belied her glib answer. I'd lived with Callie almost as long as I'd been in New York. She was my best friend, my confidante, my housemate. She told me the truth when I didn't want to hear it, and had picked me up during moments when I was at my lowest. Yes, we had our disagreements, but she was the closest I'd ever come to having a sister. The thought of her going away left me bereft.

"You know I'm rooting for you to get it, if that's what you want." This was true, but I felt sore at heart already, and she was still sitting right in front of me.

"Don't break out the mourning crepe yet. I haven't even auditioned. If I do get it, I'll miss you and everybody here, but I can't deny I won't mind getting out of town for a bit now that—"

She didn't have to finish. *Now that Teddy's gone.* "Besides," she went on, "you're so busy all the time with your police work, you probably won't even notice I'm gone."

"You can't seriously believe that. Who will I talk to, and celebrate the holiday with?" I gave her shoe a nudge with my foot. "Who will give me advice on fashion?"

She smiled. "I'll pin instructions to all your wardrobe items before I leave. And at least you have your uniform to fall back on."

"Not today. I was going to ask to borrow something to make me alluring to my coworker on the newspaper."

She blinked in confusion. "What newspaper?"

Of course—she didn't know what I'd been up to in the past two days. Now I filled her in about being yanked off the street by Secret Service operatives, and my clandestine assignment for the government. The longer I spoke, the wider her eyes grew.

"Louise, you're crazy. These people sound dangerous."

"The Germans?"

"All of them. And if you ask me, that fellow Johann was trying to warn you about something. Remember, these are men you suspect of having something to do with Ruthie's death."

"I haven't forgotten. But I don't have any proof. I'm beginning to think there isn't any."

"What does Muldoon think about it?"

"He doesn't know." I had to give Callie an update on my falling out with him too, although I left out the unflattering things he'd said about her and actresses in general.

Astonishment was written all over her face. "And you didn't tell me any of this?"

"We've both been busy. But I'm glad to have told you now, especially about my work. If I disappear, you'll know it's in service to my country."

"Sounds like you were drafted." A blond eyebrow arched. "Just how far are you willing to go on your charm offensive against this fellow Johann?"

"Nothing too outrageous. He's already acting like a wounded lover. A flash of ankle should do."

She rolled her eyes. "You're working as a government spy, not playacting in a hoary old Clyde Fitch drama."

"I'm still me, not Salome of the Secret Service."

"All right, but you need something distinctive—but subtle—to catch Johann's attention." She thought for a moment. "This might be a job for Beaux Rêves."

"What's that?"

"Perfume. Teddy gave it to me."

"I couldn't—"

She waved away my objection before I could voice it. "You're not going to take a bath in it. Just dab on enough so he'll get a good whiff. It's not a magic potion, mind. You'll have to do the rest."

She was so good at thinking of things like this. "Maybe *you* should be working for the Secret Service."

She laughed as she stood. "I'd rather not have strange men snatching me off dark streets, thank you very much."

"It's been pretty dull at the paper so far."

"From what you're telling me, it's about to get more lively." She looked me over. I was still in my bathrobe and slippers. "You'll need to wear something flashier than usual. Something to catch his eye. You should look through my wardrobe for something—anything but my new crimson velvet," she added quickly. "And maybe an accessory that lets him know that you wanted to stand out today."

Callie helped me sort through her wardrobe. As an eye-catcher, she picked out a stole she'd found in the bag I'd brought from Ruthie's. It was in surprisingly good shape, which made me suspect it had been acquired shortly before Ruthie's death. The fur was of undetermined origin—a grayish brown, not as soft as rabbit, but certainly nothing dear like mink.

"Do they make stoles of woodchucks?" she wondered aloud as she draped it around my shoulders.

"I'm not sure." I modeled it over my robe. "What do you think?"

"It'll snap up your coat a little. And if you're smart, you'll get Johann to help you with that sticky clasp."

I stood before her bureau mirror to see how it looked. Not bad. It was fitting that I'd be wearing Ruthie's stole, since it was looking into her death that had set me on this path. "Your wardrobe advice always gives me confidence."

"Just don't be too confident. Even jolly, pudgy fellows can turn wolf when they sense easy prey."

"I can handle Johann."

"That declaration has the ring of famous last words," Callie said.

Which was another reason I dreaded Callie's going away. She was usually right about men.

An hour later, doused in Beaux Rêves and bedecked in the woodchuck stole, I swanned into the office of *Das Auge*. Luck was with me. Johann looked up, and from his lingering glance I could tell he noticed the care I'd taken with my appearance.

"Oh bother," I said, following Callie's script as I stood by the coatrack. "I never can get the hang of this clasp . . ."

He bolted out of his chair. "Let me help."

Within seconds, he was standing before me, breathing in a gulp of Beaux Rêves–scented air. I could almost tell the second the perfume hit his brain.

"You must think I'm a ninny, unable to dress myself." I smiled. "Or undress myself, as the case may be."

"I'm good at this—I mean, I'm good at clasps and things. Not undressing women." His red face would have given a boiled lobster a run for its money.

"I knew what you meant." I stepped closer, tilting my torso closer to his chest and angling my neck so he could have better access to the clasp.

He lifted his hands to it, squinting in concentration. "It's just a little—"

For a moment I didn't know what had stopped him. The memory of Holger? Had I overdone the perfume? Was the clasp truly a tricky one?

Johann was staring at the stole almost as if he feared the poor creature that had given up its life for it would come back to life and bite him. Slowly, his gaze traveled up to mine. The alarm written across his face reminded me of Gerald when he'd seen Eddie.

"That"—he made a gesture toward the stole—"is yours?"

"It is now. I bought it off a peddler." I studied his face. "Is something wrong?"

He swallowed so hard his Adam's apple hurdled over his collar. "It looks familiar."

I glanced down at the stole, in part to disguise my nervous reaction. He'd seen it before—on Ruthie?

He backed away as if I were about to put a curse on him. "I'm sorry," he said, too quickly. "It's just—I'm very busy this morning."

I smiled as though I saw nothing amiss, even though my nerves were jangling as much as his appeared to be. The only reason I could see for his being discombobulated by Ruthie's stole was if he had been involved in her death. And now I was alone with him. Instinct screamed at me to drop everything and run. Curiosity—and my duty to the assignment I'd accepted—made me take up my usual post at the typewriter desk.

Not long after I arrived, Johann wrote a note and flagged down a boy off the street to deliver the message for him. Some of my colleagues at the precinct referred to these children as guttersnipes—homeless boys who scraped by on whatever work came their way, or by thievery. Their other occupation was dodging truancy officers and social workers. Unfortunately, I missed where—and to whom—the message was going. Johann was being secretive.

The thread of tension in the office remained all day, unalleviated by Johann's usual jokes or running discursive monologues. My plan to get Johann to open up had backfired, but the fact that he'd reacted so strongly to the sight of Ruthie's stole was useful in itself. Useful, and worrying.

In the afternoon, a man—he looked more like a bum than a journalist, even *Das Auge*'s caliber of journalist—came by and handed Johann a much-used envelope that went immediately into the mystery drawer. Johann looked over, catching me as I watched him lock it. I glanced away. Our visitor was still standing by the door, and Johann pulled money out of his wallet and handed it over: two ten-dollar bills. Twenty dollars for any of the scribblings that went into *Das Auge* was at least ten dollars too much.

And why would an article need to be under lock and key?

By the time the man left, I was so curious I was about to levitate out of my chair. I stood, stretching out my tired back muscles. A year in the police force had made me forget how much of a strain it could be to sit hovered over a typewriter all day.

"Would you like me to type that?" I asked Johann.

He startled as if he'd forgotten I was there. Then he followed my gaze to the drawer, his jaw hanging open indecisively. "It's . . . not an article."

"Oh, is it a notice or some other type of column? You certainly paid him handsomely for it."

He remained silent longer than seemed necessary. "To be honest, that old fellow's just some sad-sack acquaintance of Holger's. I think he was a professor in the old country. Now he writes wretched poetry, and Holger gives me money to pay him for it. Pays him far too much, as you said."

"It never appears in *Das Auge?*"

He shook his head.

"And the man never notices?"

"Why should he care? He gets paid."

If I hadn't already known Johann was lying, I certainly did now. During the year I'd worked in publishing, I'd never met an author who didn't care about seeing their words on the printed page at least as much as they cared about money. And authors cared about money a lot.

Johann spent the next hour shifting in his chair, filling his desk blotter with doodles, and checking his watch. Finally, he stood and headed for the coatrack. "I'm going to have to leave for an hour or so."

His manner was definitely strained, and he was avoiding my gaze again. "Where are you going?" I asked.

"I, um, just need to talk to a few of our advertisers about money they owe."

"I'll bet." When he drew back, clearly wondering what my comment meant, I added, "If we're handing bad poets twenty dollars, it's no wonder we need to squeeze the advertisers to pay up."

Part of me was glad he was going out. I suspected the errand was related to whatever was in that locked drawer, and that whatever was in there had something to do with either Ruthie's death or the forgery crimes that the Secret Service was interested in. I didn't have permission to bow out of the operation, but I itched to crack that lock as soon as Johann was out the door.

As things turned out, that itch would go forever unscratched. Before leaving, Johann doubled back to his desk, opened the drawer, and removed the envelope there, tucking it into a pocket inside his coat. He then relocked the drawer—though I'd seen it was empty—and headed out with an overly jaunty wave.

On impulse, I leapt from my chair, grabbed my coat off the rack, and set off after him. If I couldn't get my hands on any evidence, I at least wanted to see where Johann took it. That story about advertisers was hogwash.

I kept myself a quarter block behind Johann on the avenue, but then he turned left and headed east, forcing me to fall back more. He zigzagged again at First and continued on, barely seeming to look where he was going. Wherever he was headed, he knew the way quite well. At Seventy-Ninth he walked another long block, crossed Avenue A, and then cut down to a walkway that led toward the water. The land wasn't exactly park—but it was dotted with scrub and various makeshift buildings that were little more than shacks. Behind us, where Avenues A and B intersected, a small factory belched acrid smoke into the evening air, sending up a dark plume against the winter clouds. I'd never been at this spot next to the East River. It was a whole new world—and a very different world from the one just a block away, where a fine new apartment house, in the mold of those of Sutton Place to the south, was under construction.

A gravel path led to a short pier—not like the colossal piers at the south of Manhattan and up the island's west side, where great steamships, freighters, and cruisers slipped in and out daily, guided back out to sea by the bulldog-like tugboats. This waterfront was a more ramshackle affair, as were the vessels moored to the pier: a barge, a rowboat, and a top-heavy-looking houseboat.

I stopped dockside, lingering in the shadow of a building and looking out at Blackwell's Island just across the water. The lights of a few of the island's institutional buildings were just beginning to stand out in the early twilight. This did not feel like a safe place. The ground was littered with discarded liquor bottles, and a metal barrel that appeared to have been used as a makeshift stove stood a few feet away. Cold wind sliced down the river, causing water to slap against whatever boats were tied nearby, their riggings creating a percussive backdrop for all the other city sounds around us—traffic and gulls and a metallic tattoo coming out of the factory. Somewhere on the water, a ship's horn lowed.

Johann hurried down the rickety pier toward the houseboat. It was a queer vessel, a big boat hull sitting low in the water, with a squared-off shingled structure on its deck. I could make out a door leading to what must have been the cabin, although it was partially obscured by a clothes wire running from one corner to the bow. Shirts, pants, and a pair of red long johns flapped in the cold wind.

I knew immediately whom he was meeting—the Skipper—but I needed to verify it with my own eyes. Furtively, I moved around to get a better view, unobstructed by long underwear. From a different vantage, I was able to make out the lettering on the side of the ship's hull: *Silver Swan.*

That name had slipped my mind for days. Now I gaped in disbelief. This cobbled-together heap was the *Silver Swan* I'd been hunting for? It looked more like a half-dead goose. In a way, though, that absurdity intrigued me. The houseboat's unremarkable appearance was hiding something significant, I was sure of that.

My brain was on fire. First there had been Johann's alarm at Ruthie's stole. Now the name she'd scrawled on a piece of paper and tucked into the passports was right before me. What was Johann up to?

He called out and the old Skipper appeared, pushing aside a pair of pants that blocked the door to the hold. Johann reached into his coat and produced the envelope he'd taken from his locked drawer. It passed into the older man's possession, and the two men continued talking. I tried to figure out what this meant—Johann and the Skipper made regular exchanges of something other "contributors" brought into *Das Auge*. Passports? Even given a black market in passports, it was hard to believe they would have enough value to involve so many people. And how did Ruthie's death tie in?

I needed to get a note to Operatives Halloran and Luft, and maybe to Captain Smith. I was sure they were right about the criminal activity going on at *Das Auge*, but now I knew it'd had something to do with Ruthie. She'd known about this place, and she'd been killed. By Johann?

Before either man had the opportunity to turn and see me, I did an about-face and retraced my footsteps. I wanted to get back to *Das Auge* well ahead of Johann. Perhaps I could even gather my things and clear out for good before he got back. Whatever was going on at *Das Auge* was not just underhanded, it was deadly. Worse, Johann, I was sure, had begun to suspect me. My work in Yorkville, though incomplete, was done.

I made quick time back to the office, arriving out of breath. When I opened the door, the sight of a man sitting at Johann's desk caused me to gasp. How had this happened?

The figure turned. It was not Johann—of course it wasn't. Johann could never have moved that fast. The man at the desk was Holger, and he did not look pleased.

CHAPTER 21

"I came here to speak to you, only to find the door unlocked and the office empty," Holger said. "Does this happen often?"

"No. That is, I don't think so. It's the first time it's happened all week." I swallowed, collecting my wits. "I was following Johann. He left very abruptly. You told me to keep my eye on him."

"We need to have a little talk, you and I."

Yes, we did. I wasn't sure how much Holger suspected his employee was involved in—but surely he didn't want a murderer on his payroll. I was curious what Holger would say to what I'd witnessed that day.

"I will take you to dinner," he said. "Somewhere nice."

Was it dinnertime already? It was dark outside, but the days were so short now, I couldn't tell how long I'd been gone.

"Not too nice, I hope," I said. "I'm not exactly dressed for the rotogravure."

"You are dressed attractively enough," he said.

A ringing endorsement if ever I'd heard one.

Johann burst through the door, red-faced and sweating from what must have been a very brisk walk. I hadn't been far ahead of him. When he saw Holger, his eyes grew wide. "I'm glad you're here, Holger. I need to speak to you."

"Herr Schmidt," Holger said sternly, "you left the office open. And Leisl was not here."

"She wasn't?" Johann turned to me. "I wonder where she was." From his expression, I could tell he'd guessed I followed him. I gathered my things quickly, eager to get away. I only wished there was some way I could contact Operative Halloran and arrange a rendezvous. There was no way to use the telephone in privacy in the office now.

"Try not to leave the offices unmanned again," Holger warned Johann. "That printing press was expensive."

"I didn't think I was leaving the office empty." He colored at the injustice of being scolded for something he considered, rightly, to have been my fault. "Herr Neumann, I need to speak to you about a very urgent matter."

"Tomorrow, perhaps," Holger said. "Right now I am taking Fräulein Frobisher to dinner."

"But—"

"I *know* your concern," Holger told him sharply. "I will deal with it."

I picked up the stole and draped it around my shoulders, eager to get out of there. Something in the air between these two, and the way Holger avoided Johann's pleas, unnerved me.

Holger's lip curled at my fur stole. It seemed clear he hadn't seen it before. "What kind of animal was that?"

"*Nicht ganz* mink," I said, then glanced over at Johann. "Good night."

He barely met my eye. " 'Bye, Leisl." There was guilt in his jowly face . . . but was it the guilt of a killer?

Saying nothing, Holger took my arm and escorted me out to a waiting car. His driver—the same tall, broad-shouldered man as before—opened the back door for us.

"I need to talk to you about Johann," I said, once we were settled on the seat.

To my surprise, Holger almost chuckled. "He wants to talk to me about you, too. But that does not matter now."

If Johann didn't matter, why had I been planted at Das Auge?

I expected we would drive downtown, but the chauffeur turned the car in the opposite direction and didn't go very far before stopping in front of an old carriage house. Most of these had been converted to garages, or torn down to create more space for rapacious apartment house builders. This one had a sign swinging over its door that read *The Coach House.*

Inside, the wide-open space stretched from front door to back, dotted with round, red-clothed tables. The floors had been refinished, and the brick walls painted a light beige that glowed golden in the dim lights that hung down from the pressed-tin ceiling. The few remaining stalls had been transformed into private, bench-lined cubbies. A woodstove in the corner let out enough heat to warm the place, aided, I surmised, by stoves in the unseen kitchen. A long bar took up one side of the room. Here and there paintings of horses were hung in honor of the club's origins. The air was hazy from cigars and cigarettes. In the far corner, a pianist pounded out "Play a Simple Melody," the tune I'd loved from *Watch Your Step.* It was already a hit.

A maître d' appeared, although with his thick neck and arms he looked more like a bouncer. Even at this relatively early hour there were only a few tables open, but we were shown to a good one. The maître d' took a long look at me before pulling out my chair. Had I seen him before? I sat and inspected the café's patrons more closely. They weren't the smart set by any stretch: businessmen obviously stopping for a bracer before heading home to their wives and children or empty flats; cold-eyed men in dark suits surrounded by similar types and women in too-loud clothing; a few looked like artistic types, who flocked together at a few tables, absorbed in conversation.

Holger requested wine first thing—a Riesling, unsurprisingly—and the man nodded and hurried off to do his bidding.

The maître d' made me anxious, and that anxiety reminded me of Leonard Cain. Had I seen the man previously at one of Cain's clubs, or during one of my few other encounters with Cain? For all I knew, this place might be one of his. The man was in jail, but his businesses hadn't died with his sentencing just a few days shy of a year ago.

"Does this club belong to Leonard Cain?" I asked Holger.

"The criminal?" His eyes narrowed. "How do you know about him?"

"I read about him in the newspapers. He ran gambling dens and other unsavory places."

"I wouldn't know. This is merely a restaurant I come to sometimes." Uninterested in Cain, he studied his menu. "Veal cutlets are the thing to have here. I will order for us both."

High-handed, but what could I say? "Thank you." I pushed the menu away from me as if relieved to be unburdened by such a weighty decision. "I think you should know something about Johann."

"My main concern is that those who work for me are loyal to our cause."

The waiter buzzed up to our table, opened a bottle, and poured Holger a glass of wine, which was duly approved. The man poured wine in my glass, and Holger ordered the promised veal cutlets, potatoes macaire, and green beans au gratin. I'd eat well, at least.

Holger took a sip of wine, as did I. "You should perhaps know that Johann wrote to me this morning," he said. "About you. Can you guess what he told me?"

I froze. His face was twisted in a smile. Was this some sadistic way of toying with me?

The one small swallow of wine I'd had burned like acid in my stomach. I'd expected to be the one telling tales on Johann—but apparently I was going under the microscope, and who could say where that would lead. "*I know your concerns,*" Holger had told Johann at the office. What exactly did he know?

I shouldn't have come here. I should have made excuses and reported to Operative Halloran to get instructions before speaking with Holger.

"No guesses?" He lit a cigarette, then exhaled extravagantly. "He told me you were a spy."

I started to reach for my wineglass to quench my parched throat, but thought better of it, in case Holger was able to detect a telltale nervous tremor.

"He wrote me a note this morning to inform me of your duplicity." Laughter burst out of Holger like canon fire. "The fool thought he was telling me something I didn't know. 'I don't trust her,' he wrote." He chuckled, delighted.

Of course. Holger already knew I was a spy. A spy for *him*. Tension drained out of me.

I purposefully sagged with disappointment rather than show my relief. "I suppose this means you won't need me anymore."

"Not at all. Just because I don't need you at *Das Auge* doesn't mean you can't be useful to me in other ways. Unless you've decided you no longer want to work for my organization?"

"Is it an organization?" I asked, perking up at the chance to mine a little more information from him. "I thought it was just you, and your interests in"—I lowered my voice, although I doubted anyone could have heard me over the surrounding conversation, laughter, and the pianist, who was barreling out the "Merry Widow Waltz" as if it were a ragtime tune—"Germany."

"There are many of us working in various ways to help our cause. A girl like you could be useful. Although . . ." He eyed me critically.

"What?"

"Perhaps we need to teach you to be a better liar—so the next Johann is fooled for a little longer." I smiled and he half smiled back. "For now, let's have our dinner. Afterward, we can discuss your future. Would you like a cigarette?"

He offered me one, which I dutifully took. I tried to relax a little. Maybe my work here wasn't done, after all. Holger had plans for me . . . although whether he would still have plans when Johann was turned over to the Secret Service was something I doubted.

Holger struck a match and I leaned in to light the cigarette. I peered over the flame, down at Holger's coat sleeve. There was a button missing. The other button had a tiny eagle on it. Polished brass. Exactly like the button I'd retrieved from Ruthie's.

I inhaled, then coughed.

"Is something wrong?" he asked.

Everything was wrong. Alarms were going off in my skull. Holger had been at Ruthie's and lost that button . . . near the tub. How? In Ruthie's final struggle? I'd assumed Johann reacted so sharply to Ruthie's stole because he'd felt guilty about her death.

But I was now just as fearful that the culpable one was Holger. The button placed him, not Johann, at the murder site.

Johann had even tried to warn me—he'd liked me that much, at least until he'd realized I was spying on them. "*I don't like the way he deals with people,*" he'd told me.

In all likelihood, he had witnessed or at least knew of the way Holger had "dealt with" Ruthie.

And now, if I gave myself away, Holger might deal with me.

I reached for my wineglass, commanding myself to guard my expression. Unfortunately, at that moment my gaze latched in horror on a woman following the maître d' to a table. It was the dress that caught my eye first: a deep rosy-pink wool dress with a black lace overlay on the bodice. It was Callie's dress, but Callie wasn't wearing it. Anna Muldoon was. Worse, in the same moment I saw her over Holger's shoulder, she spotted me. Her eyes bulged, and she stopped in her tracks.

Was it too much to hope that she would read my expression silently begging her to move on without acknowledging me?

"As I live and breathe—Louise!"

"I'm not—"

Anna was already turning to her escort, a man in a dark suit, with rakishly long hair parted down the middle and a thin mustache. I was fairly certain this was the much-talked-of Alfred Sheldrake, formerly Callie's favorite director. "Alfie, look—it's Louise Faulk, Callie's roommate. You know, the police lady."

Alfred said a polite how-do-you-do.

So much for hoping I could bluff my way out of this with denials. I was caught left-footed, and Anna was too sure, too loud, for me to convincingly contradict her. How could I possibly salvage this situation? I could feel Holger's gaze burning into me, suspicious, blue eyes darkening with suppressed anger.

Anna must have noticed him, too. "Who's your handsome friend, Louise? Don't worry. I won't tell Frank." She lowered her voice to a stage whisper as she explained to the men, "Louise and my brother are undeclared sweethearts."

I stood so abruptly that my chair scraped the wood plank floor with a shriek that turned heads. "Thank goodness you're here,

Anna. I *desperately* need your help with something." I took hold of her arm. "A girl matter," I explained to the men. "You'll excuse us, won't you?"

Holger half rose, while Alfred and the bewildered maître d' watched me whisk Anna away. When we'd first entered the restaurant, I'd noticed a sign pointing to the ladies facilities up a staircase off the foyer. I led Anna in that direction. The second floor was probably where the horse groom had once lived, and my guess was that it hadn't improved much since then. The restroom turned out to be a rather primitive chamber with a smallish window, a dripping sink, and no attendant, yet the privacy suited me at the moment. I pulled Anna in after me.

"Really, Louise, I can wait outside. Alfie will—"

"Forget him."

She looked aghast at the idea. "He's an important director."

"He's a married director, with three children. Callie says he's notorious, and if you have the sense God gave a pill bug, you won't lay the foundation of your career on an illicit flirtation."

Her eyes narrowed. She wasn't going to thank me for the warning. "Are you worried I'll say something to Frank about seeing you with—" She nodded as if Holger would be just outside the door. *God, I hope not.* But there was no reason he wouldn't be. He had to know by now that he should have listened to more of exactly what Johann had to say about me.

I took Anna's hands in mine and gave them a hard squeeze. "I *want* you to tell Frank. Better yet, tell Frank's superior at Centre Street. You know where that is?"

She frowned. "I've been there once."

"Good." Hurriedly, I reached into my satchel and pulled out a pad and pencil. With a shaky, hurried hand, I scrawled a note to Captain Percival Smith. I told him I'd discovered Ruthie's murderer and the houseboat where the forgery operation was likely taking place. I gave the name of this restaurant, and where they could find Johann. I emphasized sending help with the utmost urgency, as I had been discovered.

I folded the note and gave it to Anna. "Put this on your person, and deliver it to Captain Percival Smith at Centre Street Headquarters. If Smith is not there, hunt down your brother and explain that I was on a clandestine mission and have been found out. Most of all, the first policeman you see, send him here."

As I spoke, Anna's face became more and more perplexed. "Found out by whom?"

"Never mind. Just tell him. Captain Smith and the Secret Service need to know there's a houseboat called the *Silver Swan* moored off the pier near East Seventy-Ninth that has something to do with what they wanted me to find out. Most of all, tell them that Holger knows who I am."

"Of course he does. He's your date."

I shook my head. "Tell it back to me. What are you going to do?"

She clucked her tongue. "Alfred promised me an evening on the town. Do you know how hard we've been working?"

"Never mind that. This is life and death."

"Whose death?"

"Maybe mine."

"Then shouldn't *you* find this Captain Smith?"

For someone who'd just been told she had my life in her hands, she didn't inspire confidence.

"I'll try, believe me. But if we're both looking, there will be a better chance of at least one of us having success. Promise me. Find a policeman, then deliver the note."

She took in a deep breath and let it out as if exhaling were a form of hard labor. "I promise."

"Thank you." I hurried over to the small window and yanked at the sash. It stuck at first, then flew open. Cold, sour-smelling air blew in. I glanced around, then beckoned her. "Time to go."

She dug in her heels, aghast. "You expect me to crawl out a window?"

"If you're seen leaving, it will raise suspicions."

"But—"

"We are dealing with men who have killed at least one woman, Anna. Believe me, you don't want them following you."

Her mouth closed, and she hurried forward. "All right. But I hope if I do this, you'll help me explain to Frank that having an actress for a sister isn't the end of the world."

"I've already made a start."

She smiled. "Have you? He never said!"

She looked ready to settle in for a long talk about her career prospects, so I reached into my bag and pulled out several dollar coins. "Take these and hire a taxicab. Speed is absolutely essential."

Grumbling, she took the coins, folded them in the note, and hid them in her bodice. She poked her head out the window.

"How do I get down?"

"Climb out and swing over to the fire escape. It's just a couple of feet away."

"I was my school's girl physical culture champion, but that was in seventh grade," she said. Nevertheless, she gamely hiked up her skirt and scooted out onto the sill. Her nose wrinkled. "What is that ghastly smell?"

It was full dark outside, but I recognized the odor. "The kitchen must have a back door below this, where they keep the garbage cans. Good incentive not to fall."

"So is the fact that I want to remain in one piece."

I smiled. "Good luck."

"And what will you be doing?"

"What actresses do when they've forgotten their script. I'm going to extemporize."

She looked doubtful, but then turned her attention to the task at hand. She scooted over to the right, as close to the fire escape as she could get, reached her right hand over and grabbed the railing, then swung her right foot over.

"I wish I hadn't checked my coat," she said, shivering. Then, in a display of acrobatics that gave proof to her boast about being a physical culture champion, she swung the left side of her body onto the fire escape and scrambled over the railing. She waved that all was well, and then hurried to lower the metal ladder and climb down it. Throughout this, she was a blur in the darkness, until I heard her heels hit the ground below. A clang and a high shriek went up.

"What was that?" I called down in a loud whisper.

"I think I scared a mouse," she said in disgust.

More likely a rat. I didn't tell her that, though. "Are you all right?"

"I'm fine, but I'm not so sure about this dress. I hope Callie doesn't want it back."

"You need to hurry," I reminded her. "Godspeed!"

I could just make out her arms flapping in a final wave, and then her footsteps retreated down the alley.

I straightened. Now what? Should I attempt to sneak out, too? Or should I return to the table and announce to Holger that I knew all?

An unnecessary announcement, if the look on his face when Anna had given me away was any indication.

Slowly, I lowered the sash. Someone needed to keep their eye on Holger's whereabouts. Otherwise he might slip away. If I played my cards right, I could keep him occupied long enough for Anna to get a policeman to me. I could arrest Holger on suspicion of murder right away, of course. But aside from a badge, I had nothing to back up my words. If a man had gone to extremely devious means to kill Ruthie, I doubted he would acquiesce quietly to an arrest by a lone, unarmed policewoman.

I washed my hands, and checked my face in the chipped mirror, willing a determined expression to replace my look of uncertainty. Then I unhooked the latch and swung open the door. I went down the short corridor and turned into the stairwell.

Holger waited for me on the top step. "Abandoning your escort at the table is bad manners," he said.

"I'm coming back to you now."

"Where is your friend?"

I forced a laugh. "Where do you think? The rest room is small—a one-at-a-time affair." When he studied me skeptically, I said, "Shall we go? I'm looking forward to my dinner."

His lips thinned. "Sadly, it will have to be postponed. I will take you home."

Not if I could help it. I wasn't getting into a car with him again. I needed to be back in the restaurant, among the diners, so when I told him he was under arrest, he would be trapped in plain view of scores of witnesses.

"Must you?" I asked. "I really am hungry."

He sighed. "The only thing, you really are, fräulein, is a liar." He nodded over my shoulder, and a shadow bore down on me.

I'd forgotten about the driver. I barely had a chance to wonder at how a large man had hidden himself behind me when he whirled me around like a rag doll and slapped a hand over my mouth. *Bite him*, I thought. But with the first breath I took, a sickly smell hit my nostrils, and a strange sense of disembodiment settled over me. That sweet, noxious, vaguely familiar smell was the last thing I remembered for some time.

CHAPTER 22

Salt. A hint of oil. Sharp fish odor. Nausea rose in my throat as I lay on a hard surface, my eyes squeezed shut. Part of me didn't want to know what had happened. I felt so queasy, the whole world seemed to be undulating. I had no memory of anything after being on a staircase.

Sounds. The clump of footsteps in heavy boots.

"*Was ist falsch?*" a voice I recognized demanded. *What is the matter?* It was Holger. He continued, in German, "*Why aren't we moving?*"

"*A problem with the motor,*" replied another voice in the same tongue, gruffer than Holger's. "*She's been resting for a while.*"

"*Well, she cannot rest now. Do something.*"

Who was the *she* they were referring to? Was it me?

"*I warned you about that one,*" said the other man, his voice brimming with resentment. It was the Skipper, my foggy brain realized.

"*Just do as I say,*" Holger told him.

More footsteps, even heavier now. They led away . . . and up some stairs? When they grew distant enough, I opened my eyes.

I lay on a scratchy blanket over hard wood, in a low-ceilinged cabin. The room was dank, cold, and dim, lit only by two oil lamps. I was against the wall, opposite a door that was more like a hatch accessed by three rough pine steps. I knew exactly where I was: in the belly of the *Silver Swan*. That undulating wasn't nausea, it was waves. The fishy odor emanated from the dried salt cod lying on a nearby metal table bolted to the floor. The smell turned my stomach. I sat up, holding my breath.

Gripping a shelf above me, I pulled myself to standing. I wobbled, amazed I could stay upright. I felt numb, as limbs might after you'd sat in one position for too long. But this was my whole body. My brain worked slowly, too—there was a hesitation between my seeing something and my understanding what I was looking at. A typewriter sat on a wood table. Next to it lay a shallow box full of documents. I stumbled toward it, holding on to furniture and the wall as I went.

The documents were passports. Dozens of them.

Steps came toward me again, and I fumbled backward, hitting the wall. The Skipper came through the hatch faster than I'd anticipated.

"*She's awake,*" he called out, eyeing me as if I were some type of wild animal.

Holger appeared, and I had to fight the urge to cringe. He was wearing his overcoat and hat. How long had it been since he'd caught me in the stairwell of The Coach House? Both men were bundled in coats, hats, and gloves. I particularly envied the Skipper's oilskin slicker. The cold and damp penetrated my pores. I'd left my coat behind.

"*Told you we should have tied her up,*" the Skipper said.

"*Where is she going to go?*" Holger eyed me closely, and I felt myself trying not to weave. "*She is still drugged.*"

Drugged. Yes. That explained the numbness. But my mind was churning back to life, and it didn't like the way all the pieces of the puzzle were finally fitting together. The passports. The sweet-smelling drug. I'd noticed the same smell at Ruthie's when I'd picked up the basin to bathe Eddie in. It must have been a remnant of whatever had been used to knock her out. Perhaps a cloth holding ether had sat in that basin—or a handkerchief bearing the initials HN.

I tried not to picture what had happened to Ruthie, or to imagine what might happen to me now. Panic wouldn't help me.

"I am Officer Louise Faulk of the New York Police Department," I said. "If you're smart, you'll put me ashore this moment."

"That would be rather inconvenient," Holger replied dismissively. He turned to the Skipper, nodding at the box of documents. "Take those and put them somewhere secure."

"I saw the passports," I piped up. "What will you do with them?"

"Do not worry yourself about those. You should really lie down, fräulein. You appear unwell."

I looked around at the place where I'd slept. A blanket had been strewn across several crates. Canned goods, mostly, although block letters across one read DYNAMITE. That word caused a pressure on my chest. "I suppose you'll tell me not to worry about a box of dynamite, too."

"It's all for the cause," he said.

"What are you planning on blowing up?"

"That has yet to be determined."

Good God. "And the government thinks your worst sin is forging documents," I told him. "It was the passports that led me to you. I found three in Ruthie Jones's flat."

Holger's mouth thinned to a flat line. "I do not know that name."

Liar. "Johann certainly seemed to know her. He saw me wearing Ruthie's stole and it was as if he'd seen her ghost. And then he sent a message to you, telling you I was a spy—a warning you assumed meant my spying on him for you had been discovered. I followed Johann to this houseboat, where he passed an envelope of documents to the Skipper. Maybe the passports in that box. What do you do with those?"

Holger didn't answer.

"Doctor them in some way?" I guessed. "Sell them? Is that your racket?"

That last word offended him. "This is no racket. We do not sell."

"What would you call it?"

"Patriotism. There are German sailors and ship workers all over the New York waterfront, idle. Young, healthy men who could be fighting for their country. The Germans on military vessels are forbidden to leave the country, but as mere tourists—Swedes, Englishmen, or Frenchmen—their returning to Europe is not questioned."

"Ruthie stole passports for you," I said. "You bought them from her?"

"She was one of many who bring us the documents," he said, dropping the pretense of not knowing her. "We buy them—at my expense, along with funds donated to us by other patriotic groups. Ruthie was a very useful girl. Johann knew her. He is a sloppy man of unclean habits. But Ruthie, like too many of your gullible countrymen, began to read the newspapers, the ones naming Germans as butchers. She believed all these lies and told Johann she would not work for us anymore. When he tried to persuade her to continue, she threatened to tell a certain policeman she knew of our operation. I took care of the problem myself."

I wouldn't let him dehumanize her as *a problem*. "You drugged a woman and made her death look like a suicide, slashing her wrists while there was still blood pumping in her veins. You murdered her child. You detest people calling Germans butchers so much that you were willing to become one."

"Johann told you all this?" He frowned.

"He said nothing. I saw Ruthie's flat the night she was found." I thought of Ruthie's locked room. "You went out the window and down the fire escape, didn't you? The police thought the locked front door confirmed she must have killed herself. But I noticed an empty milk bottle on the fire escape. I couldn't figure out why Ruthie would bother leaving an empty bottle outside instead of putting it by her door for the milkman. But it was you—you must have knocked it over, then righted it." Holger was a man who liked neatness.

He shrugged. "Perhaps. I don't remember."

Righting a milk bottle when he'd just killed a woman. And a baby. I shook my head. "Why'd you have to hurt Johnny?"

"Who?"

"The little baby. He was helpless. What harm could he have done you?"

"The baby wouldn't stop screaming. I was searching for the

passports, but the brat was going to bring all the neighbors up. So I drowned him and left him with his mother."

"You killed a baby for crying?"

Holger was having none of my shaming. "The son of a whore. What life would he have? He is better off."

I thought of Eddie, warm and safe at Aunt Irene's. Thank heavens for that. But he'd been deprived of his mother, his twin brother. A life cut off before it had begun. "You are despicable."

"I am a patriot."

I'd heard that patriotism was the last refuge of a scoundrel, but this went beyond being a scoundrel. This was the vilest crime I'd yet witnessed. And he'd told me all about it. Bragged, even.

That did not bode well for my future.

The Skipper poked his head down. "Herr Neumann! Someone is coming."

Holger scowled at him. "Another boat?"

"Yes. Behind us, from the city."

"A boat on the Sound is not unusual."

"It'll gain on us quickly if I can't get the damn motor started. I've got the rowboat out, though. We could use that."

The contempt on Holger's face intensified. "And leave all this—to be captured in a rowboat?"

"We could get to shore and run for it."

"Keep working on the motor," Holger said. "I need to take care of this first."

The cabin was cold and damp, but nothing chilled me to the bone like hearing myself referred to as *this*. There was no suppressing panic now. He was going to kill me, and then what? Toss me over the side? I wondered whether there really was someone behind us. *Please let it be a police boat.* The windows were curtained, so I couldn't even tell where we were. Holger had mentioned the Sound. Long Island Sound, if that's what he meant, was wide and led to open ocean. Is that where we were headed, in this rickety houseboat full of stinky fish, canned goods, and dynamite?

Instinctively, I backed away from Holger. Not that there was anywhere to go. I moved toward the little desk where I supposed the passports had been doctored—a change of age here, a few inches added to a man's height there. All to funnel a few dozen men back to the German army. In the big scheme of things, how much difference could that make? Enough to justify the deaths of Ruthie and Johnny . . . and me?

"You should have stayed asleep," Holger said.

"Are you going to bring your chauffeur in to knock me out again?"

"Unfortunately, he is not aboard, and I am all out of ether. I have no painless way to render you unconscious."

If he only wanted me unconscious, perhaps that was a good thing. Unconscious was preferable to dead.

"You could just leave me," I said. "Tie me up or something and take the Skipper up on that idea about the rowboat."

"Leaving you would not be wise."

From outside, the Skipper called to him again. "Boat's coming closer!"

My chances of getting away were looking impossibly slim. A wave of despair hit me, followed by a surge of determination. I couldn't give up. I wasn't going to be bested by a cold-blooded murderer, the man whose own hands had left Eddie an orphan. I wanted to see Ruthie vindicated, too. The men at the precinct had seen nothing of value in Ruthie Jones. But at the end of her life, when she had so much to lose, she'd made a stand for what she believed was right. She'd shown courage and had paid a terrible price for it.

If I died, the full truth of her death might die with me.

I glanced around, looking for a weapon. There was nothing. The few cooking utensils—including, I assumed, a knife—were on the other side of the cabin where the large metal table was, near the Skipper's bunk. I'd backed myself into the wrong corner. On the desk, there was only glue, ink, paper . . . nothing that would help me. The Skipper's typewriter was one I recognized from my days in secretarial school, an L.C. Smith Model 2, a clunker of a machine prone to sticky keys and a carriage return requiring the arm muscle of a stevedore.

I sidestepped around the table to position myself in back of it. I'd been to a circus once, and for a flash of a second I envisioned myself fiercely wielding a chair to fend off Holger, as the lion tamer had fended off his two large, roaring cats. Anything I could do to buy a little more time, to get ready to run. My limbs were still rubbery—jittering fear didn't help—and if I did make it topside, there would be the Skipper to contend with. I'd have to cross that bridge if I was lucky enough to reach it.

Holger sneered at my maneuvering. "Are you really going to try to play puss-in-the-corner, Miss . . . ? I've already forgotten your real name."

"Faulk. Louise Faulk."

"Faulk," he repeated, bemused. "A German name."

"It was when it belonged to my grandparents. It's been American since I've had it."

"Ah, I see. You are one of your countrymen who denies your heritage. You've also bought into the lie of American neutrality."

"No," I replied honestly, "I see your point about Wilson's dealings with the Germans. I just don't agree with your methods. You *are* a butcher."

While I spoke I tried to get a grip on the chair, but to my chagrin, the thing wouldn't budge. It, like the tables, had been bolted to the floor. The Skipper had battened down furniture as if he'd expected a typhoon on the East River.

Holger reached into his coat and pulled out a revolver. "I have had enough of nonsense, Fräulein Faulk."

Blood drained from my face in a dizzying rush. Nothing rivets attention like a firearm, especially one with its blue steel barrel aimed right at you. I tried, with my shaky knowledge of guns, to focus on detail. A single-action weapon. Probably .38 caliber. For all the good that would do me.

"It's the American method, no?" A grim smile tilted his lips. "The Wild West."

My future, I knew now, would be determined in seconds. He was armed and all I had was instinct. That, and a very deep animus against L.C. Smith typewriters. He pointed the gun at my heart. I dropped to a bent-kneed crouch, summoned every ounce of strength in my body, and hurled the typewriter at his face.

He wasn't expecting my action, but does anyone ever expect a typewriter to be lobbed at them? The surprise of it saved my life.

My aim wasn't very good, but neither was his. His gun went off as the machine struck him, and his shot went wide, hitting the wall behind me.

I scrambled around the table and nearly stumbled over him. He reached out with one arm, but I sidestepped, and then slipped. As I touched a hand down to catch myself, I spied what Holger had been looking for. His revolver. It was on the floor, a yard from my feet, closer to me than to him. We both lunged for it, and I snatched it and sprang away just in time, wrapping my hand around the unfamiliar grip. My weapons training had been minimal. Armed women were the last thing the hidebound brass of the NYPD wanted to set loose on the streets. But a group of us had been allowed a demonstration and a chance each to fire at a target. I held the revolver now, arms extended, in a two-handed grip.

Holger attempted to adjust to the power shift that had occurred in the cabin. He held both hands up, though whether in a calming gesture or one of surrender I couldn't tell. Nor did I care.

I cocked the revolver.

"Leisl—Louise—don't make an ape of yourself. You will not shoot a man."

"You were going to kill me."

"I only wanted to frighten you."

Rage rose in me like bile. "Did you say something similar to Ruthie before you killed her?"

"You are not Ruthie. That woman was a whore. You are as different as night and day."

If he was hoping to win me over with words like that, he was mistaken. "She was a mother, and a human being."

"Of course she was," he said, his tone even, reasonable. "But this is war, Miss Faulk. Do you know how many will die before it is done?"

"It's not my war, and it certainly wasn't Ruthie's. You had no right to take her life."

"And do you think you will take mine?" he asked. "Kill a man in cold blood?"

Did I have it in me to kill someone? I abhorred murder . . . almost as much as I hated him.

"Besides," he said, smirking, "the revolver's chamber is not full."

Those words caught me off guard. But if I were aiming a gun that wasn't loaded at him, why wouldn't he have rushed me already?

I stood my ground, but doubt must have showed in my eyes. He took a step toward me. "Louise . . ."

"Stop," I said.

A cloud passed over his eyes, a darkening, a deadening. That was all the warning I had. He charged as a bull might. He expected to push me over, to disarm me. He assumed I wouldn't have the reflexes, or the nerve, to shoot.

I shot.

His body reeled as if a whip had cracked him, then he stumbled to the side, falling to his knees as his face drained of color. Surprise showed in his eyes—surprise to be shot, and shot by me. Maybe he really had doubted how many rounds were left in the chamber. He was clutching his left shoulder.

I watched him, half expecting him to leap up again like a melodrama villain rising to take a bow at the curtain call. But he only groaned, which was joined by the sound of a lowing horn of a ship.

"Neumann! We need to go. Now."

At the sound of the Skipper's footsteps at the hatch, I pivoted, gun still in my hand. The old man's eyes went round.

"Help me tie him up," I said, indicating Holger.

"You're crazy." He turned and ran.

Holger sneered at me through a grimace of pain. "You thought *he* would help you?"

I scowled at him. "He's certainly not helping you."

A boat's horn sounded again. Rescue. Despite everything, my heart lifted. I was going to get out of this mess, after all. I decided to go up and investigate. Holger, who had fallen over, was hardly a threat in his current condition.

Though I'd deduced we were on Long Island Sound, seeing the lights of the city so far away shocked me. I must have been unconscious quite some time. The tallest skyscrapers were distant beacons, and the bridges just lights arcing toward Manhattan. As I faced Manhattan, Connecticut was to my right, Long Island to the left, but both were too far off to make out any landmarks—not that there were any out here I would recognize. The lights along the Long Island shoreline were only intermittent.

But it didn't matter. I could see the lights of a boat heading toward us. They weren't far.

A splash in the water alerted me that the Skipper had gone over the side. I hurried to the edge and squinted down. At least there was a moon. The old man was adjusting the oars, preparing to make his getaway.

"Stop!" I aimed the gun at him.

The whites of his eyes became visible as surprise registered, but he wasn't looking at me. He was looking behind me.

I pivoted. Holger, still holding his shoulder, had climbed topside. He was far enough away that I wasn't too worried, although keeping my attention on both of them would be difficult. "I'm not letting you get away," I said. "Either of you. You're both under arrest."

Listing, Holger laughed. He seemed more preoccupied with a barrel container on the houseboat's deck than with my gun, though.

"Dear God, Neumann!" the Skipper shouted. "Don't do it. The *Silver Swan*'s not yours."

"It will not be theirs, either. And I will not be sent to a barbaric electric chair over the death of a whore."

Their interchange perplexed me, until Holger overturned the container. Liquid surged over the deck, rushing toward me. Gasoline fumes stole my breath.

"He's crazy!" the Skipper yelled.

I didn't know how crazy until I saw Holger bring something out of his pocket. Matches.

"The Americans will never know what's on this ship."

There was only a second to decide between life and death. Fire or water. I chose water, hurling myself into the ice-cold salty ink of the Sound, diving as far as possible and then stroking toward the rowboat. The light wool fabric of my dress was like a coating of cement now, dragging at me, pulling me down. The water was freezing. I was freezing.

And then the deck of the *Silver Swan* exploded in flames. The fireball blotted out the lights of the distant city, the approaching boat, and for a moment even the moon. The fire was all I could see—I could not see Holger, though I heard a piercing scream. The horrible sound rent the air.

What was coming would be even worse, I knew. So did the Skipper. The rowboat skimmed past and I grabbed hold. "Fast," I said, struggling to stay above the waves around me. My teeth were clacking from the cold. How long could I stay alive in this water?

I worried the Skipper would dislodge an oar and knock me away. But he didn't waste time on that. He rowed, and his rowing probably saved us when the fire reached the dynamite in the cabin and the second explosion struck.

I cringed, closed my eyes, and ducked behind the rowboat. Debris flew through the air, and plopped into the water around us, some sinking, some floating. The air stank of petroleum and acrid smoke. When the shower of burning wood died down, a moan from the rowboat made me pull up and peek over the side. The Skipper was doubled over. "Something hit my eye."

I struggled to lift myself into the boat. It felt even colder out of the water than in, but I knew I wouldn't last long in the water before hypothermia set in. "Give me your hand," I said.

Still covering one eye, he reached to me with his free hand. I managed to work my way into the boat like a beached, shivering fish. "Let me see," I told him, trying to force my teeth not to chatter. He removed his hand from his face, and it was all I could do not to recoil in horror. A large splinter had hit him in the eye. "You need a doctor," I said. "The men coming on the approaching boat will take you to Bellevue."

I said this with assuredness, although I was doubtful about the identity of the boat that had been following us right up to the moment when I saw Captain Percival Smith at the prow of the tug-shaped police vessel, glasses perched on his nose as always, with a life vest over his long dark coat.

"Is that you, Officer Faulk? You lived through that explosion?"

"Yes, sir. But the main suspect didn't. It was he who blew up the boat." I pointed down at the Skipper. "This is the boat's owner, and Holger Neumann's accomplice. He needs medical help for his eye."

"Does he now," Captain Smith said. "We'll see about that."

It seemed to take forever to get transferred from the rowboat to the police boat. Once I was aboard, Captain Smith put a blanket around my shoulders, while Operatives Halloran and Lunt peppered me with questions. They wanted to know what had happened, and what materials had been on the *Silver Swan*—how many passports, how much explosive, and if I'd seen any money. I answered their questions as best I could. To be honest, I was only half listening. I couldn't take my eyes off the city as we drew ever closer to it. Never before had it seemed so brilliant, so expansive, so like my home.

"So Anna Muldoon found you?" I asked Captain Smith. I'd expected she'd actually look for her brother first, and that perhaps he would be here. I tried not to feel a stab of disappointment that he hadn't come.

Smith nodded. "Quite a capable messenger you sent. We picked up that fellow Johann Schmidt at the boardinghouse address you gave, and when he realized what hot water he was in, he immediately began to tell all."

"What you can't tell us about the *Silver Swan*, Schmidt probably will," Halloran said. "When the captain here informed him he could be charged with the murder of the prostitute, he was ready to spill everything he knew about everyone from Holger Neumann right up to Kaiser Bill."

"Quite a talkative fellow," Luft added. "What he doesn't know, he might make up."

"Schmidt told us that Neumann and this other fellow had a plan to hide the *Silver Swan* with all its contents for counterfeit and sabotage at a cabin Neumann owned outside Mattituck, on Long Island. That's how we were able to find you."

"There might be more explosives in that cabin," Smith said.

Halloran nodded. "Hopefully no one like these characters will be able to get their hands on any of it."

"Holger Neumann's gone," I said, almost in disbelief, trying not to remember that scream. A new little something for my nightmares. "The ringleader."

Halloran frowned. "We're not so sure he was the ringleader. The English say there's an old German aristocrat—supposed aristocrat—operating in this country. We were hoping to track him down through Neumann."

The Secret Service men huddled, discussing what efforts should be made to recover Neumann's body. I didn't care if they left him to a watery grave.

I turned back to Captain Smith. "Thank you, sir, for coming out to rescue me."

"You seemed to have matters well in hand. A shame you weren't officially working for the NYPD tonight. Might've earned yourself a commendation or a medal."

"Just being alive is reward enough for me."

"Good, because we certainly don't want word of this getting around. No press—I'm sure you understand."

"No, sir, I'm not sure I do."

"German saboteurs in New York City?" He took off his eyeglasses and rubbed the spray-splattered lenses with a handkerchief. "A fine panic that would cause. And we certainly don't want it to get around that a policewoman was involved in a gunfight and an explosion that took a man's life. The public thinks little enough of us without having to worry about gun-wielding females working for us."

I stared at the water turning to foam as the boat sliced through it, then disappearing into our wake. Something inside me seemed to be turning to foam, too.

"No, we need to think of another explanation for the explosion, in case some people saw it," he continued. "And I'm sure they did. It was like the Fourth of July in December. I thought you were dead for sure."

"For a few moments, I worried I was, too."

"We'll give you a week off." He patted my shoulder. "You deserve a rest. We'll tell your precinct that you caught a fever on your trip upstate."

As miffed as I was about my deeds being erased, the thought of a week off was a balm. "Thank you, sir. I'll be glad for a week."

He looked amused. "What do you intend to do?"

"Celebrate," I said. "I'm going to celebrate Christmas, and celebrate being alive."

"There's something else you can celebrate," Smith said. "You were right about Ruthie Jones all along. My detectives were wrong."

Cold as I was, and numb from all that had happened, in that moment exhilaration filled me.

"What are you smiling at?"

Was this insanity? Was it crazy to hate danger, yet feel a rush at having cheated death for the third time in my life? And—icing on the cake—I'd had my most skeptical superior officer tell me that I'd been right all along about a case. That was a sweeter melody than anything Otto could have thought up.

CHAPTER 23

In 1914, I celebrated Christmas twice. The first, early celebration took place two days after my survival of the destruction of the *Silver Swan*. December twentieth. Callie was catching the late train to Chicago, so we invited all our friends that evening for a combination holiday party and farewell send-off for Callie.

Otto helped me gather goodies for the party that afternoon. Callie stayed at the apartment, finishing packing her trunk, popping corn and tying ribbons from her whatnot box for decorations. While we were out, a letter from Teddy was delivered, which Callie waved at us as we came through the door with our bundles.

"Teddy and that maniac Hugh sold the apparatus to the English and now they're headed to France. He says they're going to have a spree in Paris"—her brow wrinkled at the page—"I don't like the sound of that. Then they're going to see if anyone there is interested in their flying expertise." She put the letter down in exasperation.

"They'll be back in a few months," I predicted. "Probably before your tour of the Midwest is done."

"That war can't go on much longer," Otto agreed. "The Germans are bound to surrender. Louise is licking the bastards right here in New York City."

Though I'd been instructed not to tell the press or my coworkers what had happened, I hadn't kept it a secret from my friends. And who knows? One of them might slip the story to a journalist. Both Otto and Callie had friends among the newspapermen of the city.

Callie tilted her head at Otto. "I thought you were pro-German."

"Not if they're going to try to kill my friends," he said.

The events of my night on the *Silver Swan* kept rising unexpectedly in my mind. The memory of staring down the barrel of the revolver would occur without warning, frightening me almost more than when I'd actually been in the houseboat's cabin. The sounds of the explosion still reverberated inside me. Yet a giddiness also lingered. It was hard to explain the complicated stew of joy at being alive mixed with horror at what I'd lived through. I certainly couldn't talk about it to my friends as we stood around admiring our Christmas tree, which began to look less forlorn as we wound Callie's popcorn garland through its branches. The dried needles that sprinkled to the floor struck me as rather rustic. It was like a natural woodland carpet, right there in our apartment.

Callie and I rolled up the rug in anticipation of dancing, mulled some wine on the stove, and put out an impressive assortment of delicacies Otto and I had spent the afternoon picking up in the neighborhood. We'd offered the Bleecker Blowers free refreshments in exchange for some Christmas songs and dance music, and as they had no job that night, they were more than happy to come upstairs and play. They arrived and in no time the apartment was filled with music, friends, and good cheer.

I'd invited our other neighbors, too, including the opera teacher next door, who promised to give us a performance. There was never a shortage of entertainment at our parties. Some of Callie's theater friends showed up—the ones who weren't in shows—and Otto had a Tin Pan Alley pal or two drop in. My aunt had a previous engagement, but I was gratified when Walter and Bernice arrived. Walter, winded from the climb, entered my dwelling with trepidation.

"Worse than I imagined," he declared, looking about him.

Callie laughed. "That's funny, the place has never looked nicer."

"Don't feel bad," he said. "Even I probably couldn't have done better. The only way to make this building spotless would be to tear it down and start over."

Bernice handed me a covered plate containing one of her caramel apple cakes. Just holding it made my mouth water. She offered to go to the kitchen and slice it up, but I steered her to a group of some of Callie's Red Cross knitting friends.

Everyone was instructed to put a decoration on the tree. My aunt had sent an angel, and Walter climbed on a chair to put it up. The gang began to sing an upbeat "Hark! The Herald Angels Sing" with both syncopation and coloratura. My people. I looked on from near the open front door, feeling a calm contentment for the first time that day.

Unexpectedly, someone tapped me on the shoulder and I swung around, my heart pounding. A defensive instinct was still alive in me. My hands clenched, but I forced myself to smile.

Anna Muldoon launched herself at me, squeezing me in a hug. "Oh, Lou, I heard all about it!" she said in a breathless whisper. "The Captain told Frank everything. And to think, if it weren't for me, you'd be dead. Drowned! I feel positively heroic."

She went on to regale me with her gallant quest two nights ago to find Captain Smith, which entailed finding a cab and directing the driver to take her to police headquarters. Nevertheless, for all her swiftness, she'd heard that the captain barely rescued me in time! And never would have, if it hadn't been for her.

And if you hadn't recognized me at The Coach House, I might not have been in that fix to begin with. It was Christmas, though, and I was determined to be positive and generous. "Thank you."

She caught me glancing over her shoulder and smiled knowingly. "Don't worry, Frank's on his way. That awful man on the first floor waylaid him—wanted to complain about some person lurking, he said."

Wally was suspicious of everyone.

Muldoon did arrive just a few minutes later, and stood behind us long enough to hear Anna launch into the subject of her heroics again. I caught his wince and smiled at him. Anna looked at us. "Oh, I see," she said, misinterpreting as usual. "Say no more, you two. I'll make myself scarce."

His gaze followed his sister till she was out of earshot, then he turned to me. "I hope you don't mind my being here."

"Of course not."

"Anna told me about this party tonight, so I decided to tag along. I thought she might want to apologize. From what she described, it sounded as if she gave the game away during your operation."

Anna, apologize? How could a man live with a sister so long and understand her so little? *Positive and generous.* "It's all right. If Anna hadn't completed her mission, I'd be spending the holiday at the bottom of Long Island Sound."

My assurance didn't seem to comfort him. "I wanted to come by the night before last, after I heard what had happened to you. But I'd been out on a case, so it was late . . . and they assured me you were safe." He dug his hands into his pockets. "And I guessed if you'd wanted me to know, you would have told me about that Secret Service operation in the first place."

"It was supposed to be a secret."

He nodded. "Captain Smith said you found the man the Secret Service had been looking for, and you cracked the Ruthie Jones case."

I half laughed. "Captain Smith is better at telling people to keep things under their hats than he is at staying mum himself."

"He knew I was interested."

"I'm glad it's over," I said. "I just hope I'll keep my job."

"If the police won't have you, the Secret Service might. Captain Smith said those operatives were singing your praises, so naturally he values you now, too. I don't think you have anything to worry about."

"The NYPD likes successes. I'll just have to remember not to fail."

He lowered his head. "Earlier I said I thought Anna had come to apologize, but it's me who really owes you an apology, Louise. I failed you. You were right about Ruthie Jones's death. If it weren't for you, her killer would still be walking the streets."

"I only wish that the cause of her death could be public," I said, still frustrated by this edict. It felt unfair to Ruthie. "Maybe now I'm the only one who really cares, but Eddie will, someday. It grieves me that he might hear the official, wrong story about what happened to his mother and brother."

"Hopefully you'll be able to straighten out the record for him in person, when he's old enough. You and your aunt."

I smiled.

He fiddled nervously with the hat in his hands. "There's something else. The last time we talked, I said some terrible things."

"You did," I agreed. "So did I."

"Everything you said was true, though. I cringe every time I think how small-minded and mean I sounded that day."

"You were worried about your sister."

"And you were telling me a truth I wasn't ready to hear. I don't think I've ever understood my little sister, or even tried to. After Ma died, I always just assumed Anna would be happy to have a house to run until she found a husband. All this time, she's been busting to get out in the world." He looked down the corridor in the salon, where his sister was turkey-trotting with one of the opera students from next door. "I'm not sure she'll find happiness that way, but I can't stop her."

"I don't think anybody can stop her. There's no stuffing the butterfly back into its cocoon."

When the dance stopped, the Bleecker Blowers began a rendition of "It Came Upon a Midnight Clear," which had always been one of my favorites.

"I'll regret speaking to you that way for the rest of my life," Muldoon said. "It was unforgivable."

"I'm sorry, Detective, but you don't get to decide what's unforgivable. If you've wronged me, it's up to me to forgive." I looked into his face, where his furrowed brow awaited my verdict. "As it happens, I already have. Not because you weren't wrong, but because *everyone* gets things wrong. The world is progressing at lightning speed, and we're all clashing in ways we never expected. It's only people who don't reflect and never change that get my goat. But it sounds to me as if you've been mulling over quite a few things."

"Friends again?"

He offered me his hand, and I took it. I'd had a cup of eggnog, generously laced with brandy, but that didn't account for the warmth that filled me, or the strong tug I felt. It wasn't as if his hand was pulling me closer to him; some invisible force was doing that. The music in the apartment didn't explain the restlessness singing inside of me, either.

But it was definitely the explosion that propelled me the rest of the way into Muldoon's arms. After the first crash made us freeze, a propulsive *whoosh* threw us to our knees on the floor.

I groaned. *Not again.* This week seemed determined to kill me.

We were in the doorway, and after a moment of shock, footsteps ran toward us. We looked down the short hallway and through the parlor. By the window, the tree was on fire, and a stampede to escape the room had begun.

Muldoon and I scrambled up and out of the way. "Call for the fire department," he told me, and ran in the opposite direction of the people running toward us.

I raced down the stairs and out the door, to the next apartment building where I knew the superintendent had installed a phone. For good measure, I called out to a boy who was gaping up at the third floor from across the street. "Run to the fire station!" I dashed into the neighbor's building and as soon as the operator spoke I told her to send a fire truck to our address. Then I dropped the receiver back in place and ran right back out.

Our guests were gathered outside the building, joined by alarmed neighbors. I saw Anna and moved toward her. "I'm glad you're safe," I said.

"Safe, but what a horror! All that noise—and smoke. This is the second dress this week I've completely ruined."

"Where's your brother?"

"I saw him bring one woman down. Quite the hero, isn't he? Two other men took her down the street to the drugstore."

I looked up at the smoke coming from the third floor and shuddered. If only the fire trucks would get here . . .

Bernice was huddled with some of the others under a streetlamp. They were all unharmed, but disheveled and stunned. As I approached, Bernice shook her head at me, as if she'd expected no better from a party of mine.

"Was anyone hurt?" I asked. "Should I call for a doctor?"

"I haven't seen anybody hurt bad. Just what you'd expect—cuts and such."

I followed her gaze, and frowned. "Have you seen Callie? And where's Walter?"

"Callie shooed everyone out but then went back in again," she said. "Walter never left."

My heart froze and my gaze scanned up to the third floor, where smoke billowed out of the broken parlor window.

I raced for the door. Wally, the landlord's son, blocked the entrance like an angry sentinel. "What the hell were you doing up there?" he yelled at me. "You said it was a Christmas party."

Pushing him aside, I ran up the stairs, past several singed saxophonists. "Are you all right?" I asked them.

Charlie, the Blower I spoke to, looked dazed. "We're okay. Just sorry about what happened to your place."

"What *did* happen?" asked one of the others, laden with saxophone cases.

"I'm not sure . . ." But I had a suspicion.

I found Otto on the third landing, agitated.

"Where's Callie?" I said.

Just then, she ran out, dragging her trunk. Her face was dark red, and her hair seemed to have taken on a layer of ash.

"Are you crazy?" I asked her. "You need to get out of the building, or at least away from this floor."

"I couldn't leave my trunk. It's got my costumes and makeup box in it."

I took my two friends by the arms and maneuvered them down a few steps. "We need to clear the stairwell. The firemen will be here soon."

"There won't be a fire for them to fight," Callie said. "Muldoon and Walter have taken care of most of it."

I gaped at her. "They're in the apartment? Still?" I looked up the stairwell, and then, cursing, turned and ran back up.

"Now who's crazy?" Callie said to Otto.

I found them in the parlor, where a confetti of ash floated through the air. Burnt ribbons, I realized. Or maybe curtains. The room stank of seared cedar and popcorn, and an acrid smell that brought to mind the *Silver Swan*'s burning. Fuel. A line of flame crawled along our old sofa, while Walter and Muldoon were beating one wall with the carpet Callie and I had rolled up not long ago, in anticipation of dancing. A section of the floorboards—the would-be dance floor—had been scorched and hollowed out, almost as if it had been hit by a bomb. The wallpaper was charred, and in places the wall had burned down to wood studs. Despite the fire and smoke, the room was cold. Smoke might be going out the window, but plenty of cold air was finding its way in.

I ran to the kitchen and filled up a pan of water, then raced back out to throw it over the sofa. I coughed, and Muldoon looked over as if seeing me for the first time. "Louise, get out."

I hurried back to the kitchen. Why should he and Walter risk their lives for my apartment? I'd barely had time to throw the water on the last of the sofa's flames when Muldoon's arm clamped around mine. "You shouldn't be here."

"He's right," Walter said, holding a handkerchief over his face. "Your aunt would never forgive me if I let you burn to a crisp."

It was more likely that she'd criticize me for risking Walter's life.

"The firemen will be here soon." I looked at the smoking ruin that was our parlor. A finger of flame chewed up a curled corner of wallpaper. "But I think you might have already saved the building."

I'd seen a building devastated by fire—the publishing house where I'd worked for ten months had been reduced to a charred skeleton. Muldoon's quick thinking and diligence had saved the apartment buildings next door, as well. Our apartment was not going to be livable for a while, but at least everyone in the building and on the block wouldn't be homeless.

"I know I said the place needed to be torn down," Walter said, crushing a red cinder on the floor with his shoe. "I didn't mean *burn it* down."

A clanging sounded from a nearby street. Thank goodness. "They're almost here."

"Good," Muldoon said. "Go."

When he turned to bang the carpet against the wall some more, I looked again where the floor had been burned. Broken glass was scattered across the floor, too, and not all of it was from glasses dropped by the guests. And then there was that hole in the window. And the smell.

Wally had told Muldoon he'd seen someone lurking.

A minute later, the first firemen appeared, striding through the door in their high boots and black uniforms. "You need to leave the building," their leader announced.

"We're police," Muldoon said. "Detective Frank Muldoon and Officer Louise Faulk." He nodded at Walter. "And Mr. Walter Billings."

The fireman eyed me curiously, but I was used to being a novelty. "This is my apartment."

"Still better if you waited outside, miss. We'll take care of this." He looked at the charred remnant of the Christmas tree, a thin black stump. "People need to be careful with flames around these trees."

The sad, dry tree had gone up like a torch.

"It wasn't the tree's fault," I said. "This was a present from Leonard Cain."

Over his handkerchief, Walter's eyes widened, and Muldoon sucked in a breath. He hadn't put it together.

"December twentieth," I reminded him.

A year to the day since the testimony I'd elicited from a witness had resulted in a judge sentencing him to ten years in Sing Sing. This Christmas present was Cain's way of letting me know he hadn't forgotten me.

CHAPTER 24

The second Christmas celebration, on Christmas Day itself, was spent at my aunt's house, where I moved after being booted out of our apartment. Callie had caught her train west the night of the fire, and while she was gone I would scout a new place for us to live. Having an incendiary-lobbing crime lord following my movements from jail would not appeal to potential landlords, so I would probably have to do without a recommendation from Wally Grimes and his mother, who were understandably incensed about the damage to the building even though Aunt Irene was reimbursing them for repairs.

Christmas morning was so perfectly orchestrated by my aunt, however, that it was hard to summon thoughts of the apartment fire, my near escape from the houseboat, or anything else negative. My aunt's house was a scene of domestic beauty and tranquillity, like a cover of *House Beautiful*. When I arose Christmas morning, the air smelled of strudel, the baked apple and cinnamon mixing with the usual morning aromas of bacon and the rich coffee my aunt preferred. I floated downstairs on that scent. In the parlor, candles were lit and the decorations on the tree shone with their reflection. Santa had arrived during the night, bringing at least two large boxes for Eddie and a few other smaller packages that hadn't been there when I'd gone to bed.

I added the wrapped parcels I'd bought for everyone and stood back to admire the display of colors. My aunt appeared next to me, rubbing her hands together. "Oh good, you're up. We can start the real fun now."

For the next hours we opened gifts, nibbled at all the wonderful things Bernice had prepared, and watched Eddie crawl everywhere in search of mischief. He loved every gift he received, meeting each unwrapping with a gummy smile and a desire to touch his new possession. He also enjoyed the boxes themselves, and the ribbons.

My aunt laughed. "Next year perhaps I'll go to FAO Schwarz and ask them to wrap up their best empty boxes for me."

Next year. I tried to imagine it. Everything seemed so up in the air. Would Callie come back? Would Otto have put on *Double Daisy*? And what would I be doing? After the week I'd had, it was hard to imagine going back and sitting with the female prisoners of Hell's Kitchen. But that was my job—babysitting accused criminals. A bit dull, perhaps, but safe.

The trouble was, safe didn't appeal to me. I only wished there was a way to do interesting, exciting work without having to worry about possibly being killed.

One thing that made me perfectly contented was seeing my aunt so blooming. Ever since Eddie had arrived, she'd become a new person. That maternal side of her might come across as ridiculous at times, but I'd never seen her happier. Occasionally I even felt a spike of envy. Somewhere in the city, *my* boy was having his second Christmas. He was walking and running now—I'd spent the previous afternoon on a certain street on the Upper East Side, doing a little spying—and his hair, my mouse-brown color, was now long and curly. Calvin Longworth was as pampered and cared for as Eddie, but if I'd kept him, the two could have been friends. Now they would never know each other. If only . . .

I gave myself a shake, bringing myself back to the celebration. After presents, we sang carols at the piano, accompanied by Walter. Otto had gone home to Altoona for a few days, and though his presence was missed, I looked forward to his bringing back a report of our old hometown. I wondered what he would say of my aunt and uncles, or if he'd had a chance to visit with my two younger cousins. Did they remember me, talk of me?

Around noon, guests began to come by, some just to drop off token gifts and goodies, others to share in the big meal Bernice was busy preparing. I spent an hour helping in the kitchen, where Bernice and I chopped, sang carols, and stirred pots.

"Do you ever miss home, Bernice?"

"I'm home right here," she said.

"I know . . . but I guess I mean having a home of your own. A family?"

She narrowed her eyes on me. "A husband, you mean? I've had those." How many she'd had varied from telling to telling. "I might find another one yet. Thing is, it's better to be happy how you are than to hanker after what you don't have."

"Count your blessings and all that," I said, without much enthusiasm.

"Never being satisfied with what you have gets you in a whole load of mischief."

"Maybe, but look at Aunt Irene. Did you ever expect her to have a son and be so happy? She must have been hankering after something else, and when she saw her opportunity, she reached for it."

"A baby's a responsibility, not an opportunity." She smiled. "But Eddie's a sweet little thing, isn't he?"

Eddie had landed in cotton, all right. After all the horror since discovering Ruthie's death, I was glad at least for this happy ending.

When Aunt Irene's dinner guests had all arrived and offered their tributes to her and Eddie, we sat down to dinner. I missed having my friends there, but Aunt Irene's guests were always a diverting bunch. I was seated between her lawyer, Abraham Faber, whom I'd met before, and a poetess named Evelyn Hartwell. She wasn't the first poet I'd met, and certainly not the first pacifist, but she was the most argumentative pacifist I'd ever come across. We weren't halfway through the meal before she and Abe Faber were in a deep, heated discussion of the war in Europe, with me playing the role of no-man's-land between their sharp volleys.

"And what do you say, Louise?" she asked me, then thought better of it. "Never mind. You're probably too young to have thoughts on political matters. At least thoughts that mean anything."

"And why shouldn't young people have political thoughts?" Abe Faber said. "They're the ones who'd have to go fight."

"Not the girls," she shot back. "Girls nowadays are all frippery and foolishness."

I weighed how much I could tell her of what I knew of war without bringing the United States Secret Service down on my head. When Holger Neumann was about to kill me, he'd claimed that it was because of the war. In that moment, I was part of the fight. Ruthie and Johnny had been casualties. The conflict, I feared, would reach us all sooner or later.

Before I could speak, however, the doorbell rang.

Aunt Irene looked up. "Did I forget someone? I thought we were all here."

Conversations resumed, but I was distracted now. I heard the front door open, and a minute later a strange couple appeared at the double doors between the dining room and the parlor, accompanied by a distraught Walter. Aunt Irene twisted in her seat to look up at them, and then, seeing Walter's expression, she rose.

The man and woman were in their thirties, and wore plain clothing obviously made by the woman's own competent but unpretentious hand. I'd never seen her, but I knew her from a picture of a woman I realized must have been her mother. Her hair was arranged in braided loops beneath a plain brown felt hat decorated with a plaid ribbon. The visitors' faces were red-cheeked from a lifetime of sun and wind. Both bore nervous expressions.

Ever gracious, Aunt Irene smiled and held her hand out to the woman. "How do you do? I'm Irene Livingston Green."

The woman looked a little confused. "I'm Sara Turner, and this is my husband, Hiram." Hiram nodded, still holding his hat in his hands—Walter evidently hadn't been able to part him from it. "We were sent here from another place downtown. We were looking for someone named Louise Faulk, but the people down there said her place burned down."

I rose. It seemed as if strings were pulling me, strings I'd put in place weeks ago and then had forgotten about. An invisible band was squeezing my chest.

"You're Ruthie Jones's people," I said, and then looked at my aunt.

"Why don't we talk in the parlor?" Aunt Irene suggested, ushering them back a few steps. "I'm sure my guests will excuse me for a short while."

The guests murmured their agreement. I hurried to join Aunt Irene before Walter shut the double doors.

The woman turned to me, her eyes bright but her expression unspeakably sad. "Thank you for writing to tell us about my sister. We came about the baby. My nephew. We're here to take him home."

The first thing my aunt did was have Walter bring the Turners tea and refreshments. The detritus of that morning's gift exchanging had been cleared away, but a large plush tiger sat on a footstool. The couple looked but did not comment. Their eyes lingered longer on Dickens and Trollope, who had been groomed for the holiday in green and red velvet bows and sat in their usual places at both ends of the sofa, panting at the newcomers. In the minutes that followed, my few attempts to start conversation petered out quickly. I'd never been so happy to hear the rattling of the tea tray as I was when Walter appeared again.

"You've come a long way," I said as Aunt Irene poured out two cups.

"Nebraska," the man said. "South Junction, outside Elbart. Don't suppose you've heard of it. Took us shy of three days to get here. Had to overnight in Chicago."

"I wish we'd known to expect you," Aunt Irene said. "We could have made arrangements for you. You're staying in a hotel?"

The man nodded. "The Hotel Manhattan, on Fiftieth. Good thing they gave the city's streets numbers, else nobody'd ever know where they were. Darnedest place I ever saw."

"I hope you're comfortable," I said. "At the Manhattan."

"Oh yes," his wife assured me, in a voice that made me suspect just the opposite.

"Doesn't matter," the man said, "we can't stay long. We only came for the child."

"Ruthie's boy," his wife added, as if that were necessary.

"We weren't sure you . . ." My throat felt so dry I could barely talk. "When I didn't get an answer to my letter, I thought maybe . . ."

The woman's eyes widened. "You didn't receive my letter?"

"Maybe we got here before it," her husband said. "As soon as that photographer fellow came out to the farm, we knew we'd be coming out here. Just had to find somebody to look after the cows and such."

"We have a little farm, and a dairy," Sara explained.

"Milk gets taken to Omaha by train every morning, right from South Junction," her husband said.

"It's the same farm Ruthie grew up on, but Hiram's made all sorts of improvements. Especially with the dairy." Sara looked at Aunt Irene, then turned back to me. "Ruthie never knew Hiram. She was always a high-spirited girl, and she never got along with our stepfather. Especially after Mama died. Our stepfather wasn't a kind man . . ."

"I saw the picture of him Ruthie had, which I assume was of him and your mother?"

She nodded. "When she ran away, Ruthie took that with her. I guess because of Mama's likeness."

"I can return it to you."

"Thank you. I'd like to have it again as a keepsake of my mother. I also didn't care for my stepfather too much. He was a sour man, and broke Mama's spirit."

"You don't have to go over all that, Sara," Hiram said.

"We'd like to hear however much you feel like telling us," my aunt said.

"Well," Sara said, "like I said, a while after Mama died, Ruthie ran away. For a long time I didn't know where, and my stepfather forbade me to answer after the one time Ruthie wrote to me to tell me she was here. New York City seemed so far. She stole all the seed potato money, but even so it must've cost her most of it for the train ticket.

"It was awful at home without Ruthie, but then Hiram came along to work for my stepfather, and the old man died. To my surprise, the farm was passed on to me. And Hiram started helping me make all sorts of improvements. We got married last summer, and I wrote Ruthie and begged her to come home. But I never heard from her again. I didn't know why . . . until I got your letter, Miss Faulk. I suppose she thought she couldn't come home again, because of the babies. I gather there was no husband."

I shook my head.

"It's true, people would talk, but Hiram and I wouldn't have minded that. We wouldn't have held it against her, if she'd promised to set herself on a better path. Ruthie always was proud, though."

I nodded.

Sara smiled. "Can I see him now, the baby? You said his name was Eddie. That's the name Ruthie gave him?"

"Yes," Aunt Irene said, standing. "I'll bring him down."

I wondered if the Turners noticed the slightly stiff way my aunt moved, or the moisture in her eyes. "Let me go, Aunt Irene," I said, but she waved off my offer.

"Stay here with the Turners, Louise. I need to pack a case for Eddie. I know where all his things are."

When she was gone, Sara turned to me. "My grandfather's name was Edward. I guess Ruthie didn't hate her family so much after all."

"Was your other grandfather named John?" When she nodded, I told her that there had been another twin who'd died. I didn't give her the particulars surrounding Ruthie's death, and she didn't press me. I would write her the details someday soon, but I had an inkling that today, Christmas, she wanted to remember her high-spirited little sister the way she'd been when they were younger.

"The boy will never hear a word against Ruthie," Hiram said.

I nodded, then lifted the teapot's lid. "Let me warm up this tea. And would you like some more strudel?"

Hiram nodded. "I wouldn't say no. Best food we've had since leaving South Junction."

I hurried to the kitchen and made a small plate of food from what was in there, because I knew Aunt Irene would want me to.

Bernice was nowhere to be seen, but I guessed she was upstairs helping my aunt get Eddie set for his next journey. I was too cowardly to go up and check on them myself.

The guests in the dining room were still at their meal, oblivious to the drama. I could hear the poetess shouting about the brotherhood of man. I hurried back to the parlor. Hiram Turner had just finished a slice of roast beef when Aunt Irene appeared with Eddie.

He was dressed like a little squire in a tweed jumpsuit and cap, with brown booties. It was his least outlandish suit of clothing. Aunt Irene had put some thought into his outfit, wanting him to get off on the right foot with his relatives. She was smiling—a perfect hostess—but I detected redness in her eyes.

Bernice put a suitcase down and then turned to go back to the kitchen before I could catch her gaze.

"Here we are," Aunt Irene said, placing the baby in Sara's arms. "Reunited with his family. Of course you'll need to take him to New York Foundling. I'll have Walter escort you. The sisters will arrange for you to be his official guardian. There won't be any trouble, I'm sure."

As she held her little nephew, tears flowed down Sara's cheeks. "Look, Hiram. He's got Ruthie's eyes. Aren't they just like her picture?"

The man peered at the little boy, then turned to my aunt. "You say he doesn't make a sound?"

"He can hear just fine," Aunt Irene said, "but he's mute."

"Doesn't matter," Hiram said, patting his wife's shoulder. "Having a good heart's what matters." He looked at my aunt again. "Does he like animals?"

"He plays with my dogs."

Hiram flicked another glance at Dickens and Trollope as if he wasn't sure they qualified as part of the animal kingdom as he understood it, but after a moment he seemed satisfied. "We have a dog, and chickens, and the cows, and as much land for a boy to roam and play as he could want."

The Turners stayed a bit longer, and to me each moment was an agony. Aunt Irene kept the conversation from flagging, and sent me up at the last moment to get Eddie's stuffed bear. When I came back down, they were all in the foyer. Hiram took the bear from me and said, "Before I left I was going to take some money to that hospital you mentioned in your letter, to thank them for taking care of Eddie. But now it seems Mrs. Green here's done most of the looking after."

"Not at all," Aunt Irene said. "The hospital merely asked if I would foster him during an outbreak of illness there. And of course we wanted the poor boy to have a happy Christmas."

They thanked her again and were gone, with Walter agreeing to escort them to the hospital as Aunt Irene had promised.

Laughter drifted from the dining room through the closed double doors. Aunt Irene drooped, and for a moment I thought she would break down. But she straightened. "At least we can cool it off in here now."

I felt like weeping for her, but I followed her lead, swallowing back tears. "Your guests were looking a little poached earlier."

"I'd better see to them," she said, nodding toward the dining room. "They'll be clamoring for dessert."

"I can step in as hostess, if you'd rather."

Her eyes, still slightly red, widened. "I couldn't abandon..." Her voice choked, and she lifted a handkerchief to her face.

"Aunt Irene, I'm so sorry." I didn't know what else to say. "If only I'd never written that letter."

"No." Gathering herself again, she put her hand on my arm, as if I were the one who needed comforting. "Remember Sara Turner's face? How joyful she was. That woman got back a piece of someone she loved, and Eddie will be with family. Giving him a family—isn't that always what we wanted?"

I nodded, not trusting myself to speak.

She patted my arm. "Thanks to you, Ruthie's orphan has been given a happy ending."

Happy endings were always Irene Livingston Green's specialty. I only wished I'd managed to make one for her.

"Now put your company face on, and smile. And tonight, after everyone leaves, we'll stay up late, and talk, and I'll do my best turban and tell your fortune."

"Oh, Aunt Irene. I wish I could believe in all that."

"You will when everything I tell you comes true." She took my hand, turned it palm up, and gave it a quick examination. "Look at that—1915 will be a good year for you."

"Merely good? I'm not sure that will make me a believer in the occult arts."

She dropped my hand, then hooked her arm around my waist and gave me a squeeze. "Oh, I'm just getting started, sugar plum. Wait till I've had a few more cups of Walter's eggnog."

ACKNOWLEDGMENTS

All my thanks go out to the wonderful people at Kensington Books who work with me on the Louise Faulk series, especially my editor, John Scognamiglio. Thanks also to my agent, Annelise Robey, for cheerleading me through the rough spots. I'm grateful as ever to my sister Suzanne Bass for critiquing my first draft, and to Joe Newman for being my go-to proofreader.

I sought German-language help from my dad, Bill Bass, and Evelyn Staton. *Vielen Dank!* Any errors appearing in the published book are mine.

While *An Orphan of Hell's Kitchen* is a work of fiction, a few aspects of the story were sparked by real events that occurred in and around New York at the outbreak of the First World War. For instance, there really was a passport scheme to help German sailors return to Europe, although its discovery unfolded in a different manner than what happens in this book. The true story of German spies and saboteurs in the U.S. during World War I has been written by many historians, but my favorite references were *The Detonators: The Secret Plot to Destroy America and an Epic Hunt for Justice* by Chad Millman, *Sabotage at Black Tom* by Jules Witcover, and *New York at War* by Steven H. Jaffe.

Connect with U s

Visit us online at
KensingtonBooks.com
to read more from your favorite authors, see books
by series, view reading group guides, and more.

Join us on social media

for sneak peeks, chances to win books and prize packs,
and to share your thoughts with other readers.

facebook.com/kensingtonpublishing
twitter.com/kensingtonbooks

Tell us what you think!

To share your thoughts, submit a review,
or sign up for our eNewsletters, please visit:
KensingtonBooks.com/TellUs.